DEVIL'S GOLD

Julie Korzenko

Medallion Press, Inc.
Printed in USA

DEVIL'S GOLF

Julie Korzenko

DEDICATION:

To Robert. Thank you for believing in me and loving me
unconditionally, for my front porch and all the sunsets—
past, present, and future.

Published 2009 by Medallion Press, Inc.

The MEDALLION PRESS LOGO
is a registered trademark of Medallion Press, Inc.

Printed in the United States of America
Typeset in Adobe Jenson Pro

Library of Congress Cataloging-in-Publication Data

Korzenko, Julie.
  Devil's gold / Julie Korzenko.
    p. cm. -- (Zebra chonicles ; 1)
  ISBN 978-1-934755-55-6
  1. Women zoologists--Fiction. 2. Viruses--Fiction. 3. Security,
International--Fiction. 4. Special forces (Military science)--Fiction.
5. Yellowstone National Park--Fiction. 6. Niger River Delta
(Nigeria)--Fiction. I. Title.
  PS3611.O74915D48 2009
  813'.6--dc22
                        2008045684

10 9 8 7 6 5 4 3 2 1
First Edition

ACKNOWLEDGMENTS:

I would like to acknowledge the perseverance of my children, Chelsea and Nicholas. Thank you for laughing at the less-than-perfect lunches. Yes, I know. Two slices of bread does not make a PB&J. You two are troupers. I love you.

I am indebted to the brilliance of Dr. Michael A. Davis for his ingenious ability to understand what it was I wanted. Without his diabolical mind, CPV-19 would never have been conceived. I take full responsibility for all scientific flubs and inaccuracies. Thank you, Dr. Mad. You may step into my Hall of Heroes.

I could not have succeeded without the support of Catherine Berlin, Stephanie Bose, and last but not least, the Bats, specifically a few that hold a permanent place in my heart: Valerie Parv, Shara Jones, Sheila Holloway, Ann Wesley Hardin, Bronwyn Parry, Pam Payne, Anne Lind, Karen Kerns, Kate Rothwell, Meg Allison, Laura Hamby, Grace Tyler, and Angie Martin. Cavey of me to only name a few Bats . . . but space is sparse, and I *am* Dread.

CHAPTER 1

Gardiner, Montana

EDWARD FISKE STEPPED FROM THE SHADOWED RECESSES OF THE front porch. The worn planks of the farmhouse creaked and groaned beneath his feet as he made his way down the rickety stairs and into the sunshine. It was a glorious morning. He paused, inhaling the sweet scent of dew and cottonwood trees. Emerald spears of late spring grass beckoned bare feet as they danced in the wind, ending in a graceful sweep at the banks of Yellowstone River.

The serenity of the homestead sent a warm tingle through Edward's body, tugging his normally stern mouth into a slightly lopsided smile. He shook his head at the irony of life. Beauty and tranquility were nothing more than a mask for the evil that slept below.

Edward concentrated on centering his emotions. It wouldn't do at all to allow his technician to see the excitement that bubbled furiously in his gut. He was an impassive man. The itch of anticipation was not something he normally felt, but last night he had surpassed the Christmas Eve eagerness of his childhood. Each time he had stirred from sleep, his watch had mocked him. It had ticked through a layer of molasses, slowing the large hand to an infuriating snail's pace.

But he'd managed.

He'd held himself in check.

His feet crushed the grass; the tender blades bent and broke beneath the soles of his sneakers. He resisted the urge to race across the lawn but stepped up the pace and ignored the biting pain that clutched his upper chest.

After the sale, he'd lose weight. He'd have to. Touring the country and lecturing on his creation would take energy and a physical fitness he currently lacked. Edward brushed a stray strand of hair over the balding area of his head, pushing on toward his dream.

He rounded a grove of quaking aspens and halted. The dilapidated log cabin was a poor monument to the significance of what rested beneath its rotting logs and disintegrating roof. A worn and chipped cornerstone marked the front doorway. His eyes scanned the chiseled numbers, and he nodded to himself, puckering his lips in satisfaction. The date-stamp on the cabin reflected an era when men battled wilderness, forging past the obstacles created by forces unimaginable. It resembled a time of progression. Similar to him, Lewis and Clark were men of evolution. The success and failure they struggled through as they charted a waterway across North America coincided with Edward's vision of his own career. It seemed fitting to have a cabin dating back to their era acting as a shield for his baby.

Pushing on the heavy front door, he scurried within and stopped inside the darkened room, allowing his eyes to adjust. The scent of mold and decaying flesh assaulted his senses. A corner of the room was littered with the carcasses of small rodents killed as they ingested the poison he'd laid out to trap the menacing creatures. Wrinkling his nose in disgust, he crossed the hard-packed earthen floor toward the far wall and opened a small metal box, punching a sequence of numbers into the lighted keypad.

A brown cloud of dust particles rose from the floor as the doorway to the lab slid open. He hurried to the edge of the four-by-four opening, turned around, and began his descent down the steep metal stairs. His pudgy fingers grasped the railing. Concentrating on not missing a rung, Edward descended at a slow pace.

His mind whirled with visions of how he'd present his creation. He'd have to be careful because what lay below had Satan's signature scrawled across it in blood-red letters. That thought stopped him. He liked it. It had an almost poetic tone, one that would fit nicely in his memoirs. With a mental note to write that thought in his journal, he continued his descent into what had once been a typical cellar.

The dawning of a new era was about to take place. His era. It was time for Edward Fiske's name to be written next to Albert Einstein's. When Isaac Newton's principles of relativity were discussed, so would Edward Fiske's DNA modification be expounded.

Yes, his heart beat faster. This day brought forth endless visions of scientific recognition.

"'bout time, Eddie," a muffled voice called from the end of the room.

Edward pulled a handkerchief from his back pocket and mopped the sweat dripping down his forehead. He quickly surveyed the laboratory. Black granite work surfaces were littered with an array of equipment, the far right corner more congested than normal. The night before he'd shoved the three-sided laminar flow station against the back wall. Its air filtration system was no longer adequate. Stacks of unused petri dishes scattered the interior of the flow station, discarded and unnecessary.

A grin tugged at Edward's lips.

His benefactor never questioned funding requests. Life, the past few years, had been damn near Nirvana. He inhaled, releasing his breath slowly to calm the excited jumble of nerves, the tinny scent of humming electrical equipment overlaid by alcohol sterilization as sweet to him as his mother's roses in spring.

Edward's fingers tickled the cool ceramic of a white cylindrical container. He verified that the controls on top of the cryogenic storage tank were correct, then paused, splaying his fingers around the sides of the containment unit. His success lay inside.

"Eddie?"

His assistant's voice broke the moment of silent self-worship. His lab technician was hunched over a large microscope, his hands shoved into robot-type arms that stretched beyond a thick glass pane and into the negative airflow chamber.

"Well?" Edward moved forward to stand beside the younger man.

"Take a look, boss." Jason stepped away from the scope, scratching his ass. He shuffled in place and pushed loose strands of greasy hair behind his ears. Edward grimaced, grateful he'd soon be free of this throw-back-to-the-sixties slice of humanity. If Jason weren't so damned clever with DNA replication, he'd have dumped the kid years ago.

Bending forward, Edward peered into the lens. He adjusted the microscope. A brilliant red and green cell came into focus, moving ever so slightly within the solution smeared on the slide. Bingo. His version of Fifth Disease sparkled in the center of the cell. The modified genetic composition of CPV-2 that he'd spent his entire lifetime perfecting weaved itself into the cell like Christmas lights on a tree. He'd done it.

This human cell now sported the canine virus parvo.

All the interminable hours of waiting while Jason processed these little babies suddenly vanished. He glanced up, taking a second to freeze this moment in time. His technician smiled and laughed and Edward grinned, clapping him on the back.

"It's finished. Five years of trial and error, and we've finally succeeded."

"Yep, Eddie. We're through. How soon until you meet with the big guys? I want my bonus."

Edward narrowed his eyes. Money wasn't his motivation. It was the look of astonishment from his colleagues he craved. They wouldn't turn their backs this year at the conference. No. His strain of Fifth Disease would win the National Medal of Science, maybe even the Nobel, and the accolades of his brotherhood.

"We must show our investors our results." Lost in thought, Edward tapped his forefinger against his mouth. He continued speaking, not really concentrating on what he said. "That's what the grant outlines. A demonstration and then final payment." His mind pictured rapturous applause. Recognition and respect. "However, we need to reverse this procedure and develop an antidote prior to releasing CPV-19. No need to run the risk of exposure." The whining tenor of Jason's voice sliced through his inner reflections, and Edward snapped his attention back to his assistant.

"Why?" Jason asked, tugging at the edge of his shirt.

"Excuse me?"

"We've an entire chamber of results. Why do we need a demonstration? Just send a picture."

Edward curled his lip, disgusted by the younger man's greed. Controlling the surge of anger, he faced the glass that separated the main part of the lab from the negative airflow chamber. The wolf remains, bloodied and trailing gore from all extremities, were piled haphazardly against one wall. "The results in this laboratory were never the objective. It's the procedure and technology that the board seeks. This is a great leap forward in disease prevention and cure. The steps taken to achieve CPV-19 combined with the creation of the antidote will provide our benefactors with the humanitarian rewards they desire." Lecture over, he crossed his arms over his chest and waited for more complaints.

Jason stopped, scratched his ass again, and sighed. "I'll get right on the antidote. That is, after a few hours of shut eye. I'm wiped."

"Not before you dispose of the bodies." Edward headed back to the metal stairs. He began to climb. Stopping halfway up he cleared his throat and turned around, watching the younger man secure his specimen and shut down the scope. Edward gasped for air in short, fast gulps, his nostrils flaring to draw in more oxygen. He'd only climbed the bottom part of the ladder. Swearing, he calmed his breathing and summoned a commanding voice. "I noticed the wolf pens were empty. Did you destroy the last two?"

Jason shot a quick look in his direction, then lowered his eyes and bent down to dig out the cover for the scope. "I took care of 'em." He slipped the heavy plastic over the machine and offered Edward a lopsided smile.

"Good," Edward said and climbed the rest of the way up. Whistling a little tune, he popped his head into the center of the log cabin. Suddenly, the insidious scent of rotting flesh no longer bothered him. A perfume of success now lingered in the air. Nothing could stop him now. Nothing.

CHAPTER 2

Niger Delta, West Africa

THE STALE SCENT OF AIR-CONDITIONING TICKLED CASSIDY'S nose, and she fluttered her eyelids several times seeking to diminish the burning dryness of her eyes. A voice, spoken an octave too low, interrupted her moment of contemplation.

"Dr. Lowell?"

Cassidy pushed back from the edge of the wall, her fingers sliding from the smooth metal surface of the window sill, and turned to face the president of New World Petroleum. She hid her disgust for Robert Cole behind a polite smile. He was a wisp of a man, hardly a physical threat. The onyx of his hair reminded her of the oil slicks his company refused to clean up. He was her enemy.

Unfortunately, in a roundabout way, she worked for him.

"I hope this meeting hasn't inconvenienced you." Cassidy brushed a stray strand of hair off her forehead and hooked her thumbs into the back pocket of her jeans.

He walked toward her, tapping his hand against the backs of the chairs surrounding the conference table as he passed them. Cole paused beside her and surveyed the room, a loud sigh emanating from his lips.

"I'm used to much better accommodations. Was there a reason you requested this room?"

"I felt we'd avoid the glare from the large windows in your upper
conference room." Her gaze slid from the confined space to the narrow
window and followed the path of sunlight sparkling across the water of
the Gulf of Guinea until it settled on the shores of West Africa. From
her vantage point on NWP's corporate floater, the environmental dev-
astation was barely visible. She heard the machinations of active oil
rigs. They hummed and banged and echoed above the gulf, twisting
her gut as they bled the region.

"I see. Your request was a pleasant surprise. I hope you've brought
me what I need." The tight smile that crossed his face didn't warm
his eyes.

With quick strides, Cassidy maneuvered toward the table and
waved her hand at the man seated behind an array of computer equipment. "I assure you, I've done my homework," she responded. Pressing
her palms against the surface of the conference table, she wiped the
nervous sweat off her hands. "Please signal Atlanta that we're ready."
The technician nodded. Cassidy pulled out a worn fabric chair and slid
into it. Drumming her fingers against the table and ignoring Cole, she
waited for the video connection to be made.

A small computer screen extended upward from the end of the
table, and within a few seconds the hum and crackle of static air confirmed a link to the video conferencing room of ZEBRA headquarters
in Atlanta, Georgia. The face of Dr. Drew Sharpe appeared. He
glanced at Cassidy, confidence and pride apparent in the smile he offered. She grinned back and felt an overwhelming sense of gratitude at
his virtual presence.

"Mr. Cole. Dr. Lowell. It's a pleasure to see you both. I understand
from the Nigerian Oil Ministry that there's a necessity to escalate the results of our project. Dr. Lowell, where do we stand on your findings?"

Cassidy inhaled, preparing herself for the tantrum that would certainly follow her report. "Dr. Sharpe, I have discussed in great detail with Mr. Cole the futility of this project. Under no circumstances does the presence of New World Petroleum or its sister organizations have a positive influence within the Niger Delta. In short, sir, oil drilling is killing this region." She sat back and waited for the fireworks.

An angry red flushed Robert's neck as he directed his attention at Drew. "Sharpe, our corporation has not donated close to a million dollars to your agency in order for them to determine we're harming the environment." He leaned toward the screen and stared directly at Drew.

Cassidy narrowed her eyes and focused on the man across the table. She allowed her words to remain unheated and unemotional. "I hadn't realized this was a pre-bought report. If you wanted fiction, then you hired the wrong organization." A fake smile tilted her lips upward when Robert twisted in his seat and glared at her.

"Cassidy, be careful." Dr. Sharpe warned. She glanced at her boss. He sat still, no fidgeting or paper shuffling. The stern set of his mouth and cold stare created an expression she'd never expected to see applied to her.

She felt her own cheeks heat with anger and frustration. "I cannot in any professional manner create a positive report. The Niger Delta is dying. The only way to salvage the region is for oil production to cease all activity." Cassidy paused and drew in a shaky breath. She gazed across the length of the table and spoke with deliberate slowness. "Your refusal to clean up the spills is unacceptable."

"Refusal?" Robert pushed away from the table and slowly rose out of his chair. He ran a tapered finger along the edge of the conference table, continuing this movement as he stepped around the circle of mahogany and stood directly beside her. "I warn you, Dr. Lowell, to cease and desist with your false accusations."

Cassidy willed herself still. The tight control of her temper radiated down her body and released itself through a series of frustrated foot tapping hidden beneath the table. "False accusations? Mr. Cole, I'm not an idiot. You only have to look beyond the shoreline to find the problems." When he merely quirked a brow, she turned toward her boss. "May we speak in private?"

Dr. Sharpe pursed his lips and glanced at Cole. "Mr. Cole, do you mind?"

He shrugged and offered Cassidy a tight, cold smile before turning toward the video screen. "Get your employee under control, Drew, or you won't like the consequences."

Cassidy grinned when she recognized the don't-mess-with-me glare emanating from Dr. Sharpe's face. "Threats don't work, Robert." He glanced down at a stack of paper and with swift precise movements spread the pages out on the table. "Leave the room, please. I need to confer with Dr. Lowell."

Robert Cole tipped his head down in a stiff nod and signaled for the computer technician to follow him out of the small conference room. "I'll be in touch, Drew."

Dr. Sharpe smiled and stared at Cassidy. "Well?" He leaned slightly forward, resting his elbows on the edge of the table.

She sucked in stale air through her teeth and swallowed against the sudden dryness in her throat. "Sir, there is no possible way I can complete this contract per the terms of the original agreement. I've tried to explain this to Mr. Cole, but he's adamant that we respond with positive results." Cassidy sat on the edge of her chair, the worn fabric no longer a cushion against the sharp metal that dug into the back of her thighs. She folded her hands and concentrated on not fidgeting.

"I've glanced at this report you faxed over. Can you not twist any of these details into a better light?"

Cassidy felt her mouth drop open, and she snapped her jaw back up. Rolling her eyes to the ceiling, she bit on her lower lip. "Okay.

Let's see—by creating gas flares that burn 24/7, New World Petroleum has provided a constant hot plateau for baking bread and drying clothes. The natives are extremely grateful. However, one must not get too close or else one burns to death."

Steel blue eyes hardened and no longer offered the comfort she'd sought in the beginning of the meeting. Sharpe pointed a finger at her and spoke harshly. "Cassidy, stop being sarcastic."

She refused to bow to the intimidation flowing across the satellite link and plowed on. "Or how about, New World Petroleum has demolished all the pesky mangroves and provided new roadways. We'll leave out the part where the mangroves provide erosion control and a livelihood for the locals. Roads are much more exciting." She smacked her palm on the top of the table and pointed back at Sharpe. "How's that?"

"Your zeal is appreciated but unacceptable."

She met her boss's gaze. His mouth was tight, and a thin white line surrounded lips that were twisted down in anger. "What?" Cassidy felt the heat of her own anger burn her cheeks. She cursed silently, wishing for the geological survey Charles promised. It held concrete evidence to the downfall of this region.

"Can you, for once, think outside the box?"

She began to tell him exactly where to stick his damn report, but she glanced out the window instead, allowing the sun to smooth back her irritation. "The reason you hired me was because I consistently think outside the box. Drew, you trained me. I'm the best zoologist on staff. How can you expect me to see any positive in this ecological nightmare? I can't find any trace of the pygmy hippo or close to a dozen additional species that previously inhabited this region." She stared at the screen, not really wanting to see the expression on Sharpe's face. He was her mentor. A man she admired above all others.

Dr. Drew Sharpe, the life force and creator of the Zoological Environmental Bio Research Agency, more commonly referred to by its acronym "ZEBRA," was a man whose mere presence commanded undivided attention. His unwavering dark eyes and angular features, his clipped New England accent, and his bearing reinforced a military background that didn't tolerate insubordination. His left eye twitched, and a shadow of ink-blue veins protruded from his neck at her defiance. She'd crossed the line into enemy territory.

Cassidy refused to believe he was asking her to lie.

She held her breath and waited. After what felt like an eternity, Dr. Sharpe nodded and pushed the stack of papers on the table away and out of her line of vision. "You have ten days to wrap up whatever loose ends remain, and then an extraction team will bring you home."

Her heart flipped out of her chest and dropped to the floor. She couldn't breathe. "What?"

"You're needed back at corporate."

A high-pitched buzz rang in her ears, and she shook her head to clear the panic that numbed every corner of her being. "Excuse me?"

"Cassidy, your field time has stretched beyond acceptable limits."

Inhaling a deep breath, Cassidy smiled. "Very funny." Dr. Sharpe stared at her, and she felt every ounce of confidence crack and fall away. "You're serious?"

"Quite."

"But I haven't even begun to determine the long-term ramifications nor started on any resolutions for the oil conglomerates. There's months of work here to be completed. Years, maybe. The multitude of species within this region have barely been recorded. Drew, please, this place will be dead unless someone fights for it." Cassidy opened her palms and tilted her head to the left. "Please."

His lip curled in a sad smile, and Drew closed his eyes for a second. When they opened, they were void of emotion. "It's no longer your concern, Cassidy. I'll see you at debriefing on . . ." he dragged over his calendar, "the Friday after next."

Cassidy stared, too shocked to say anything. He offered her one last parting smile and then hit the disconnect button. The room dimmed. She sat there, ears ringing and body numb. Her eyes burned from more than the thin stream of cool air flowing through the vents. Unshed tears pricked and demanded release.

She fisted her hand and slammed it on the table. The pain shooting up her arm from the contact didn't even register a *one* on the Cassidy-pissed-off scale. "Damn." A long blond curl fell against her cheek. Pushing it off her face, she yanked her ponytail holder from her head, twisted the stray strand in with the rest of her mass of disorganized curls, and refastened her hair. "Damn! Damn!"

The door cracked open and Cole peered into the room. "Problem?"

She glanced at the smug expression twisting the president of NWP's mouth into a fake smile and bit her tongue before she stuck it out and blew a raspberry at him. "No, sir. Is the boat ready to take me back to shore?"

Principe, West Africa (an island south of the Niger Delta)

Jake Anderson wiggled his toes. He stared beyond the edge of his worn rope hammock and watched in fascination as a school of flying fish burst from the crest of the frothy white wave, flicking their fins rapidly and sailing through the air as graceful as birds. The fish dove back into the aqua waters of the South Atlantic and disappeared from sight. A gentle breeze ruffled the spiky leaves of the palm tree he'd tied his hammock around, causing a soft rustling noise.

Closing his eyes, Jake allowed the crashing waves and cries of the sea birds to lull him into a semi-trance. The ocean smelled of fish and brine that pulled him back through time with the ebb and flow of the tide. Memories of his sun-drenched youth collided with those of his intense Special Forces training, leaving behind an odd emotion of satisfaction and regret. Water. Time. It all boiled together as the sun beat upon his face.

It took Jake a few seconds to distinguish the high-pitched peal of his cellular from the raucous noise of the tropics. Sighing, he shifted in the hammock and retrieved a thin-lined silver phone. He pushed a lock of black hair off his forehead and listened to the voice on the other end. Jake rocked himself out of the rope bed, jumping to his feet in one graceful motion honed from years of tactical training. "You are the man, Walter! I'll be there before the beer warms."

Whistling a Willie Nelson tune, he pulled an olive green T-shirt over his head and tucked it into the waistband of his khaki shorts. Jake gathered the rest of his belongings—flip-flops, sunglasses, sunblock, and an empty water bottle—then jogged toward a black and white striped pickup truck parked beyond the sandy beach.

Opening the truck door, he smacked the palm of his hand against the faded ZEBRA logo emblazoned upon its door. A bright colored globe with a black slashed "Z" across the top symbolized an organization Jake was damn proud to be a part of. He climbed behind the wheel and sped onto the narrow road, climbing upward toward the highest level of the small, tropical island.

A cluster of metal buildings framed by heavy canvas tents came into view. A kaleidoscope of personnel dressed in an assortment of clothing, from lab coats to hiking gear, moved around the camp, intent on their individual assignments. Reaching a rectangular building with the ZEBRA logo painted against the rusty brown backdrop of its corrugated tin sides, Jake slammed the brake on and shot out of the truck.

He waved absently at a few men gathered to the left of the cantina. They appeared relaxed and comfortable, but Jake's expert eye spotted their concealed weapons and wary eye. He nodded his approval and ran into the metal building before him. Jake halted, allowing his eyes to adjust to the interior. This was his inner sanctum—a state-of-the-art laboratory designed in Atlanta and flown piece by piece to West Africa.

A small man wearing silver wire-rimmed glasses greeted Jake by handing over an ice-cold beer and clapping his hand on Jake's back. "Thanks for coming so quick."

Jake slugged back half the bottle and wiped his mouth in appreciation. "Whatcha got, Walt?"

His lab assistant pulled him toward the center of the room where a large computer screen dominated a narrow metal conference table. "That orchid you brought back the other day?"

Jake ran a finger along a pencil sketch of the flower that rested on top of a pile of papers. "This one?"

"Yeah." Walter sat down before the computer screen and typed in several commands.

Jake sat beside him, stretching his legs out and propping them on the table. He pulled another yeasty mouthful of beer from the bottle and sighed in appreciation as the cool liquid slid down his throat. "What about it?"

Walter raised his eyebrows and pushed his glasses farther up the bridge of this nose. "It's not listed." His hair and mustache were painted with silver, and there was no mistaking the intelligence sparkling in the lab assistant's eyes.

Jake placed his beer on the tabletop and grinned. "Yeah, I guessed that by your call." He dropped his feet to the ground and leaned forward to study the computer screen.

Walter turned the monitor in his direction and pointed at a small grid displaying a list of numbers and a colored twisted helix. "See? The genetics don't match anything in the database."

Jake studied the computer-generated DNA, then pushed back from the table and stood up. He walked toward a small refrigerator in the back of the room and retrieved two more beers. Returning to the table, he handed one to Walter and flipped the cap off his own. "Where does that put us on the board?"

"One up on Dan."

Resting his hip on the edge of the table, Jake laughed and knocked his bottle against Walter's. "Where is our man from Down Under these days?"

Walter slid his fingers across the keyboard once more. "In Spain. Donana National Park."

Jake nodded, remembering the national disaster several years ago caused by a large toxic spill. He finished his beer and tossed the bottle into a nearby garbage can.

A wave of heat emanated from the front of the lab as the door swung open, signaling the arrival of another body. Jake and Walter both turned to face the entranceway. Jake stood and returned the salute of a young soldier. "At ease," he said.

"Sorry to interrupt, sir."

Jake ambled toward him, stretching the kinks out of his neck. "Is it time?"

The soldier met him halfway and handed him an eight-by-ten black and white photograph. "Yes, Captain."

Jake studied the picture and even through the grains and slight fuzziness, the beauty of the woman stole his breath. She knelt beside a riverbed, a thick braid of hair falling across her shoulder. It wasn't the curve of breast or graceful arc of arm that drew his attention so much as the intense gaze into the camera lens. Jake knew she was unaware of the photographer, but something primal and intuitive drew her sight in the camera's direction.

He whistled through his teeth. "Nice piece of sugar."

The soldier glanced at him. "Sorry to contradict, Captain. But she ain't sweet. She's the reason we're here."

Jake's eyebrows shot up to his hairline. "This is the zoologist?"

"Yes, sir."

He exhaled and whistled again, this time in exasperation. "Kinda young to have New World Petroleum by the balls, don't you think?" The soldier paused before speaking. Jake moved his head to indicate the man had his permission to continue.

"She's causin' a ruckus all right."

Flipping the photograph over, Jake studied the printed type on the back of the picture. He ran a thumb along the stubble of his early evening beard. "Dr. Cassidy Lowell." Glancing up and chuckling, he handed the picture back to the soldier. "Let's go rescue Dr. Doolittle before she creates a worldwide incident."

CHAPTER 3

CASSIDY CLOSED HER EYES AND ALLOWED HER BODY TO SWAY to the rhythmic movement of the small speedboat. She inhaled the briny scent of the sea; it poured into her senses as dread invaded every pore. She'd been yanked from her assignment. The disappointment on Drew Sharpe's face played over and over again. It was haunting. Debilitating.

Failure.

No. Not a failure. Cassidy opened her eyes, straightened her shoulders and faced the fast approaching cluster of barges. She was right. It didn't matter that Dr. Sharpe didn't agree. He wasn't here. He didn't see. But her photography and videos would explain what words couldn't. Whether she remained or worked the angle stateside, this was an ecological crime that required a resolution.

She raised her hand and shielded her eyes against the brilliant sunshine. "Red, would you run me by that last rig over there?"

The old black man nodded and turned the wheel of the small speedboat in the direction of one of New World Petroleum's oil rigs. After leaving NWP's headquarters, she'd decided to investigate several of their installations. The boat slapped against the choppy waves, kicking up a salty spray that cooled her skin.

"This rig's attached to the gas lines," Red explained to her.

They approached the rectangular shaped rig, its sides bleeding with rust. Cassidy's eyes scanned the tall, thin round chimney that blasted poisonous gases thirty feet into the air. It burned bright and steady. "Is that so?"

"Yes'm." Red tossed a weathered rope to one of the workers, and together they secured the speedboat against a narrow floating dock. Cassidy accepted Red's helping hand and disembarked. "I'll stick with you, Doc. These types don' always take to strangers."

Cassidy winked at the man, grinning as his wrinkled face transformed into a thing of beauty when he beamed a large smile in her direction. "Thanks, Red."

Together they climbed rusted metal stairs that clung to the side of the ship. The noise of the rig was deafening as machinery slammed against each other and engines screeched with the strain of forcing a foreign object through the earth's crust. Topping the edge of the main deck, Cassidy paused and waited for Red to catch up with her.

She inhaled sharply as a gorilla-sized man approached. He wore the dark green shirt of a New World Petroleum foreman, tree trunk arms swaying forward with each step he took. Cassidy placed a congenial expression upon her face and straightened her shoulders. The man didn't scare her. Much.

He turned his gaze toward Red and nodded in recognition. "What's ZEBRA want here?"

Red tilted his head and pointed toward the gas exhaust. "Cole's given her access to the rigs to measure air quality."

Cassidy bent her head to hide a smile. *Given* was an overstatement. Cole'd about had an epileptic fit at her request. But he'd acquiesced in the end, rushing her off the ship because of some unscheduled

19

appointment he'd been informed of by his head of security, Nick Fowler. Cassidy shivered at the mere thought of Fowler. The guy gave her the creeps.

Focusing her attention on the foreman, Cassidy reached out her hand and introduced herself. "I'm Dr. Lowell. I appreciate your coop- eration, Mr. . . ."

"Smithy." The man's eyes heated slightly as she moved past him. Cassidy narrowed her own gaze, silently warning him against any inap- propriate behavior.

"Tell me, Smithy," she said, pointing at that gas flare, "why is that still burning nonstop when you're hooked up to the new gas lines?"

"We ain't hooked yet."

Cassidy flipped open her notebook and scanned the reports handed to her by New World Petroleum. "It says right here that you are." She tapped her finger against the memorandum from Cole.

Smithy glanced at the sheet of paper; then his neck disappeared as he heaved his shoulders upward. "Ain't never seen that. We're a porta- ble unit, smaller than all the other rigs 'round here. Far as I know, this baby's going upriver in a month or so. They didn't want to waste time connecting to the lines. Guess some other jerk'll take this spot and si- phon the methane."

Cassidy stared at him, taken aback by that knowledge. "What's upriver?"

The oaf shrugged beefy shoulders. "Dunno. I ain't no informa- tional computer."

Snapping her notebook shut, she scribbled on the cover and turned away from the foreman. "Red, let's go. There's nothing more for me here."

Red appeared startled, his forward motion coming to an awkward stop. "You don' wanna measure the air?"

Cassidy bit her bottom lip and lifted her head to glare at the burn- ing gas. "Nah. I know what I'll find." What she wanted to know is why the hell NWP was hauling an established rig upriver. "Let's get off this piece of floating poison." She turned and headed back to the stairs but not before she caught a glimpse of the foreman speaking into his walkie-talkie. Cole, no doubt, was the voice on the other end.

Cassidy stretched her fingertips toward the sky, pulling on the knots and bunched muscles caused by too much worry and not enough sleep. Red navigated the speedboat up the mouth of the Niger River. Glancing to the right, the coastline of Port Harcourt drew her attention. Mammoth gray hulls of recently emptied oil carriers dotted the harbor. Without the weight of their liquid gold, the oxidized bases rose high above the waves, an ugly testament to pollution. The boat swung to the left and headed deeper into the Niger River. Cassidy clung to the railing, bracing her body against the impact of boat on wave as the coastal city faded from view.

Several wet drops hit her skin, and she glanced upward. It was the rainy season, and the weather slipped constantly from clear skies to walls of water. Yanking a yellow slicker from her canvas bag, Cassidy tugged it on and prepared for the drenching she knew lay seconds away.

Several small fishing boats dotted the river. Men in bright colored shirts flung nets into the water. Toss and drag, toss and drag. Their movements graceful with the rhythm of repetive motion. Cassidy tilted her head and smiled as the men's voices rang loud and clear, good naturedly taunting one another.

Red slowed their progress so as not to send unwanted currents in the fishermen's direction. The boat tipped to the right, and she trailed her fingers along the crests of the waves, its biting water reminding her that the simplicity of the scene she witnessed lay in the vision and not the task. These men were battling for survival, not enjoying a pleasure cruise.

A flat-bottomed boat full of heavily armed soldiers shot from the shore and cut toward the fishermen. Red slipped behind the militia and jammed the throttle forward. "We don' wanna mix with dem," he called back as the wind picked up with the speed of the boat and tore his voice into a whisper.

Cassidy swore and twisted in her seat, watching in despair as the militia forced the fishermen to pull in their empty nets and head back to shore, defenseless against the threat of muscle and gun.

Rain shot from the skies, pelting her with watery bullets. She bowed her head, fighting back a sudden wave of depression. "Those men weren't doing any harm," she yelled at Red.

Red wagged a finger at her. "It's not for you or me to decide, Doc. Stick with NWP and you'll stay safe."

Red's words didn't soothe. They infuriated. Cassidy detested the idea that she was left untouched because of the initials plastered to the outside of the speedboat. They banked to the right and headed in the direction of a long wooden dock. Wrapping her arms around her waist, she leaned forward to avoid being drowned by the sudden downpour. Red killed the engine as it rode a small wave into a designated slip. The ferocity of the shower lessened somewhat as the boat rested between the piers.

Red tossed ropes to anchor it in place.

Cassidy gathered her bag and pulled the top of her hood farther down over her forehead. She leaned over and dropped a kiss on Red's cheek. "Thank you. You know, if you ever want to leave NWP, ZEBRA is always looking for hard working employees."

The blush that tinged his onyx skin tugged a smile from her lips. "Thanks. But I'm too old to be goin' elsewhere, and my pay's on time."

Cassidy gripped his shoulder and squeezed gently. She accepted his arm and used him for balance as she clambered up from the rocking boat and onto the pier. "See you, Red." It took a moment for her feet to find the rhythm of the dock. The rickety wood moved with the current, making her walk in drunken sailor style. Her eyes locked onto solid shore, and she wove her way down the length of the walkway.

The village market buzzed with activity. Women swathed in brightly colored cloth carried baskets and bowls, filling up on necessities for their families. It the first village beyond Port Harcourt, and tourists brave enough to risk the Kill-and-Go methodology of the local militia flocked here in search of authentic souvenirs. Stands laden with carved masks and woven baskets of all shapes and sizes were scattered across the center street.

Cassidy paused, picking up a small round bowl. The intricate weaving of multi-toned natural fiber cast a dizzying circle of jagged peaks around the upper rim. She lifted the lid and peered inside. The craftsmanship was inspiring. Cassidy patted her pockets and withdrew a sodden five-dollar bill, shoving it at the artist. Cradling her purchase, she moved beyond the stands.

The acidic scent of the constant gas flares burned Cassidy's nostrils. She walked quickly through the throng of natives and jumped behind the wheel of her Jeep. Turning the ignition and releasing the emergency brake, she slammed her foot on the gas pedal and sped onto the road away from the river. She ignored the rusted pipelines and oil-crusted riverbeds that flanked both sides of the street. It was sad, and she was angry.

Cassidy sifted through a million ways to explain to her camp that they'd be closing up shop. "Damn, damn, damn." It all sounded as if she were raising the white flag and laying her weapons down.

As the vehicle bumped over the uneven road, Cassidy gazed beyond the dying mangroves and poor vegetation. She envisioned the Niger Delta as it was more than forty years ago, before the never-ending burning sky. The lush tropics full of chattering creatures called to her soul.

Africa.

She connected with the endless plains covered with nothing but dust balls during the dry season, and with the mountain ranges that held century-old tribal secrets that continued to feed the world with new species. A precious corner of Earth was dying, and no one cared.

Pulling off the road, she followed the bend of a dry riverbed, remnants of an oil leak still present in the blackened soil. The small haven of her encampment came into view. Modern tents were erected in a half moon, circling a constant burning fire pit. Cleaned and polished concrete buildings scattered beyond the line of tents marked the rehabilitation of a dead village.

She stopped the vehicle and soaked in the view. The engine rattled and heat rose from the ground in waves of humid fog, but she remained. She'd been here for six months, and it hurt to think of the damage her announcement would do to the pride and sense of achievement these natives felt about this renovated township.

Cassidy inhaled. The rain abated, leaving behind a sense of renewal. In this tiny patch of land carved into a diminishing mangrove outcrop, the Niger Delta flourished. Mangrove roots were cleansed of suffocating oil and clung to the edge of a thin stream that remained free of pollutants. Her heart hurt. If given enough time, she was certain these steps toward environmental resurrection could be successfully implemented throughout the entire region.

On the left, a small band of locals worked the water filtration system she'd introduced. Tears burned behind her eyes. What would happen to these people when she left?

Running her fingers through her hair, she yanked her ponytail loose. The wind and rain had created a clumped and tangled sodden mess of it. Cassidy allowed herself a brief second to fantasize about a hot shower and scented soap. Instead of igniting a yearning, though, the vision spurred anger.

It wouldn't be long until that fantasy became reality.

"Damn."

A young woman dressed in stained khaki's and a ZEBRA T-shirt raised her arm and waved. Cassidy sucked in her bottom lip and briefly closed her eyes, seeking patience and guidance. "Double damn," she said softly. Inhaling a deep breath, she slid from behind the wheel of the Jeep and plastered a smile upon her face. "Time to stick a pin in the voodoo doll of reality."

Jake waited. The interior of the laboratory was dark, lit only by the glow of the multitude of lab equipment humming on the counters. He lounged in a chair at the center work table, his fingers drumming an impatient beat on the hard metal surface. Lifting his arm, he pushed a small button on his watch lighting up the dial. As if his motion triggered a signal, the computer screen flickered to life displaying a message to accept a satellite signal. He leaned forward and moved the mouse over, completing the connection.

Jake frowned as an empty room came into focus. A hand flickered on the monitor, displaying an index finger pointing upward indicating for Jake to wait. He sighed, leaned back in his chair, and crossed his arms behind his head. Muted voices echoed from the computer and filled the dark corners of the laboratory with sound.

"Anderson?"

Feeling slightly stupid talking to an empty chair, Jake sat forward and rested his elbows on his knees. "Here, sir."

"Wait one doggone second, son. These morons have me all discombobulated."

Stifling a chuckle, Jake nodded at the empty room and waited for his superior officer to make an appearance. Finally, Colonel Price moved into view. He settled himself in the empty chair Jake had been staring at. "Evening, sir."

Price braced his hands on the edge of the table and focused on Jake, his features sharp and angular. "Talk to me."

Jake pointed to Price's head. "Going for the Kojak look, Colonel?"

Price rubbed a hand over his smooth shaven scalp. "Celia likes it." The slight widening of the colonel's eyes explained to Jake that the colonel himself wasn't yet comfortable with the entire Mr. Clean persona.

"Celia's a smart woman, sir."

Price waved a hand and shook his head. "I'm not wasting our taxpayer's dollars discussing my hair, or lack thereof, with you like two old hens. Anderson, what in tarnation is going on over there? I've gotten more hot-headed jerk-offs trying to crawl up my ass this afternoon than Nixon had tapes."

Jake raised a brow and tilted his head to the side. "How's that, sir?"

"Fuel and Energy Commission's been informed of the possible shutdown in oil production in the Niger Delta. They're not happy."

Jake frowned and scratched at the beginning of a headache attacking the corner of his right eye. "NWP's ordered a hit on ZEBRA."

Colonel Price narrowed his eyes and leaned toward the monitor. His image wavered slightly as the camera refocused. "Repeat that, son, and add a few more details for my old senile mind to comprehend."

The corner of Jake's mouth tugged upward in a cocky grin. "Here's the expanded version for your ancient ears." He laughed when Price flipped him the finger. "About an hour ago we received word that a Kill-and-Go squad had been personally handpicked by the senior security officer of New World Petroleum. My informant's indicated ZEBRA's camp is the target."

"When?"

Jake paused for a brief second. "Tonight."

The colonel closed his eyes and bent his head, rubbing the center of his temple with his thumb. "Jesus H. Christ. Why can't everybody

26

play nice for once?"

"This is Africa, sir. I don't believe they understand those rules."

Price snickered. "Smartass. What's your plan?"

"I'm leading two tactical teams out of here in about twenty minutes. First unit will extract all ZEBRA personnel. The second unit . . ." Jake paused, knowing this would probably not pass muster with the colonel.

"The second unit?" the colonel prompted, leaning back in his chair and crossing his arms over an ample chest and belly showing the telltale signs of good food and abundant drink.

"The second unit, sir, will secure the safety of the remaining members of the camp."

Colonel Price slammed his hand against the desk and stood up abruptly. "Dammit, Jake. We're not to involve ourselves in local governing. You're supposed to be a *biologist*."

"Sir, NWP ships solely to the United States. I think they've already involved us in this so-called governing."

Price paused his pacing and sat back down. "I don't like it. The Nigerian Oil Ministry's been very specific about what we can and cannot do there."

"Sir, I believe that's why Black Stripe is here."

Price swore to himself and nodded. "Full report upon completion of your mission," the colonel said, pausing and staring at Jake, his gaze unwavering. "In person."

Damn. Jake nodded, even though his insides tightened at the thought of leaving Principe's tropical paradise and returning stateside. "Yes, sir." Jake clicked the mouse and disconnected the satellite link. He sighed, stretching the kinks out of his muscles. The lab door opened, allowing a stream of late afternoon sun to flood the interior of the room. Jake turned and glanced at Walter.

"Lab's all yours, Walt. I'll be heading home after this extraction."

27

CHAPTER 4

CASSIDY STEPPED FROM THE INTERIOR OF HER TENT AND PAUSED for a moment, appreciating the subtle change from day to night that colored the sky in brilliant hues and softened the spiny edges of the mangrove. The bustling activity of camp ceased and settled into a more leisurely pace.

A cluster of personnel gathered to Cassidy's left, and she ambled in their direction. She heard her name being called and twisted around to find her assistant, Anna, waving at her from the direction of the bird-cages. Cassidy smiled as a rustle of leaves and screeching signaled the presence of a group of monkeys. Searching the small canopy of leaves above her head, she spotted a Sclater's guenon.

Over the past several months, the tiny primates that topped Niger Delta's most endangered species list had begun to reappear around their village, stealing food and entertaining the children. This particular guenon was named after Philip Sclater, a zoologist from the early twentieth century. Cassidy studied the guenons. They had wide, red-brown eyes surrounded by bright patches of white, and a crown of muted browns and greens covered the head and splayed across the back. She wasn't certain if having a small monkey named after you constituted an achievement or failure.

Cassidy snapped her pen off the edge of a clipboard and quickly jotted down the location and brief estimate of their numbers, then headed toward the tall wire cages that housed several Black Crowned Cranes. They stood tall, some with one leg tucked beneath each heavy round body. Long necks swept upward in a lazy graceful curve. They startled easily, swaying their black tufted heads back and forth. A strong scent of oil and feces wafted in her direction, causing her to wince.

"Dr. Lowell . . ." a man dressed in sweat-stained khakis and sporting a large straw hat signaled from beneath a large tent they used for group conferences.

"Yes, Charles?"

"I received your e-mail regarding the future of this camp. Are you positive we're all to relocate?"

She nodded and offered the geologist a sad smile. "Yes. All of us."

"I see. And we have how long?"

Cassidy reached out and squeezed his shoulders. "Ten days." She twisted to her left, intent on continuing her trek toward Anna.

"Dr. Lowell . . ." The man huffed and moved to block her from walking away. "I've found something unusual on the geological survey."

She paused and tilted her head. "Will it help keep us here?"

Charles sighed and moved one shoulder in a halfhearted shrug. "I can't say, but it should definitely be contained within your report to OPEC. I've sent David upriver, but he's not checked backed in. I'm worried."

Cassidy closed her eyes against a sudden surge of frustration. Without hardcore, kick-ass facts, she'd never convince Sharpe to recant his decision. "Well, if David shows up with a miracle, let me know immediately."

"I think I'll head upriver and help him out." Charles turned away and started to head back toward the cluster of tents.

She caught his arm and shook her head. "Not tonight. I don't like anyone traveling that river in the dark. It's too dangerous."

"But David?"

With a frown, she shook her head. "Keep trying him on the radio."

"Cassidy . . ."

Anna's panicked voice jolted her from the sudden worry Charles' concern over his partner elicited. "Wait until the morning, Charles. That's an order." Turning, Cassidy ran toward the birdcages.

Anna Kuffae, her black skin contrasting with the white, sweat-soaked T-shirt clinging to her body, knelt within the center of the birdcage wrestling with a dirty and irate crane. "Could you please give me a hand?"

Cassidy opened the wire gate and slid inside the cage. She crouched down and inspected the bird's wings. They were coated with a thick layer of sludge. "Another one?"

Anna shifted her weight and pushed the bird toward Cassidy. "How many of these aren't we finding? You'd think my government would at least do something about its national bird." Anna sighed in exaspera-tion. "Oil's everywhere. I can't hold it long enough to do any good."

Cassidy slid her fingers across the slick feathers, cooing in soft tones. She gathered the bird tightly against her chest and rose to a half crouch, using her body weight to deliver it to a large tub of water Anna was filling with warm, soapy suds. "Clean it the best you can. If the lungs are clear, we'll be in luck."

Anna began rinsing the slick oil off the body of the bird, revealing white feathers. "Charles handed in a preliminary report. I put the flash drive with the geological survey you requested on your desk. You're right. Port Harcourt is sinking."

Cassidy cupped a handful of water and assisted Anna with the cleans-ing of the feathers. "Lot of good that'll do us, but I'll take a look and add it to my findings." She scowled at the dirty water quickly filling the tub. "He said something about an unusual finding. Did you see anything?"

Anna bit her lower lip and scrubbed at the underbelly of the bird. "I didn't even look at it. He did emphasize that it wasn't complete, though."

"I wish he'd give me something to uncover NWP's corporate bullshit."

"Who pissed you off this time?"

Snorting through her nose, Cassidy wiped the back of her hand against her cheek. "That obvious?" Anna nodded and raised a brow, waiting for an explanation. Cassidy lifted her chin toward the sink tap, and her assistant quickly twisted the nozzle to an off position. Glancing at the bird, she ran gentle hands across its cleaned feathers. "Met with Robert Cole today."

"New World Petroleum's president?"

Cassidy rolled her eyes. "Yeah. He's refusing to clean any of this up and insisting I write that damn report for OPEC."

"You can't do that."

Cassidy stared at her assistant. "I know. They've reassigned me, Anna. ZEBRA's pulling out in ten days."

The expression drained from the other woman's face; then her features changed, distrust and accusation shining from her eyes. "Giving up are you?"

Cassidy picked up the bird and released it into the cage. She reached for Anna's arm and held tight. "Not on your life. I'll be back. But right now, this is what I must do."

Anna bent her head and slumped her shoulders. "I know. I'm sorry. It was wrong of me to accuse you like that. It's just . . ." She glanced around the village. "We've come so far."

"I know. I know." A ring of childish laughter filled the night air, and Cassidy turned in its direction. "That's what I need right about now."

Anna laughed softly as a young boy ran up and wrapped his arms around her legs. "This is our life, Cassidy. Don't blame yourself for our mistakes."

Cassidy turned her face away from Anna's son, purposely ignoring him. "It shouldn't be—not under these conditions." Unable to hold out any longer, she glanced down and grinned. "Who's this handsome little man?" Georgie giggled and tried to hide behind Anna's body. "I don't suppose you'd be interested in anything I might find in my pockets?" Georgie giggled again and held out his hand.

"You spoil my son."

Cassidy patted her pockets, pretending to have lost something. "It's one of the greatest moments of my day." She finally dug her hand into her jeans and retrieved a handful of wrapped bubble gum. "Want these?"

Georgie yelped with joy and threw his arms around Cassidy's neck. She accepted the sweet and innocent embrace, blinking back a startling blur of tears. "I need to finish my report. I'll see you in the morning, Anna." Cassidy sniffed and focused on the tip of her shoes to hide the tears. Shaking her head, she turned and walked toward her tent. The familiar noise of camp slipped beneath her skin. Its rhythm, once soothing, drove stakes of guilt into her heart.

The suffocating humidity of her tent surrounded Cassidy. It was near midnight, and she'd closed all her flaps against the preternatural light created by the gas flares. Stripping off her pants and shirt, she padded barefoot to her desk. Settling in the chair, she inhaled the dank air and snorted at her attire. Tank top and bikini pants were a far cry from the flannel pajamas and fuzzy slippers her mother raised her in. Wyoming's climate certainly was the polar opposite of West Africa's.

Yellowstone National Park. The playground of her youth.

Tapping a pencil against her lips, Cassidy stared at a picture positioned precariously on top of a stack of scientific journals. Her parents, vibrant and alive, smiled at her from behind the smudged and dirty glass of the frame. Behind them the peaks of the Tetons cut a jagged edge into the horizon.

It was late. She stretched her arms to the ceiling of the tent and yawned. One more item on the agenda. Moving her shoulders to shake out some of the stiffness, Cassidy reached for a small manila envelope. Slitting the edge, she removed a tiny flash drive and inserted it into her computer.

Clicking on the appropriate icon, she opened the geological survey prepared by Charles. A detailed sketch of the earth's layers beneath the surface of the Niger Delta flickered on the screen. Cassidy glanced at it briefly and scrolled down to find the fine points on Port Harcourt. Nigerian scientists reported several years ago their concern for the city, and she'd wanted to confirm the theories and potentially gain more positive interest from President Nuna.

Before reaching the section on Port Harcourt, Cassidy paused and began reading a blurb about the Jurassic period and its impact on the Niger Delta. She reread the same paragraph four times before finally giving up. Sleep called. There was something in the text that sparked her curiosity, but her brain lay in a fog of exhaustion and refused to fire off the neurons that would puzzle out her questions.

Pushing away from the desk, Cassidy moved to sit on the edge of her cot. She refused to dwell on everything that had happened that day, instead turning her mind to pleasant thoughts and preparing for sleep. Flipping off the small halogen lamp on the edge of her desk, she lay down. No covers tonight. Fatigue quickly shut down her consciousness as she slipped into the comforting embrace of oblivion.

Cassidy shivered.

Trying not to rise too far out of her sleep stupor, she turned and snuggled deeper into the warmth of her pillow. A gentle kiss of air fanned her face.

She blinked her eyes, rubbed her cheek, and mumbled incoherently, intent on finding the comfort of sleep again.

A swish of fabric, barely audible, echoed within the tight confines of her tent. Her breath caught and she froze, alarm signals jangling across every inch of her body, firing up nerves and muscles. Her senses were on full alert.

She wasn't alone.

———

Nick Fowler crouched beyond a thin line of mangroves. A distant gas flare cast a faint orange glow to the camp, shadows from the tents weaving irregular shapes along the hard-packed ground. Closing his eyes, Nick tilted his chin up and inhaled.

He could smell her.

Tonight the edge of his knife would sink into her skin, slicing skillfully through her perfect complexion. It would reveal the beauty of muscle and tendons entwined with fear-engorged veins of dark, crimson blood. She'd plead for her life first, then cry and whimper like a scared bitch. When reality dawned and Blondie faced her own mortality, she'd scream. Loud and long. Its music would wrap around him and lift him to a higher plain of existence. He craved this. He needed this.

"Mr. Fowler?"

Nick snapped open his eyes, releasing himself from the fantasy that had plagued his mind since that fateful moment six months ago when her perfect beauty had invaded his world. "Yeah?"

"We're ready."

Nick glanced past the large black man and scanned the line of trucks laden with a mix of local militia and NWP oil workers. This was Kill-and-Go, Fowler style. Handpicked for their ruthlessness and bloodlust, these men would massacre the village leaving behind an unmistakable "don't fuck with oil" message.

He gave the signal to move out and jumped into the cab of the lead truck. "Remember," he said, his voice a low growl, "the girl's mine."

Cassidy remained still, only her eyes moving to scan the capsule of her tent.

A hand pressed against her mouth.

Panic slammed into her chest, and she inhaled using the fear-induced adrenaline to heave herself off the cot. Her attacker swore and scrambled to regain control.

Cassidy ducked under his arm and kicked at the back of his knees.

He outmaneuvered her, pinning her to the ground and lodging his forearm firmly beneath her chin. "Dammit, be still." All she could see was a pair of brilliant blue eyes peering at her from a camo-painted face.

She paused, recognizing a familiar Southern cadence in his voice. "Who are you?"

He shook his head and placed a finger to her lips. "Hush."

A gunshot rang, splitting the night air with its resounding echo. Screams filtered through the flaps of her tent. Cassidy's eyes widened, and she swallowed against a lump in her throat. What the hell was going on? She and her captor remained still for what felt like hours until he nodded and released his hold.

"Who are you?" she asked again.

He moved toward the front of her tent and peered through the slight gap in the flap. "Hush. I'm the good guy." His voice was deep and menacing. He certainly didn't sound like a good guy. Screams filtered through the opening, echoing within the small enclosure.

She was frightened and feeling out of her element. Inhaling short deep breaths, Cassidy tried to convince herself she was in the midst of a nightmare and would awaken any second.

Silence. Then more gunshots.

"It's the Kill-and-Go squad."

Cassidy shook her head. She didn't want to acknowledge any of this. "You're wrong. We're protected."

He ripped up the sleeve of his camouflage T-shirt to reveal a tattoo of a jagged black "Z" striking the center of an American flag. "Not anymore."

Cassidy squinted at it, trying to decipher the meaning. Could this situation get any more bizarre? Perplexed, she glanced at his face. His features were undistinguishable beneath heavy camo paint, but his gaze was steady and unwavering, making her feel a bit like Alice down the rabbit hole. Her mind tumbled through the significance of his tattoo, but nothing clarified the mystery. "Zorro Squad?" she asked, unimpressed with this display of masculine pride and struggling with the fear that slammed her heart against her chest, making it difficult to breathe.

His shoulders dropped, and he rolled his eyes at her.

She shrugged, her fear turning into anger. "I'm not psychic, you know."

"Zebra. Black Stripe."

Her breath caught. The "Z" on his arm was suddenly more deadly than lightning and no longer amusing. She moved her head from side to side. "No way."

A sarcastic grin tugged at the corner of his mouth. "'fraid so."

"You're a myth. You don't exist."

She flinched when he reached out to take her arm. "Some days I wish that were true." A bullet split the top of her tent, and he slammed her to the floor. "No more time for pleasantries." His words were a rush of hot air against her cheek. She scrambled to find her pants, but her fingers only connected with air.

Her thigh slammed into the edge of the desk, which wobbled and caused the laptop to slip and tumble to the ground, smacking her on the head. She winced and reached over, releasing the flash drive. She heard him muttering and swearing as he pulled on her arm. "Just a sec." Making a fist around the miniscule plastic hard drive, Cassidy crawled behind him. At least she'd save some evidence.

Whipping out a knife, he cut the base of the tent, reached back, and grabbed her around the waist, pulling her forward and shoving her through the hole. "Move!"

Cassidy ignored the sharp bite of rocks and rough ground and scrambled to her feet. He pushed her from behind, and she stumbled. A scream rang above the chaotic gunfire, making Cassidy cry out loud. "Anna! That's Anna! We have to get Anna and Georgie!" She struggled against the arm holding her and pulling her away from the camp.

"Doc, my orders are to get you out. Let's go."

Cassidy screamed at him. "No! Anna and Georgie! I won't leave without them!" He pulled her tightly against his chest and prevented her from running.

His eyes glittered dangerously beneath the orange haze of night. "The Kill-and-Go are here for you. Understand?"

Shock froze her. She gazed into his face, trying to latch onto something familiar and grounding. "No." Cassidy swore when her vision blurred. She shook her head, refusing to allow the tears to fall.

His face softened, and he offered her a halfhearted smile. "Sorry, Doc. We need to go." Bullets shattered the branches of a tree behind them. "Now!"

Cassidy spun around, spotting the Kill-and-Go. A group of heavily armed soldiers, faces pockmarked with the cruelty and destruction of their trade, wove through the camp shooting at anything, man or beast, that moved. Leading the mass of angry men was a figure she recognized, the jagged scar that ran from the edge of his cropped dirty-blonde hair down across his chin and below his neck unmistakable even at this distance.

As if in response to a silent signal, his head swung in her direction.

Their eyes locked and he lifted an arm, pointing at her. Nick Fowler. Her security guard. Why was NWP targeting their camp?

Revulsion and fear coursed down her spine, and her hands came up clutching onto the man from Black Stripe as if he were the last person alive on earth. Nick Fowler's howl of rage rang through the camp, and the evil and danger buried in its tone struck at Cassidy's heart. Her gaze dimmed, and brilliant sparks of light flickered before her eyes.

She heard a muffled swear, and suddenly Cassidy felt her body being lifted and then the sharp edges of Zorro's shoulder cutting into her abdomen. They were moving. Her eyes wouldn't focus. She tried to speak, but her mouth couldn't work its way around coherent words. She heard him yell, and then the deep baritone of other male voices drifted through the haze of absolute shock.

She closed her eyes tightly, then reopened them. Misty figures ran behind them, firing machine guns at a heavily armed pack of militia. Cassidy recognized the figures of her biologist and ecologist colleagues; then she lost sight of them as she was lifted off the man's shoulder and swung in a circle.

Cold metal slammed against her back. Her teeth snapped together, followed by the bitter taste of blood. Shaking her head, Cassidy realized she'd been tossed into a helicopter. She scrambled back against the door, gripped the outside edge, and bent forward, offering her hand to the other two ZEBRA employees being pushed inside.

Although dazed, Cassidy heard Anna's cry for help. "Anna! Anna! Run, dammit, run!" Her voice cracked and disintegrated against the whirring sound of revving helicopter props. Panicked, she glanced at the faces within the chopper. "Where's Charles?" The other ZEBRA scientists shook their heads, indicating they didn't know.

Cassidy swung around to search the camp and watched in desperation as Anna raced across the ground, little Georgie cradled against her chest. A small band of militia ran to intercept her. Cassidy screamed at the men inside the chopper. "Help her!"

The helicopter lifted. Cassidy grabbed the edge to steady herself, ignoring the arm that anchored her in place. A man, black as a panther, knelt on the earth below. He lifted his elbow, pointing a rifle across the field. Cassidy followed the angle of his arm. Screams ripped from her throat.

Anna glanced over her shoulder, then spun and lifted Georgie toward the helicopter. "Oh my God," Cassidy pleaded, tears coursing down her face and blurring her vision. "Please, I beg you! Go back! Please go back!" A gunshot snapped, an alien noise against the rhythmic thud of the helicopter blades. Her friend fell to her knees.

"Anna!" she sobbed. Fear flooded Georgie's small face. A red stain spread across the left corner of his mother's shirt. She bent her head and crumpled against the ground, protecting her son from the rain of bullets.

Cassidy leaned over the edge of the helicopter, trying in vain to reach her. But they were airborne and nothing but a cold blast of air entered her embrace. She spun around and pounded on the nearest soldier's arm. "Go back! What's wrong with you people? Go back!"

Horror gripped her chest, making it difficult to breathe and racking her body with uncontrollable shakes. Cassidy's eyes connected with the hard gaze of the Black Stripe soldier. An emotion kicked in her gut. One that was all too familiar. One that she'd fought against the last nine years.

Hate.

It bloomed within. Fired by the power of evil that invaded the land below and fueled by self-loathing. If she'd been better, been stronger, been smarter . . .

CHAPTER 5

Gardiner, Montana

Edward Fiske paused in the center of the circular gravel drive, the toe of his shoe grinding into the tiny gray rocks. The entrance to Livingston Golf Course and Country Club lay before him, its wrought iron gates mocking his poor attempt at proper golf attire. Patting down the strands of hair once again whisked away from his bald spot, he breathed deeply. He didn't belong in places like this.

Edward tugged at the pleat on his tan corduroys and prayed his inexpensive white button-down shirt wasn't too full of wrinkles. He knew his clothes were out of place among the bright colored golf pants and polo shirts decorated with designer logos.

A man beyond the gates lifted an arm and waved him forward. Edward hitched his overburdened messenger bag more comfortably on his shoulder, sniffed, and almost sneezed as the scent of freshly cut grass assaulted his nose. He walked toward the gentleman. Counting each step as it crunched on the stone drive, Edward concentrated on not allowing his nerves to publicly display themselves.

He'd never met this particular board member. Actually, he'd not been aware that there was a member of the corporation positioned this close to his laboratory.

"Mr. Jacobs?" Edward asked, attempting to sound confident and at ease.

Mr. Jacobs nodded and extended his hand. "Edward, on behalf of the board and myself, let me be the first to congratulate you on your success. I'm sorry that we were unable to convene at a more respectable arena. Everyone is extremely anxious to learn of your results. However, it has been left to me to speak with you personally."

Edward frowned. This was a first. Normally, the board barked orders and pressured him for results via e-mail and video conferencing. Never had they ever expressed any gratitude. Returning the man's handshake with enough strength to avoid the image of being weak, he assumed that these men finally realized the importance of his discovery. "Mr. Jacobs, thank you very much." Edward glanced around. His eyes scanned the span of perfectly manicured grass. In the distance a small lake glittered beneath the sun, affording a scenic landscape. "Where would you like me to set up?"

"Set up?"

Edward shifted his weight and refrained from sliding his sweat-soaked palms against the edge of his pants. "Yes, sir. I've blown up my notes and created a diagram to explain the procedure. Also, I have a three-dimensional computer program that explains more detail on the genetic compound and mutation."

Mr. Jacobs walked toward a golf cart, jumped behind the wheel, and signaled for Edward to join him. "Actually, Edward, what we're most interested in is the composition of CPV-19."

Edward moved his bag from one shoulder to the next and followed Mr. Jacobs. He eyed the green and white cart and for one brief second envisioned it popping nuts and bolts and disintegrating into a pile of junk the second he sat down. "I don't understand." Edward said a silent prayer and shuffled onto the white vinyl bench. The golf cart rocked beneath his weight but didn't break. "CPV-19 is simply the byproduct of the successful mutation. The process is what must be patented." He clutched his bag to his chest as the golf cart swung off the driveway and sped across the fairway.

The wheels hit a narrow gravel path, crunching and grinding the small rocks into the dirt. Mr. Jacobs eased off the pedal, and the cart slowed to a crawl. Edward inhaled and continued his mini-lecture. "You see, with this procedure many scientists will be able to utilize their existing gene therapies, apply my mutation series, and then reach cures for inherited blood disorders and anomalies. For example, we could find a way to cure sickle-cell anemia."

As Mr. Jacobs nodded absently, Edward fumbled in his bag and pulled out a detailed sketch of CPV-19. "You see, sir, I modified the gene in the canine parvo virus to recognize the transferrin receptor of the human version of parvo, Fifth Disease."

The golf cart crept to a complete stop. Edward glanced around quickly, not certain of their location. They appeared to be beside some type of watering hole. There was a funny red metal stand beside a large, green, metal container with a dispenser of paper cups on the side. Edward tilted his head and studied the red stand. A puddle of water muddied the sand at its base, adding to the puzzle.

Mr. Jacobs reached his hand out and pulled the diagram from Edward, scrutinizing the sheet. "Transferrin receptor?"

Snapping his attention back from the mystery of the metal pole, Edward realized he needed to simplify. "Every virus has this protein affixed to their genetic compound." He climbed out of the cart, leaving his bag behind. "For example, take this red stand."

"The ball washer?"

Mystery solved. Edward smiled and placed his hand on the ball washer. "Yes. This ball washer. Both the ball washer and this green dispenser contain the same product, right?"

Mr. Jacobs lifted one shoulder. "Water?"

"Yes, water. But they're not the same, really; are they?"

"Of course not. Dr. Fiske, what exactly are you trying to say?"

Edward stood between the two metal stands. "Even though these units contain the same liquid inside, their outer shell or metal containers determine specifically what they are used for." He walked back toward the golf cart, swatting at a fog of gnats attacking his eyes. "Essentially, parvo and Fifth Disease are identical except for the proteins marring their surface which determine what cells to attack. Inside is the same, but not outside."

"So you made the outside the same?"

Edward became excited. Finally, the man beside him was interested. "Kind of. I genetically modified the DNA to contain both protein strains. Wove them together like a braid."

"Which does what?"

"Actually, it's rather a bad thing. These two diseases merged into one are highly contagious. The amazing thing is not this new virus but the fact that I was successful in manipulating the protein. Imagine— we could cure any immune deficiency with this technology."

"How?"

"Immune deficiencies can be caused by a missing gene or one that's been eradicated due to disease. We could inject that gene and tell it exactly where to go by attaching the right protein. See?"

"I see." Mr. Jacobs neatly folded the large piece of paper and handed the diagram back to Edward. "But what is CPV-19?"

Edward thought for a moment. "An extremely volatile and highly contagious virus."

"What does it do?"

Sighing, he fought against his dismay. The man didn't understand. "It kills intestinal cells in both humans and canines, resulting in death by dehydration and nutrient malabsorption."

"Excellent," Mr. Jacobs said. "How soon can we have this product to market?"

Edward felt his stomach twist into knots. "Market?" He shook his head. "This isn't something to market. I don't think you understand. The procedure is what we need to market, not the virus."

Mr. Jacobs patted Edward's knee. "We want the virus as well. How soon?"

Shock vibrated from the tip of Edward's tailbone all the way up his spine and across his scalp. A fresh batch of sweat sprung from his pores, and he wiped the back of his hand across his forehead. "Well, I'm currently working on an antidote. The details on the procedure will take some time for me to articulate on paper for the patent."

"Now, Dr. Fiske, it's you who doesn't understand. I don't give a fuck about the procedure." Mr. Jacobs smiled. "I want the virus."

Although the man's expression was pleasant enough, Edward noticed steel behind his gaze. He hid his shock, his brain scrambling for an answer to this dilemma. "It's not stable enough to reproduce."

Jacobs slammed his foot on the gas pedal and swung the golf cart in a hundred and eighty-degree turn. "I thought you said it was."

Think, Edward. "Well, you see—the difference between B19, Fifth Disease, and CPV-2, parvo, is that they infect different cells. B19 attaches to erythroid progenitor cells; those are the ones that make red blood cells." Good. Jacobs' eyes were beginning to glaze over. "CPV-2 attaches to cells in the immune system and intestinal lining. I have to find that perfect balance where CPV-19 functions in both areas. Right now, I have verified how canines handle the virus, but not humans." Edward gripped the metal bar holding up the plastic canopy that comprised the top of the golf cart and hoped Jacobs was buying into his story.

"I understand. However, the board will not be happy about this. We require CPV-19 to be delivered no later than the end of this month along with the antidote."

"But I . . ."

Mr. Jacobs narrowed his eyes. "Mr. Fiske, this is not a polite request."

"And the patent?"

Jacobs waved his hand in the air. "Whenever you see fit to finish the paperwork." The man shrugged. "The end of the year is fine for that."

This was a nightmare. "But . . ."

"Have no fear; that's yours to keep. Hell, we'll even process it for you, if you like."

Relief eased the uncomfortable vice grip on Edward's chest. The patent was his. "I would appreciate that. Thank you, Mr. Jacobs."

"You're more than welcome, Edward. Fax the specifics to head-quarters, and we'll run with it. In the meantime, you get busy on the production of CPV-19." Jacobs pulled the golf cart in front of Edward's sedan and waited for him to jump out.

"Yes, sir. I will. Thank you for this opportunity." He scurried to-ward the driver's side of his vehicle, sliding his key in the lock. He didn't lift his head or glance back as he heard gravel crunch beneath the tires of the golf cart. Dust kicked up by the electric vehicle floated across the air, tickling his nose and making him sneeze.

Slipping behind the wheel, Edward bent his head forward and rest-ed his forehead on the steering wheel. He released his breath in short, quavering gasps and ignored the sweat than ran down his cheeks in rivers of panicked fear. It could be worse, he told himself. It could defi-nitely be worse.

Edward hung up the phone, sighed, and tilted back in the ancient swivel back chair. This day felt endless. He'd confirmed with his contact on the board Mr. Jacobs' request to produce CPV-19. The fact that his benefactor was no longer interested in the patent set off all types of bells and whistle. But he ignored them.

Glancing down at the newspaper spread out on his desk, Edward's face creased into an even deeper frown. Another dead wolf. He bent forward and rested his chin on his hand, reading the black newsprint for the fiftieth time that morning. This couldn't have anything to do with CPV-19. They'd been extraordinarily careful. Unless . . .

What crossed Edward's mind caused his fingertips to tingle and face to feel numb. "No!" He stood up and waddled out of his office as fast as his short legs would carry him. *Please, please, please,* he prayed silently, *let me be wrong.*

The sun still sat high in the sky, causing a thin layer of perspiration to spring to life on his face. A sharp pain in his chest and leaden feel to his legs reiterated the degradation of his physical condition. Edward quickened his pace, concentrating on putting one foot in front of the other without twisting his ankle. The grass faded to worn dirt as he neared the log cabin.

He reached the entrance to the lab and clambered downward, the tinny sound of Jason's radio echoing up the steep stairwell.

His feet touched solid ground, and he sighed in relief. One of these days, he feared he'd slip on the slick metal and plummet to his death. "Jason?" He inhaled, trying to calm the pounding of his heart. He wasn't sure whether it was from panic or the mad dash he'd just finished. His eyes adjusted to the interior, and he spotted his lab assistant in the far corner, pouring over a stack of computer printouts. "Jason." He repeated.

"Yo."

He walked over and pulled out a rolling lab chair, its wheels making a low scraping sound against the tile. Sitting down next to his assistant, Edward grabbed the stack of paper and pulled it away from him. Jason sighed and finally gave him his attention.

"Whazzup, Eddie?"

"Wolves, Jason. Apparently, Yellowstone is in a crisis. Their wolves are disappearing."

Jason tugged on the end of his ponytail. "That's too bad."

"Yes, it is. Now tell me what you did with the specimens we had here." Fear tickled the back of Edward's neck. Jason's eyes roamed the interior of the lab. They went everywhere, except the one place Edward wanted them. Jason refused to look him in the eye. "Jason, I need the truth." The scent of stale smoke surrounded his lab assistant, making Edward's nose sting. He maintained his calm, allowing the smooth surface of the countertop to cool his sweating hands.

The lab assistant shrugged. "I got rid of 'em like you told me to."

"How?" No answer. Edward narrowed his eyes. "Did you release them back into the wild?"

Jason hung his head. "They're beautiful, man. That black one? His eyes were the soul of the universe. I couldn't burn him. It was wrong. Bad karma."

Edward stood and paced in a tight circle. "I see."

"Eddie, it was wrong. You get that, don't you? They were fine. Healthy."

The tight whip of control snapped, and Edward spun to face Jason. "They were contagious!" he screamed, watching in fascination as his spittle flew across the room in tiny dewdrops of venom. That's what they'd unleashed on the unsuspecting habitants of the greater Yellowstone region. Tiny dewdrops of incurable venom.

CHAPTER 6

One week later
Atlanta, Georgia

CASSIDY WELCOMED THE TREMBLING OF OVEREXERTED MUSCLES. She heaved in gulping breaths and stood with arms dropped at her sides in exhaustion. Blinking, she ignored the rivulets of sweat that snaked down her forehead and blurred her vision. With a quick dip of her head, she swiped her arm across her face and cleared her eyes. Her gaze narrowed, and she reached a gloved fist toward the gently swaying punching bag, touching her padded knuckles lightly on the surface.

The faded and worn leather goaded her.

Blue eyes glittered in her mind. Inhaling deeply through her nose, she welcomed the scent of her own sweat mixed with the chlorine that floated across the gymnasium from the lap pool. It symbolized the beginning of retribution. Cassidy twisted her shoulders and shook her arms, battling against the numbness from the past hour spent beating the bag into subservience.

Stance.

Fists up.

Power.

Her fist slammed into the unforgiving leather. Her muscles

quivered as the shock of contact wove from her wrist up through her shoulder muscles. Picking up speed, she jabbed with her left and spun on her heel smashing her foot firmly into the imagined face. The bag swayed away from her vicious attack.

She hopped back, jogged in place, and went back to work. Her mind was blank as she attacked the surrogate enemy. Strike. Retreat. Strike. Retreat.

Strength in pain.

This was her new mantra. Strength in pain. Never again would she allow herself to be vulnerable and directed by outside forces.

In the background, a pounding rhythm poured from the speakers that littered the corners of the gymnasium. Sun glittered through the floor-to-ceiling windows, making Cassidy squint and forcing her to turn her body and begin working another section of the bag. The resounding thud of glove to leather laced its way into the beat of the rock song.

Next time someone attempted to take control of her, she'd think quicker. Act faster. Be more deadly than any man. Her gut twisted, and she advanced at a quicker pace, slamming her fist harder into the bag. Jumping back, she leapt and struck at the inanimate enemy with both feet, trying to drown out Anna's cries and her own guilt.

Landing gracefully, she spun upward and sliced the middle of the bag with her left foot. Damn Black Stripe.

Her right fist followed and jabbed six inches above where her foot landed. Damn her cowardice.

She hopped back and then attacked with a vengeance, her fists pummeling the bag in rapid succession. Damn New World Petroleum.

Cassidy's vision blurred and she paused, bending forward and drawing in deep breaths. Her ponytail had come loose sometime during the workout, and strands of sweat-soaked hair plastered themselves against her forehead and cheek. Biting the straps on her wrist, Cassidy tugged her gloves off. She pushed her hair out of her face, her hands shaking from the force of her attack against the punching bag.

A towel flew through the air, falling against the back of her neck and draping over her left shoulder. Gripping the edge of the rough cotton she wiped it against her face, inhaling the familiar scent of detergent and antiseptic.

"Nice workout, Cass. What crime did that poor bag commit?"

Cassidy struggled for air. Lifting her chin, she gazed to the side and grinned at the man standing beside her. He lounged against the wall, arms crossed over his chest as if he didn't have a care in the world. She narrowed her eyes and focused, reading him like only a best friend could. His wild mop of brown hair fringed light green eyes that were clouded with concern and his rakish smile that never failed to make her grin wasn't as wide or lighthearted as usual.

Steve Pullen unfolded his arms and held them open. She didn't hesitate and flung herself at him, needing the embrace of the only person on the planet who loved her. "Hey, stranger. It's nice to see your ugly face." Cassidy rested her head against his chest and allowed herself a brief second of feeling safe.

Steve kissed her forehead and patted her back. "Right back atcha, kiddo. What's cooking?"

She stepped back and allowed Steve to guide her off the mats and toward the doors that led into the changing rooms. Cassidy scanned the room, searching . . . dissecting. The walls flickered with the shimmering reflection of the lap pool that spanned the entire back of the athletic center. Was it possible that the hulk-like man eating up the water with long, steady strokes was Black Stripe? A pounding noise echoed from above, and her gaze traveled upward. Three women ran around the suspended track, their steps in unison, their breathing unchallenged. *What about them?*

"Earth to Cassidy."

She felt Steve's elbow nudge her stomach and snapped out of her scrutiny. "Just releasing some pent up anger."

Steve punched her shoulder, then pulled her tight against his chest. "Missed ya. I can make it to the top of mini-Everest in less than sixty seconds." He motioned to the tallest and most vertically challenging of the four climbing walls that jutted out from the far left wall.

"Yeah? Prove it."

He sighed and cocked his head. "Not this time, sugar. God would like a moment of your time."

"Is it Friday already?" Cassidy asked, allowing a playful pout to mar her face.

Steve grinned and shoved her toward the door marked for women. "No. But I think the circumstances surrounding your hasty retreat from Africa moved your briefing up just a tad."

Anger flushed her face. "If you only knew . . ." Her voice caught, and she swallowed. Her emotions were still too raw and unstable. "Any contact from Charles and David?"

"Not yet."

Cassidy narrowed her eyes, a flash of uncertainty triggering distrust in her friend. *Could Steve be Black Stripe?* She sighed and moved past the unaccustomed emotion but not before Steve noted the expression on her face.

He reached out a hand and rubbed her shoulder. "I'm on your side, remember?"

She tipped her head back and closed her eyes tightly. When she refocused on Steve, she smiled, trying to alleviate the concern from his face. "I'm okay. Just tired. So tired."

"Run away with me, then."

Cassidy winked, enjoying the familiarity of their old game. "To where?"

Steve frowned, pretending to think hard on his answer. "Iowa."

Laughter bubbled up and burst from her lips, freeing her mind temporarily of the burden of memory. "Now that's a new one. And what will we do in Iowa?"

"Farm and raise a family."

Cassidy snickered. "The family thing might be a bit hard seeing as there's not an ounce of attraction between us. But I'm game to try my hand at farming. We could grow corn and make little husk dolls."

Steve sighed and shrugged his shoulder. "Gee, what fun. You must've been my grandmother in a previous life. That's the only way to explain this thing we've got going on."

Cassidy patted his cheek, then offered him a light hug. "I wouldn't trade this relationship for the hottest love affair in the world. I need you just like this."

Steve rolled his eyes and shoved her through the door. "You're a better person than me, Cassidy Lowell. I'd drop you in a second for a steamy, torrid love affair."

The humidity of running showers enveloped her, and Cassidy grinned to herself, chuckling at Steve's last statement. "Yeah, you probably would." She didn't know how he did it, but after a few moments in his presence the world brightened to an almost functional level.

Cassidy hummed a Garth Brooks melody, ignoring the rock in her stomach. The elevator lurched upward in fits and starts. ZEBRA's office complex needed an entire overhaul. Because it was a multinational government organization, its funds were carefully allocated. Dr. Sharpe placed tremendous pride in their used desks and worn carpet, insisting that the United States wouldn't appear wasteful or wanton. The athletic center was his only concession.

She exited the elevator and veered to the left. A quick stop at her office was required before venturing into the lion's den. The scent of buttered popcorn filled the corridor, making her mouth water. One of the disadvantages of having a spacious corner office was that it sat within ten steps of the break room. Reaching her door, she picked off the Post-it notes left by the department's administrative assistant. Cassidy scanned them, satisfied that there wasn't an emergency.

Turning the doorknob, she moved to enter her office. Her door wouldn't open past a few inches. Puzzled, she pushed against it. It wasn't locked. Something was jammed against the inside wall. She pressed once more, then smacked her shoulder and hip against the wooden veneer, putting all her weight against the stupid thing until finally it budged. After squeezing through the narrow gap, Cassidy froze.

"What the hell?" She dropped the Post-its and knelt on the floor. A worn canvas travel bag sat before her. Lifting a shaking hand, she trailed her fingers along the familiar fabric. "And where did you come from?" Unzipping the top, Cassidy searched its interior. She sighed in gratitude at the picture of her parents, then kissed the frame and hugged it to her chest. Digging deeper, she discovered all her notes and her laptop.

How could this be? She was certain these things were all destroyed by the Kill-and-Go militia. The stench of unwashed clothes hit her dead-on. It smelled like wet towels left in the washing machine for a month. Wrinkling her nose, she quickly zipped the bag back up. "Yuck. That's ripe."

Cassidy's intercom buzzed, and Drew Sharpe's voice barked from the receptacle. "My office. Now."

"Aye-aye, Captain." She huffed and jumped to her feet.

Reaching behind her, Cassidy snagged a folder off her desk. She flipped open the file and glanced at the preliminary report she'd written. "Let's go ruin my career."

Kicking the bag away from the door, Cassidy left the soothing interior of her office and jogged down the hall to Drew's.

"Cassidy!" Sharpe's voice boomed from behind double wooden doors.

She rolled her eyes at his secretary and entered his office. It was three times the size of hers and came complete with antique Persian rugs and a fully stocked minibar. "I'm here. Sorry." Cassidy approached the imposing executive desk that dominated the entire back wall of windows.

Drew Sharpe sat behind the shiny mahogany, his stature slight but not overwhelmed by the oversized piece of furniture. A scowl slashed his brow and flicked a feather of fear in Cassidy's stomach. "You're late."

Checking her watch, she refused to surrender to intimidation. "I found my bag from Africa. How'd it get here?"

He stepped from behind his desk and walked toward her. "Really?" Pointing to a chair, he raised one eyebrow and silently commanded her to sit.

A brief flash of hope brightened the day. "You've had no contact with the Black Stripe unit that pulled me out?"

"None. As far as this office is concerned, they don't exist. Sit."

Cassidy covered the disappointment on her face by concentrating on the view outside his office. Modern buildings graced the skyline with tops of gilded metal and bronzed arches. Sliding into a leather chair, Cassidy decided to take the offensive position. "I know you're upset about the lack of a report."

"You think?" Sharpe sat back down behind his desk, leaned forward, and folded his hands. "What can I do to salvage this operation?"

"Salvage?" Cassidy frowned. "Like how?"

"I would still like to submit something to New World Petroleum for OPEC regarding their standing within Nigeria. What do you suggest?"

Cassidy flipped open her folder and shuffled through several sheets of paper. "I've begun a brief outline of my recommendations. First and foremost, all oil corporations operating within the Niger Delta must adhere to the same regulations as those operating within the United

States and the rest of the world."

"I thought you understood my position, Cassidy. I'm not looking for negatives but positives."

Cassidy stood up, irritation making her restless. "And I thought you understood mine. There are no positives."

"Dammit, Cassidy. What am I to do?" Sharpe smacked his palm against the desk. "NWP donated a very large sum of money to ZEBRA."

Straightening her back, Cassidy gazed at her boss. "NWP sanctioned an attack against our camp."

Sharpe shook his head. "There's no proof of that. This is a political game, Cassidy. One that's fought on battlefields of financial give and take. Taxpayers don't pay for our high-tech equipment, laboratories, and missions. It's about marketing, selling, and finding contributions. It doesn't behoove New World Petroleum to piss us off right now. They need us."

Cassidy didn't move. "I know what I saw."

Sharpe's eyes didn't flicker. He stared straight at her, not one iota of emotion showing. "I contacted Robert, and he has no knowledge of the attack. He's deeply sorry and hopes you'll be able to compile something that'll sway OPEC."

Her brain screamed at him, *Bullshit!* Cassidy glanced at her notes and collected her temper enough to speak professionally. "I won't lie."

He rested his forehead against the top of his desk. Straightening, he stared at her. "I don't want you to."

She re-crossed her legs and tapped the toe of her shoe against his desk. "Why don't we twist the report and offer our opinions as to how they can present themselves in a more positive light? Clean up the spills. Transfer the never-ending gas flow into pipes that can be channeled for power. Abolish the Kill-and-Go mentality and assist the natives in protecting their homes." Cassidy shrugged and then sighed. "I'm not good at politics. I'm sorry. This is all I can offer."

Sharpe gazed at her for a second, his bland expression masking his thoughts. She uncrossed and crossed her legs again, feeling like a misbehaving school child. His refusal to accept her version of the Kill-and-Go hit spoke volumes of her position within ZEBRA. Her job was vulnerable. After several excruciatingly long minutes, he nodded and tossed a sealed eleven-by-seventeen envelope at her. "These are the specs for your new assignment. It's in a place you're quite familiar with."

She ripped open the edge of the envelope. "Oh yeah?"

"Yellowstone."

Cassidy's heart skipped a beat. She gripped the edge of the envelope, no longer curious of its contents. "What's going on in Yellowstone?"

"Wolves are disappearing."

This couldn't be happening. She'd been yanked out of Africa for a bunch of wolves? It didn't make sense. "What?"

"Read the papers, Cassidy. Your team is already in place, gathering background information. You're scheduled to fly out on Friday. In the meantime, take a few days off and decompress."

Although worded nicely, she knew he wasn't suggesting vacation but ordering her to mentally regroup. She'd disappointed him. Cassidy smiled but knew the smile didn't reach her eyes. "I'm sorry, Drew."

He rubbed a hand against the back of his neck. "Whatever for?"

Sharpe spoke as if amused, but she knew better. He was shutting her out, diminishing her contribution. With a sick feeling sticking in her gut, Cassidy shrugged. "I'll see you in Jackson for the briefing on the wolves?"

"I'll be there."

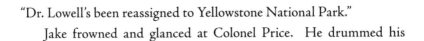

"Dr. Lowell's been reassigned to Yellowstone National Park."

Jake frowned and glanced at Colonel Price. He drummed his

fingers against the cool metal of the makeshift conference table. The clanging of pipes and rushing water echoed within the tiny basement room in the deepest recesses of ZEBRA's corporate headquarters that Black Stripe used as their central command.

A paneled wall separated Jake from the inner sanctum of Black Stripe. He didn't need to be behind those doors where advanced technology monitored the safety of the United States. He was field. The rules were clear. Sighing, Jake shook his head. "Have the grizzlies been warned?"

Price tipped his chin downward in an attempt to hide his smile. "You're going with her. Strip your fatigues and attitude, soldier. It's time to put on your jeans and use that degree we paid for."

"Shit." Jake rubbed a hand through his hair, pushing it off his face. "I'm going as her biologist?"

Price winked. "Smart man. Besides, I'm sure the grizzlies will appreciate your backup. She have a beam on you?"

Shrugging, Jake considered lying, then decided it wouldn't do him any good. "Nah. The light was funky, and I was in full camo. What's going down at Yellowstone?"

"Wolves are disappearing."

Jake grinned. "Is this some kind of terrorist plot by the prairie dogs? Take out the wolves first and next the entire country?"

Price snorted his soda through his nose. "Smartass." Jake laughed, following the colonel with his eyes as he stood and grabbed a piece of paper from inside an old beaten file cabinet. Jake knew the second they left, the file cabinet would retreat behind the wall into the safety of central command. "Myrtle spit out these facts. Steve can't trace the origin of the wire transfer."

Glancing at the sheet, Jake lifted an eyebrow in surprise. "Why would ZEBRA wire this amount of money to the Nigerian government?"

"They didn't. They laundered it for NWP, who then sent it on to the Nigerians."

Whistling through his teeth, he set the paper on the table. "This amount is much larger than the usual bribe. What gives?"

"Find the answer, and you win the game. Right now, Dr. Lowell is our only lead."

"Because she worked over there for six months?"

Price rested his palms on the table and leaned forward. "No. Because they want her dead."

Jake pushed back from the table, the bottom of his chair scratching against the linoleum. "Why not bring her in for questioning and just ask?"

"You and I both know the truth rarely exists for public scrutiny. That's why Black Stripe is effective. We damn well make sure that whatever this international environmental organization gets its hand into, it's in our country's best interest."

"You think ZEBRA's slipped?"

"I'm thinking I don't like bad-ass militants snuffing out American scientists. And more importantly, I don't like it when that order appears to be connected with the organization we're associated with. ZEBRA allows us access to countries we'd normally be banned from. The president is adamant that our involvement in ZEBRA remain as is. Nothing is to tip the scales. Find the truth, Anderson. Find out what this cluster fuck is really all about."

Jake thought about what the colonel had said. Africa stunk. His gut felt it; his mind agreed. "Yes, sir."

Cassidy left Drew's office, struggling to come to terms with what had transpired. The entire Nigerian assignment appeared on paper to be straightforward but in reality was riddled with contradictions and misguided goals. Ten years of successful operations for ZEBRA and now this? It didn't make sense. Nothing connected.

There was one little item regarding her time in Africa she decided to clarify. Passing her office, she entered a small computer lab. "Steve?"

Steve spun around in his chair and smiled at her. "There's my prettiest and bestest friend!" His exuberance contagious, Cassidy grinned back.

"I come seeking information."

He rubbed his chin and pretended to be deep in thought. "That'll cost you. Myrtle here . . ." he said, waving his hand at the large computer screen hanging from the ceiling, "doesn't come cheap."

"How about margaritas and fajitas?"

"Sold! To the lady in tight jeans and shirt displaying an odd breed of zebra."

Cassidy glanced at herself, twisting around to see her butt. "My jeans are not tight, smartass."

Steve laughed loudly, and his smile lit the entire room. "Glad to see your sense of humor is still intact. Come. Sit down, and let me amaze you with my computer magic. What deep dark secret do you require knowledge of?" He cracked his knuckles, waggled his brows, and pulled a chair over for Cassidy to sit on.

"I want to know about Black Stripe."

As quickly as it had appeared, Steve's smile faded.

CHAPTER 7

As Nick made his way to the door of the Italian bistro Drew Sharpe had suggested, Atlanta's humidity wrapped around him in a vice grip of still, stagnant air. After months in West Africa, Nick thought he could handle any heat on earth, but this was different. Here there wasn't a constant breeze from the ocean washing away the humid air. This heat sat above the sidewalk snatching at exhaust and human pollution, until Nick felt his lungs seize.

Nick pulled open the glass door and sighed as a flood of cool air escaped from the restaurant. After his eyes had adjusted to the dim interior, he took in the ocean of white tablecloths adorned with candles and crystal. Brass railings lined several levels and soft, luminescent lighting created an intimate ambiance within the bustling eatery. He inhaled the scent of garlic and oregano mixed with a blend of yeasty bread and fresh tomatoes. Nick's boss, Robert Cole, adored fine Italian cuisine, and it smelled as if this place would deliver a meal Robert's palate craved.

Nick scanned the bistro and found Drew seated at a table toward the back of the restaurant. Making his way through a throng of impatient patrons, Nick indicated with a flip of his hand to the maitre d' that he was expected at that table. Weaving among the tables, he adopted a casual and relaxed manner even though his eyes swung from corner to corner searching out any possible threat.

Nick affected a warm smile and reached across the table to envelop the director of ZEBRA's operations smaller hand within his. "Drew." The man was nervous. Sweat glistened across his brow, and Nick scrambled inwardly to mask his disgust at Drew's clammy hand.

With a nod of his head, Drew indicated for Nick to sit. "I was surprised when your secretary called to say Robert was in town. Will he be here soon?"

Nick pulled back a chair opposite of Drew and sat, his body tipped forward, ready to strike if danger approached. "He has high hopes that this meal will contain a positive report for OPEC?" He narrowed his gaze as a deep flush brightened Drew's face.

The man choked and gulped a large mouthful of water. He glanced quickly at Nick's face, then cast his eyes downward, shaking his head.

"No?" Nick sighed and signaled for the waiter. "Did you get . . ." He paused, not wanting to say her name, but even that small attempt at distancing his emotions didn't quell the sudden flutter of excitement as he pictured her wide-eyed and frightened against the backdrop of gunfire and burning oil. He'd have another chance at her. "Did you get the zoologist off to Wyoming?"

Nick picked up the small leather binder on the table and scanned the list of available wines. He pointed to a 1982 merlot and then turned his attention back to Drew Sharpe. Cold beer would be better, but he needed to maintain this image Robert Cole insisted he perfect.

Sharpe cleared his throat and tapped a finger against the white linen tablecloth. "Yes. I still don't understand . . ."

"It's not for you to question." He ignored the flicker of anger that sparked in Drew's eyes.

"Cole's complicated the entire mission by sending in your goons."

Nick's affable manner slipped, and he leaned forward, piercing Drew with a sharp gaze. "Don't make accusations you can't prove." *Fuckin' idiot.* Didn't he know who he was dealing with?

Drew sat back, sighed deeply, and laced his fingers together, resting them lightly on the edge of the table. "I'll place another signature on the report."

Turning back to Drew, he felt his anger simmer to an acceptable level. "You can't replace her name, you jerk! That'd alert OPEC."

Drew raised his hands in the air in an act of defeat. "I've sent her to Yellowstone. She's out of the way, so just tell me what you want me to do. I'll do whatever you ask."

A half smile tugged at the corner of Nick's lips.

Cassidy flipped her wrist over, checking the time. One o'clock. She hurried into the bedroom. Her duffel bag sat on the bed, the faded olive-green canvas with its numerous stains and frayed seams alien amidst the floral prints and muted spring colors of her quilt. Her windows were shut tight against the hot air outside, but a lingering scent of lemon from the candles she'd burned last night mimicked the perfume of the budding magnolia tree that knocked gently against the glass pane.

She opened her closet and dumped a minimal amount of clothing into the bag. Reaching onto the top shelf, Cassidy ran her hand across the wire rack until her fingers connected with smooth plastic. She retrieved a clear tote stuffed with miniature toiletry samples that she always bought by the dozen from her local discount store. She tossed that across the room, and it landed next to her bag. With a quick glance around, she snatched up a pair of worn work boots and shoved them into the now burgeoning interior. It didn't take more than five minutes to complete her packing. She was low maintenance and proud of it.

Cassidy hauled her duffel off the bed and dumped it next to the front door. She then did a quick walk through her apartment, verifying all lights were off and there were no overlooked dirty dishes hiding. That didn't take more than sixty seconds. She'd moved into this apartment twelve months previously, and everything but one box of kitchen items remained packed.

This wasn't home.

Her dedication to her career was reflected here, in this barely inhabited apartment situated not far from ZEBRA headquarters. A paper infested desk in her office welcomed her more warmly than her ghostly silent bedroom and sterile kitchen.

No life, no love, no commitment to anything but her job.

Shaking those morbid thoughts from her head, she picked up her bag and left the apartment. By the time she reached the lobby, a black Crown Victoria slid into the small pick-up and drop-off zone in front of the ornately trimmed front doors.

"Leaving us again, Doc?"

Cassidy nodded and waved at the security guard. "Sorry, Joe. This was just a short trip home. But we're still on for that poker rematch, right?"

He grinned. "Yes, ma'am. I hope they pay you good. You're gonna need it."

Laughing, Cassidy left the apartment building. She squinted against the sudden burst of sunlight that caused her eyes to water and signaled to the driver of the Crown Victoria. She dumped her canvas bag in the trunk and slid into the cool interior of the vehicle. "How's the traffic?"

The driver shrugged. "Typical of the lunch rush out of the city. We'll be at Dobbins within the half hour."

They headed north up I-75. Cassidy gazed out the window, not really seeing the throngs of people hurrying along the concrete sidewalk; her mind was turned inward and wandering back to Africa. She'd replayed that last night a million times and still couldn't fit together the pieces of the puzzle. Her heart clenched at the vivid memory of Anna; then came the familiar burst of anger and hatred toward the individuals, including herself, responsible for leaving her behind.

Steve hadn't offered any insight to the mysterious Black Stripe squad. Never one to leave a puzzle unsolved, Cassidy decided to pull in a few favors. She hummed to herself, and a Cheshire cat smile spread across her face. "I've got friends in high places . . ."

The car exited the interstate and turned left to loop back over the highway. Dobbins Air Force Base was located about twenty minutes north of the city. ZEBRA leased a small section of warehouse space and had flight privileges for its fleet of planes, making it a convenient ingress and egress route from Atlanta. As much as she traveled, Cassidy gratefully kissed the bureaucratic butt that prevented her from having to navigate through Hartsfield-Jackson International Airport.

The Crown Victoria deposited her outside ZEBRA's warehouse. The black and white striped transport plane sat on the runway, awaiting departure. A familiar figure scurried around the ground beneath it. Cassidy grinned and lifted her arm to attract his attention. "Steve," she yelled.

He turned and waved back. She grabbed her bag and jogged toward the plane.

"Hi, Cass. They've let me out of the office."

She tossed her bag to one of the maintenance crew. He, in turn, tossed it up the stairs, where it was retrieved by the pilot and stored onboard.

"Do they know how dangerous you are?" Cassidy teased.

Steve motioned for her to follow him toward the tail end of the plane. A camper-like vehicle was being driven up a ramp. "This is our latest mobile unit. We figure Yellowstone will be the perfect test ground for its unique capabilities. Hence, my release from jail."

Pushing her hair back from her face, she tried not to breathe too deeply. The hot Atlanta air was stifling. "You and your toys." Cassidy noted that the strange camper had a Ford heavy-duty truck base that supported a boxy upper structure.

Steve cringed as metal banged against metal and the vehicle was roped and tied in place. The ground crew triple-checked the cables, then signaled for everyone to vacate the storage area beneath the plane. Cassidy and Steve walked back down the ramp and watched as it slowly rose and sealed their equipment inside.

"What does it do?"

They headed toward the stairs at a slow, leisurely pace. "It's pretty cool. On the outside it resembles a regular camper, but inside it's full of state-of-the-art equipment including top-notch computers and a miniature laboratory. And it expands to provide a fully stocked necropsy lab."

That piqued Cassidy's interest, and she paused to glance over her shoulder at the back of the plane. "Really?" She hated dissecting in the field. Their results were never as clean as the ones they'd be able to obtain in a lab. "Now I'm sold. But let's hope we don't have to use it on this trip."

"You're kidding, right? We have to use it. Otherwise my valuable time and intellect will have been wasted."

Cassidy cocked a brow at him. "You really need to work on your self-confidence. Besides, they let you out all the time, so quit your whining."

"Bitch."

She growled and launched her fist in his direction, missing on purpose. He laughed and ducked her sucker punch, then jogged up the stairs and into the plane before she could reach out and really smack him. "I hate it when you call me that."

"I know."

"Cassidy?"

Cassidy lifted her nose from the stack of documents she'd been lost in for the past four hours, and blinked at Steve. "What?" The hum of airplane engines acted as a soothing anesthetic, causing her to yawn.

Steve laughed and shook his head. "You're not speaking to me."

She tilted her head and quirked one brow. "You're so sensitive. The fact of the matter is that I'm plowing through this invigorating report on wolves compiled by our enthusiastic research center." Waving the stack of documents at him, she smiled. "Besides, I hate flying."

"You're angry."

"Am not. I made you fajitas and margaritas the other night, didn't I?"

He leaned forward and snatched the documents out of her hands, stuffing them into a black leather messenger bag at her feet. "I can't tell you anything more about Black Stripe."

She sighed and gazed out the window. They were three-quarters of the way from Atlanta to Jackson. Secretly, Cassidy had been thrilled when she'd spotted him at Dobbins. His analytic brain was more precious than the entire ZEBRA mainframe. But she was pissed at his lack of forthrightness regarding Black Stripe, and being in such close quarters with him the past few hours made it hard to hide.

"Right," she huffed.

"Cassidy," he sighed. "I can't."

She leveled an I-don't-believe-you stare in his direction and reached down to reclaim her reports. "All you know is that they are a military division assigned to track our organization?"

"Yep."

"That's it?"

"Yep."

She stared at him, noticing the way his foot tapped against the floor. Steve was in constant motion, but the systematic rhythm of his toe bothered her. "You're lying." She stood up and paced in a circle, running her tongue across her teeth. She needed gum. The plane's passenger compartment was outfitted to afford the most comfort, with overstuffed chairs arranged to promote conversation and a small kitchenette in the back.

Cassidy made her way to the back, rumbling through the cabinets and finding a pack of salted nuts. From the half-sized refrigerator, she snagged a bottle of water she figured would be enough to eliminate the sandpaper feel of her mouth.

Not wanting to continue her discussion with Steve, Cassidy sat down at one of the work centers and logged onto the corporate network. She skimmed through her e-mail. There wasn't anything of importance, and most of it she deleted as spam. Even with the high level of security at ZEBRA, jokes and chain mails still managed to filter in.

It irritated Cassidy.

Turbulence shook the plane, and her stomach knotted. "I can do this," she said. Steve twisted in his chair and glanced back at her, patting the seat next to him. She disconnected from the network and sighed. "Crap." Making her way back toward the front of the jet, Cassidy concentrated on deep breathing exercises to calm the current uncomfortable sensations in her belly.

"Cassidy, calm down."

She glared at Steve and felt the plane bank to the left. Clutching the headrest of the seat, she lowered herself into place and buckled her belt back up. With a quick glance out the window, she swore violently when a string of mountain ranges came into view. "The Almighty certainly has a wicked sense of humor."

Steve chuckled. "How's that?"

Her memories surfaced, and she rubbed her temple. "'He'll only give you what you can handle' is what my mother always said."

"Wise woman."

She snorted. "I can't handle this. First Africa. Now Jackson. I thought my bravery at returning home would be enough martyrdom. This flight seems like an unnecessary evil." Cassidy shook her head, gritting her teeth against the painful burning in her chest. Against her better judgment, she scooted into the seat beside the window and pushed up the blind. They flew through shadows. It wasn't clouds blocking out the sun but thousands of feet of jagged rock.

The Grand Tetons.

Breathtaking. Majestic. Deadly.

Watching the mountains pass by, Cassidy rested her head against the cool window. She'd be a wreck by the time they landed. Triple damn. The plane bucked against the increasing turbulence, causing Cassidy to grip the arms of her seat in a panic.

The pilot's voice boomed over the intercom. "You might want to buckle up; it can get a bit dicey through this stretch."

"No shit," she said, quickly tightening her seat belt. A morbid sense of curiosity prevented her from closing the blinds.

"Stop it, Cassidy."

Steve's voice startled her, and she turned toward him. "Stop what?"

"Whatever it is that's burning a hole in your chest. Look at you! You're an emotional basket case. What's the matter?"

Slamming the blind down, she unbuckled the seat belt, scooted sideways, re-buckled the belt, and poked a finger into Steve's chest. "This is how my parents died." The plane rocked and shuddered. She bit her lower lip and continued to stare at Steve.

"Bullshit." They slid to the left as the plane dipped. Her stomach dropped, and she suppressed the need to wretch. Not good. This was not good at all. She wrenched her seat belt tighter.

Cassidy glared at him. "At twenty-four, I resigned from Yellowstone National Park and accepted a position with ZEBRA."

Rolling his eyes, Steve clucked his tongue in dismay. "Tell me something I don't know."

The plane plummeted what felt like five hundred feet but in reality was probably only fifty. She gripped the arms of her chair and closed her eyes tightly. Cassidy bent over and lowered her voice to a menacing whisper. "Nine years ago, my parents flew through these very same skies." Her flesh puckered up in a series of chilling goose bumps.

"Uh huh." Steve said, his voice void of emotion.

Cassidy ignored him. "Right when they were about to land . . ." she rounded her eyes and swept her arm down, "a huge blast of air shot down from the icy glaciers above and smashed them into the side of the Tetons."

Steve inhaled. "Holy shit. Why didn't you ever tell me this?"

"You never asked."

"I asked plenty; you just shut me out." Steve clamped his teeth down and stared at her.

The plane vibrated, and Cassidy breathed deeply. "Don't play all wounded puppy on me. You seem to have your own horde of secrets you refuse to share."

"It's classified, Cass."

"Yeah? Well, you'd better start praying that God's not classified us in the same category He did my parents." Cassidy felt the dip of the private jet as it circled left in preparation for landing.

Home.

A loud thud signaled the drop of landing gear, and she squeezed her armrest. She never should've eaten those peanuts. "Remember," Cassidy prayed, "this Lowell doesn't want to crash. She's not quite done here on Earth. You've got my parents; let's not be greedy."

The pilot's voice boomed from the intercom. "Hang tight; this landing's gonna be about as smooth as a ten-point buck slamming into your behind."

"What?" Steve squeaked.

Cassidy leaned over and flipped up the window visor. She swallowed past the lump in her throat. The plane was eating up the runway, and there was nowhere else to go but the side of a mountain. "I'm sorry, I'm sorry, I'm sorry," she chanted, laughing when she heard Steve mimicking her words. Grasping his hand, she held tight.

An ear-piercing screech filled the cabin, and her world spun out of control as the wheels slid off the runway.

CHAPTER 8

JAKE LAY SPRAWLED ON THE HOOD OF THE ZEBRA-STRIPED JEEP. His hands were linked behind his head, resting on the glass of the windshield. He tilted his face toward the sky, soaking in the warmth of the late afternoon sun. A thin trickle of sweat ran down his bare chest and tickled his belly button. He sat up, scratched, and raised his arm to shield his eyes from the bright sky. In the distance, the sun sparkled off the silver wings of an approaching plane.

Dr. Cassidy Lowell.

Hell and damnation if this wasn't going to be the most frustrating assignment. He'd spent the past few days solidifying his cover and reading spreadsheet after spreadsheet regarding wolf habitat and migration. It didn't take him long to realize there'd be very little scientific involvement on his end. This was nothing more than a damn babysitting job. Not even a rogue Isotria to be logged.

He squinted and watched as the plane's wings banked sharply to the left. Jake frowned and snatched his sunglasses off his T-shirt. He focused on the landing and swore loudly. "Sonofabitch."

Jake's heart thumped against his chest as he watched the approach of the black-and-white-striped corporate jet. The pilot miscalculated the air density, making the plane veer too sharply. Snatching up his shirt, he shoved it over his head and jumped behind the wheel of the Jeep.

The high-pitched squeal of rescue vehicles carried down the runway, and he pulled behind them, driving at breakneck speed.

Jake cringed when the jet spun off the tarmac, its tail skidding sideways, kicking up dirt and grass. When the plane came to an abrupt stop, undamaged, Jake let out a sigh of relief. He maneuvered his vehicle between the fire truck and ambulance.

The cabin door opened, and stairs unfolded. As the engines settled into silence, voices from within the plane drifted down. A woman appeared at the top of the stairs, pushed aside the pilot, and tossed a moss green duffel bag down the steps. The bag landed on the grass with a resounding thud.

Dr. Cassidy Lowell. He'd never seen her in proper daylight. She was tall, as thin as a whip, and had a halo of golden hair that made a grown man want to get down on his knees and pay homage. Jake let out a low wolf whistle and headed in her direction. She sure was pretty.

"That was some sorry-ass landing," she snapped.

He remembered the tone of that voice and shook his head, glad he wasn't on the receiving end.

"How the hell'd you get your pilot's license?"

Another man exited the plane and scooted Cassidy down the stairs. Jake grinned when he recognized the familiar face of Steve Pullen. The rescue team made their way up the stairs, stopping the doctor's downward march as they verified everyone was safe and sound.

"Dr. Lowell?" he called from the base of the steps. Poor pilot. The man looked like he needed a drink. Actually, he looked like he could down an entire twelve pack and still need a drink. A brisk wind swept across the tarmac, stealing the bite of heat from the runway.

"Yeah?" The face of ZEBRA's lead zoologist stared down at him.

"Who the hell are you?"

No recognition. Good. "Jake Anderson, ma'am."

She jogged the rest of the length of the stairs and stopped before him. Her head tilted up slightly, and deep emerald eyes returned his appraising gaze. "And who is Jake Anderson?"

"I'm your biologist."

"Where's Liv?"

"Liv Somers is currently en route to Cuba."

She folded her arms across her chest. Jake tried to keep his eyes from dropping to the enticing skin exposed at the base of her neck, but he couldn't resist. When his gaze traveled back up, there was a notice-able frost in her eyes. "Too bad," she said coldly.

"I'm sorry your landing was rather rough."

Her face flushed bright red. "Rough? Is that your definition of al-most kissing the side of a mountain at 120 miles per hour?"

She was sassy. He liked sassy. Instead of fueling her temper, he shrugged and waved at the pilot. "You know, I'd expected a different person," he said. "Is this normal behavior for you?"

Cassidy raised her brows and shrugged. "Normally I'm an insuf-ferable bitch. I think I'm being rather pleasant today."

Steve walked up behind Cassidy. "I can vouch for that."

"Thank goodness for small blessings," Jake answered, picking up Cassidy's briefcase. "Good to see you again, Steve."

"Right back atcha." Steve answered.

Cassidy turned her attention toward Steve, and Jake watched in amazement at the transformation of her face. It went from guarded and unfriendly to open and trusting. Harsh to beautiful in under three seconds. "I suggest you check the belly of the beast," she said. Jake's eyes widened when she patted Steve's cheek. Cassidy continued, "I'd hate to think all your intelligence and hard work were wasted because of that piss-poor landing."

"You reading my mind again, boss?" Steve winked and turned, signaling to the pilot to drop the ramp.

Cassidy turned, and her gaze hardened. "Give me the briefcase, Hercules. You can grab my duffel bag." She climbed into the Jeep. "But be careful. It contains fragile items."

Jake eyed the bag that she'd sent sailing out the plane's door. He grinned and went to rescue it from the barren ground. With the likes of Cassidy Lowell around, this assignment suddenly didn't seem quite so boring.

Cassidy watched Jake out of the corner of her eye. She didn't like his type. Too masculine. Narrowing her eyes, she scrutinized him. He certainly didn't carry himself like any biologist she'd ever met. Shaggy black hair hung past his shoulders, softening the sharp angles of his face.

Laugh lines crinkled when he smiled. He and Steve were tossing insults at one another via the two-way radio. She twisted in her seat and waved to her best friend, his face barely recognizable behind the tinted glass of the modified camper.

Wind whipped strands of hair against her cheek, and Cassidy held it back from her eyes. She loved the feeling of riding in the open-topped Jeep but refrained from allowing it to show in front of her biologist. Something about him struck a caution cord.

She cocked her head, thankful that her sunglasses masked her scrutiny. Strong hands. Strong arms. Confident to the point of cocky. Nope. She'd never met a biologist like this before.

Sighing deeply, she rooted in her handbag for a ponytail holder, quickly gathering her hair and pulling it through the loop. Better. Maybe now she could focus on the road instead of blinking back tears from wind-whipped hair.

"You okay?" Jake's question interrupted her thoughts.

"Fine."

"You're very quiet. Don't you have any questions regarding where we're at with our investigation?"

Sighing in exasperation, Cassidy snapped, "Shut up, Jake Anderson. I'm concentrating on my personal anguish."

"You're what?" The glare she tossed him over the rim of her glasses quelled any further response. Good. She had no desire to talk, about either herself or the assignment.

She felt the mountains closing in. Cassidy chewed on her bottom lip; she'd thought she could handle it. Had convinced herself, in fact. But now, with the familiar backdrop of peaks and plains, she felt her heart hammer against her chest with such intensity she was certain it couldn't be healthy.

You're a weak one, Dr. Lowell. She hummed the tune from *The Grinch*, trying to find words that would make her laugh and not weep. "This is my job. I can do this. It's only Jackson."

"Excuse me?" Jake said.

"What?"

He leaned across her toward the glove compartment, his arm brushing against her thighs. "You said something."

If this was his idea of flirting, she wasn't impressed, nor was she interested.

Flipping open the compartment, he retrieved a pair of sunglasses and popped them on his face. "So, what did you say?"

"Nothing."

"Yes, you did. Something about this is my job . . ."

She crossed her arms over her chest and bit back the irritated none-of-your-business blurb, not wanting to sound like a complete idiot. "I tend to talk to myself." Narrowing her eyes, she dared him to comment further.

Jake glanced at her quickly, her reflection wavering in his mirrored glasses. "Nothing wrong with that," he said. "I do the same. Actually, I'm such a social moron that most of the time I'm the only person interested in listening to what I have to say."

Cassidy bit her lip, but it was too late. Laughter bubbled up and spilled from her mouth in waves of pent up emotion. She couldn't believe how horribly she'd been behaving. It wasn't like her. "Yes," she hiccupped. "I think that's it exactly."

"Friends?"

She eyed him, squinting against the sun that poured through the windshield. She rubbed her forehead and tilted her face to the warmth of the rays. "No. I'm the boss, and you're my biologist. But considering we're both in the same proximity, we might as well appear slightly sane and speak to one another instead of ourselves."

The corner of Jake's mouth twitched up in a grin, and he shook his head at Cassidy. She put on her sweetest smile, waiting for him to say something that would no doubt piss her off. Cassidy didn't like the sudden affinity he'd created; she'd do her best to keep her guard up.

He winked. "Strictly business then. Last week the pre-unit arrived and began gathering data from the locals."

Cassidy focused her attention on his words, snatching a small pad from the side of her messenger bag in case she needed to take notes. "Locals?"

"Park Rangers. The local authorities responsible for all aspects of Yellowstone."

"I know what the Rangers do."

Jake nodded. "Right. You worked here, didn't you?"

"It was a job." He cocked his head in her direction, and she figured he was probably shooting her a very nasty look behind those aviator glasses. "Continue."

"We've verified the statistics. And you won't like them. In less than a week, more than sixteen wolves have dropped off the radar."

Cassidy fell into silence. Her mind whirled around facts, figures, and possible answers. "That's impossible."

"My thought exactly."

The entrance to Yellowstone loomed ahead. Wooden guard houses paused traffic, collecting fees and handing out maps. Jake slowed the vehicle, and Cassidy averted her eyes from the large timbers that marked the entrance and stared at her hands, feeling a sudden wave of insecurity.

Jake flipped open his identification wallet, and the guard waved them through without demanding an entrance fee.

Cassidy gave up trying to prevent her eyes from feasting on the familiar surroundings. Even though she didn't want the pain, she couldn't fight the call. The depth of green that painted both sides of the road drew her attention. Behind the dense brush and hundred-foot lodge pole pines hid a vast array of wildlife. She'd been fascinated as a child, intrigued as an adolescent, and incurably addicted by eighteen.

This is what had shaped her.

Her passion for animals had begun right here, at her father's side. She missed him.

Cassidy needed to concentrate on her assignment. But the geysers called. She could almost feel the mist of Old Faithful, and the sulfur scent of the hot springs that surrounded Yellowstone's hydrothermal basin crept into her senses. It felt like a champagne cork had exploded, allowing her memories to shoot out and touch the crystal sky above.

Scooting forward in her seat, she gripped the edge of the dash.

"How does it feel, Sunshine?"

"What?" Her mind was only partially on the conversation.

"To be home?"

Cassidy bit her bottom lip and sat back in her seat. A million memories flickered through her mind blinking on and off rapidly, leaving her confused and slightly disjointed. The buzzing of whispered words long past rang in her ear. She inhaled and shredded the mist that threatened to emotionally cripple her. Glaring at Jake, she pointed a nail-bitten finger in his direction. "My feelings or lack thereof are none of your business. I'm here on assignment, and that's all you need to concern yourself with."

His shoulders moved in a slight shrug at the sharpness of her words, and he turned to face the road again. "Whatever you say, Sunshine."

Irritation scratched the back of her neck. The ghost of summers past had a hold on her, and it was making her ultra-sensitive. She mentally smoothed away her annoyance and focused on the facts of the assignment.

Wait one damn second.

There was definitely something about Jake Anderson that warranted this sense of aggravation. She frowned, thinking about their conversation.

Did he keep calling her *sunshine?*

Her mouth dropped open, and she snatched her glasses off, glaring at him. "You're a real condescending jackass," she finally said.

"I think, Goldilocks . . ." He reached over and tugged on her ponytail, causing her to pull back and smack her funny bone on the hard metal of the Jeep door. "You bring out the best in me."

CHAPTER 9

When Jake pulled in front of Lake Yellowstone Hotel, Cassidy's breath caught. Her eyes followed the length of the bright white pillars supporting the four-story front porticoes. Its history dated back to the late nineteenth century, and she could recite it as easily as she could the Lord's Prayer. Pale yellow paint decorated the antique building's exterior, an odd contrast to the dark, woodsy setting.

Memories played through her mind, unnerving yet comforting.

She'd spent most of her childhood romping across the long slope of grass that dipped toward Lake Yellowstone, making this place a home away from home. She was here, and she'd better deal with it. Running her hand down one of the imposing columns, she let her eyes sweep upward to where it connected with the roof leaving a comfortable corner for nesting birds. She closed her eyes and imagined the past, remembering the scent of fresh sawed wood laced with burnt pine from the ever-steady fire that disintegrated discarded debris. It seemed so real that a tickle of warmth and comfort filled her chest.

She felt the heat from Jake's presence against her back and then the touch of his hand upon her shoulder. "Snap out of it, Sunshine. The day's a wasting."

She sighed, slipping back into the present. "Nostalgia's an evil thing." Cassidy needed to concentrate and focus. A truck backfired in the parking lot and she jumped, her hand clutching at her chest to stop the pounding of her heart.

Jake patted her back. "Easy, kiddo. It's just a bum muffler."

Cassidy moved away from his touch and swore beneath her breath. This had to stop. If every bang and jolt brought visions and nightmares of Africa, she'd become a raging lunatic before autumn had a chance to smack the mountains with color. "Sorry. I must still be a bit raw from that landing." She stepped away from the pillar and snagged the messenger bag Jake dropped by her feet.

Steve pushed between them. "Need to drain the main vein," he said.

Cassidy groaned, and Jake chuckled. "Take a left down the main hall and follow the signs to the presidential suite," Jake called after him.

"Ten-four." He waved and disappeared into the lobby.

"Do you know this is the oldest standing hotel in Yellowstone?" She walked slowly past him and headed toward the front entrance.

Jake glanced around and shrugged. "It sure has a nice view." He kept pace with her.

"That it does." Walking toward the glass door, Cassidy continued her history lesson. "The building was first completed in 1891. Of course, the architecture was less sophisticated than what you see today, but still it was mighty impressive. Stagecoaches would pull right up here, next to the front doors."

Jake pulled the door open and allowed her to step through. "In 1903," she continued, "Robert Reamer decided it needed a facelift and added his own colonial touches. Those false balconies and dormers outside were his idea, as well as additional columns."

"And you would know this because?"

Cassidy paused, ignoring his question. She absorbed the large, gracious lobby with hardwood floors that gleamed in the late afternoon sun. The scent of fresh brewed coffee wafted from the lounge to the left. A wavering reflection of the lake played through the full-sized windows that arched across the front. She ignored his last question and continued to soak in her surroundings. "This place declined drastically over time until it was known as nothing more than Bat Alley."

"Bat Alley, huh? I guess there were more than cobwebs hanging from the rafters."

Cassidy moved toward the heart of the lobby and stopped in front of a large picture. Tapping on the grainy surface of a face that rose behind a group of men, she smiled. "This is my father. He helped bring back Robert Reamer's dream. It took these men almost ten years of triumphs and failures to realize that man's vision. But it was worth it, wouldn't you say?"

"Yes," Jake said softly. "I'd agree." Dropping her duffel bag, he peered closer at the picture. His scrutiny didn't sit well with her.

Squaring her shoulders, she stepped back and looked at her biologist. "And here ends our history lesson for today. Shall I get checked in so that we can get on with this game?"

Jake picked up Cassidy's bag and headed down a side hall. "No need. We're in the presidential suite." Shock kept her rooted in place as she watched him walk down a wide hallway carpeted with thin multicolored commercial Berber. After a few seconds, he turned to look at her. "Coming?"

"We? Did you say *we*?"

"Yes, Sunshine. But don't worry, there's two bedrooms. The sitting room has been relegated to command central. We drew straws for room assignments, and you won." He shrugged. "Or lost, depending how you view it."

Jesus, Cassidy. Could you be any more touchy? she asked herself, feeling guilty. "Sorry . . ." She offered him a half smile. "That'll be fine." These weren't unusual circumstances. ZEBRA missions meant close quarters and intense coordination of personnel. But she needed to square one small item away. Pointing at Jake, Cassidy narrowed her eyes and put on her best demanding boss impersonation. "I swear if you use *Sunshine* as a proper noun one more time, I'll do something drastic like stick shaving cream in your hand while you sleep." She moved past him and headed toward the presidential suite.

Jake laughed, filling the hall with his lighthearted voice.

With her back to him, Cassidy allowed herself an honest smile, one that lifted her spirits and made amusement tickle her chest. It felt good. Damn good.

Following the signs to the presidential suite, Cassidy felt an itch of excitement as she neared their room. Work sounded wonderful. Drowning herself in the wolf mystery would help re-center her skewed emotions. She grinned like a fool at the thought of hiking to one of the many observation posts and spending a solitary night with nothing more than her blanket and, hopefully, a pack of gray wolves.

She stood before the wooden door, placing her palm against the smooth grain of the polished surface. It vibrated. The room beyond was frantic with activity. She could smell it.

Jake reached around her and twisted the knob, urging her through the entryway with a nudge of his shoulder. "They won't bite. I promise."

Cassidy rolled her eyes as she stepped into the center of a typical ZEBRA mission. The room was filled with about a half dozen people spread out in front of computers and ringing telephones. She immediately snapped into work mode, weaving through tables and employees to reach the safety of a small, narrow conference table.

The scent of fresh brewed coffee drew her attention to the far corner, where Steve was already attacking a computer keyboard with the dedication of a master pianist. There was a food cart to the left of him, but before she could take one step toward the much needed caffeine,

Jake turned her shoulder until she faced the other end of the room.

Dr. Sharpe sat at the head of the small conference table. Cassidy immediately recognized his impatient frown and offered Jake a grateful smile. She waved him away and walked over to sit beside her mentor.

Dr. Sharpe focused on Cassidy, and Cassidy noted the tired lines around his eyes and wondered what troubled him. He absently rubbed his hand over his roughly sheared salt and pepper hair and pursed his lips thoughtfully.

"Tough landing, I hear?" he said, his voice gruff with concern.

"It's already forgotten."

He tilted his head and cast a sly grin. "You're a real pain in the ass, Lowell."

Cassidy laughed softly and tapped her pencil against the back of his hand. "Yeah, I know. But I'm good at what I do."

Drew flipped open his notebook and scanned a piece of paper, taking his eyes off the document after only a few seconds. "Did you by any chance order a geological survey of the delta?"

Confused by the sudden change in topic, Cassidy opened her mouth to explain why she'd gone over budget and flown Charles and David to the Niger Delta. However, the memory of Charles' last statement about the results of the survey along with her retrieval from Africa and reassignment here had her quickly changing her words. Something wasn't right. "Why do you ask?"

"Thought I saw it on your expense report."

Weirded out but not willing to express her wariness, Cassidy lifted her shoulder in a careless shrug. "Don't believe I've had the chance to turn that in yet."

Drew held her gaze for a beat too long, then dismissed the conversation by returning his attention back to the document in his hand and speaking to her in an offhand manner. "Then I suggest you do. Payroll hates playing catch-up."

Cassidy rose from the table. "I just need a few minutes to review the latest stats that Dr. Anderson provided; then I'll be ready to make the presentation." She didn't like his reserved attitude.

Sharp glanced up. "Okay. I'll inform everyone to convene in approximately fifteen minutes."

Spreading her data on the table, Cassidy scrutinized the figures. The printout she'd been provided with prior to take-off notated a gradual decline in wolf population. The back of her neck tingled. She glanced over her shoulder and stared at Jake. "Must you stand so close?" He grinned and stepped to the side.

"I didn't realize you had personal space issues."

"I don't. Do you have the updated information?" He was still standing too close.

Leaning over her shoulder, he placed a spreadsheet on the table. "Right here."

About to demand he move away, Cassidy stopped. The numbers on the sheet caught her eye. She grabbed a highlighter and began marking up her schematic of the park. Nearly every quadrant containing wolves had been depleted. "This is unsettling."

Jake pointed to an area on her map. "I wonder if something has contaminated the water system and then transferred from pack to pack. See how heavily populated the area past the north entrance was? Is it possible that the packs returned to certain quadrants that are fed from the same water source?"

Cassidy chewed her bottom lip and frowned. "Maybe. But I'm certain that would be the first thing the rangers tested. Besides, a contaminated water source would leave numerous species dead. Not just wolves. Let me get through this briefing, and we'll head out to grab our own sample."

"All work no play makes Dr. Lowell grumpy all day."

She grinned. "My work is my play." Cassidy folded up the schematics and stats, shoving them back into her briefcase. "I'm ready," she announced to Dr. Sharpe, laying a folder full of transparencies on the table. He nodded, and his attention turned to the rest of the crew now taking their places around the table.

Cassidy followed his gaze. Michelle Allen, their chief ecologist, slid into the seat next to her. Her brown hair was pulled neatly into a ponytail, and she sat primly behind the table, prepared to take notes. Michelle had been with ZEBRA longer than Cassidy and had about ten years on her age-wise. Cassidy returned her smile, wondering why Michelle had never advanced higher in the organization.

Steve flung himself into the nearest chair, flipping her the finger and dropping a flurry of disorganized papers on the table. She stuck her tongue out at him and grinned. His long, slender physique should make him ungainly, but he was as limber as a monkey, constantly in motion and burning more calories just sitting still than the average person did walking a mile. He winked. She crossed her eyes. Catching an amused expression on Jake's face, Cassidy blushed and twisted in her chair to face her administrator. "Valerie, do you have copies of the preliminary report for everyone?"

Valerie had a one-inch stripe of shock-white hair that contrasted with the rest of her black bob, and Cassidy tried not to stare at it as the older woman tucked it behind her ear. "Yes, they're right here." She carefully distributed the detailed reports down the table and nodded to Sharpe when she was done.

When everyone had a copy of the report, Drew stood and clapped his hands together. "Okay, ladies and gentlemen, you are officially now members of Pod Gray Wolf."

A soft chuckle spread around the table. Dr. Sharpe referred to all his group assignments as pods. The term originated from one of their earlier expeditions where they complained that the close quarters made them feel as if they were all just peas in a pod. Sharpe demanded equitable teamwork and liked the idea of reinforcing that idea by naming each handpicked team as a "pod."

After the noise settled down, he continued. "As you know, all reports and communication shall be labeled as such." He turned his chair and flicked a few switches. The lights dimmed, and an overhead projector outlined a sketch of Yellowstone National Park.

"We've been assigned to assist park personnel in determining why their gray wolf population has suddenly decreased in number. The team leader for this expedition will be Cassidy Lowell. She is an expert on the gray wolf and was one of the team leaders that initially reintroduced the species to Yellowstone National Park. At this point in time, I'll turn the projector over to her, and she'll explain a few more details."

"Thank you, sir." Cassidy flipped another transparency on the screen, displaying a picture of a proud male wolf, his vibrant golden eyes gleaming fiercely from the screen. A mask of brown, gray, and black hair outlined the eyes cupped by soft, downy white fur that spread from his nose to beneath his ears, producing the effect of a wide, cheeky grin.

"This is canis lupus, more commonly referred to as the gray wolf. In 1973, the population in North America plummeted to four hundred due to a long history of hunting, trapping, and poisoning. The gray wolf was one of the first species listed as endangered in that same year, and all hunting has since been prohibited. Unfortunately, there are many ranchers that still uphold the view that these are dangerous beasts." Cassidy took a breath and scanned the room to make sure she still held everyone's attention. Her mouth watered when another whiff of coffee filtered across the table, and she occupied her caffeine-starved brain by refocusing on the lecture.

"There are roughly thirty-five hundred gray wolves now residing in the lower forty-eight states, primarily in Minnesota, Wisconsin, and Michigan. In 1995, I had the privilege of taking part in the reintroduction of thirty-one gray wolves to Yellowstone. That count has steadily increased, and in the last survey the population was noted at approximately a hundred and twenty adults. Last month," she said, pausing and looking through the dim light at her team, "the count was reported at fifty-five. And as of this morning, GPS can find no positive response from any of the collared wolves." A soft gasp and instant buzz could be heard throughout the room.

"Has the wolf been removed from protection under the Endangered Species Act?" Jake asked.

"Not yet," Cassidy answered. "However, federal regulators have proposed a lower level of protection that places them close to being removed. This is exceptionally dangerous, as we will no longer have any control over their fate."

"This might sound like a dumb question, Cassidy," a soft voice spoke from the side, "but if the wolves are confined to Yellowstone, why are the ranchers so against them?"

Cassidy smiled at Michelle. She always saw the upbeat side of every ecological success; maybe that's what prevented the ecologist from promotion. It would be beyond her ability to believe that any positive accomplishment would result in negative responses, and that hindered the out-of-the-box thinking required to lead a successful mission. "Michelle, as you know, we can't control wildlife. The wolves have wandered out of Yellowstone territory, and there's nothing we can do to stop them. Many ranchers have been, and still are, alarmed at the reintroduction of a natural predator to the surrounding land, threatening their livelihood. They are mollified, somewhat, by the reimbursement for dead livestock, but we're still forced to shoot any wolves that decide to dine on domesticated animals."

Cassidy watched Jake stretch his legs beneath the table and rub his chin in thought. "Who's to say half the Yellowstone population hasn't migrated?" he queried, interrupting her thoughts.

"About twelve out of the twenty or so packs have migrated beyond

Yellowstone boundaries. However, all the packs have numerous collared wolves. The packs are monitored constantly through GPS. Also, they're clinging very close to Yellowstone. They're still in what is considered undeveloped wild country."

"You said they were collared?"

"Yes. Even though a tagged wolf would be considered inferior to the rest of the pack and killed, Yellowstone has had great success with radioed collars. About 75 percent of the population is tracked, and all packs can be located through GPS."

"How are the others counted then?" he persisted.

"Visually. Just like you and I, each wolf has individual markings and is assigned either a number or name based on its description. Pictures are taken when possible and a detailed log maintained."

Jake tapped a pen against the desk. "What about other wildlife?"

"As in?"

"I'm not sure. Have there been other inconsistencies that might point us in a direction to begin the investigation?"

Cassidy shrugged. "I haven't gone over Yellowstone's spreadsheets yet. However, I did send a bulletin out to all the local veterinarians and wildlife organizations within this area and haven't received back anything substantial." She flipped over a few pages and squinted at a printed e-mail. It was hard to read in the dim light. "The only response sent was from a vet's office in Gardiner. He's been experiencing a higher than normal influx of parvo . . ."

Pausing, she held the letter under the light of the overhead projector. "It says that he didn't feel it to be a concern because almost all of the dogs originated from the pound. They've tested the remaining animals in the facility and cleaned the area. The dogs were all treated successfully." She glanced up at Jake. "That's it."

Dr. Sharpe flipped off the overhead projector and turned the lights on. Cassidy squinted and rubbed her eyes.

"Okay, Cass, what's your take on this? Environmental or man?"

"I don't know, sir. The numbers are really scary. Almost all the population gone or missing? It could be anything from a poisonous plant to migration to illegal hunting, but I agree that we need to investigate."

"That's what the feds want as well. I don't believe that disease is involved, due to the fact that no bodies have been found. Therefore, I'll refrain from involving the CDC. Yellowstone wants to maintain its image as a safe haven for wildlife and has asked that we keep a low profile and try to avoid any negative publicity." Sharpe cleared his voice and pierced Cassidy with a demanding look. "Chief Ethan Connor is your contact."

Cassidy smiled brightly at her boss and nodded . . . another aspect of her past brought present. *Ethan.*

"All right then, I consider this pod officially briefed. I'll be returning to Atlanta in approximately thirty minutes. Are there any questions?"

The room was silent, and Sharpe glanced at his watch. "I believe, Cassidy, that a joint briefing is taking place at park headquarters tomorrow morning."

"Yes, sir."

Cassidy gathered her notes and rose from the table. She absently acknowledged the other departing team members as she stretched out muscles that screamed for a quick workout. "You ready to gather that water sample, Jake?"

He grinned and nodded toward one of the closed doors. "Why don't you go freshen up, and I'll order us some lunch first. Then we can get to work."

She nodded, silently relieved that she'd have a few moments to herself. Before she'd reached her bedroom door, she stopped and turned. Dr. Sharpe was standing in the middle of the parlor staring at her. She couldn't read his expression, but it sparked alarm.

"Sir?"

"I want to make sure that neither the death of your parents nor your episode in Nigeria will affect your performance."

Cassidy's entire body tingled then went numb. Heat flashed to her face, more than likely making her look like an overripe tomato. She didn't dare glance at Jake.

"No, sir." Her voice cracked, and she inhaled to garner some control. She couldn't be any more mortified if she were standing stark naked.

"You'll do whatever's necessary. Is that clear?"

"Sir?"

"If you need to fly in and out of that airport where your parents died, then that's what you'll do. I'd be disappointed if you required rescuing again."

Embarrassment laced with anger left her speechless. She'd never been the object of Dr. Sharpe's concerns before, and his reference to her personal tragedy was both unprofessional and unwarranted. Not to mention that his allusion to Nigeria remained totally unjustified.

"Dr. Sharpe, I'm certain that won't be necessary." Jake stepped over and took her elbow, leading her toward the bedroom. He shoved her inside and slammed the door closed. She felt like a little kid, her body unable to respond to the conflicting signals her mind kept screaming.

What the hell was the matter with her? Cassidy inhaled deeply, then pounded one shaking fist against her open palm. She closed her mind to insecurity and guilt, focusing on her center balance. Yanking the door open, she opened her mouth to tell the men to shove it where the sun doesn't shine but faced an empty room.

She stood gaping at the paper-strewn conference area. She was alone. Tears burned her eyes but this time not from old ghosts. This time, they were tears of disillusionment. Her failure in the last mission must have placed her on Sharpe's watch list. She'd known deep down of this possibility, but it stung when reality bit her in the ass. The thought that she'd lost his respect and trust fired up her guilt over

Anna another notch.

This was the reward for sticking to your ideals.

Cassidy rested her head against the doorjamb, trying to find justification and reassurance from some small crevice of her soul.

Instead, she found coffee.

A slow smile spread across her face as she moved forward, drawn to the carafe of caffeine that finally lay within reach. Pouring a large mug full, Cassidy rested her hip against the conference table. Allowing the heat and rich hickory of the slow-roasted beans to weave its healing powers around her jangled nerves, she thought about everything that Drew had said that afternoon. The puzzle became larger, the pieces more elaborate.

"What game are you playing, boss?"

CHAPTER 10

CASSIDY BRUSHED OUT HER TANGLED CURLS AND QUICKLY braided her hair, securing the end with a black ponytail holder. She leant forward and scrutinized her face. An extra spattering of freckles littered her nose, making her reach for her purse to find the sunscreen. Her fingers slid against its edge but failed to latch on, and the bag crashed to the ground. Rolling her eyes at her clumsiness, Cassidy knelt down to gather up her things. A small green metal square caught her attention.

She reached forward and snagged it off the carpet. Staring at the flash drive, a tornado of thoughts filled her mind. Cassidy began collecting her scattered belongings. She held her cell phone in one hand and the flash drive in the other. With a resigned sigh, she dialed Charles' number and prayed he'd answer, make her laugh at her foolish thoughts of his endangerment, and give her some answers. *Stupid man.* He and David were probably halfway around the world engrossed in another geological mystery. But she needed them now to enlighten her as to why Drew was suddenly interested in the geological survey they hadn't bothered to complete.

The phone rang four times and then flipped into voicemail. Cassidy prepared to leave a message but frowned when an automated voice indicated Charles' voicemail was full. "That's odd."

Before she had an opportunity to digest the meaning of yet another dilemma, Jake pounded on her door. "Food's here."

"I don't want anything."

Her bedroom door opened, and Cassidy hastily tucked the flash drive into her back pocket, then scooped up the rest of her belongings. Jake glowered at her. "You're going to eat."

"No!" Cassidy shouted, then cringed at the ferocity of the word. He didn't understand. There was something chewing at her brain, and she needed to figure out what the hell it was. The flash drive had triggered a memory, but the edges were fuzzy and the picture distorted. Drew's interest in the survey stored on the drive sent up a slew of warning signals, but the reason eluded her. She counted backwards to control her irritation. "I'm sorry. I didn't mean to yell."

He stood before her, hands on hips, a very determined expression on his face. "I ordered all this food. You have to eat something."

She rose and followed him out of her room and into the main conference area. Jake walked around a heavily laden trolley, inhaling and sighing in appreciation. He uncovered steaming plate after steaming plate. With a quick bow, he waved her over to admire the bounty. She rolled her eyes at his dramatic presentation. It didn't matter that her stomach churned and growled at the scent of the food; Cassidy wanted control. And that meant eating when she determined it was time to eat. "I'm not hungry." He continued to circle the baking dishes, ladling spoonful after spoonful onto a plate.

"Sit."

"Look, Anderson, I don't want to eat. However, if you need me, I intend on sitting at *that* table over there." She pointed to the conference table he'd shoved aside to make room for the food cart. "And when you're done stuffing food into your mouth, you can join me. I'll be working." She walked to the table, pulled the stack of files that Steve had left for her, dropped into a chair, and flipped open the top one, ignoring her biologist.

She'd work through the meaning of the flash drive later. For now, the wolves were top priority. Scanning the first sheet, she quickly became absorbed with the updated wildlife statistics the park provided. There didn't seem to be anything unusual.

Jake pushed something into her hand. It smelled heavenly. Out of habit, she took a bite and stifled a sigh of appreciation as the warm bread and succulent beef slid down her throat. Maybe she should eat just a bit.

"Watcha got?" he asked, pulling a chair up next to her. She ate another bite of the sandwich and ignored the self-satisfied smile that crossed his face.

She wiped the edge of her mouth with the napkin she found on her lap. When had that gotten there? "Nothing."

"Bummer."

"Uh huh." She chewed, swallowed, and placed her half-eaten sandwich on the corner of his plate. Snatching a fry, she popped it in her mouth and laid the paper she'd been studying on the table between them. "Here." She stabbed a finger at a graph. "See the dips in wildlife population over the past few years? The rise and fall is absolutely normal."

"That's good."

"For them; not for us. I was praying for a bit of enlightenment."

Jake handed her back her sandwich and gently tipped her elbow toward her mouth, indicating she needed to finish it. "I suppose that means we have to find ourselves a pack of wolves."

"Exactly," she nodded, waving the last bit of bread and beef in the air. Jake smiled, pushing his plate closer to her. She grinned and finished off the fries. "I'll need the GPS stats first thing in the morning in order to determine what post to observe from."

"I'll notify Steve to have them on hand before we meet with the rangers."

He's usurping my authority again. "I'll do that," she said. Damn, this man irritated her.

"Suit yourself."

Cassidy pushed the papers to the center of the table, faced Jake, and crossed her arms over her chest. "Tell me why you seem attached at my hip and determined to be in charge."

Jake didn't say anything for a few minutes. She almost smiled at how quickly his brain seemed to be running through scenarios. He leaned forward and stared intently, his face twitching with amusement. "I think you're pretty?"

Rolling her eyes, she sighed in exasperation. "You don't look like any biologist I've ever worked with before."

Jake's answering smile lit his eyes, and it was damn hard not to smile back. Cassidy bit her bottom lip, waiting for some answers. Call her ultrasensitive, but there was something about this man that had her nerves on constant high alert.

"I needed a hiatus," Jake said.

Cassidy narrowed her eyes, thinking back to her conversation with Steve. She didn't voice the silly rumor about Black Stripe invading missions like ghosts, but it crossed her mind for one brief second before rational thoughts returned. Black Stripe was government, and government provided soldiers. Jake Anderson might be buff and tough, but by the way he handled himself in the meeting with his comprehension of the wolf statistics, Cassidy recognized that he knew his science. "A hiatus from what?" she asked.

Jake hung his head and ran his fingers through his hair. He peered at her and shrugged. "My last assignment was tough. I didn't particularly care for the results."

Africa had been one of many rough assignments, which led a shred of credence to his explanation. "I can understand that. Being on American soil is like taking a vacation, isn't it?" She only half bought this act. However, she didn't push him. It could wait. She'd asked Steve to run his bio. Until then, Cassidy would reserve judgment.

He tilted his head and continued his disconcerting scrutiny of her face. The verbal pause heightened her senses, causing a funny sensation to ripple down her spine. Nerves.

Jake leaned forward and rested his elbows on the table, studying her with a cool detachment. "I'm not an idiot, you know. My doctorate isn't fake."

Cassidy swallowed against the sudden dryness in her throat and pushed a little farther away from the table. "I never considered that." She rose and placed her hand on his shoulder. "Let's blow this taco joint. My legs are screaming to be stretched."

Jake's eyebrows shot to his hairline. She hung her head and took a deep breath, kicking herself mentally. *I can't believe I just said that.* "Get your mind out of the gutter. You know what I mean." He chuckled, and she punched him in the arm as he passed by her.

"Ouch. Don't beat the help." Jake grabbed a black bag, waved it at her, and held the door open. "Have test kit, will travel."

Edward Fiske pushed the disconnect button on his cell phone. An unsettled feeling caused his stomach to clench. He didn't like this new arrangement. Maybe it was the fact he'd been up all night finishing the paperwork for the patent, or maybe he had a valid reason for his concern. Twisting his neck to the left and right, he stretched his tightened muscles. Even the quick swig of his favorite soft drink hadn't helped infuse any energy; it'd tasted flat in the confines of the sterile lab.

He sighed and bent to peer into the narrow lens of the microscope, the metal of the eyepiece warm from his hours of verifying the contents of each vial. Jason had done as promised. The past fortnight of long hours resulted in the accumulation of the necessary number of spores as well as a substantial backup. Now he had to deliver the product. However, the antidote had yet to be field tested.

They'd been ready to head into Yellowstone this morning to attempt to locate the infected wolves and inject the antidote, but the board called and demanded all the vials be prepared. They didn't care that CPV-19 ran rampant in Yellowstone or that the antidote had yet to be properly tested.

That was the noose that tightened around his neck.

A muffled noise penetrated the steel ceiling of the laboratory. Edward spun around in his chair as the trapdoor opened. Jason slid down the steep metal stairs, entering the lab in the fashion sailors used on submarines. The scent of dirt and outdoors followed him, an odd acrid smell trailing behind. It reminded him of burnt hair. Edward wrinkled his nose then pulled out a neatly folded handkerchief, holding it beneath his nose before he sneezed and contaminated the countertops.

Jason noticed his expression. "Smoke's gettin' bad."

He blew his nose and nodded, wadding up the dirty cotton and shoving it into his back pocket. Right. He'd forgotten about the summer fires burning to the north of them. "I checked with forest services yesterday afternoon and they indicated the fire wouldn't be anywhere near our location."

"Still stinks."

"That's not the only thing." He didn't want to admit his concerns, but he felt Jason should know.

"Whazzup?"

Edward pushed away from the table and crossed his arms over his chest. He absently plucked at the soft linen of his shirt. "The board doesn't want to wait for the antidote to be tested."

"Yeah, so?"

Could the kid be that stupid? "It means we're releasing a biotoxin with no guarantee of a cure."

Jason used his palms to heft himself onto the counter. He sat and stared at Edward, swinging his feet back and forth. "That's bad cuz?"

Exasperated, Edward focused on the pendulum motion of the lab assistant's well worn work boots. "Jason, the investors are requiring us to hand over the virus to them in quantities that could possibly kill millions." He picked up a pen and uncapped it, staring at the dried ink on the end of the tip.

"That sucks." Jake leaned against the glass pane separating the working lab from the negative air flow chamber, absently twisting his thumbs around one another. "Don't do it."

Snapping the pen cap back in place, Edward dropped it on the table. "It's not that simple." He rose and stretched his arms to the ceiling, stifling a yawn.

"Why?"

Edward stopped his movement, suddenly self-conscious of his girth. "I won't get my patent."

"And?"

He stared at Jason, wondering if he was truly this ignorant. "Without that, I can't introduce my findings to the scientific community. We will have wasted five years for nothing."

Jason whistled softly. "You could introduce it without the patent."

True. But it went against everything Edward craved. "No."

"Don't sweat it, boss. We've had a good run here. It's time to move on. Just give them what they want. As for me, I'm looking forward to sticking my feet in some warm sand and soaking up rays."

Edward paused before heading up the metal stairs, his stubby fingers wrapped around a metal rung and his grip tightened in anger until he could feel every line and indentation on the stair tread against his palm. "It's always been about the money for you, hasn't it?" He concentrated and released his hold, wiping the painful marks away with his thumb.

Jason cocked a brow. "Like what else is there?"

With a shake of his head, Edward turned and climbed up the ladder in disgust. He didn't deny the brilliance of the kid's mind, but he detested the lack of professional achievement. What a waste. "I'll see you later."

A soft laugh echoed up from the cellar, followed by a shout. "Peace!"

CHAPTER 11

THE INTERIOR OF A BUILDING NEVER FELT THIS WARM OR WEL-
coming. Cassidy rested her back against the wall, feeling as if she'd run
five hundred miles with a thousand pounds strapped to her back. She
glanced sideways and watched Jake insert their room card. "I think I'm
tired now." Not even the rhythmic music filtering down the hall from
the bar could entice her to move in any fashion that didn't get her closer
to a shower.

Jake pushed open the door and slid her a snarky grin. "Oh I think
there's at least one more streambed or watering hole we haven't covered."

Rolling off the wall, Cassidy stumbled into the room. "No. I think
we've traipsed to every water source from here to Idaho. And if we
haven't, I don't care." Light from a streetlamp filtered through the window, bathing the conference area in a soft fluorescent glow. "You won't
mind if I skip polite and jump straight into rude and head for bed without so much as a see-you-in-the-morning, do you?" Cassidy heard Jake's
answering laughter; it filled the vacant space with warmth. His company today had been tolerable, but she craved solitude.

"I'm going to run these samples."

With her hand on the knob to her bedroom, Cassidy paused and glanced over her shoulder. "You're kidding, right?" Damn. If she attempted to leave after her shower, she was convinced he'd insist on joining her. And she didn't want company, nor did she feel like fighting about it.

Jake winked at her and dumped the case containing three dozen water samples on the conference table. His hair was mussed and sweat stained the edge of his t-shirt, but other than that he appeared rested. "No. I'm a night owl." He moved toward his bedroom peeling his shirt off and displaying a disconcerting amount of muscle and skin. "I'll shower, then work for awhile. I'll keep the lights to a minimum, so you shouldn't be disturbed."

Disturbed? Lights weren't disturbing. But his naked flesh was certainly distressing and created all sorts of violent reactions from her stomach to her toes. Cassidy thought about the punching bag back at headquarters and her commitment to remaining in control and dismissed her hormones, irritated at herself. "Do whatever you please."

He glanced over his shoulder at the sharpness of her tone. "You okay?"

Rolling her eyes, Cassidy entered her bedroom and slammed the door. *Jackass.* First he ruined her perfectly planned evening by staying up and working, and then he purposely paraded his masculine buffness before her like a damn trophy. *Jackass.*

Moving toward the bed, Cassidy set the alarm on her cell phone. She'd take a two-hour nap after her shower, and then maybe Jake would be asleep and she could slip away for a few moments of much deserved peace.

⇒━━

Cassidy's eyes fluttered open as the soft peal of her phone alarm rang beneath her pillow. She stretched and yawned, then rolled on her side and glanced down at the bottom of her door. No glow, which meant no lights on in the conference room.

Smiling, she slipped out of the comfort of her bed. Her shoulders burned, and she muffled a wince. The constant bending and twisting today had used muscles she'd left dormant for awhile. *Note to self: bend and twist more.*

Tiptoeing to the door, she turned the handle and prayed it wouldn't squeak. Peering into the conference room, Cassidy verified it was empty and there was no light shining from beneath Jake's door. She sighed in satisfaction and quietly pushed against the knob until it clicked and locked.

Padding over to the window, Cassidy unlocked it and slid it open. Due to the bitter cold winters, there wasn't a huge bug population in Wyoming and screens were rarely used. She slipped outside, rubbing her arms against the sudden chill. Reaching back through the window, Cassidy snagged her sweatshirt, then closed the glass.

She grinned, did a little jig, and jogged toward the front parking lot. Not bothering to glance upward at the brilliant night sky, Cassidy concentrated on finding the Jeep. Her stomach flipped in excitement as she reached the vehicle. Finally, alone.

Locating the key Jake left beneath the steering column, Cassidy gunned the engine and drove away from Lake Lodge Inn. She needed Old Faithful. Driving past it earlier today had about killed her. She wanted to touch, to feel, and to do this without anyone around to witness her raw emotion.

Thirty minutes later, she reached the parking lot of Old Faithful Inn. Jumping out of the Jeep, Cassidy walked toward the geyser and settled herself on one of the many viewing benches to wait for the blessed moment. It was nearly midnight, and she was glad she'd remembered her sweatshirt. The chill night air swept across her face, causing goose bumps to rise on her arms.

Very little light emanated from the building to her left. Tourists, exhausted from a day of hiking and sightseeing, were all sleeping soundly within the comfortable confines of the inn. Shaking her head, she couldn't help but smile at her sweet success in escaping the ever-present Jake Anderson.

Soft plumes of smoky water bubbled to the surface, escaping the prison of bleached volcanic rock. With a sudden sulfurous blast, Old Faithful erupted. Towers of misty fingers reached for the brilliant stars that sparkled and winked in a canopy of diamonds. Leaning forward, Cassidy studied this miracle of nature. She felt the spray of warm water kiss her cheeks and inhaled the memorable scent of the slightly sulfuric water, allowing it to carry her backward in time. Happiness of her youth made her heart tingle, and then the black hole of despair killed that joy.

Cassidy closed her eyes, determined to find a balance between the love for her parents and anguish at their death. It hurt. She gazed at the familiar sight of Old Faithful and prayed for peace.

It was a solitary moment, one she'd been seeking all day.

Her mind felt like it tripled in size in an attempt to absorb all the factions of the past twelve hours.

Nine years since she'd last seen this glorious miracle of nature. It didn't seem possible. That would mean—she quickly calculated backward in time—that next month she turned thirty-three. Was that true? She frowned, repeating her math. Thirty-three? Cassidy looked down at the ground, carving a circle in the fine gravel with the tip of her sneaker. She certainly didn't like the feeling that her internal clock suddenly seemed to be whipping its hands around in fast forward.

As Old Faithful bubbled down into a frothy mass, Cassidy checked her watch. She squinted to see the numbers glowing softly on its face and decided to wait another eighty minutes to enjoy an encore performance before returning to Lake Lodge.

Her thoughts were lost in the past.

Conversations of babbles and sputters trickled across the plain from mud pot to mud pot as geysers and hot springs soared to life then faded back to sleep. A long wailing cry pierced the gurgling murmurs. Cassidy jumped in surprise. Grinning, she pulled a small notepad from the back pocket of her jeans, quickly jotting down the direction of the wolf song. If the GPS stats didn't show her anything, that's where she'd begin her research.

First, however, she needed to meet with the Yellowstone officials.

"Therein lies the problem," she said to her shadow.

Her insides knotted, and her head pounded.

Ethan.

It didn't matter. Life wasn't about *what ifs*. She'd chosen her path, accepted her future. *Don't look back.*

Cassidy turned her mind to the circumstances that had brought her home. Tapping a finger against her notepad, she tried to think of something within the ecosystem that might cause this problem. Nothing. Her thoughts kept revolving around the phantoms of summers past and not the culprit of diminishing carnivores.

"Snap out of it, Lowell. This is no way to start an investigation." Cassidy cleared her throat, tipped her head back, and inhaled the crisp night air. She was here to banish her ghosts. At least, that's what she hoped. A little time alone would buy her the harmony she required to work within the boundaries of Yellowstone.

She glanced around and caught sight of movement beneath the great wooden pillars bracing the portcullis of the lodge and determined it was probably time to leave. The sensation of being watched made her frown. She didn't sense any physical threat, but the emotional vulnerability she felt was reserved for her own private scrutiny and not available for public inspection. Cassidy turned her face away from Old Faithful Inn and scanned the winding path to her right.

What to do about her unresolved emotions for Ethan?

Forget that she used to love him. Forget that she blamed him for her parents' death. Forget what an adolescent idiot she was to run away.

That thought alone dropped her guts into her socks. "Yes ma'am," she spoke softly. "Super size that number one combo of shame and regret, and add a side of embarrassment."

"Damn." Rising from the bench, Cassidy selected the more remote path and walked slowly among the steamy holes and sulfur-scented crevasses. "The past is the past." The underbrush rustled with activity as the pika, a small rodent resembling a very fat and furry rat, gathered food and socialized with its neighbors. Cassidy frowned and listened intently to the voices in the dark.

Her ears rang with the high-pitched yipping and screeching of a pack of coyotes chasing their dinner, but the lone wolf cry had never been answered.

She climbed behind the wheel of her Jeep. She was tired. It felt like years since returning from Africa, not days, and her back burned with taxed muscles. Thirty-three was a joke; right now ninety-three sounded about right. Cassidy turned the key, listened to the purr of the engine, and felt only slightly better. *So much for banishing my demons.* She should've stayed in bed.

"This place means nothing to me anymore." The suffocating band of memories tightening around her chest, however, blatantly contradicted her words.

A fist hammered loudly on the bedroom door, wrenching Cassidy from sleep. She bolted upright in bed, startled and confused. It took her a moment to absorb the luxurious surroundings of 1920s decor. The weight pressed against her body was nothing more than a cozy goose down comforter protecting her from the cool, early summer breeze blowing softly through the window.

Her heart slowly ceased its erratic percussion as her mind slipped around the fact that she wasn't in a pungent-scented, gnat-infested tent in Africa, and a hot shower was only a step away. Relief followed by a quick stab of guilt had Cassidy sinking beneath her covers in frustration. Another round of boxing ensued against the door, this time followed by a deep threatening voice demanding she exit her little cocoon of warmth and comfort. Cassidy stuck her tongue out at the intrusive noise, climbed out of bed, and yanked open the door.

"What!"

"Good morning to you, too. Have you conveniently forgotten our 8 a.m. briefing?" Jake pushed through the open doorway and strode into her room. "I'll just wait here and escort you personally."

"I can find my way." She yawned and stretched, ignoring the flush that crept up his face as her tank top tightened against her skin. She blinked innocently and shrugged a shoulder, silently complimenting herself on her unplanned payback for his bare-chested display from yesterday.

"Sorry, Goldilocks," he said, shaking his head. "I don't trust you. I've been informed that the minute you see what awaits you outside that window, you'll be off and running with no instructions for the rest of us lowly creatures. I can't work that way."

"I'd never do that. Now move along and let me take a shower."

"No time."

"What?"

"It's 5:45."

Cassidy stared incredulously at his snarky smile. Double damn. She felt a sudden urge to punch his smug, arrogant smile right off his smartass biologist head. But he was right. If the morning managed to catch her eye, she'd have her backpack on and gear in place before anyone could rope her into the briefing.

She sneered at Jake, grabbed her clothes, and entered the bathroom for a quick wash and change.

"Where were you last night?" he called through the closed door.

Startled at his question, Cassidy played her cards straight. No sense in lying. "Out," she slurred through toothpaste, squinting in the mirror at her tangle of blonde curls and sleepy green eyes.

"No kidding? You could've used the door. I wouldn't have stopped you."

She felt a flush heat her face. Embarrassed, she slid an apologetic smile in his direction. She exited the bathroom, patting him on the cheek. "Sorry."

"So where were you?" he insisted.

"No time to play twenty questions, handsome. We've got a meeting to attend. It'll take us almost two hours to drive to park headquarters."

Cassidy's long legs easily matched the pace Jake set. They walked in companionable silence through the carpeted halls of the inn, heading to the front of the complex.

"Rest of the pod waiting on us?" Cassidy asked.

"Yes," he said, tilting his head to the side and looking at her. His hair slanted across his eyes, and she resisted the urge to push it away from his face.

"Does Steve have my GPS stats?"

"Yes."

As they passed through the lobby, she glanced out the huge glass windows framing the front entrance. Dawn lightened the horizon, but the sun remained hidden behind the snowcapped peaks of the Grand Tetons. Heavy fog lay in billowing mists upon Yellowstone Lake, dissipating slowly as tendrils of early morning light kissed its surface.

Cassidy stopped to admire the view, wondering what had ever drawn her to the humid embrace of Atlanta, Georgia. Faces never forgotten swam before her eyes. She hadn't been drawn to Atlanta; she'd run. At full speed. Chased away from a place she loved and called home her entire lifetime by a nightmare too ugly to live with. ZEBRA had been her salvation, a Band-Aid to protect her shattered soul.

"Careful; don't let the demons invade your work," she said softly, twisting her head away from the serene landscape.

"What was that?" A frown marred the chiseled features of Jake's face.

"Nothing," she said, surprised he'd heard her. "I'm just muttering about the injustice of being woken up by a brute such as yourself."

"You're sure it has nothing to do with returning home after nine years of flitting around the world saving wildlife?"

"That's none of your concern, Dr. Anderson. Besides, I don't flit."

Jake laughed. "Your file says otherwise."

He'd had her checked out? She'd trump his card. He wasn't the only curious member of this team. "At least I've only been flitting for nine years. You've been flitting for ten." *Hah! See how he likes having his past scrutinized.*

He raised one eyebrow. "Touché. Did you find anything of interest in my background check?"

"Nope. You're boring. How about me? What did you find out about me?"

"You're boring, too."

Cassidy faked a shocked gasp. "Am not." She stumbled slightly, her toe catching the corner of an out-of-place piece of luggage. She bumped into the paneled wall, and he placed a hand on her arm to steady her. She ignored the small electric spark snaking across her skin where his warmth seeped into her. "You're pushing your luck, Anderson. I'm cranky when I don't get my shower in the morning."

"Or your coffee?"

"How'd you guess? The aroma of Columbian beans would probably put you back in my good graces."

"Let me see what I can do. I'll meet you out front in five."

She nodded energetically, and he snapped a mock salute, turning toward the small café at the edge of the lobby.

Chuckling softly, she paused before heading out the front entrance. This wasn't so bad. If nothing else, the man was a distraction from her troubles. If all went well and the GPS stats coincided with what she heard last night, she'd head immediately to one of the observation posts in the northern quadrant. It wasn't that far from Mammoth Hot Springs, the location of park headquarters. With an intense resolve, she refused to dwell on the upcoming briefing with Ethan. Her hands shook slightly, the only sign of her emotional distress.

The scent of lemon polish tickled her nose, and the aroma of coffee had her salivating. She missed her morning routine of hot shower and hot coffee, but the day called. Her tummy twisted and she grinned, surprised to realize the emotion was excitement.

She was home.

Cassidy was pleased to find her group already convened in front of the lodge where their Jeeps were parked. Stopping beside the muddy-brown vehicles, she dropped her backpack on the sidewalk. Battered and faded to a light mossy green, the bag's interior was stuffed to the zipper with paraphernalia she required for her observation later that day.

Jake came up behind her, shaking his head at her packing ability, and handed her a cup of coffee. She smiled sheepishly. Picking up the lumpy distorted mushroom of clothes and necessities with her free hand, she tossed it into the back of the closest Jeep.

Jake and Cassidy climbed aboard the first vehicle. Steve followed behind with Michelle and Valerie. Although only about seventy miles away, it would take just under the two hours allotted to reach park headquarters due to strictly enforced speed limits, and the never-ending wildlife attractions that didn't always remain on the grass and out of the road.

He drove north toward Norris Junction, and Cassidy smiled at his roving eyes seeking the scenic view. She didn't bother asking to drive;

he'd never allow it. It was a sure bet that *control freak* was an understatement when referring to Jake Anderson.

It didn't bother her, though. Part of being a successful team leader was playing to the strengths of your team. If Anderson's strength included the need to be in control of the vehicle, then so be it. She turned her head to gaze out the window. Then again, he'd better not cross the line and attempt to take control of her.

"This is amazing country," Jake said. "I've never been here before."

"Did you know . . ."

"Oh no, Doctor. Another lesson?"

She laughed. "It might help you acclimate faster."

"Okay, Dr. Jeopardy. Teach away."

Cassidy took a deep breath. The love and awe she felt for the park resonated in her voice. It allowed Jake a small window into her soul, but she didn't mind. This time. She'd captured his attention, and surprisingly that pleased her.

"Six hundred thousand years ago a huge volcanic eruption occurred, spewing forth more than two hundred and forty cubic miles of debris. The central portion of the park collapsed, forming a twenty-eight by forty-seven mile caldera, or basin in layman's terms, which is home to a variety of wildlife. The Grand Tetons surround the greater Yellowstone ecosystem, which also includes the Teton Range and Jackson Hole. This is the largest, essentially intact natural area within the United States. That last part, I'm sure you knew."

Jake nodded, absorbed by the sight of a herd of bison grazing leisurely beside the road. He pulled onto an embankment, intent on obtaining a closer look.

The beasts were massive, their shaggy brown coats caked with mud, dirt, and a horde of buzzing insects.

"Keep your distance," she cautioned.

Jake nodded and crouched at the edge of the grass. He laughed when one bellowed menacingly at a calf intent on snaking a sweet grass patch away from it.

"This gives you a definite appreciation for the hunting talents of the Indians. These animals are huge."

Cassidy knelt down beside him. She pointed to a large bull, his protruding horns a symbol of age. "That male right there weighs pretty close to eighteen hundred pounds."

"Amazing."

"Did you know that Yellowstone is the only place in the lower forty-eight states where bison have existed since prehistoric times?"

Jake grinned. "You are full of all sorts of little facts, aren't you?"

Steve rolled down his window and waved his arm wildly, signaling them to come over. Cassidy groaned. *What now?* Her mind refocused on the forthcoming briefing, and she reluctantly followed Jake to hear what Steve had to say.

"Hey man, guess what Grand Teton stands for?" Steve quirked his head and wiggled his brows then nodded knowingly at Jake, who shrugged and raised his own eyebrows in question. Steve cupped his hands in front of his chest and moved them up and down. After a half second of stunned silence, Jake burst out laughing and turned to Cassidy for confirmation.

"Yes, leave it to this shameful excuse of a man to figure it out, but it's true. A French explorer named them." Cassidy sighed and fidgeted.

Michelle peered up at the mountain range and frowned in concentration. "What was he thinking?" she whispered.

Steve looked at her in disbelief. "Sex, Michelle. He was thinking about sex."

Cassidy shook her head, smiling at the ecologist's shocked expression.

"Let's get this show on the road, gang, or we'll be late." She turned to head back to her Jeep, but Steve grabbed her hand.

"You okay, Sugar?"

Sunshine. Sugar. What was with these guys? "I'm fine."

"I'm here if you need a friendly shoulder to cry on."

She smiled and disengaged herself from his grip. "Thanks. But, really, I'm okay."

Cassidy climbed back into her own Jeep, and they headed toward Mammoth Hot Springs.

"You're a bit uptight," Jake said.

Good grief! She bit her lip to prevent the snippy comments from flying out of her mouth. It would only act as a display of how very on edge she was. "Told you I don't do well without a shower."

She glanced out the window, refusing to look him in the eye.

"That's an excuse. I'll pull the truth from you, Sunshine. Never fool with a patient man."

As they drove, she knew he only pretended to be mesmerized by the number of elk and an up-close encounter with a male moose. But his lightheartedness and boyish charm pulled her out of her nagging thoughts, and she smiled, surprised that she was actually enjoying the ride.

Jake maneuvered the vehicle into the parking area in front of Yellowstone National Park headquarters. The group had managed to reach Mammoth Hot Springs in record time.

The morning was still crisp and cool, not yet heated by the summer sun. Exiting the Jeep, she grabbed her jean jacket from the backseat.

Time to face the past.

She turned slowly and smiled at the waiting group now overshadowed by a man whose face triggered a movie trailer of memories.

Chief Law Enforcement Officer Ethan Connor.

CHAPTER 12

ETHAN HADN'T CHANGED AT ALL. HIS SUN-BLEACHED HAIR was cut in short wavy locks that framed a tanned, ruggedly handsome face. Piercing brown eyes nailed her with their fierce demand for recognition. Accusation glowed brightly within their depths, faltering any forward motion Cassidy had begun to make. He was angry.

She burned with apprehension and took deep breaths to calm her nerves.

She was a grown woman, not a foolish girl.

She could do this.

She had a job to do.

There were wolves to save.

Cassidy repeated her thoughts, and they gave her strength with every step she took. By the time she reached her team, she was furious at Ethan for making her feel insecure and galled by the thought that she'd allowed him to crawl beneath her skin. She could feel the flush of anger creep up her face and welcomed its emotional mask.

"Dr. Lowell." His outstretched hand reached for hers, and she couldn't prevent herself from grabbing it.

"Chief Connor." Cassidy squeezed firmly, refusing to be the first to pull back from his iron grip.

"Welcome back to Yellowstone."

"Thank you." He released her hand. "You never returned my calls or my letters."

Cassidy stared at the ranger emblem stitched onto the pocket of his shirt. "Ethan, let's not do this now. We have work to do." This was worse than she'd imagined. He was confronting her.

Relieved when Ethan addressed the rest of her pod, she glanced at her team and caught Jake's expression. She turned her back when he sidled up to stand beside her.

"What was that all about?" he asked.

"The past," she answered softly, stepping farther away.

"You're shaking."

"It's nothing but a few unexpected nerves. I can't wait to head out to the observation post." She smiled reassuringly and urged him forward.

"No titillating details?"

"No details," she stated flatly. "It was a lifetime ago." Her heart clenched, and Cassidy realized the ache of loss suddenly felt unbearable. It must be Anna's recent death that had ripped off the seal from the pain she'd spent all these years fighting against. Mom and Dad were gone. Ethan's voice irritated the loathing that lay curled in her chest. Cassidy didn't want to live this way: one foot on hate, the other on regret.

She shrugged, trying to dislodge the memories that floated uninvited in her mind and indicated with a quick nod of her head that they should follow Ethan into the building.

The park headquarters featured several small offices and a tiny front hallway. The door slammed behind Cassidy, enclosing the small group in a tight, almost suffocating arena.

Ethan stood in the center, commanding their attention. "Welcome, everyone, to our humble abode." His voice boomed loudly within the confines of the hall. Cassidy rolled her eyes at his comment and was rewarded with a scowl from Ethan.

"All the park facilities and resources are at your disposal," he continued. "Any questions?"

"Where are we meeting?" Cassidy had been scrutinizing the floor, avoiding any form of eye contact but was forced to glance up when there was no response to her question. She was startled to find her eyes in line with Ethan's chest. She tilted her head, not backing down to this silly attempt at intimidation. Her sudden emotional see-saw shifted to annoyance.

"One of the deputies will be available shortly to provide you with any information you require. I, however, am in the middle of an important investigation and will not be available."

"That's convenient." Cassidy's eyes widened in dismay as Ethan's gaze darkened in anger. It was cruel to patronize him, but she couldn't help herself. It was her best defense.

"Dr. Lowell, my investigation will not overshadow yours. Don't worry your pretty little head over official park business."

Cassidy saw red. "Don't you dare speak to me that way, Ethan Connor. I've worked damn hard to achieve my position within ZEBRA, and I resent the tone of your voice." Why the hell was she explaining herself? After ten minutes together, she'd allowed him to usurp her authority and dent her professionalism. Punching bag. Punching bag. She fisted her hand and glared at him.

Ethan leaned forward and placed his hands on her shoulders. "I know you have, honey."

A blanket of pure white fury suffocated her. Cassidy could hear Jake's protests in the background. She saw a large hand grab Ethan's arm; then suddenly he was gone. Air, wonderful sweet air, surrounded her. Shaking her head, she focused on the two men standing before her facing one another with the testosterone of two rams in rut. Night and day. Their differences were as startling as their beauty.

"Jake, it's okay. I can handle this."

Jake speared her with a glare, and she narrowed her eyes. Stepping forward, she pushed between the two men. This wasn't at all how she'd envisioned her reunion with Ethan Connor. She could fight her own wars, thank you very much. She flung Jake a don't-mess-with-me look and then faced Ethan.

"I'm sorry, Ethan. I'm certain your investigation is extremely important, and I'll respect your position." She was going to ream Jake a new one for making her apologize.

Ethan offered her a genuine smile. "No problem, Cassidy. It's a drug investigation, so I caution you and your team to be careful. There're some unscrupulous characters roaming around Yellowstone."

"Drugs?"

Ethan grunted and shook his head. "That's all I can say."

"Thank you for the warning," Cassidy said.

Jake gripped her shoulder and pulled her away from Ethan. His touch shocked her, and she pushed against his hand. He glanced down at her, his mouth set and firm. Blue eyes bright with anger glared, and Cassidy bit her bottom lip at the reaction they provoked. Before she could analyze her feelings, Jake spun and faced Ethan. "Don't touch what doesn't belong to you."

───◆───

Cassidy's stomach fluttered between anger and anticipation. Impatient for the comforting embrace and relaxing ambiance of the wilderness, she bit back the words that were burning a hole in her cheek. *Damn Jake.*

If Steve hadn't hurriedly ushered them out of park headquarters and into their vehicles, she'd have laid his arrogant ass flat on the ground. How dare he? She wasn't a commodity. Cassidy gritted her teeth as he maneuvered the Jeep off the main road and ground to a stop in a blur of dust and gravel.

"Spill it," he demanded as they both jumped from the vehicle onto the dried streambed. The park was in desperate need of rain.

Cassidy huffed and tugged her backpack from the backseat. "Spill what?"

Jake stood on the side of the road, peering up the path. He shook his head and turned to her. "What's your history with Dudley Do-right?" Observation Post 29 lay at the top of that overgrown, boulder-strewn trail, and he wasn't about to let her pass without an explanation.

"Ethan?"

"Is that his name? It must have slipped my mind somewhere between the magnificent display of your cowardice and his testosterone overload."

"I don't owe you an explanation."

He nodded. "No. You don't. But maybe it'll help."

"With what?"

"It's my experience that if you talk a problem through, then it ceases to take on the life form of a one-eyed gorilla out for vengeance."

She didn't know how to respond. Cassidy paused. She inhaled deeply, swept her fingers across her brow, and used them to shield her eyes against the sun's glare. "Leave it alone. It's none of your business."

Jake didn't move. "Yes, it is. If you're incapable of separating your personal emotions from this assignment, then I'll have to request that you be transferred."

Cassidy's mouth dropped open. Her heart thudded against her chest and even though it galled her, she couldn't deny his accusation. "You're right. I behaved badly." She narrowed her gaze and pointed a finger at him. "But so did you."

Jake grinned. "Suppose I did. Want to talk?"

Cassidy inhaled deeply. The pine scent of millions of acres of nature soothed her temper. She decided the best avenue would be to ignore Jake's bizarre behavior and redirect his attention to something other than her relationship with Ethan Connor. "Forget it," she spoke softly, mentally praying he'd leave it at that. The thought of discussing this part of her past had Cassidy's cheeks burning with embarrassment.

He stared long and hard into her face, his expression impassive. "Okay." He stepped back and walked to the other side of the Jeep. "Water samples were all negative."

"Not surprised. That would've been too easy." Cassidy sighed and raised a questioning eyebrow at the Glock 9mm that suddenly appeared in his hand. She closed the gap between them, cocked her head to look into his eyes, and dropped her bag at his feet. With a flick of her wrist, she grabbed the gun. "What're you doing with this?"

"What I always do with it."

"You carry a weapon on your assignments?"

Jake frowned. "Yes. It's company policy, oh fearless one."

"But here?" Cassidy glanced around in concern, the echo of machine gunfire still fresh in her mind.

Jake smiled and took the weapon back. He shrugged. "I don't think there's anything to worry about."

Cassidy breathed deeply. She'd forgotten how wonderful the clean air of Yellowstone smelled, and she pulled it into her lungs praying it would clear the haunting memory of Africa. The light, pungent scent of wildflowers mixed with pine teased her senses, tugging her away from distasteful memories.

He handed the gun to Cassidy. Her brows knitted in concern, and Cassidy glanced at the weapon with disdain. "I don't want this."

"Take it. Obviously you left yours back at the inn." His eyes darkened, and she felt a kick of fear. "You know and I know that you're breaking all the wilderness hiking rules by insisting on going up there by yourself."

Cassidy sighed, planted her feet, and squared her shoulders. This argument she was prepared for. "ZEBRA supersedes any park regulations that might be in place. I'm more than capable of doing this by myself."

"Still . . ."

Cassidy didn't back down an inch. "Jake, this is my job and it's what I do. Don't go all macho and insist on the buddy system. It's condescending." She lifted the gun beneath his chin. "Now, why would I need this?"

He paused before answering, his eyes moving to gaze up the steep path. Jake shifted the weight of his feet and glanced in the other direction. "There's something that has my neck hairs standing at attention."

"I hate guns."

"Take it anyway."

"I can't shoot."

Jake barked laughter. "Yeah, right."

She'd taken the required gun course, but it didn't change the fact that she honestly couldn't shoot. With a sigh, she decided not to argue. "If you insist."

"I insist," he reiterated, checking his watch. He glanced back at her. "You'd better get going. What specifically will you be looking for up there?" Jake lifted his chin toward the trail.

"Any type of trail or marking," she said. "This is a huge park, but the wolves are carnivores. Did you know that before we successfully reintroduced these little beasties, Yellowstone was in a huge ecological crunch?" She tried not to laugh when he rolled his eyes.

"How's that?"

"Because the wolf is an integral part of this ecosystem, the lack of the packs had created an overpopulation of their prey. The deer, moose, bison, and elk just about destroyed the park vegetation."

"Is this why we're here? To prevent it from happening again?" He tilted his head and gazed into her eyes.

"Well, the wolves never had the fully desired effect regarding the ecosystem. They did, however, offer a few astonishing impacts. This is what I'm personally concerned with. If the wolves are disappearing, what's this doing to the other animals? The ones that rely on the wolf's kill for survival? We could be facing an even greater problem than what had existed before we reintroduced them."

"Such as?"

"The elimination of the wolves from this park could seriously endanger the existence of the beetles that grow within the carcasses of their kill."

"And that would be a bad thing, because?"

"The smallest creature can create a broken link in the food chain, Jake. Magpies and other assorted birds rely on these beetles."

"I know; I was only kidding. Do you have any theories?" Jake asked.

"Not a one." Cassidy offered up a lopsided grin, shaking her head and hefting her backpack over her left shoulder. She opened an outside zipper of the canvas bag and placed the gun inside. The weapon didn't make her feel secure or safe; the slick metal caused more angst than reassurance. But she refused to waste anymore time arguing with Jake. "But hopefully that'll change after tonight." She peered back over her shoulder and waved to Jake. "I'll see you in the morning, right?" Now why had she said that?

"You betcha. Coffee in hand and a smile on my handsome face."

"You make sure of that. The coffee that is, I couldn't care less whether you're smiling or not."

His laughter followed her up the steep trail.

She hiked slowly. It'd been years since she'd been to the park, and her lungs responded with the burning of oxygen deprivation. The trail twisted in odd angles as it wound upward. There were sections of lightly grassed, sparse plateaus then a sudden incline through thickly pined, snake-thin ravines.

Cassidy paused often to snag dearly needed gulps of water from the canteen slung across her shoulder. It bumped and slid against her hip like a jackrabbit in a trap each time she hauled herself around an especially difficult cut in the trail. She inhaled in frustration, transferring the canteen to her other shoulder and securing the strap to her backpack. With the water forced into a more secure and less mobile position, she concentrated on her surroundings.

Her eyes absorbed the beauty of the terrain. Crystal blue skies blanketed thick woods that danced with Quaking Aspens and Lodge-pole pines. The snowcapped peaks of the Tetons offered a constant background to the serenity of the park.

Cassidy's mind, however, continued to replay her conversation with Jake. She needed to focus and stop this damnable internal tug-of-war. "This," Cassidy raised her voice and called to the mountains, "is why I never wanted to come home!"

Nick Fowler felt the familiar tickle of little legs creeping slowly beneath the cuff of his pants. He gritted his teeth and silently urged the figure he was tailing to climb back in the Jeep and drive away. Nick lay sprawled within the tall grasses of the plateau. He couldn't remember a point in time he hated more than this very instant. His nose twitched to expunge the sickening sweet scent of hay, and his balls itched mercilessly in their sweaty prison of jeans and boxers.

He was frozen. The spider crept higher, his nostrils dripped, and his jeans grew even hotter and more uncomfortable.

His subject, Jake Anderson, stood as still as a statue. Blondie was gone. Long gone. Yet the man continued to stare up the path like a kid pining for his lost toy. Nick hadn't been sure of which party to continue tailing. If Anderson drove away, he'd be tempted to hike after what he desired.

Nick shut his eyes tightly, willing the uncomfortable sensations of his body into the background, and focused upon the memory of the hot little ticket now pounding a lonely path up the hillside. What he wouldn't give to wrap his fingers through her golden curls, pulling them tightly back, and watching as her eyes widened in fear and leaking heavenly tears. She'd beg, he knew. Beg for her life.

But, unfortunately, pleasure had to wait. His lip pulled up in a growl. Nick didn't like complications, and the man before him was a grade-A, first-class, walking shit-kicker.

There was no conclusive evidence, but within certain sectors it was rumored that ZEBRA had a darker secret. Over the past twelve months, the benign organization had been dispatched to North Vietnam, Syria, Cuba, and Russia. They answered the call of the wild, both animal and human.

Nick had a thick dossier on the organization. As of this date, he'd been unable to connect them to any particular speculative government force. As far as he was concerned, however, behind ZEBRA's success they left a trail of destruction. One that burned slow and low like a candlewick. Quadrant by quadrant, ZEBRA successfully eliminated terrorist groups and factions of unrest that threatened the United States. Jake Anderson's name was linked to each operation.

He had discussed this with Cole after the Niger Delta cluster fuck. But Cole had dismissed his concerns, focusing on the failure of the mission and redirection of Blondie.

Nick cursed violently beneath his breath. His enemy stood less than fifty feet away. He wouldn't want to meet the imposing presence of Anderson in face-to-face combat, but with a slight movement of his finger, he could lay open the operative's head like it was nothing more than a ripe peach. His hand itched to pull the trigger, but the kill would compromise his instructions.

Too bad.

Nick released his grip on the deadly weapon as the echo of a car door reverberated through the valley. He slid it silently to the side and rolled over. The Jeep finally pulled away. He didn't know whether to slap, blow, or scratch first. He leapt to his feet, shook his pants leg, readjusted the family jewels, and wiped his runny nose against his upper arm. He'd not follow Jake Anderson anymore today. He knew where to find Jake.

Throwing a longing glance up the trail, he sighed. For the second time in twenty-four hours, she lay within reach. Last night at the geyser, with her face framed by the erupting Old Faithful, he'd fantasized that he'd taken her there, amid the heat and steam of the geysers.

The wonders of a woman were up the trail. He'd have hours of private time to explore, destroy, and dissect at random.

But not last night and not today. Not until he was given the green light.

CHAPTER 13

"You almost blew it," Steve said.

Chewing on a straw, Jake leaned against the wooden railing that separated the boardwalk from the geothermal fields in Lower Geyser Basin. When he'd returned from dropping Cassidy off, Michelle had suggested the pod view a recently formed geyser that might be throwing the ecosystem off in the park. Glancing at the barren, hard-packed ground, he watched as the ecologist walked the edge of the fields, taking heat measurements with thermal monitoring equipment.

Turning, he looked at Steve. "Blew it?"

"Yeah, your little showdown at headquarters."

"Oh, that." He frowned and picked at a splinter of wood, noting that the techie had shed his nervous, geek persona and slipped into a skin Jake was more familiar with. The only reason he allowed him to speak in such a manner was that he trusted the man with his life. It was also the reason he'd specifically requested him as backup.

Steve was Black Stripe.

"Yeah, that." Steve said. What gives?"

"I didn't like the way that park ranger manhandled her."

Steve laughed out loud and smacked Jake on the arm. "I don't think I've ever seen you behave like that."

Jake straightened, pushing away from the railing. How had he acted? "The job is the most important thing, and she lost perspective. I just set it right."

"And my Aunt Fanny looks like Angelina Jolie. Is it possible that our resident zoologist has found a hole in your armor?"

"Don't go there, Pullen. You've got the wrong idea. Half of that was making sure my controlling macho cover was in place." Wasn't it? "Besides, you're the one with the buddy relationship."

Steve grinned. "Jealous?"

"No."

"Yes, you are. But I'll be a friend and tell you that she's like my sister. Shit. She doesn't even confide in me. I didn't have a clue her parents died in a plane crash."

Jake crossed his arms over his chest and faced Steve. "Plane crash?" Steve turned his head away from Jake, following the figure of a curvaceous redhead. Jake didn't care about the eye candy, but the sudden sick feeling in his stomach signaled information he wasn't going to like. "You were saying?" Jake pulled the straw from his mouth, glanced at the chewed end, and stuck it back in.

With a sigh, Steve refocused on Jake. "Yeah. They died at Jackson Hole Airport. That's why she was so freaked yesterday after the landing."

Jake hung his head, running his hand through his hair. "I didn't know." He hated when he became his own worst enemy. "I practiced my macho-asshole act on the ride to Yellowstone so she'd think my need to follow her around like a control freak was genuine. Damn. I bet she categorizes me as head of the jerk class." He swore louder and kicked the edge of a wooden post. "I had her so cornered yesterday, she felt the need to sneak off to Old Faithful in the middle of the night."

Steve's face sobered. "You let her out of your sight?"

Rolling his eyes, Jake worried the straw between his teeth. "Nah. Ruined my sleep though."

"Good." Steve sighed and glanced across the plains, his face creasing in a worried frown. "I don't like the idea of her alone at the observation post."

Jake didn't either but he wasn't about to voice his feelings, afraid Steve would read more into his concern than professional interest. "I couldn't push to go along. It didn't make sense."

Steve nodded. "I know. But still . . ." his voice trailed away, and they both dropped into a thoughtful silence.

Jake swore again and tossed the straw into a small metal garbage can. "After seeing how Connor spoke to her, I bet she hates me. I've been a typical male ass." A soft breeze drifted from the plains, ruffling his hair. An ocean of rock spread and rose before him in small crests of sandy brown waves that on any other day would've had him appreciating the jagged and uneven edges of what history carved into this land.

Steve smiled, stretched his arms to the sky, then worked his shoulders in slow circles. "Sounds like you're off to a winning start. Good thing you don't care about her feelings."

The glare Jake tossed at Steve silenced any further comments, but Jake saw his friend's lips twitch with amusement. Steve turned his attention elsewhere, pointing a finger toward a crew of carpenters constructing a large set of bleachers. "What do you suppose they're doing?"

Planks of wood were being secured onto metal frames. "Have no clue, but I guess we might as well find out." Jake stepped back from the railing and led the way over to the crew of workers, the rhythm of hammering barely audible above the sound of the air compressors. "As soon as we're done, I'm going back to park headquarters."

"Another meeting with Chief Connor?" Steve asked.

"Not exactly. I want to see whether they have a master system that tracks the campsites and their occupants."

"I received a report this morning that one of Cole's henchmen was spotted at Vini Vidi Vici's with Drew several nights ago."

The wooden boardwalk leading toward the construction crew groaned beneath their heavy steps. "And the circle closes in," Jake said. Before reaching the group of men, his cell phone buzzed. He glanced at it, smiled when Cassidy's name appeared on the small screen, and waved Steve toward the workers. "Let me answer this, and I'll join you in a second." Turning away from the noise of the hydraulic nail-guns and power saws, he clicked on *reply*.

He couldn't help the grin that spread across his face when she answered. "Miss me already?"

"Hell no. I'm loving the quiet solitude of a lonely mountaintop."

Jake watched the graceful curve of a hawk as it floated on a downward draft, and the connection with Cassidy made him pause and find enjoyment in the sensuous dance of air and feather. "Then what are you calling for, Sunshine?"

The connection went dead for a second, then a soft voice reached his ears. "I'm thinking."

He closed his eyes, imagining her leaning against a tree, ankles crossed and fingers absently plucking at grass. He swore silently. "Yeah? About what?" His train of thought needed to end here. When exactly had she crawled beneath his skin?

"If the GPS collars suddenly went dead together, is it possible that it's a technical malfunction?"

Jake's eyes trained on the tradesmen, and he watched Steve razzing the construction workers. He caught a few barbs regarding rival football teams and turned his attention back to Cassidy. "I'll ask Steve to check it out. I wish he'd had luck with the GPS locators. The thought of you spending the night in a spot that might not have any wolves but possibly has drug dealers doesn't sit so well."

"That's damn sweet of you to care, Anderson. Thanks." There was a long pause. "I'm sure it's not the collars. I mean that just seems too cut and dry."

"What do you mean by that?"

He could hear her crunching on something and figured she must be eating trail mix. "Ethan's a class-A anal retentive jerk. He'd have checked that."

"We'll double check then."

"Okay." He heard her release a quick breath before she switched gears and responded in a lighter tone. "Where are you?"

He glanced around, forgetting momentarily the name of his location. He tilted his head back to read a sign posted against the side of an administrative building. "I'm at Lower Geyser Basin watching Michelle measure temperatures surrounding a new geyser that's supposed to erupt within the next week."

"Really? A new one? How big? How far out on the plain? Have they named it yet? Do they know the exact date of eruption?" Her rapid fire questions brought a smile to his lips.

"Whoa, Sunshine, hold on. I think that's what Michelle's looking for. Could this have any connection with the wolves?"

Silence again.

"Sunshine?"

"Hold on; I'm thinking."

"Oh no, not that." he said, laughing when she retorted with a few choice words of her own.

"Unless the movement in the earth's crust that triggered this geyser also released some sort of poison creating an environmental anomaly, I can't see how the two would connect. But . . ." He heard her stretch and yawn. "We have to cover all bases," she concluded.

"I'm sure we'll know more once Michelle's done with her exploration. Any sign of wolves?"

"A few tracks. It's hard to judge how old, though. It's so dry up here. I'm about to do a perimeter search, and then I'll settle in for the night. Hopefully, I'll see something around dusk."

"Goldilocks?"

"Oh, for Pete's sake, quit with the names already."

Not on your life, he thought. "Be careful." He considered continuing the conversation, holding the satellite link between them for a bit longer, but the intimacy felt dangerous. "Anderson out." He killed the connection.

Jake turned to find Steve heading back in his direction. "Anything?"

Steve shrugged. "Apparently this geyser thing is a really big deal."

"Yeah, it seemed to excite our zoologist."

Steve reached Jake's side and leaned a hip against the wooden railing. "Are you sure it wasn't your deep and sexy voice?" he said, a mischievous grin lighting his face.

"Steve," Jake shot him a warning glance. "What did the laborers say?"

"Okay, for a bunch of nail bangers, they're pretty well informed. Apparently this geyser will be bigger than Old Faithful. The bleachers are being constructed for an assembly of scientists due to arrive the day after tomorrow. I need to clarify a few things with Michelle, but apparently they can determine the exact hour of eruption based upon the heat that builds beneath the fissure in the earth's crust, or something like that."

Jake stared at the bleachers, turned, and trained his sight on the slight mound rising from the plateau. "I want a complete rundown on every scientist and their entourage due in for this event . . ."

Steve raised his hand, stopping Jake mid-sentence. "New World Petroleum is one of the sponsors of this event."

"What?"

Pointing over his shoulder at the carpenters, he nodded. "They're securing NWP plaques on all the bleachers."

"Jesus, this is bizarre. I need to contact Price and figure out what the deal is. This seems way too coincidental. What gives?"

Steve shrugged. "I have no clue."

Jake glanced at the garbage can, wishing he hadn't thrown the straw away. "I'm heading back to the room. Will you locate the GPS station and verify all is in proper working order?"

"Sure, Captain." Steve nodded and turned to rejoin Michelle and Valerie. Before he reached the edge of the boardwalk, he called back to Jake. "Up for a game of chess later?"

Jake glanced at the young Special Forces officer and smiled. "Have you saved your money?"

"No need. Have you saved yours?"

Steve laughed and waved. Chess would be good. He might even be able to sleep a few hours before picking up Cassidy.

Jake's eyes snapped open. His internal clock signaled that dawn fast approached the horizon. Stretching, he worked his muscles until they were limber enough for him to gracefully exit the bed. If he ignored this ritual, years of strenuous activities coupled with several battle wounds guaranteed a rough landing once his feet hit the ground.

The narrow spot between his shoulder blades itched, signaling trouble. Jake moved quickly through his morning routine, an inner urgency pushing him forward and twisting his gut into an uncomfortable tangle of nerves. He forced himself not to run down the hall and into the lobby. What was wrong? His instincts were screaming at a decibel level he couldn't ignore.

Leaving the quiet inn, the disharmony of the waking park seized his ears in an angry storm of chirps, croaks, and bellows. He inhaled the crisp air, mist, and pine, the rich scent acting as an analgesic for his panic.

With a tilt of his head, he surveyed his surroundings. It was dark. The sun hadn't begun lighting the sky, but everything seemed normal.

He thought it must be the strange surroundings that scraped at his anxiety.

A sudden vision of a dark, remote corner of the forest made him realize why he felt apprehensive. The thought of Cassidy spending the night alone amidst miles of uninhabited land unsettled him. He'd been a fool to allow her to go. Did it stem from his stubbornness to ignore the attraction that sparked and fired between them?

She was the leader of the pod and could do as she saw fit. Frowning, he tried to determine a way he could've joined her without blowing his cover. Nothing came to mind. Cassidy was in peak physical condition; he'd scrutinized her stats in the personnel file. She'd be fine. Besides, he'd given her a gun.

He walked slowly to the Jeep, the echo of his footsteps out of place among the natural waking forest. He opened the back and grabbed a gift bag containing the thermos he'd bought yesterday. It looked like a bear. Jake ran his thumb across the plastic nose and sighed; this was a bad sign. He'd given in to whimsy.

Trudging back into the lodge, Jake concentrated on clearing his thoughts. He absently filled the thermos with hot coffee from the silver urn to the left of the lobby. With a twist of his wrist, he screwed on the bear's head, then paused, suddenly unsure of himself. He'd promised Cassidy coffee but had no clue what she put in it. He grabbed a few packages of creamer, their edges moist with condensation, then snatched up some sugar and artificial sweetener.

He drove the forty-five miles to the spot she'd been dropped off yesterday. It was almost 4:30. Better early than late. Jake stepped lightly onto the scattered gravel that acted as an unofficial parking area.

A familiar scent lingered in the air. Sniffing, he recognized the faint remnants of tobacco. Odd. He scanned the deserted road and surrounding plateau. Nothing.

With a glance over his shoulder, he moved toward the base of the trail. Something was wrong. His shoulders burned. Grabbing his gun from its holster, he proceeded using well placed steps to soften the echo. He couldn't hear anything. Not even the sounds of wildlife.

Jake allowed years of training to lead him as he melted into the night. His eyes absorbed every nuance. A broken twig. Looking closer, he discovered several strands of blonde hair snagged on the jagged edge of the stick. Cassidy could've easily done this yesterday, but a picture of her trudging up the path with her hair securely braided flashed through his mind.

What he saw next caused a myriad of frightening images to rear their ugly heads. A cigarette butt lay next to the path. Clicking on a small pen light, he shined its narrow beam on the tobacco remnants, confirming his first impression. The cigarette floated in a large pool of blood.

CHAPTER 14

CASSIDY LAY SPRAWLED ON HER STOMACH, MOTIONLESS WITH-in the confines of the observation platform. The hard plywood dug uncomfortably into her hip bones. And her elbows, rubbed raw from supporting the high-density night binoculars, ached with exhaustion.

Her vision blurred. She moved her face away from the binoculars, closing her eyes tightly in the hope of finding some relief from strain. As her eyelids fluttered open, the first light of dawn crowned the majestic range of the Grand Tetons. It was late, or early, depending on whether or not you had spent the night diligently maintaining your vigil or comfortably cocooned in a warm bed. Either way, morning arrived and the wolves hadn't. She rested her forehead against the wooden floor and fought against the tears of frustration and exhaustion.

This urge to cry was becoming annoying. In reality, an unsuccessful first night shouldn't bother her. This assignment might take months to complete. No. She wanted the mystery solved now. The day she could fly out of here couldn't come quickly enough.

A twig snapped, piercing the air like a gunshot, and she raised her head slowly, peering over the edge of the platform. Her eyes strained to see what she prayed padded below. Dark gray shadows moved within the swirling morning mist and passed beneath her as silently as a school of fish. A grin played across her face while she mentally calculated the total number in the pack. *The wolves are here.*

The pack drifted beyond the observation platform, silent and graceful. She squirmed and strained her neck forward to achieve a better surveillance position. Cassidy silently counted to herself. Eight. The alpha male led the pack, his haunch at least three inches taller than that of the smaller boned females. Coloring and collars couldn't be made out in the dim light of dawn.

A deep rumble reverberated against the wooden deck, and it was several seconds before Cassidy's brain registered what it was. The wolves snaked through a grove of aspens, disappearing beyond the edge of the ridge. She swiftly yanked the cell phone from her belt hook, swearing softly at the text message displayed. It was Jake.

She rested her head back on the platform, shutting out the brilliant blue eyes and cocky grin that had invaded her mind all night. Cassidy couldn't remember the last time she'd been fascinated by a man, let alone this feeling of a sophomoric crush on the varsity football star. If it weren't for his uber-macho attitude, she might actually consider the validity of her attraction.

She glanced at her phone again and hesitated. Knowing him, the 911 symbolized his demand for an update. Cassidy decided to let him sit and stew. If it'd been important, he would've called rather than used text.

Cassidy cursed louder as she gingerly sat up. Her muscles were as tight as a whip from the long hours spent in one position, and her bladder shot bolts of pain through her groin. This was the worst: the morning after.

She climbed hesitantly down the side of the platform, careful not to misplace a foot; an injury this far in the wilderness could cause serious—even fatal—problems. Once her feet were firmly planted on the ground, Cassidy proceeded to stretch each muscle, reintroducing the flow of blood to several numbed body parts.

Morning calisthenics completed, Cassidy climbed up the platform to retrieve her belongings. She unpacked a bottle of water and bag of trail mix. As usual, she was late. It was time to begin the four-hour hike down from the ridge. With any luck, Jake would be there with an offering of delicious hot coffee.

This was Cassidy's favorite part of the day. Her fatigue melted away with the milky white morning mist. She nibbled and slurped her way down the mountainside, intent on making just enough noise to not startle an unsuspecting bear but still quiet enough to appreciate the hidden treasures buried within Yellowstone National Park.

Lost in the beauty of her surroundings, Cassidy quickly forgot Jake's message was the reason she'd decided against following the wolves. Her phone remained clipped to her waistband, the urgent message left unanswered.

The sun crested the snowcapped peaks, shining brightly and illuminating the beautiful scenery surrounding her. Trees, heavily laden with various shades of green, painted a picture of a perfect July morning. A soft breeze tickled wisps of hair at the base of her neck, but she was oblivious to the touch, her attention drawn by the graceful dance of a full-grown, male bald eagle.

Brilliant white feathers masked his head as he soared majestically on the currents, screeching of his freedom. Cassidy paused and absorbed the sight of the huge bird. Her brain automatically acknowledged that he would be hunting for food to feed his young. She scanned the surrounding area in search of his nest and mate but couldn't locate either.

Someday she would be able to spend hours observing wildlife purely for pleasure. Right now, however, she had a job to do.

This was her specialty.

Suddenly, the eagle's cry sounded too close to the human pain that plagued her nightmares.

Africa. She shuddered. It would take a long time to forget. As her eyes followed the elegant dips and turns of the bird, she inhaled, mesmerized by the winged ballet. The air was crisp and scented with a mixture of composting leaves and sweet wildflowers.

A far cry from Atlanta. A lifetime from Africa.

Remembering the horror, Cassidy squeezed her eyes shut. It would fade with time.

She smiled when the bird perched on top of a rotting tree. His magnificence drew her mind from the suffering and helped reaffirm her commitment to ZEBRA. She didn't agree with all their policies, but the organization held an important place in pursuing world peace. Dedication and loyalty were like children. At first, full of unconditional love. Then abuse, disillusionment, and emotional pain turned them bitter and shaky, making it difficult to find a clear path.

Her commitment to ZEBRA's mission statement remained solid. But the combination of Drew's odd behavior toward the Niger Delta assignment and Charles' disappearance, had her questioning the organization. Something wasn't right.

Cassidy crouched and ruffled the grass. It felt good to touch Yellowstone soil. If the death of her parents could somehow be compartmentalized behind all of the other wonderful memories of Jackson, she might be able to call this place home again. And she needed a home.

Her mission in Africa was compromised. Despite Drew's denial, NWP had attacked their camp. Every bone in her body knew this, but she lacked concrete evidence. The fact that she'd witnessed Fowler at the scene of the attack wasn't enough. She'd find a way to uncover the truth and seek recourse on Anna's behalf. If she could locate the Black Stripe operative that had pulled her from her tent, maybe she'd unearth some answers.

Her side vibrated. As she detached the phone, Cassidy hissed in annoyance. These things were worse than a leash. She hated being tied to reality, when her work consumed all her energy. That wasn't entirely true. It'd been deliberate on her part not to return the message because of who had sent it. That, she realized, was unprofessional.

Cursing her stupidity, she checked her watch. She'd been on the path for three hours. It was almost nine o'clock. She sighed deeply, knowing that a long lecture was going to be delivered when she met up with Jake.

The rustle of underbrush and scattering of rocks stopped her movement. Years of training had her instantly frozen in place, her ears straining to hear what moved below. Heavy footfalls bounced back through the morning air, along with deep ragged breaths as if someone were racing up the mountain. Crouching at the edge of the trail, she waited, not wanting to call attention to herself. Whoever was jogging this trail must be in excellent physical condition and definitely someone she wouldn't want to encounter in such a remote area. With disappearing wolves and drug smuggling at the park, Cassidy intended on being cautious.

The intruder rounded the pass, stopped, and with incredible instincts looked directly at her.

CHAPTER 15

"JASON?" EDWARD'S VOICE DRIFTED UPWARD THROUGH THE rectangular hatch. He cringed at the fear that resonated in the hesitant, shrill tone of his words. Edward hated the small confines of the laboratory. He was claustrophobic. Another sound echoed from above, and his breath hitched. "Jason?"

"Right here, Eddie." Jason stepped onto the top rung, braced his feet against the side of the ladder, and slid down to land gracefully on the hard linoleum floor below.

"What were you doing up there?"

Jason shrugged. "Just checking to make sure we hadn't left anything we might need." He moved forward toward Edward. Clearing his throat, he smiled his usual silly grin and stepped closer. "All done?"

Edward frowned and scooted his chair toward the counter. He grimaced as the wheels scraped against the linoleum, shooting a shiver straight up his spine. "Yes and no. I ran several more tests and discovered an amazing but disturbing occurrence."

Jason shrugged. "Whatever it is, I'm sure you'll plug it into your report. Relax, man." He lifted a hand and signaled toward a metallic silver briefcase. "Is that the briefcase containing the vials of CPV-19?"

Edward glanced over to where Jason pointed. "Yes. But you really need to witness this."

"Eddie ole man, I think that *you* really need to witness *this.*" Jason pointed a semiautomatic handgun at Edward and waved it in a small circle. "Isn't it cool?"

Panic and fear skittered along Edward's skin and he stood, slow and cautious. "Jason, what on earth is going on? Put down that gun."

Jason snorted in disbelief. "Time's up, Doc." He winked. "You've been sold out."

Edward froze, shock overshadowing fear. "I don't understand," he stammered.

Jason shook his head. "Ya know, I believed in what we were doing. I really did. But a better offer came along and . . ." He paused, sighing and lifting his left shoulder in a halfhearted shrug. "I went with the better offer. Now move it. Get up those stairs."

Edward saw no other option. His mind whirled with escape ideas, but until something solidified he would do as he was told.

Humming a Beach Boys tune, Jason grabbed the briefcase and hurried up the ladder behind Edward before he had a chance to gain any distance.

"Don't even think of trying something stupid, Eddie. I'll be happy to blow a hole in you right now."

Edward turned and glared down at Jason. "Then why don't you?"

Jason shook his head. "Because, Eddie, you're too damn fat to haul across the yard."

They scrambled out of the laboratory, Edward's lack of physical fitness a hindrance. He swore silently and cursed himself. He was a walking coronary.

Jason shoved the gun in Edward's back, its round chamber sinking into soft flesh and biting the muscles beneath. Jason grabbed the back of his shirt, stopping him before he moved too far ahead. Edward paused, allowing his eyes to adjust to daylight as his captor forced him outside.

"Come on, Eddie. Let's walk."

Edward stumbled. "Don't be stupid, Jason. We can work out a new arrangement. I'll add your name to the patent."

Jason bent forward, smacking his free hand against his thigh. "You don't get it, man, do you? I don't give a rat's ass about the patent or saving humanity." He shoved Edward in the back. "Pick up the pace, you stupid son of a bitch."

They reached the clearing around the incinerator. Jason pushed Edward hard and sent him flying forward. "Sorry, man. This is the end of the line." Edward lay on the ground. Thoughts whirled and whirled in his head, but nothing jumped out to solve the situation. He stared back at Jason and felt himself cowering like a pitiful pound puppy. Clucking his tongue, Jason stared, his eyes glowing with maniacal pride, relishing the feeling of God-like power. He controlled Edward, and he knew it.

Winking, Jason gave Edward one of those half-smiles that the kid thought made the ladies all hot and bothered. "Lights out." He aimed and fired.

The kid was a class-A screw up. Edward squeezed his eyes against the pain in the right side of his head. It felt ready to explode. He stifled a moan, his ear burning like he'd dipped it in molten lava. Fear still ran through Edward's system, mimicking the dip and dive of the river rapids shooting past the front of the property.

Jason hadn't bothered to check whether or not the bullet hit home, assuming because of the amount of blood and lack of movement that he'd succeeded in striking a killing blow. Edward supposed he should be grateful that all the years of making Jason redo tests because he'd skipped a step or forgotten to write down pertinent data never sunk into the kid's pot-damaged brain. Carelessness granted Edward an upper hand.

He lifted his head, fighting a wave of nausea and dizziness. If he didn't act fast, his system would shut down from shock. Edward spotted the gun lying about five feet from his leg. Jason opened the door to the incinerator, and Edward took advantage of the blast of heat that temporarily blinded the kid to move sideways and grab the gun. Edward quickly scooted back and braced himself against a tree, not trusting his legs.

What was the idiot doing?

At the sound of the chainsaw, Edward's chest tightened. He had to give the kid a few points for creativity, not to mention guts. The mere thought of Jason hacking his body to pieces brought forth a conundrum of nightmares.

As Jason turned in his direction, Edward pointed the gun at the kid's chest and willed his hand to stop shaking. He could do this. It was a game of survival.

Jason stopped short, pointing the chainsaw in Edward's direction. "You gonna kill me, Eddie?" His voice rang loudly above the whirring of the power tool.

Edward nodded.

"Nah. I don't think so. What would the scientific community say?"

Edward frowned. Jason had a point. He couldn't very well kill the boy and then call 911. He'd have to explain about the laboratory and then CPV-19 and then . . .

"I don't care." Edward said, as convincingly as possible.

Jason flipped the switch on the chainsaw and silence descended, creating a preternatural calm. "Of course you do. Your patent hasn't been filed yet, man."

Edward narrowed his eyes. "How could you know that?"

Jason dropped the chainsaw and lifted his hands as if in surrender. "Well, you see, I wasn't bought off by another group wanting CPV-19. I was paid by New World Petroleum to watch you and filter back your process. They don't care about the patent, and because of that you're disposable. Besides . . ." The lab assistant shrugged, stepping forward. "CPV-19 is already running free."

Edward froze, his mind trying to sort through this last piece of news. "It couldn't have spread so quickly."

"Well, see, that's where we were wrong. According to my main man, it's spreading—spreading real quick. Which means, Eddie . . ." Jason bent forward and dropped his voice to a soft whisper. "Yellowstone is about to have a few very bad weeks. And you are out one highly prized patent. They ain't never gonna give you any awards for creating something this nasty. As a matter of fact, they'll probably put you right in jail."

With a jolt, Edward realized Jason had moved too close. "Stop. Don't take another step."

"Tsk tsk, Eddie. Afraid?" Edward's eyes widened as Jason's face transformed into a maniacal monster's with only one item on the agenda. Murder.

Edward felt as if he'd fallen down a rabbit hole. He had one clear thought: in order to survive, Jason must die.

Before he chickened out, he fired the gun. His head snapped back against the tree as the shock of the weapon vibrated from his fingers through his arm. Sulfur tinged the crisp air, and the shot echoed through the valley, transforming the two-second episode into slow motion.

Blood spread rapidly across Jason's chest. He staggered then collapsed to the ground, pressing his hands against the mortal wound. Several gurgling gasps for air, and then all became still.

Edward hurried over, holding the gun in front of him. The gun wobbled violently, and he tried to steady his hand as best he could. Bending, Edward checked for a pulse. Nothing.

Glancing around, his gaze rested on the chainsaw. There was no way he'd be able chop the kid up. His stomach just wasn't built for that type of thing.

He'd leave him.

Edward pressed his hand against his own wounds and staggered to his feet. He needed to act fast. With hesitant steps, he made his way toward the main house. Each movement forward sent slashes of pain searing through his head. *Damn Jason. Damn him to hell.*

Entering the small half bath on the first floor of the house, he surveyed the damage to his head. The bullet grazed his temple but not before shattering the top of his ear. Actually, that was probably a lucky thing. The amount of the blood from the ear wound was what had convinced Jason his shot had been true. He reached beneath the vanity and searched blindly for the first-aid kit.

Swearing, Edward bent down to locate what his fingers couldn't find. Pain strangled his head, and he fought against the blackness that threatened. He spotted the white plastic box and with shaking hands went to work.

He stitched the three-inch gash above his right eye, sucking sharp breaths in and out as the needled pierced his skin. Finished, he swabbed the wound clean and pasted a Band-Aid over the stitches.

The ear was a mess.

Edward splashed disinfectant on the shattered skin, then wrapped it as tightly and with as much gauze as he could.

Finally done with first-aid, he retraced his steps back toward the incinerator. The case containing the CPV-19 vials and antidote lay propped against a tree. Edward retrieved it and made his way beyond the quaking aspens and into the log cabin. Each step required reaffirmation that everything would be all right. His head pounded, his hands shook. Life wasn't looking so bright.

Entering the lab, he gathered the data from the last test. Edward verified there was nothing else of importance he needed. The lab had been stripped down over the past twenty-four hours. There was nothing here that would reproduce the genetic mutation process or CPV-19.

His patent was safe. But the suitcase he carried meant he stepped into the world of the hunted. Edward needed to reach New York and have his lawyer file the patent before NWP caught up with him.

His stomach lurched. He felt sick. To be truthful, Edward didn't know how far the board's power spread. He'd accepted their money with gratitude, never once questioning their motivation.

He'd allowed his greed for recognition to cloud his judgment. What a stupid man he'd been!

Climbing the stairs out of the lab, Edward sealed the door and exited the cabin. Squinting against the brightness of the sun, he noticed a peculiar pattern flickering on the grass.

Dark shadows moved in and out of his line of vision. Edward gazed upward and gasped at the tornado of vultures circling high in the sky. They'd smelled death.

This wouldn't do. It could draw attention to the property. He didn't know when and where Jason was supposed to hand over the virus; it could have been within the hour, or it could have been the next day. Everything needed to appear normal.

He moved as quickly as possible toward the incinerator. Jason's body was sprawled on the ground, the pool of blood bigger than when Edward had left.

Glancing around in a panic, his gaze fell on the river. That would work. The rapids would carry the body downriver, and by the time it was discovered Edward would be long gone.

He grabbed Jason under the arms and began dragging him across the grass to the riverbank. *Don't think about death.* It'd been necessary. Still his heart felt heavy, and his head felt as if it'd been split in two. If he focused on remaining conscious, the guilt of his murderous actions faded to a soft whisper.

The strain of using muscles he didn't have forced blood to pump from the wound on his ear. Sweat poured from his forehead, blocking his vision.

Murder was an uncomfortable thing.

After an interminable amount of time, Edward reached the banks of Yellowstone River. The water sped past the loamy shore. He needed to drag the body past the row of kayaks piled to the left that Jason had collected over the past five years.

He hauled the body into the river, inhaling sharply when the frosty bite of the river seeped into his clothes. Edward made certain he'd waded far enough offshore before releasing his hold on the lab assistant. He watched, mesmerized as the river tossed the remains of Jason from one icy wave to another. The choppy surface swallowed death in a matter of seconds.

Edward headed back to shore, an unusual patch of white catching his attention. He frowned and squinted at the thing lying close to the edge of the embankment. As he approached it, a flash of fear caused his heart rate to increase and beads of sweat to form on his brow. His body alternated between shivers from the icy water of the river and shakes caused by the dead wolf at his feet.

He knew what he had to do. Edward calculated the time it would take for him to retrieve his medical kit and obtain blood samples from the infected animal. It would be well worth it. This was an opportunity to study a live second-generation virus sample. The importance and impact on his research outweighed the half hour he'd expose himself to capture.

CHAPTER 16

"WHERE," SAID JAKE, HALTING, HIS WORDS STRAINED FROM EX-
haustion, "have you been?"

Cassidy gazed at him in shock and surprise. She couldn't believe
that he stood not more than ten feet from her. His face was flushed,
and his nostrils flared with the joint effort of recapturing his breath and
controlling his anger. She stood rooted, watching him bend over, inhale
deeply, and gather his strength. A tremor ran through his body, and
she responded on instinct. Sliding down the trail, she gently touched
the side of his neck, checking his pulse.

His arm snaked out of nowhere, pinning her to his chest. Cassidy
struggled, but there was no lessening of the pressure.

"Jake, let me go."

"In just a moment." His voice, husky with lack of oxygen, sent shivers
down her spine. "I don't want to fall down. That damn trail is steep."

She felt his breath on her hair, hot and fast. She moved her head
to see his face. Blue eyes, dark and dangerous, gazed back. An edge of
familiarity sparked in her brain, then quickly faded beneath the heat
their bodies ignited. A lump formed in her throat, and swallowing be-

came difficult.

Time slammed on the brakes.

It felt as if nature's force surged from the ground, twisting her heart and ringing in a vision of the future different from any she'd ever imagined.

Cassidy shoved at his chest, jumped back, and fell flat on her ass.

Jake reached down and hauled her to her feet, brushing dirt from her behind. She swatted at his hands and glared at him.

"Do you have your phone?" He spoke very softly and enunciated each word with great determination.

"Yes. You know I do. Why?"

"Ever consider answering my message?" His patient words rang warning bells in her head. Cassidy, once more, cursed her own stupidity for not replying to his text. Smiling shyly, she tried to lighten the mood with a joke.

"And why would I do that, when I have you to run them up the mountain? Besides, if it'd been important, you would've called."

Jake swiped his hand through his hair, sweat making it slick against his head. "Because I was running up the mountain, signal was limited. I thought a text would reach you better."

Cassidy gazed at his face, chewing the edge of her bottom lip. "Oh."

"You," he said, clenching his jaw, "just cost me ten years of my life." Jake walked to the side of the trail. "I was worried." His voice remained soft.

"Why? What happened?" He appeared to be scouting for something. "What are you looking for?"

He didn't bother to glance back. "Tracks."

Cassidy glanced around and shook her head. "No. You won't find any here. I don't believe the wolves have crossed this area in the past month."

Jake crouched down and pointed to a spot off the main trail. "Human tracks."

"I don't understand."

"Bloody human tracks." He turned and faced her. "There's a body." His jaw tight with emotion, he pointed down the trail. "There."

She followed his gesture and sat down suddenly as understanding swamped her. He'd thought she'd been in danger. "What?"

"In addition to the body, there's a trail of blood that runs down toward where it was discovered."

Cassidy swallowed. "I'm sorry about the phone." She brushed her hair out of her face. She'd allowed personal feelings to affect her judgment. *Damn.* "It was wrong of me not to answer." She took a deep breath, and words spilled from her mouth. "But I assure you I was not in the least bit of danger. Whatever happened didn't occur anywhere near me." His tense stance and white-knuckled fists signaled exactly how in control his temper remained. Cassidy smiled hesitantly. "So you see? No worries, mate."

"We're a team" is all he said.

She counted herself lucky that he didn't let loose the torrent of angry words she deserved. "I understand." She'd broken a ZEBRA cardinal rule, removing herself from contact.

He nodded and examined the side of the trail.

Straightening, Cassidy started to stand, then sat with a thump when another man stepped into the clearing.

Jake ran through several mental exercises that released his fear and worry. Cassidy thought he was angry. *Good.*

He wasn't.

He'd been certain that what lay at the top of this trail was another mangled and lifeless body. The past hours of hiking up a trail laden with footprints and blood splatters caused disconcerting thoughts.

The panic that seized his insides and froze his mind began to dissipate. Goose bumps spread across his skin.

He wanted her in his arms.

He'd better find a way to forget that last thought.

Kicking an invisible rock, he swore. If this wasn't a tangled nest of irritated rattlers, he didn't know what was.

"Ethan," he called and headed over to the park ranger. Cassidy sat on the side of the trail, eyeing the other man with consternation. "There's another set of prints over there." Jake pointed behind him and nodded in satisfaction when the chief went to measure and mark. He'd called him the second the trail of blood had led him to a body.

Jake hadn't been more than a mile up the trail when he'd heard the sirens and voices of the park rangers. The high altitude had worked against Jake, and it hadn't been long before Ethan Connor was only a click behind him.

"Sunshine," Jake said softly. "Snap out of it." He crouched in front of her and touched her shoulder lightly.

"I'm so sorry."

"Okay. It's over, and I'm almost sorry to say that it's good to see you alive and well." He stood and pulled her to her feet. "Come on, Betty Boop. Let's get down this mountain and grab some coffee."

The small clearing suddenly filled with people as a multitude of officials arrived. Chief Connor directed everyone to the other prints and dismissed Jake and Cassidy with a nod. This wasn't ZEBRA territory yet. He'd make sure Ethan Connor provided him with a detailed report of his findings. The itch that spelled danger spread.

Cassidy blew out a mouthful of air and allowed Jake to lead her down the trail and away from Ethan Connor and his rangers. She needed to clear the air with Ethan and put the past where it belonged: in the past. The thought of disappointing Jake and her pod paralyzed her. *A fool. A jackass.* With a snort, she spoke beneath her breath. "Definitely Betty Boopish."

"Huh?" Jake said.

"Talking to myself."

He smiled and gave her a slight nudge. "Did you find anything last night?"

This was a comfortable area. And she realized that in the stress of the situation, she'd forgotten all about the wolves. Cassidy beamed at Jake. "Yes, I did."

He walked next to her, lifted her backpack off her shoulder, and swung it onto his own, and suddenly the world skittered back into place. The tightness in her chest lessened, and she could breathe. A little emotional hiccup brought on by shock and adrenaline was no reason to spin into a full-fledged *I-want-this-man* panic.

"Tell me," he coaxed and stepped in front of her.

Cassidy followed him down the path. She'd glanced behind once or twice and reassured herself that Ethan wasn't following. She needed to deal with that situation, but not now. Not yet. It didn't bode well that he hadn't said a word since yesterday. If she wasn't careful, the memories Ethan provoked would distract her and she'd jeopardize her job. That was unacceptable. *I'll call him tonight,* she told herself.

Decisions made and emotions back in alignment, Cassidy began to soak up her surroundings.

"A pack of approximately half a dozen full-grown wolves crossed the outpost. I didn't follow them because"—she rolled her eyes in his direction—"somebody interrupted me."

Jake shrugged a shoulder and offered her a half smile. "Were they collared?"

Cassidy paused and frowned. Jake stopped beside her and waited for her answer. "You know, I couldn't say. It was dawn, and the light was bad due to fog. But we know they're in this quadrant. I'll try another location tonight." She started walking ahead of him and took a moment to gaze around at the scenery. "Did you know . . ."

Jake groaned, and she reached back and punched his arm. "Knowledge is power, Jake." He rolled his eyes, and she laughed. "Did you know that from November to early May most of the park roads are closed, making this region isolated from civilization?"

"Nope, didn't know that." Jake said with a deadpan face.

He didn't fool her; Cassidy saw the interest spark in his eyes. His soul craved solitude and wilderness whether he wanted to admit it or not. "It was one of my favorite times of the year. My father and I would ride our snowmobiles through the designated trails. You wouldn't see another soul for hours."

Jake surprised her with a nod of agreement. "My dad and I love taking out four-wheelers when we're lucky enough to get snow. A hundred acres of nothing but white. It's beautiful."

For some reason, family didn't seem like one of Jake's assets. It made Cassidy curious. "Where's your land?"

"About sixty miles north of Atlanta."

"Do you live there?" It seemed unfathomable to Cassidy to actually have a home and maintain the level of work required of ZEBRA field personnel.

Jake laughed. "Don't look so shocked. Beneath all this muscle, I'm a real homebody at heart."

The warmth of his smile was genuine, and that little kick of she-didn't-know-what attacked her stomach. Maybe the trail mix was causing indigestion.

"Tell me about your childhood," he urged.

Too close.

Cassidy shrugged and offered a smile, hoping it covered her panic.

"Maybe another time."

They reached the base a little over an hour later. She'd concentrated on idle chatter, refusing to allow him anymore access to her inner self, as well as distancing the conversation on anything that might make her see Jake Anderson as anything other than an irritating coworker.

Cassidy rounded a bend, balancing herself against the steep incline by leaning back. Yellow tape flapped in front, surprising her. As she focused on the area, the chalk outline of a body had her quickly shuffling backwards and smashing her back against Jake's chest. "Easy girl," he said against her ear, sending a shiver of awareness down her spine. Damn him.

Mistake. Move forward. Find air.

She stepped forward, putting at least five paces between them. "I'm fine. It just took me by surprise." Crime scene tape flapped in the wind, and after a quick glance around, she selected a trail down an incline outside of the cordoned off area.

It was almost 10:30 and the midmorning sun beat down relentlessly, springing rivers of sweat to life that ran in tiny trickles across Cassidy's brow and down her cheekbones. Jake moved in front of her, and she reluctantly accepted his hand as he assisted her in stepping around a prickly patch of loose rock and dirt.

"Who found the body?"

"Me."

She paused. Scrunching up her nose, she glanced at him. "Ick." He shrugged and signaled her to keep moving. "Cause of death?"

"Indeterminable, but I bet it has something to do with blood loss."

She shot him a puzzled look. "Why?"

He pointed to the area in the center of the taped off quadrant, and Cassidy inhaled sharply at the size of the puddles and sodden ground.

"Time of death?"

"Around 2 a.m., I believe. Why?"

Cassidy gazed at the crime scene. "Why didn't I hear anything?"

"You were twenty miles up, Sunshine. If, like you said, she was nowhere near your location, you couldn't possibly have heard a thing."

"Noise travels these trails like rumors at a cocktail party. I should've heard something."

Jake glanced at her thoughtfully.

Cassidy pointed toward the path they'd descended. "The silence that surrounds the observation post is complete. My ears are tuned to any variance in noise. I was perched directly above the crime scene." She turned and stared at Jake. "Any strange sound should have carried straight up to me."

"That far?"

Cassidy shrugged. "An average person might not differentiate an odd tone, but I'm a trained observer and certainly should've heard something."

"You've got a point. I'll be right back."

She waved him away. A little peace and quiet before facing the real world was just what she needed. Cassidy stepped out of the woods onto the road. She watched Jake speaking with a man in a black windbreaker. *FBI. Now what are they doing here?* Jake lifted his head and returned her gaze. The heat in his eyes stole her breath.

She needed space.

Shaking her arms in an attempt to shed the uncomfortable attraction for Jake, she cursed and paced in a tight circle.

"This isn't good, Lowell."

Jake joined her. "Talking to yourself again?"

"Yep, Goofy. I am." She smirked when he raised one eyebrow at the name she used, and they walked to the Jeep. "What's with the feds?"

"They're trying to tie the dead body into the drug ring that's plaguing Yellowstone. Apparently, the dealers are crossing state borders in different spots each time, making tracking complicated."

Cassidy climbed into the Jeep. "Huh. Sounds like Ethan has his hands full." She rested her head against the back of the seat, sighing at the comfort of its padding. As Jake drove away from the trail, exhaustion, both emotional and physical, finally took hold. Oblivion closed upon her mind, shutting it down as easily as flicking a switch. She shifted her weight away from the uncomfortable presence of Jake and placed her forehead against the window, slipping away from the present and allowing sleep to claim her.

CHAPTER 17

Jake drummed his fingers on the sleek surface of the conference table. The rhythmic motion aided in untangling the convoluted information dump of the past twenty-four hours. Leaning forward, he grabbed his pen and scribbled on several index cards. He picked them up, fanned them like a deck of cards, then placed each on the flat surface. Beams of late-afternoon sun sparkled on the wood finish, making several of the cards difficult to read. He adjusted them.

Wolves. Post 29. Cassidy Lowell. Niger Delta. Ethan Connor. New World Petroleum. Murder.

All separate, yet undeniably linked.

Tapping the card labeled Ethan Connor, he tried to focus on what bothered him about the man. Both times he'd been in the park ranger's presence, his senses had kicked into high alert. Why? Something rested within the depths of the man's eyes that didn't shoot straight with Jake. Snapping open his cell phone, he punched in a number. The automated system routed his call and when requested, he entered his security code. A few seconds later, his call was routed over a secure line.

"Identification?" A computerized voice asked.

"Anderson, Jake. Delta Squad. Black Stripe." He then spouted his identification number and answered several more questions. There was a brief pause, and his call finally connected.

"Captain Anderson, what can I do for you?"

"I need a complete background check on Chief Ethan Connor employed by Yellowstone National Park with specific focus into his connection with Dr. Cassidy Lowell, ZEBRA, White Stripe."

"Priority?" The detached voice asked.

"Red." He disconnected.

The humming noise of water-filled pipes stopped, and after a few minutes he heard Cassidy's bathroom door open and close. She'd been exhausted after last night, and he'd insisted she nap. With his head tilted to the side, he listened as she rummaged through her stuff. Jake chuckled when her voice floated through the wall in an indecipherable litany of sentences. Her habit of talking to herself amused him.

He picked up the card with her name scrawled across its white surface in bold letters and traced his finger along the black pen marks. Jake sifted through what he knew. Cassidy graduated with a bachelor's degree in biology from Principia College and fast-forwarded through her doctorate in zoology from the University of Georgia, returning home to participate in the release of the gray wolves into Yellowstone. Her parents died the summer after the wolves were released while day-cruising on an ultra-light.

ZEBRA attempted to woo Cassidy into their fold from the time she began her graduate studies in Athens, Georgia. After her parents' tragic accident, she ran back to Atlanta and dove into the organization with such dedication it made Jake's tenure in the armed forces seem like a vacation. Cassidy's zoological successes spanned the globe, making her one of the leading authorities on endangered species.

Jake lifted his head and stared at her bedroom's closed door. He heard her moving around, humming a song that seemed familiar, but her voice drifted off before he could identify it. Her biography was black and white. The woman, however, remained a kaleidoscope of contradiction.

The scent of shampoo and soap tickled his nose, and he smiled when Cassidy's bedroom door opened. Jake inhaled in appreciation. Her sun-blushed face glowed and glistened, a perfect picture for the frame of damp locks that cascaded around her shoulders.

He pointed to the chair beside him. "Join me." She walked over, but her eyes were apprehensive. "Get enough sleep?" he said in an attempt to ease her sudden hesitancy and shyness. Chemistry and attraction threatened his impartiality. He knew control over his desire to flirt with her must strengthen because without her trust, he'd never gain the information his assignment demanded.

"Yes, thanks. What's all this?" she asked as she settled in the chair next to him.

He pushed over the carafe of coffee resting next to his elbow and slipped the cards marked Niger Delta and New World Petroleum into the palm of his hand and out of sight. "Our mysteries." Cassidy snatched at the silver-plated pot like it was a million dollars. Scanning the table, she gave up on finding her own mug and took his. He watched her, enjoying the graceful movement of her hands.

Closing her eyes, she inhaled the aroma. After several sips, Cassidy turned her attention to the cards on the table. Narrowing her eyes at one of the cards, she picked it up. "I'm not a mystery."

Jake shuffled the stack, placing Ethan Connor's name first, then the card marked *Murder*, then slipped hers from her fingers and stuck it beneath.

Her brows rose almost to the tip of her hairline, and she placed the coffee cup back on the table with a thump. "You don't think Ethan had anything to do with the murder?"

"I don't know. He appeared at the crime scene only twenty minutes after me." Jake tapped the card, furrowing his brow. "There's something about him that bothers me."

"And?"

"His ranch is more than an hour away. I checked."

Cassidy leaned forward and touched his arm. "Jake, Ethan has family all across Jackson Hole. He could've been in any number of places. Don't look for reasons; look for evidence."

He stared at her face. Ignoring the physical attraction, he shrugged. "His attitude toward you is evidence."

"No." She shook her head. "His attitude toward me is unprofessional. It doesn't label him a murderer." She picked up Ethan's card and ripped it in half. "What else have you got?"

"Not a damn thing. A lot of uncomfortable vibes, but other than that, nada."

Cassidy reached beneath the table and snagged the hidden index cards from under his thigh, flipping them at him. "Explain these." Her face was expressionless except for the flicker of anger lighting her eyes and staining her cheeks red.

Damn.

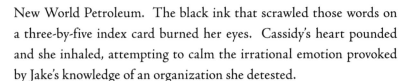

New World Petroleum. The black ink that scrawled those words on a three-by-five index card burned her eyes. Cassidy's heart pounded and she inhaled, attempting to calm the irrational emotion provoked by Jake's knowledge of an organization she detested.

Jake's frown when he picked up the cards she'd tossed did nothing to mar the attraction of his face.

Damn the man. The small amount of trust she'd felt for him vanished.

"I'm waiting." Cassidy tapped her fingers against the polished wood of the conference table. "Cat got your tongue?"

"Your last assignment turned dangerous."

"My last assignment has absolutely nothing to do with this one or with you for that matter. And I'd appreciate it if you quit delving into my background." Cassidy was pissed. Who the hell did he think he was?

Jake grinned. The spark of amusement in his eyes caused the hair on the back of her neck to rise. "Whatever," he said, picking up the cards and ripping them in half.

Cassidy narrowed her eyes, not believing in his easy retreat. She'd play his game for now. "Fine. Let's move forward. Where were you while I slept?"

His teeth flashed, and he smiled like he'd won some kind of bet. It irritated her. "I went to headquarters to see if they had any reports on this morning's little surprise."

"What did you learn from Ethan?"

"Chief Connor didn't make it back while I was there. But I had an opportunity to talk with the coroner."

She leaned forward, resting her elbows upon the table. "And?"

"There was some sort of rash on the woman's face and chest. And . . ." Jake paused and gazed into her face. "You sure you want to hear this?"

Typical male. Cassidy rolled her eyes and pasted a sweet smile on her face. "I'm not squeamish. Spill it."

He sighed. "Okay. There was profuse internal bleeding that spilled pretty much out of every orifice and onto the ground. In addition, she was severely dehydrated."

Cassidy frowned. "Any results from the lab on body fluids?"

Jake shrugged. "Nah. Too soon for that. But they promised to fax it as soon as they have them."

"Wow. I'm impressed at the level of cooperation you received."

He winked. "I've just got it like that."

She wagged a finger under his nose. "Ah-ha. The coroner was a female, wasn't she?" Cassidy sat back and crossed her arms. "You little player," she accused, half amused and half she-didn't-know-what. Jealous? *No way.*

Jake leaned forward, and for a panicked moment Cassidy thought he was about to embrace her. Instead, he grabbed a file. By the wicked grin tugging at his lips, she knew he'd caught her reaction.

"Don't worry Sunshine, you're the only one on my mind."

She caught the fish disease, as her mother used to call it, and Cassidy found herself opening and closing her mouth like one of the cutthroat trout that inhabited Yellowstone Lake. Her insides were fluttering and jumping around in an annoying mix of excitement and nerves.

"This is the latest data from the GPS system," he said, handing her the file he'd retrieved.

With something to focus her attention on, she ignored his full-fledged smile and the glint lighting his eyes. She stared at the graph, scanning the page. "It doesn't show the pack I saw at Post 29."

"Interesting, don't you think?"

She nodded. "Is it possible there's an entire pack roaming around without any tracking devices attached?"

Jake shrugged. "I don't know; that's your department." He pushed back from the table. "Let's get outta here."

Cassidy glanced at him as he rose and strode to the door. "Where to?" she asked, even though she was already moving to follow him.

"A walk."

"Didn't you have enough outdoorsy stuff this morning?"

"Don't you want to see the geyser?"

She exited the presidential suite; a ripple of excitement skimmed her stomach. Hell yes, she wanted to see the new geyser. "That's not a walk. We have to drive."

He smiled and took off at a brisk pace. "We have to walk to the Jeep."

"I really should stay and scour through these reports."

"You're too tired to read."

"I am not tired," she said, biting her lip to stifle the yawn that threatened to call her a liar.

Jake escorted her to the vehicle. "Reports can be read later."

Cassidy jumped into the passenger side, snapped down the visor, and scrutinized her face. Yep. Her messy hair still damp from the shower and dark circles lining the bottom of her eyes were a definite giveaway. She was tired. "Don't think I've forgotten about your little indiscretion."

Jake eyed her for a second, then switched his attention back to the road. "And what would that be?"

"Those totally inappropriate note cards."

Jake stared at her for a minute then shook his head. "Drop it. It was a mistake. I'm sorry if I intruded where I shouldn't have."

Another smooth retreat. "Right." She didn't bother to disguise the sarcasm in her tone.

He glared at her. "Take the apology and move beyond this, okay?"

Like hell. "Sure."

The car swayed gently to the left, and she wondered where his line of thought was going. "How about we cut to the chase and you explain, in detail, why you wrote those cards?"

"Give it up, Sunshine. I've already told you I looked into your background, and I've apologized for that. Let's leave this bone unpicked, okay?"

Cassidy sighed, not liking the distant tone of his voice. He switched personalities faster than a superhero. "You know, I wouldn't be this persistent if that assignment didn't still bother me. I have one of those" —she waved her hand in the air—"premonition thingies."

That seemed to spark his interest. "Define that."

"There're so many inconsistencies from that assignment." She furrowed her brow, then decided her brain hurt. "I'm probably just tired and overreacting." Cassidy refused to glance in Jake's direction. Let him think she was looney; who cares?

Cassidy spotted Michelle the moment she hit the rickety boardwalk surrounding the geothermal plains.

She waved and walked to stand next to the ecologist. "So tell me all about this."

Michelle smiled, pushing her chin-length hair back from her face. "It's amazing. This has the potential to blow higher and stronger than Old Faithful."

Cassidy eyed the area. It looked like nothing more than a small mound of crusty dirt, but she knew the power that bubbled and surged beneath this last layer of the earth's crust. "Do you think it's relevant to the wolves' disappearance?"

Michelle shook her head. "I doubt it. The plains surrounding Old Faithful and the other geysers are constantly monitored for advanced geothermal activity. They've had an eye on this new baby for quite some time."

Jake joined them. "How do they know when a new geyser exists?"

"Infrared imaging equipment. Apparently, several years ago there was a minor shift in the second porous rock layer. It created a crack that allowed water from an existing hot spring to seep down and be heated. Based on the calculations of Old Faithful, Yellowstone officials have determined that the first eruption is due to take place within the next ten days."

"Really?" Jake asked. "The construction workers indicated that the scientists are all flying in for a viewing the day after tomorrow."

A frown marred Michelle's small, heart-shaped face. "I don't know about that. I'll have to talk and ask more questions, not to mention take more readings. I've ordered a specialized thermal reader. It'll arrive tomorrow."

Cassidy leaned over the railing and eyed the geyser. It didn't appear to be any larger than a prairie dog's burrow, but heat that gathered under the cover of rock and dirt could peel the skin from a man's face with one blast of exploding water. "So we're still at square one."

Michelle sighed and shrugged her shoulders. "Yep."

"I need to find Steve," Jake said. "Do you know his whereabouts?"

"The last I heard, he was in his room setting up the communications system. He didn't want to leave Myrtle in the main suite. Too much commotion, he said."

"Thanks. I'll find him. What's your next move?"

"I'm off to gather soil samples. I thought I'd begin in the quadrant where Cassidy was last night. My map indicates that she was north of Craig Pass toward the Continental Divide. Then I'll head southeast toward Lewis Lake."

Cassidy smiled. "That's right." She frowned, worrying her bottom lip. "If there's any sign of danger, protocol states we need to pair up." Gazing into the distance, she mulled over the past twenty-four hours. "I think a dead body classifies as danger."

"Thanks for the concern, Cass, but I'm a lot tougher than I look." Michelle swung her equipment over her shoulder and stepped off the plateau and onto the boardwalk.

Jake bent over and slipped his hand beneath the straps of Michelle's canvas bag that sat next to their feet. He hauled it over his shoulder and slid his free arm around Cassidy's waist, guiding her toward the parking lot.

"Nevertheless, we're pairing up. Jake?"

She moved away from him, and he had the nerve to grin and wink at her as he opened the door to Michelle's Jeep and tossed in her bag. "Yeah?"

"Why don't you go with Michelle?" She was damn proud of herself for figuring out a way to place some distance between them.

Michelle stuffed the rest of her gear in the back of her vehicle. Slamming the door, she glanced at Jake and Cassidy. "Nah, I'll grab Steve." She winked. "He owes me fieldwork time for helping set up Myrtle."

Cassidy's smile faded. "You sure?" She waved her arm to the left. "Jake's right here."

Laughing, Michelle nodded and drove off, leaving Cassidy and Jake standing by their own vehicle. "That little witch. She did that on purpose." She glanced at Jake only to find him gazing at her in an uncomfortable, I-can-see-right-through-you manner. "What?"

Jake continued to scrutinize her. She refused to fidget. Finally, he sighed deeply and jumped behind the wheel of the Jeep.

She didn't move. A familiar logo beamed at her from the back of the newly constructed bleachers. Cassidy twisted and glanced at Jake. "What is NWP doing here?"

CHAPTER 18

JAKE AND CASSIDY STOOD AT THE BASE OF THE TRAIL LEADING to Observation Post 26. She pushed up the sleeve of her ZEBRA logo sweatshirt and verified the time. Stretching her arms to the sky, she twisted the kinks out of her back. The brief nap stolen while Jake coordinated data with Steve had revitalized her sagging energy. He hadn't been able to answer her question about New World Petroleum's presence in Yellowstone other than their sponsorship of the new geyser. In fact, his response had been entirely too distant and out of character.

"You don't really need to join me," Cassidy protested for the tenth time that afternoon. "Steve offered."

Jake swore beneath his breath and tossed her backpack out of the Jeep. "He's still out with Michelle. You're stuck with me."

She bent and picked up her belongings, ignoring a sudden twinge of excitement. "Fine."

The beginning of the trail wound around the south arm of Yellowstone Lake. Water glistened brightly in the dying sun. Inhaling, she smiled. A prophetic tingle ran up her spine as fresh air filled her lungs. Home. Her eyes soaked in the surrounding vistas. Early evening burned with breathtaking beauty, the vivid blue of the lake a cool blanket for the crimson sky.

Cassidy led him west toward the southern bend of the Continental Divide. "Did you know that in the summer, wolves usually set out in the early evening and return to their den by the next morning? If this were winter, we'd be facing a greater obstacle."

The path widened, and Jake stepped up next to her. "How's that?"

Cassidy didn't agree with the way her body responded to the man beside her. He was too close. "Without pups to care for, they wouldn't bother to cross back and return to their dens." She paused and sniffed the air. "Smell that?"

Jake inhaled. "Fires, right?"

"Part of Mother Nature's way of killing the old and bringing in the new. The Lodgepole pines can only reseed once they're burned."

"Really?"

Cassidy stopped and pointed to a grove of pines. They looked like a fur-topped army lined up in precision. Each member the same height as the next. "During the fires of '88 that area burnt to the ground. The new seeds were released and grew at the exact same rate. Amazing, don't you think?"

Jake walked past her. "Fascinating, Dr. Doolittle."

She tossed him what she hoped was a nasty look. "Anyway, those fires are miles away. But the scent will keep the wolves close to home in case their dens are threatened."

"How far to the post?"

"What's the matter, Charlie Brown? Tired?"

Jake shot her an amused grin. "Very funny."

She tromped ahead of him, flipping her hair over her shoulder. "I thought so. Actually, it's not too far. We'll park ourselves at the edge of this tributary from Yellowstone Lake. There's a prominent watering hole just over that ridge that attracts wolf prey." She pointed to a section against the horizon. It was a steep trail flanked by a mixture of pines and aspens that swayed in a graceful dance, inviting them forward with their leafy limbs. She calculated the distance to be approximately three miles up the trail. "I think we'll see action tonight."

They proceeded in silence. Steeply inclined passageways exhausted their energy and left them breathless. Jake reached for Cassidy, aiding her in difficult bends. He decided to give up and be himself. Jake figured that considering her awareness of their attraction, she'd think him out of character not to react to their chemistry.

Entering the clearing surrounding the post, he sank down, leaned against a tree, and contentedly watched her through half-shuttered eyes. Brilliant slashes of blood red painted the horizon with the last light of day. Cassidy moved, bathed in its soft glow, from one corner of the clearing to the next.

She scrutinized the ground, gently pushing leaves and natural debris to the side to check for any recent tracks or signs of wolf habitation. He tilted his head to the side, smiling when she bit her lower lip. Jake recognized that sign now. The thoughts whirring in that intelligent mind of hers were in direct contradiction to what her emotions were signaling. He bent his head to the other side, cracking his neck.

Cassidy was a diversion he hadn't been prepared to navigate.

She rapidly scratched notes on her pad. With a toss of her head, Cassidy flipped stray strands of hair from her face, bent, and tied flags around low branches, tracing a possible trail. He didn't allow his eyes to follow her fingers as they brushed a thin line of perspiration from her brow.

"Goldilocks?"

He smiled when she paused at the title he'd used. "Yeah?" Stopping her markings, she looked at him expectantly.

"What happened in Africa?"

"Nothing," Cassidy responded tightly. "Quit badgering."

"Sharpe mentioned that it'd been tough for you. He thought maybe you shouldn't be here." Her eyes flashed daggers at him. Grinning back at her, Jake pushed even further. "Actually, he said that ZEBRA seemed to be sapping you of all life." She stalked over, pinning him with blazing green eyes. Jake inhaled.

"It's none of your business." Through clenched teeth, her voice came out a husky rasp. Undeterred, he continued prodding.

"What happened in Africa?"

"I'm not answering."

"Are you broken, Sunshine? Have those adventurous wings been clipped?" He gazed steadily into her anger-flushed face.

"I'm not broken. My wings are intact, but Africa is off limits." Sadness crept across Cassidy's face; she knelt next to him and drew small circles in the dirt at his feet. "Because I couldn't keep my distance. The loss of life, both human and animal, was terrifying. Those people live with disease and inhumane conditions but maintain a love that puts my pitiful existence to shame. I think I'm helping, but I'm not. I'm invading." Reaching forward, Jake took hold of her hand. Silencing its nervous movements, he stroked the soil from crevices that denoted her difficult job. "We bring false hope," she whispered.

"You're helping, Sunshine. You know you are."

The expression on her face stabbed his heart. Her eyes were wide and unveiled, inviting him to witness the hurt and betrayal she felt. She didn't bother to wipe away the tear that slid silently down her cheek. "Am I?"

Holding her shaking shoulders tightly, he murmured comforting words. "Some things in life aren't easy to understand. Whatever happened, it wasn't your fault." Pulling away from his embrace, Cassidy sighed deeply. He allowed her the distance.

"That's it? You're not going to interrogate me, Popeye? Don't you want the truth about what a miserable failure I am?" She paused, inhaled a few breaths, then focused emerald daggers on his face. "You know what I want? I want to know what the hell the largest oil producer in the Niger Delta is doing playing around in my own backyard."

Popeye? She was a piece of work. "Truce. I can't answer your question, but I promise to quit badgering." At least for a day.

She stared through slightly glazed eyes. He refrained from snapping his fingers in front of her face.

"Maybe Sharpe's right," she said. Maybe I am done." Anger replaced her grief as quickly as the sun dropped behind the steep mountain peaks. "Why would he say those things to me yesterday?" Twilight descended in a gray blanket of fuzzy darkness.

Holding tightly to her hand, Jake stopped Cassidy from rising. "You're not done, and he was out of line."

Her lips twisted into a tight smile. "Sharpe is never out of line. He's like a father to me."

Why didn't that sit well with him? To combat the awkward twist to his gut, Jake jumped to his feet. "Show me what to do," he said and pulled her to her feet.

She stumbled and fell against his chest. He steadied her, inhaling the light honey scent that clung to her hair. She gazed into his face, her eyes wide and emotions vulnerable. "Come on," he said softly, releasing her. "Let's get to work, shall we?" She gaped at him in surprise, causing him to laugh out loud. "You do know how to work, don't you?"

"Yes." Her face flushed bright red. "Let's get our gear topside and settle in for the night."

"You're the boss."

She smiled and moved past him. He watched her put up her gear and scramble lithely up the wooden ladder. The spark of longing in her eyes unhinged him and he frowned, kicking the toe of his boot into the dirt. Damn if she wasn't becoming something he needed.

He quickly gathered his backpack and climbed after her.

They worked in silence. The platform was small at seven-by-seven, forcing them to brush and bump against one another as they organized the site. Scent-free tarps were laid out across the plywood with a second layer prepared to cover their prone bodies. Notepads, camera, infrared binoculars, all lined up at attention. Testing the air, Cassidy appeared satisfied that they were apparently upwind from the trail she'd picked up behind the lookout post.

"With any luck," she said softly, "the pack'll walk right beneath us . . . just like Post 29." Handing him a large plastic container, she grinned up at his puzzled expression. "Need to pee?"

Jake closed his eyes at his stupidity. "I'd forgotten," he admitted reluctantly, "about that part of the job."

"Wouldn't want you scaring away our subjects, would we?" He could hear her giggle as she turned her back. Swearing softly, he grabbed the bottle.

"What about you?" he called when he'd finished.

"I took care of that earlier away from this spot. Based on the markings, if they hit my scent, it'll push them in this direction."

"You could've told me."

"What? Miss the fun of watching the great Dr. Jake Anderson blush? Not on your life."

He glared at her smug expression, securing the offensive container in its designated position. "I'm only blushing because I feel foolish about forgetting this aspect of observation duty. If you hadn't distracted me, I'd probably have remembered."

"Excuses, excuses," Cassidy taunted. "Don't use me as the scapegoat. Do your job, Eeyore, and forget about me." He watched her gracefully stretch out on her stomach and pull the scent-free tarp over her shoulders. Her hair spilled from its imprisoning clip, flowing freely over her shoulders. Intent on positioning herself correctly, Cassidy allowed it to remain unbound.

She was having fun playing the name game. He wondered what she'd say if he explained the reason he never used her name.

Fear.

Jake was afraid of the intimacy, the longing that her name would arouse. His gaze drifted from the top of her head, down her spine, to the very tips of her shoes.

A stab of desire slammed into his gut. That he could handle. It was the skip in his heart that worried him.

Lying next to her would be too much of a distraction. He settled himself at the back of the platform, leaning against the support post and extending his long legs toward Cassidy. Drawn by the rustling of his scent-free tarp, she glanced over her shoulder. Even in the gray of twilight, her emerald eyes burned brightly.

"Why aren't you in position?"

Jake rolled his eyes. "I am in position."

"You can't see the wolves from there."

"This is where I'm comfortable." He watched her settle back and regretted speaking harshly. It wasn't her fault he couldn't control his libido.

As crimson sky washed out into muted tones of the gloaming, Jake listened to the creatures of the night awaken. Bats flickered against the fading light, swooping and gobbling millions of bugs. The shrill call of a screech owl wove through the trees and echoed back.

Sudden silence woke Jake from his quiet meditation.

A loud gunshot followed by a yelp shattered the tranquil evening.

Jake was on his feet, down the ladder, and racing in the direction of the noise before Cassidy struggled from beneath the tangled tarp that was frustratingly wrapped around her legs. He could hear her exasperated curses followed by the soft pounding of her boots attempting to catch up with him. His mind was focused on the chase.

He slowed around a particularly dangerous bend and listened intently to his surroundings. Evening crickets hadn't yet returned to their melodious chirps, which signaled a continuing disturbance in the area. Dusk quickly disappeared beneath the blackness of night. A rustle of underbrush and a snapping branch drew his attention to the left. Un-holstering his gun and flashlight, he pointed the beam of light and muzzle at the commotion. Nothing.

Cassidy slid to a halt behind him. She peered over his shoulder into the lighted area. "What is it?"

"I don't know," he said beneath his breath. "Just listen." They stood absolutely still, straining to hear any kind of noise that would direct them to the hunter. Cassidy was pressed tightly against his back; light breaths tickled his neck enticingly, causing Jake's concentration to waiver.

Another shot pierced the air. Jake moved with agility honed by years of covert operations. He pulled Cassidy to his front, pushing her to the ground. A branch above their heads snapped and broke, shattered by the path of the bullet. The moon speared the black forest with soft beams of light. Her body radiated heat beneath him, and he could feel her struggle against his weight. He bent forward so their faces were a nose length apart. Jake held his right forefinger to his lips to silence her protests.

She frowned and nodded, and they lay prone against the base of a tree. Jake shifted from Cassidy in an attempt to ease the pain she must be feeling from the sharp rocks and protruding roots. The sound of muffled footsteps reached his ears. He motioned for Cassidy to remain where she was and slid away from the tree.

The movement below guided him through a thick grove of pines. He used them for cover, sliding his fingers across their rough bark to steady himself over the steep rocks. An eye-watering stench filled the air. Jake coughed and covered his face as he stepped around an angry skunk. He'd missed the direct spray. Its tail twitched a warning he ignored, intent on finding the intruder.

The gun fired for a third time. He felt the bullet whisk over his shoulder, startling a screech owl from its post. The bird swooped down in an angry ball of feathers and claws. Jake jumped to the side, ducking the creature. His foot hit a rock, and in an instant the world turned into a roller coaster of thick underbrush and pebbled earth.

Branches slapped at his face. He heard Cassidy yell his name as he plummeted down the steep slope. Dirt filled his nose, and spider webs clung to his face and hands. With a thud, he smacked into a tree.

His head snapped against the trunk, and he fought the blinding white lights that tugged him toward oblivion. Jake used the tree as a crutch. He stood, battling the wave of nausea from the concussive slam into the bark.

Deep breaths and a quick body check uncovered no more than a million areas that would contain ugly bruises in the morning. Nothing broken. He crouched and tried to listen through the startled animal noises caused by his spiral down the hill.

A shadow moved. Jake reached for his gun and swore silently when he realized it'd dropped during his fall. Training his eyes on the spot of movement, he deciphered the faint outline of a man hiding behind a grove of aspens. The man's face tilted upward. Following the line of vision, Jake swore beneath his breath. Not more than fifty feet above lay Cassidy.

Where was he?

And why did she feel caught in a bizarre déjà vu incident? Something about this was painfully familiar.

Damn. Damn. Damn.

She daren't call Jake's name again, because she thought she'd caught sight of something below.

Reaching for her knife, she paused when Jake's voice rang up the ravine.

"Shoot, Cassidy!"

Shoot? Oh no, he didn't understand what he asked. She shook her head even though her heart pumped in fear. The shadow moved closer and in the light of the moon, she saw the muzzle of a gun.

"Dammit, Cassidy. Shoot!"

Her hands shook as she pulled out the gun Jake had insisted she carry. Cocking back the release, she aimed and fired, the noise more deafening than the crash of underbrush as the intruder barreled down the slope. He was running away.

"Go after him, Jake!" Why hadn't he moved?

The woods settled into silence, and Cassidy slipped down the ravine to where she could see the shape of Jake's body.

"I can't," he said. He sounded a bit ticked off.

She crouched next to him and glanced at his face. The woods were now bathed in full moonlight, creating a canvas of muted colors and dark shadows. Cassidy peered closer and noted his complexion was a bit pale. "Why not? Are you hurt?"

He gritted his teeth and pointed to his leg. "You shot me. How could you do that? I was nowhere near the guy."

Cassidy bit her lip and stared at his leg. Her stomach flipped, but she wouldn't show him that she cared. "You were in the same direction." Pushing her fingers around his flesh, she ignored his indrawn breath. "It only grazed your skin. Quit your whining." She smiled hesitantly and ripped the hem off her T-shirt. "I tried to tell you yesterday that I don't do guns." Wrapping the torn material around his thigh, she tied it tight to ease the flow of blood.

The trees above them rustled with activity. Relying on instinct, she snatched her knife from her bootstrap and threw it through the branches, sinking it with a thud. A muffled cry echoed down.

"But you do knives?" Jake said, his voice rising in astonishment.

"Hush. I'll be right back."

She crept up the slope. Whatever she'd hit, it wasn't human. Her knife pinned a small creature against the trunk of a large tree. She reached it and let out a sigh of despair. It was a young rabbit, no bigger than the palm of her hand. The poor thing was in the wrong place at the wrong time.

If she'd maintained her wits earlier, the knife would be buried in the back of their midnight intruder. With a quick look around, she searched for the source of what she'd heard. A branch snapped behind her. She yanked the knife from the tree and turned to protect herself. With a sigh, she relaxed. Jake had followed her up the slope.

"You can throw a knife so that it spears a rabbit at two hundred feet, but you can't shoot a damn gun?" He sat beside her. "I think I'm in shock."

She touched the side of his neck, checking his pulse to make sure he was only kidding. "I tried to tell you about the gun, but you wouldn't listen. You insisted I have it. Besides, the rabbit was an accident. He crossed paths with my knife at the wrong time."

"Why didn't you just throw your knife at that guy?"

Good question. She winced and admitted to her brain malfunction. "Because you told me to shoot."

Jake bent his head, and she tried not to grin at the pitiful picture he made. He glanced at her through a thick mop of hair. "When did you tell me you couldn't shoot?"

"Yesterday. When you gave me this thing." She waved the gun in the air.

Jake snatched it out of her hands. "You have to take an arms and ammo class when you start at ZEBRA."

Cassidy smiled. "I took it." She reached over and checked his bandage. "But I never passed."

"Ouch. Stop that."

She helped him to his feet. "Quit being a baby, Raphael."

Jake paused. "Raphael?"

"Didn't you ever watch *Teenage Mutant Ninja Turtles?*" Cassidy was relieved to see him walk with only a slight limp.

Her heart had come close to bursting when she'd realized he'd been shot. By her, no less. *Of all the stupid things to do.* Jake must think her a complete idiot. *Keep moving. Keep talking.*

"I'm a turtle? At least the names I call you are pretty."

She smiled and led the way back to the observation post. "Raphael's pretty."

Jake grunted and mumbled beneath his breath. He passed her, scanning the woods as they went. "You can bet I won't be calling you Annie Oakley."

Cassidy smothered her laughter and pushed at his back. "Hurry up. If we can settle things down, we still have a chance at a dawn sighting."

"I have to call this in." He twisted and grabbed her hand, pulling her around a narrow ledge. "I'm certain being shot at in the middle of nowhere isn't constituted as normal behavior in Yellowstone."

"It was probably just some poacher."

"Nice try at avoidance. We need to call the rangers, Sunshine. That guy aimed at us."

She stopped and tugged back on his hand. A sweet, acrid scent assaulted her nose. She fought against the reflex to gag. "What do you smell?"

"You mean besides myself?"

"Yes," her voice dropped to a low tone.

"Blood," he said. "I smell blood."

"Me too," she answered. "Move slowly and look carefully; maybe we'll find the target of that bullet. That should help explain what the hell he was doing up here."

Jake smiled tightly and turned his attention to the woods. She followed as he patrolled the area, searching for the source of the smell that had her nostrils twitching and sixth sense screaming.

Jake and Cassidy silently worked their way back up the path toward Post 26. The stench continued to attack their senses, but no source could be located. He stepped into the clearing surrounding the observation platform and halted at the horror that was painted before him.

He spun around, trying to locate Cassidy. He wanted to block her from the gruesome spectacle, but it was too late. Cassidy stood with arms hanging loosely by her side, staring at the clearing. She swayed slightly, and Jake lunged to catch her before she crumbled to the ground. Her eyes bright with pain, she stared up at him. "What would cause such a thing?" She whispered through a voice thick with unshed tears.

Jake didn't have an answer and just shook his head slowly. "Stay here," he commanded. "I need to check the site and call it in."

He left her leaning against a tree. He could see that her mind struggled to comprehend the monster behind whatever had twisted Post 26 into a blood-splattered spectacle of gore. His thoughts, however, were more concentrated on Cassidy's safety. He scanned the area, looking for moving shadows and listening for telltale signs of human habitation. Nothing. The night was ghostly quiet and unnervingly empty of life.

CHAPTER 19

NICK FOWLER RAN THROUGH THE WOODS. BRANCHES CLAWED his clothes, digging their skeleton fingers into his sweater. He swatted at the ones intent on holding him back. The moon glittered through the canopy of leaves, allowing him to see the twisted path down the mountain. His chest felt like an exploding volcano, each breath a stream of lava that seared his lungs. He skidded on a slick rock and smacked his palm on a tree to slow his forward motion.

Damn wolf.

Gasping for air, he stopped and rested his aching side. He didn't consider himself a man of fear. A shiver of revulsion shook his shoulders at the memory of the wolf that had charged him, eyes wild with pain, and blood dripping from its fangs. And the face. *Fuck.* That was enough to guarantee several lifetimes of nightmares. He knew all about CPV-19. The image of the female he'd found the night before while monitoring Blondie flashed through his mind.

He'd tossed his cigarette down and run. Away from the body. Away from the disease.

Tonight's knee-jerk reaction was to shoot the fucker, which is exactly what he did.

Then he'd heard Anderson and Blondie race toward him and his casual observation duty of their assignment went south.

Nick tilted his head back and banged it lightly against the trunk of a pine tree. It didn't matter which way you pointed the knife, he'd about gutted himself tonight.

If he'd been caught or injured, Cole would've eliminated him with a nice clean bullet to the brain. On the other stinking hand, he couldn't kill Anderson and Blondie without experiencing the exact same repercussions. He'd been lucky, and Nick didn't believe in luck.

Nick's cell phone rang. He snatched the phone off its belt clip. "Yeah."

"What the hell happened tonight?"

Resting his palm on the trunk of a tree, he inhaled several deep breaths. "A wolf almost ran right over me. I shot it. The shot alerted my targets, and I got the hell outta there. What the fuck's your problem?"

"My problem"—the voice dropped down an octave—"is that the report that came over the radio indicated multiple dead wolves. I'm on my way to check it out. For your sake, you'd better not have left behind evidence. Fowler, I know I don't need to explain to you that we're close to firing off all the ducks we have in a row. Don't screw it up."

Rolling his eyes, Nick pumped his fist up and down. *What a real jerk-off!* "No. I didn't leave any evidence. The wolves were all infected. A stray one caught my scent and went ballistic. I tossed him onto the heap with the other dead." A shiver ran up Nick's spine. "Jesus, that stuff is bad."

A soft chuckle filtered through the satellite connection. "No shit."

Nick sniffed and ran his hand under his nose. His eyes widened. "How contagious are those wolves?"

Edward drove through the remote hills of the Wasachi Range. He'd been on the road since early evening. After cashing a large check at his local bank, he'd bought a used car, packed all his gear, and driven straight through Yellowstone National Park and past Jackson, Wyoming, into Idaho.

Thinking like a criminal afforded Edward a mental challenge. He relished it. *Don't use credit cards. Don't leave behind anything that will attract attention.* Enough cash remained to purchase several plane tickets out of Salt Lake City and all additional supplies he might require.

Edward crested a bend and noticed a soft glow of city lights below. Civilization. He pulled the car off to the side of the road and snapped open his cell phone. It finally showed reception. Another phone lay on the passenger seat. It was a pay-as-you-go he'd recently purchased in Gardiner. This call, however, he wanted the board to know about.

Dialing the number to his New York attorney's home, he waited as the phone rang on the other end. Finally a voice husky with sleep filtered across the line. "Hello?" Edward began the first step to masking his whereabouts.

Step One: Mislead the enemy.

Finished with his conversation, Edward closed the phone and yawned. Tired of the dim lights in his car, he decided to finish the rest of his plan once he reached Salt Lake City. This was enough information to mull over for the next sixty miles.

He stared out the car window. The top of the ridge was flat and treeless, with the road curving downward toward the soft shimmer of city lights. Could it be this easy?

Step Two: Reach your destination.

A flicker of doubt caused his heart to jump. He needed to devise a way of explaining the release of CPV-19 into Yellowstone without becoming a suspect.

He needed to shine as savior, not madman.

This would be a challenge. Pulling onto the road, Edward began to mentally distill and ferment his plans.

Step Three: Achieve success.

CHAPTER 20

CASSIDY KNELT DOWN, HER KNEES SINKING INTO THE DEW-dampened leaves. A soft thud drew her attention to the ground behind her. Jake had tossed over her gear bag, and she quickly slipped the zipper open and reached inside, searching for a pair of latex gloves and protective mask. Snapping the gloves and blue cotton nose and mouth cover into place, Cassidy concentrated on the wolves.

She extended her hand and stroked the fur of a dead wolf. Trailing a finger along the edge of the wolf's jaw line, she bent down and peered at the snout. She sighed and attempted to see beyond the horrendous suffering that shadowed the once peaceful clearing. There appeared to be a half dozen dead. Puddles of congealed blood darkened numerous patches of earth.

"I've found our bullet." Jake walked over and pulled her away from the body. "I don't think it killed the wolf, though." He frowned, and his eyes were troubled above the rim of his own protective mask.

Cassidy shook her head. "Let me guess: loss of blood?"

"Yeah. From everywhere. Its mouth and rear."

They walked to the edge of the clearing, ripping off their masks and discarding the plastic gloves. "We need to leave this undisturbed until we can mark the perimeter and photograph everything." She turned toward Jake, switching the subject back to the wolf. "Eyes and ears bloody as well?"

"Yeah . . ." He hesitated, running a hand through his hair.

Cassidy narrowed her eyes and challenged him with a direct stare. "Snout?" Jake glanced at the full moon, then back down at her. She attempted to remain serious but burst out laughing when he lifted one brow and opened his eyes wide.

"I'm not saying anything that will incriminate me."

Shaking her head, she pointed at a couple of the dead bodies. "That one and that one have elongated snouts and a protruding lower jaw line."

"Werewolves aren't in your theory, are they?"

Cassidy's immediate response was to offer an emphatic "no" but she paused, worrying her bottom lip, allowing some unconventional thoughts to drift through her mind. "Not in the sense you're talking about."

Jake nodded. "I've never witnessed anything like it."

Cassidy frowned, trying to concentrate on what was tugging at her brain. It slipped away, and she shook her head in annoyance. "Me neither. And I thought I'd seen it all." She leaned against a tree, picking absently at the bark. "Did you verify that Ethan is providing transport for the pod?"

"They're on their way. And bringing extra lights."

"Good. We're going to need them." She stared at the remains of the wolves. They lay randomly among the clearing, their bodies sprawled upon the dirt and leaves. "What the hell caused this?" She gazed from wolf to wolf. "It's as if they died within seconds of one another. How's that possible?"

"I don't know." Jake said, his voice trailing to a whisper.

Cassidy glanced at him. "What're you thinking?" He crouched

down, balancing his elbows on his knees. She watched him scrutinize the scene. "If you're not careful, your brain will catch fire."

Jake sighed. "This is familiar."

That caught her attention. "How?"

He glanced up at her. "The woman we found yesterday, she bled like this." He stood and waved his arm. "It was everywhere, remember? I found her because there was a cigarette floating in a pool of blood."

Cassidy's mind churned his words. "It was floating?"

Jake pierced her with an intense gaze. "Why didn't the blood seep into the ground?"

Alarm bells rang along every nerve, making her ears buzz and fingers tingle. She turned and walked back toward the wolves. Snapping a twig off a low-hanging branch and holding the hem of her shirt over her nose, Cassidy shoved it into one of the blood stains. It wasn't coagulated, as she'd initially thought . . . it was thick like oil.

She swore at her own stupidity. Cassidy grabbed Jake's arm and pushed him out of the observation area. She flipped open her phone and dialed headquarters, speaking rapidly to the person on the other end. The rhythmic thumping of helicopter blades chimed in the distance. "Come on." She ran through the woods toward the designated landing zone.

"What's going on?"

She glanced over her shoulder. Jake was right on her heels. "I called the CDC." Cassidy spotted the helicopter as it crested the small rise. "We need to make sure everyone is in full decontamination suits before entering the site." She ran faster and broke into the clearing as the rungs of the first chopper touched ground.

Ethan Connor jumped out, followed by several other rangers.

"Ethan," Cassidy raised her voice to be heard over the helicopters. "We need hazmat gear." She moved her hands in front of her face to signal what she was saying. He nodded and ran back to the chopper.

Glancing to the side, she grabbed Jake's hand and shuffled him toward the side of the helicopter. "We need to shower down."

Jake grimaced and nodded, then pointed at one of the rangers unloading medical equipment. Cassidy smiled, and together they walked over. With a wave of her arm and a knife slashing motion across her throat, she indicated to the ranger that he needed to move away. Jake dove into the chopper and retrieved a portable decontamination unit. "Handy little things, aren't they?"

Cassidy eyed the metal cylinder and plastic attachments. "I don't think you'll be saying that in a few minutes."

Jake pulled open a large square bag and retrieved a black metal platform. With quick adept movements he snapped a white pipe in place, hooked up a plastic shower head, and screwed the container of water to the edge of the hose. "Just about done."

Cassidy moved past him and peered into the helicopter. "There should be three washes." She jumped into the interior and found three one-gallon bottles labeled with bright fluorescent stickers.

"Three?" Jake rolled his eyes and shook his shoulders in a fake shiver. "You first."

She glanced at the makeshift shower, down at her clothes, up at Jake, around the bustling vicinity now swarming with spacesuit-clad personnel, and back at Jake. No matter how you faced the situation, bashfulness didn't belong in this arena. "Turn around."

Jake quirked one brow and slid her an evil grin. "Don't you think shooting me in the leg deserves some type of retribution?"

Cassidy returned his penetrating gaze with one of her own, slipping out of her jeans and tugging her t-shirt over her head. Jake inhaled, and it was her turn to lift a brow and grin maliciously. "I suppose." She wasn't brave enough to play the seductress and turned around before shedding the rest of her clothes.

"Sunshine, this ain't fair."

Cassidy twisted the water nozzle and shrieked as a blast of cold water streamed from the shower head and spurted from several other areas of the pipe. She struggled with the cap of the first wash and swore violently as her hands kept sliding off its surface. She jumped when a warm hand clutched her shoulder, pinning her in place. "Let go," she gasped, her breathing made difficult by frigid fingers of water.

"Hold still," Jake grunted, ducking as she flailed a halfhearted punch in his direction. He poured the first wash over her and spun her around beneath the water.

Cassidy closed her eyes, numb to embarrassment and praying for the shower to end. She felt his hands everywhere and reached out to grip his arm. The feel of bare skin shocked her into opening her eyes and gazing up at Jake's face, ignoring the rest of his naked flesh. His jaw was set and he narrowed his eyes, daring her to fight him. Cassidy inhaled and reached for the wash to aid Jake in his own decontamination. "Wow, some first date, Aquaman."

Jake bit back a strangled laugh and shook his head. When he finally, thankfully, and mercifully cut the water, Cassidy exhaled the breath she'd been holding.

"Clothes," he snapped, his voice deep and commanding.

Cassidy tossed him a decontamination suit and slipped into one of her own. "Jaccuzzi," she responded, mimicking his tone of voice.

"Quit dreaming. The faster we work, the quicker we can properly shower and put on our own clothes."

The choppers finally shut off, leaving the clearing in dead silence. Jake bent forward and wiped a strand of wet hair off her cheek. Cassidy smiled, holding his gaze for a beat too long. He cleared his throat and backed away from her. "I'm going over to organize our troops."

"Okay." Cassidy turned to find Ethan standing a few paces behind her. She signaled with one hand for him to keep his distance. Pulling a mask over her face, Cassidy carefully placed their contaminated clothing in plastic bags and sealed them with hazmat tape. Next she strung the skull and crossbones tape across the opening of the helicopter, signaling that possible contamination existed. CDC could deal with the wash down of the metal bird. Finished, Cassidy moved toward Ethan.

He stared at her from behind the protective shield of his decontamination suit. "What's going on?"

She didn't know what he'd witnessed and frankly, at this point in time, didn't care. "I don't know. But I've called in the CDC. We have six dead wolves all with profuse internal bleeding. Blood has seeped from every egress available. And the composition of it isn't natural."

"Like the body at the base of Post 29?"

He always did follow her line of thinking. "Exactly. Any lab results yet?"

Ethan kicked at the ground. "I didn't even think to check before responding to Jake's call. This doesn't make any sense. What disease affects humans and wolves but nothing else?"

"Not anything natural."

The whites of Ethan's eyes glittered behind the plastic eye shield. "What are you saying?"

She placed her hands on her hips and shook her head in frustration, hating that she had no answer. "I don't know. But I'm going to find out. In the meantime, we need to activate hazmat protocol."

Ethan swore and turned toward his men, barking orders through the intercom of his suit. "As you can see, we've got a possible biological situation, boys. Let's proceed with extreme caution."

Cassidy glanced around and noted that the rest of her team were in protective gear, including headlamps that illuminated their path up to the observation site as they moved slowly up the trail carrying a generator and lights with them.

"There was a man up here. He shot one of the wolves, then used us as target practice."

Ethan spun on his heels. "Shot at you? Your buddy there didn't mention that the perpetrator actually opened fire on you. He indicated it was a poacher."

Cassidy rubbed her mask; a burning headache increased in intensity. "He was probably leaving all the nasty details for later. We ran," Cassidy twisted around and pointed to a small rocky ledge. "That way."

"All right. I'll see if I can't find something."

She began to head past him, but Ethan stopped her with his hand. "Cass, I'm sorry about the other morning. I was out of line."

Don't do this now, Cassidy. "Yes, you were. But I suppose I wasn't much better." She'd done it. *Why can't I learn to listen to my own advice?*

"I'd like to start fresh." Ethan glanced anywhere but at her.

She'd opened the door for communication; she supposed she'd better either shut it or leave it cracked for another time. Cassidy decided to shut it for good. "Ethan, there's a whole bunch of good between us and a truckload of bad." He opened his mouth to argue, but she shook her head. "Bad always sticks its head where it's not wanted before Good even has a second to speak. I've been listening to Bad for ages; I don't know what Good sounds like anymore."

Ethan's eyes softened. "I know what you mean."

She tilted her head, the corner of her lip curving upward. "I want to come home without guilt, without regret. Until this trip, I hadn't realized how much I miss being here." Cassidy turned and gazed beyond the ridgeline. "I'd like to be able to come home and visit." She turned and stared into his face. "But I want to be here without your shadow. I don't want the ghost of us." Cassidy swallowed.

"Wow," Ethan said, then let out a shaky laugh. "I guess honesty is still one of your things. This is your home, Cassidy. I hope you always return and enjoy the beauty of the place. Your parents certainly did." He stepped back, a sadness shining in his eyes she wished wasn't there. "You should be able to cherish those memories, not ignore them. As for us," he scratched his head and studied her. "There hasn't been an *us* for years."

Even though his eyes denied his words, they were the words Cassidy wanted to hear. She couldn't heal his wounds. He'd have to do that himself. Flipping the light switch on her headlamp, Cassidy finally laid her past to rest and jogged after her pod.

Stopping at the edge of the clearing around the observation post, she watched her team work. Steve assisted Michelle in obtaining soil and other natural resource samples. Jake had already bagged three of the carcasses. She stepped forward to help him. They worked in silence, the protective masks making verbal communication an alien voice.

Jake signaled to Cassidy that he needed to make a phone call. She nodded and grabbed a bag from their equipment, moving toward the next wolf. On his way out of the clearing, he tapped Michelle on the shoulder and indicated that she should follow. She walked behind him, carefully placing her collection of soil samples on the ground when they stopped.

"I want you to head down that path." He pointed to the footpath he and Cassidy had run down early in the evening. "You'll reach a large tree with two mammoth boulders resting on its far side." Michelle nodded. "If you follow the southerly angle, you should be able to make out a disturbance in the leaves that looks like someone fell. The full moon and your light will help, but you'll still have to search closely for the right spot."

"Is that how you hurt yourself, sir?"

Jake frowned. "What?"

"Your leg . . ." Michelle pointed to where Cassidy had shot him. "I noticed you were limping."

He'd forgotten all about his injury. It throbbed and burned, but the decontamination wash had dried the wound out and he doubted it had the nerve to bleed after being exposed to the harsh soap. "Before the spot where I decided to use my ass as a toboggan, there's a low rise."

Michelle nodded and smothered her smile.

"Search it. I want to know who the hell shot at us tonight." Jake watched the park rangers combing the area. "Be careful. I don't want to alert them to the proper location. Pretend you're taking soil samples or something."

"Why, sir, that's exactly what I am doing." She grinned and sauntered off in the direction of the area where he'd spotted the shooter.

He watched Cassidy. Each second that passed, he hated himself more for this deception. If she knew that every member of her pod was Black Stripe, she'd not only skin him alive but probably retreat behind an impenetrable shell and lose what little faith she had left in ZEBRA.

He unclipped his cell phone and dialed Colonel Price.

"Anderson."

"Sir, I need further clarification on this mission." Jake waited. This was his second request. The call he'd placed yesterday had been met with a curt need-to-know and it was stated that he didn't need to know.

"What status change has prompted this request?"

Jake stared at Cassidy as she moved from one wolf to the next. She kept rubbing her arms through the material of her suit, and her hands shook slightly. Exhaustion. Post-adrenaline fade. It could be any number of things creating those symptoms. However, the fear of earlier contamination by some foreign substance concerned him.

"Dr. Lowell and I played hide and seek with some bullets this evening. And we've discovered a slew of dead wolves that appear to be infected with some form of blood-thickening toxin. Other than that, it's business as usual."

Colonel Price sighed. "You're looking for any connection between ZEBRA and New World Petroleum."

Jake frowned. "Tell me what I don't know."

"It's been confirmed New World Petroleum is funding ZEBRA. We want to know why. I believe Dr. Lowell is the key. You're there to determine exactly what lock she fits."

"And Cole's affiliation with Yellowstone? Coincidence or brilliance?"

"I haven't unearthed anything that might lead us to believe his motivations lie in a different direction than simply spearheading one of the greatest discoveries on American soil in the past decade."

Jake sighed, feeling a strong surge of exasperation. "What are you saying?"

"Follow Dr. Lowell very carefully."

His heart caught, but he needed clarification. "Is she considered a hostile?"

"I don't know, son. The bodies of two of her team members have washed up in Port Harcourt." The colonel disconnected, leaving Jake feeling alone and confused. He'd combed through her background file, and there was nothing to signify that she was anything more than what she said. A zoologist. And a damn good one at that.

CHAPTER 21

Cassidy stretched, reaching toward the sky and wiggling her fingers. The evening was blocked by layers of plastic which had been erected to prevent any further spread of whatever possible disease might shadow these woods. Every muscle in her neck and back felt like they'd been ripped to shreds. The mad dash through the forest earlier, combined with the past three hours of bending and crouching, worked areas of her body she didn't know existed.

Leaving the cordoned-off and sealed area around Post 26, she approached Jake. He leaned against a tree, relieving the weight off his injured leg. Her breath caught again. She couldn't believe she'd shot him. Touching his shoulder, she stood on her toes and whispered in his ear. "Want me to put a proper bandage on your leg?"

He turned his head and grinned at her. "Only if it means a full body massage."

The light banter eased her frayed nerves. "Well, I have this handy-dandy little medical kit over there that comes equipped with antibiotic and gauze pads, but I'm afraid no exotic oils or sponges." Cassidy verified they were well outside the tented contamination site and stripped off her gloves and mask, inhaling and twisting her neck to stretch out tight muscles.

He reached for her hand and held it between his. Jake ran his thumb across the ridge of her knuckles. "You're trembling."

Cassidy sucked in sharply. "Well, it's not because you're touching me."

Soft laughter rumbled in his chest. "Don't I wish? No, I noticed it earlier when you were bagging the wolves. Your head hurts too, right?"

"Don't worry yourself, big guy. It's a plain and simple case of exhaustion."

He stared at her, then glanced over her shoulder. She turned and watched Steve drag the last stretcher loaded with bagged wolves out of the observation area.

"Come on, Sunshine. I think the party's over."

She followed him from the clearing. "Thank goodness for small favors."

Jake tugged on her hand, and she allowed him to pull her along. "Did you speak with Ethan? He didn't know that the poacher aimed and shot at us."

"I guess I left that out."

Cassidy frowned. Jake didn't strike her as being the forgetful type. "I filled him in on our suspicions regarding the blood and connection with the dead body."

"I know," he said and helped her around a difficult bend, invading her personal space again when he moved behind her.

"I requested that he isolate the area and post guards."

Jake stopped fifteen feet from the helicopters. "I know."

Cassidy lifted a shoulder to indicate she'd only been trying to make conversation and walked past him, irritated and tired. "Aren't you just a know-it-all then?" She headed toward the helicopter containing the wolves and her pod. Ethan's men were still working the site, searching for evidence of the poacher. The lights bouncing off the trees gave a preternatural feel to the night.

Together, they entered a small tent split into several sections. A CDC chopper sat off to the left, obviously the benefactor of this mobile decontamination unit. Cassidy went through the three wash cycle once with her suit on and then once more stripped bare. The difference, this time, was privacy, hot water, and clean sweats.

She was the last one to exit the tent and moved to join the rest of her team. Steve lifted an arm down and helped her into the body of the rescue chopper they'd commandeered for this mission. She bit her bottom lip and refused to think about the last time she'd been aboard one of these things. This one wasn't as big, though, and contained none of the dull metallic paint she remembered from her previous ride.

Seating herself against the back wall, she reached beneath the bench and retrieved a medical kit. She patted the empty spot beside her. "Come on, Anderson; let's see to that cut." Action helped her remain focused on facts and not the horror of the evening.

Jake bent his head, and his shoulders shook. He was laughing at her. "Yeah, Sunshine. Let's see to my cut."

"Am I missing something?" Steve asked.

Jake glanced at her and winked. "Nope." He sat down and stretched his injured leg across her lap. She pushed up the bottom of his navy blue CDC issued sweatpants leg and went to work, cleaning and disinfecting. The helicopter blades began their rotation and Cassidy focused on Jake's leg, blocking out the memory of Africa: the fear in Georgie's face, the brutality of the scene below.

"That looks bad," Michelle said. "What happened?"

"I'm a klutz."

Cassidy smiled. His protectiveness over her mistake made her feel all warm and fuzzy. Nibbling the bottom of her lip, she concentrated on the task at hand. Deliberately adding too much antibiotic, she smacked Jake's thigh when he squirmed.

She hated warm and fuzzy.

Finished, Cassidy pushed Jake's leg off her lap.

"Hey, I was comfortable."

She smiled sweetly. "I wasn't." Poking him in the arm, she decided to ask a few questions. It would help wash away some of the mental pictures of the past few hours. "Did you know that the Black Stripe crew is real?"

Jake was in the process of chugging water, and her question caused him to spew it out his nose. She raised a brow. That answered that.

Wiping excess water from his face with the back of his hand, he gazed at her. The brilliant blue of his eyes was a faint beacon within the dark confines of the helicopter. "Yeah, as a matter of fact, I do."

Cassidy chewed on her lower lip. "Ever met any of them?"

"Yes, ma'am."

"Care to tell me about it?"

"Well, I would . . ." He nudged her shoulder with his. "But then I'd have to kill you."

Cassidy glanced over at Steve, and he gave her a told-you-so wink. "Very funny, Dr. Anderson." She reached across his legs, and tapped Michelle on the knee. "Did you know Black Stripe is real?"

Michelle frowned and shook her head. "Nope." She squirmed in her seat and lifted a shoulder. "They don't let me out much."

Cassidy chuckled and pointed a finger at the ecologist. "You don't fool me, Michelle Allen. Behind that soft-spoken voice and innocent expression lies one of the most intuitive minds I've ever known. Don't knock yourself down because of your limited field assignments." An idea sparked. "Would you mind probing the computers for me and seeing what you can dig up on Black Stripe?"

Michelle frowned at her. "Have Steve do that."

Cassidy glared across the chopper in Steve's direction. "Already did. And he won't help."

"I don't think I can help, either. I'm not even sure they exist." Michelle responded.

"Oh, they exist, all right. But getting anyone to talk about them is like teaching your cat to sit." Cassidy sat back, frustrated. Her senate contact hadn't been able to provide any knowledge of Black Stripe. She'd exhausted all her leads. Asking for Michelle's help was an act of desperation.

"What's with the interest in Black Stripe, Sunshine?"

She glared at Jake. "Cassidy. My name is Cassidy. Or if you prefer, Dr. Lowell will work as well."

The corner of his lip curled up in what Cassidy mentally labeled his snarky smirk. Dark lines smudged the space beneath his bottom lashes, lacing his face with a predatory glint. "But you're such a ray of shining loveliness, especially this early in the morning."

Cassidy narrowed her eyes and muttered a few obscenities at Jake. He quirked his brow and she followed his line of vision, noticing the moon's movement across the sky. Checking her watch, she couldn't believe how quickly time had passed.

"PITA," she said.

He offered her a quizzical expression. "Peter?"

"P.I.T.A." She spelled out the letters and smacked him hard in the arm. "Pain in the ass."

Jake tossed his head back and laughed. She couldn't help her answering smile. After their gruesome evening, it felt good to settle into normalcy. Lack of sleep, she decided, was making her giddy. Better to laugh than to cry.

Cassidy clung to the edge of her seat as the helicopter dipped then dropped down to land with a thud. The blades slowed and by the time they'd exited the chopper, they were completely silent.

"I brought the RV over to load up on additional lab equipment," Steve called and jogged over to his camper contraption. He jumped behind the wheel, backing it up to the storage compartment beneath the helicopter. He leaned out the window and waved at Jake. "Come on, PITA. Help me get those wolves loaded."

"Cute," Jake answered.

They dragged the bags out of the helicopter and tossed them in a storage container beneath the main floor of the camper. Cassidy followed Jake into the interior of the vehicle, curious as to what she'd find. Steve hadn't been exaggerating when he'd said state-of-the-art.

The width of the center aisle was no wider than three feet. On the left side of the aisle pristine counters contained a variety of mounted lab equipment, while on the right side two computer workstations were set about four feet apart from one another.

Steve brushed past Cassidy and pointed to the upper walls. "These overhead compartments extend five feet out like airplane wings and can be used as sleeping bunks."

"Cool." Cassidy liked this little vehicle.

"This"—Steve motioned to what looked like two oversized closets that extended a few feet beyond the back of the camper—"is your necropsy lab."

"I always considered myself as having a pretty decent imagination, but explain to me how two closets become one lab."

Steve grinned, enjoying this little show and tell. "These *closets* extend eight feet out and are supported by hydraulic legs. Once unfolded, everything is pretty much drop down, plug, and play. The center floor slides out from beneath the bed of the truck. Your operating table rises up from its flattened position, and these two areas against the wall have all the equipment and storage containers you require."

Cassidy still felt dubious; however, she'd be able to see it actually fit together in a few hours. "I'll believe it when I see it." She glanced at the bag Jake carried and grabbed his arm. "What's with the yellow tape on this one?"

"That's the bullet-sporting wolf. I figure we'll need to get that over to Chief Connor ASAP."

"I guess that makes you a smart PITA?" Cassidy laughed and slapped him on the butt. His arm snaked out, grabbing her around the waist and pulling her tightly against his chest.

"Don't touch the goods unless you mean to explore them." Blue eyes challenged, a mixture of emotion swirling within their depths.

She gasped, finding it difficult to balance between soaring hormones and outrage. She shoved against his chest. His eyes darkened, and she felt her face flush beneath his scrutiny. "I won't touch again. Thanks for the warning." Cassidy squirmed from his arms and walked to the end of the camper, muttering a mixture of sailor language and animal parts she'd like to see attached to Jake Anderson.

"What's with you and Jake, Cass?" Steve stepped from behind the black-and-white-striped vehicle.

"Not a thing."

"Looks like a thing."

She put her hands on her hips and glared at him. "Well, it's not."

"Gonna stomp your foot next?"

Cassidy stuck her tongue out at him instead. "Get these bodies loaded, and head back to the hotel. You're going to show me how this cool necropsy lab magically appears and then sprinkle fairy dust on your computer and find me some answers to this blood anomaly." She paused when Steve turned to say something to her. "Don't you even call me a bitch," she warned.

"Wouldn't dream of it. Can we maybe get a little sleep first?" Steve accepted the last bag from Jake and slammed the storage compartment shut.

"Put the coffee on. This can't wait."

He grabbed Michelle's arm and steered her toward the truck, helping her with the last of the gear. "See you back at the hotel."

Cassidy watched the vehicle pull off the airport runway. A sudden blast of air snagged her curls. She instinctively ducked as the helicopter rose from the tarmac and banked in the direction of Yellowstone.

"Sunshine?"

She spun around to find Jake standing less than five feet away, moonlight bathing him in a soft glow. Her pulse did an irritating two-step. "Yeah?"

"We have a minor problem."

Annoyance at his ability to provoke irrational feelings made her words sharp and clipped. "What's that?"

"It appears you just let our ride drive off."

Cassidy twisted around, gazing at the now empty landing strip on the northern side of Jackson Hole Airport. The ZEBRA plane filled one section, but there were no vehicles in sight. Their Jeep was at the base of Post 26.

She blew an exasperated lungful of air out. "Well, heck." She frowned and chewed on her bottom lip. "Let's go see what other little toys lie within the belly of that airplane." The silence surrounding them itched Cassidy's nerves. She didn't want to be alone with Jake.

Swearing softly, she tugged at the end of her braid. Actually, she did want to be alone with him. That was the problem. "What about our phones?"

"Mine's in there." Jake pointed toward the red taillights of the camper that were being swallowed up by the night. "Yours?"

Cassidy felt her pockets and came up empty. "I think I left mine on the chopper." Her cheeks flushed with embarrassment.

Jake began walking toward the ZEBRA jet, and she followed at what she considered a safe distance. "Don't suppose you have the keys?" he called over his shoulder.

"I have the access code."

"Access code?"

Cassidy realized walking behind him and watching the way his jeans clung tightly to his butt wasn't helping her pulse settle. "Your memory isn't one of your better qualities, is it, Popeye?" She increased her pace and caught up with him, frowning at the startled expression that crossed his face. "You know? The access code. Whenever we take one of these babies and keep it on site, we're given the cipher code to retrieve all the equipment stored within."

"Oh, the cipher code, of course." Jake answered. "If you'd said that in the first place, I'd have understood."

———

That was close. Cassidy tossed him a strange glance but seemed to ignore his foot and mouth disease. In truth, he'd never required the use of a ZEBRA jet. But he understood they were standard issue for the majority of assignments. If he was who he claimed to be, a simple biologist, he should have known this.

Cassidy walked beneath the airplane. A soft breeze rippled across the tarmac, ruffling the strands of loose hair around her face. He closed his eyes for a second. Counting backwards from ten, Jake shut out the image and locked away the sudden flash of desire her movements ignited.

Back in control, he waited. She flipped on a small flashlight, locating the keypad, and pushed in the appropriate numbers. The tail of the plane split in half, as the bottom portion lowered to the ground.

Jake jogged up the ramp to scan the interior. There wasn't much. The RV had taken up most of the room. Standard issue parachutes and miscellaneous tools that might be required on a field assignment were secured along the outside walls. Several large boxes containing additional lab equipment and computer systems sat against the far wall. He followed a length of straps that were secured to the ceiling and floor. A ripple of excitement exploded in his chest. "Come to Daddy, you beautiful hunk of metal." Jake grinned and sauntered toward a large black motorcycle, running his fingers along the smooth metal. He felt rather than heard Cassidy approach behind him. "Your chariot, mi'lady."

"Wow, look at that thing. I wonder who Sharpe paid to build us that?" She walked around the jet-black crotch rocket. "Harley?"

He unbuckled the straps. "It appears so." Jake swung his leg over the seat and revved the engine. This was his kind of toy. "Nice of them to leave the keys," he called over the roar of the muffler.

Cassidy jogged down the open ramp and waited for him to ride the motorcycle out. He stopped a few feet from the plane as she raised the ramp and verified everything was locked. She moved with the grace of a lioness, all muscle and mane. Walking from beneath the plane, she grinned at him. His heart skipped several beats, making him swear silently. He tossed a helmet at her and patted the seat behind him.

Her leg swung over and Cassidy settled against his back. "This has Steve written all over it."

Jake twisted around and grinned. "This has fun written all over it." *And heat. Too much damn heat.* This was going to be a long ride back to Yellowstone. She wrapped her arms around his waist, then patted his chest to let him know she was ready. The awareness transferring between their bodies lit trails of desire along every nerve ending.

"Why is it that the guys always get to drive?" Her voice was soft and husky, filtering through the small microphone in her helmet.

He rolled his eyes and thought of anything but her. "You don't drive a Harley, Sunshine. You ride." With that, he snapped it into gear and they sped across the tarmac. Speed, and lots of it, was the cold shower he needed right now. It seemed to work beautifully until her laughter rippled across the distance.

CHAPTER 22

Back at the inn, Cassidy jumped off the bike the second Jake flipped the ignition switch. She'd loved the breakneck speed and exhilaration of racing through the night holding onto nothing but the wind and Jake. Pulling the helmet off her head, she shook her hair out and grinned at him. "That was just what the doctor ordered."

An owl hooted, and she could hear the gentle slapping of water against rock from the lake to their left. Dawn pushed at the horizon, the stars strained to shine through the last of the night sky. Pine and water mixed together, creating a fresh crisp scent. She tilted her head and gazed at Jake. He hadn't dismounted from the bike.

His eyes glittered beneath the yellow glow of the hotel lights. Jake gazed at her face, reached for her, and pulled her against his chest. Before she had a second to clear her thoughts, his lips found hers and the world went black, then white, then black again.

Oh Lord, she was on fire. Her stomach flipped then twisted into a huge ball of sizzling heat. Her toes curled, and she reached up to grip his shoulders before her knees gave out. He tasted like heaven and hell, sweet and dangerous. Everything about this endless moment in time was a contradiction. His arms crushed her against his chest in anger and frustration, but his lips caressed her with fire and passion.

Jake released her. She stumbled backwards, trying to find balance.

Cassidy trembled, but the anger at his quick dismissal flashed white hot. She watched him swing his leg off the motorcycle then point an accusing finger in her direction. "You need to keep your distance." He'd raised his voice, and it echoed loudly within the near empty parking lot.

He swore and twisted on his heel, striding toward the hotel and leaving her standing alone with only her confused emotions and hyperactive hormones.

"I need to keep my distance?" Cassidy charged after him, smacking him on the back. "You have a lot of nerve."

He whirled around, and the fire in his eyes stopped her short. "Give me space . . ." He inhaled and exhaled, his breath ragged. "Cassidy."

Her eyes widened, and she covered her mouth with her hand. "Damn you," she whispered and pushed past him.

Entering the presidential suite, she noted Michelle and Steve already at work running tests. Steve glanced up and rose to his feet, sending his chair toppling backward. "What's the matter, Cass?"

"Nothing. I'm fine." She shook her head and cast him a warning glance that she prayed would shut him up. He narrowed his eyes when Jake entered the room, crossing the floor and slamming his bedroom door behind him. Cassidy held up her hand. "Don't ask."

Steve furrowed his brow but adhered to her wish for privacy. "The necropsy lab is prepped and ready for you. I'm combing the Web for anything similar to the consistency of the blood samples found on the ground, and Michelle's dissecting the natural debris she bagged."

Cassidy rubbed her forehead. "Fine. I'm going to grab a quick shower, and then I'll get to work in the lab." She headed toward her bedroom, then paused. "Check with Ethan to see whether or not any of the lab results have come in on that human body, please."

"Yes, ma'am." Steve mock saluted.

She smiled and sighed. "We have a lot of work to do before CDC arrives."

"When's their ETA?"

Glancing at her watch, she was shocked at the time. It was past five in the morning. "They'll be here for lunch."

Cassidy entered her bedroom. With shaking hands, she retrieved her toiletries and headed toward the shower. Jake Anderson was an enigma. She didn't know what to think about their little indiscretion. However, she was certain it would never happen again. Nope. Too much feeling, too much emotion.

And way too much heat.

Cassidy flipped the shower to hot, waiting for the steam to thicken in the bathroom. She'd wash away his touch. You fight fire with fire, right? She'd burn him out of her memory.

By the time Cassidy exited the front of the inn, morning had chased the night away. The ground rustled with nocturnal animals seeking shelter. Birds chattered and gossiped, competing with one another for the loudest song. She nodded to several couples laden with backpacks and camping equipment, intent on grabbing an early start.

She made her way around the edge of the inn and walked across the parking lot to the area Steve had indicated. Spotting him waving at her from inside the back of the mobile lab, she picked up her pace, careful not to spill the coffee she was carrying.

"Here." Handing a coffee up to Steve, she felt rewarded by his grateful smile.

"Thanks. Come on in."

Cassidy stepped up the metal stairs and into the back of the camper that now appeared to be twice its original size. The necropsy lab was just as promised: a simple metal gurney in the center with all the tools of the trade secured against the wall and ceiling. Steve had pulled the mobile lab to the camper section of the inn and attached it to power and water. Anxious to begin work, she waved him away.

"This button right here, Cass, is to be used when you're done. It'll cleanse the inside via ultraviolet rays." Steve paused before jumping out the back of the mobile lab. "Do you want help with the wolves?"

Jake stepped into the confined space. "I'll help her." He moved toward the storage container and lifted the lid, retrieving the first bag.

Cassidy's pulse raced, but she bit her bottom lip and refused to acknowledge the effect the biologist created.

"Do you think that's appropriate?" Steve asked.

"I'm the biologist. I need these blood samples and body fluids. You need to be coordinating our data."

Cassidy closed her eyes against the testosterone flinging around the room. "It's fine, Steve. Jake's right; we need to work this together." She guided him out the door and kissed his cheek. "Thanks for being a good friend."

"I've got your back, Sugar."

She smiled and nodded. "I know you do."

When Steve rounded the corner, she re-entered the lab. Jake tossed her a mask and helped her into protective clothing. She did the same for him, tying the back of the long gown. They worked in silence, neither wanting to rehash what had occurred earlier.

Jake placed the first animal on the table, and Cassidy went to work. Her knife slid across its underbelly, making a "Y" shape from the upper chest to the lower abdomen. She peeled the skin apart, cracked the rib cage, and began removing internal organs.

"This pup is severely dehydrated. And note the damage to the intestinal lining? If this were a standard necropsy without anything unusual, I'd say he had parvo." Cassidy glanced at Jake. She loved the way his eyes mimicked the thoughts processing through his brain, intelligence deepening the shade of blue.

"Parvo? Here, grab me that tube of blood. I'll run a test." Jake accepted the tube of blood from Cassidy and moved beyond a clear Plexiglas divider into the computer lab portion of the RV.

He snagged a chair and rolled over toward a large microscope cabled directly to a flat panel monitor. Drawing some of the blood from the tube, he placed it on a slide. Adding a few drops of solution, Jake peered into the microscope. There they were. But something was odd. He sent the information from the scope to the monitor and ran an analysis.

"Well?" Cassidy's voice carried through the intercom system built into the RV.

"It's definitely parvo. But a strain I'm not familiar with."

Cassidy entered through the door, sealed it behind her, and stood behind him. She glanced at the computer printout. "You're right. What's that?" Pointing to a small section within the virus, she didn't realize how close they were until Jake spun in his chair and gazed up into her face.

"I'm sorry," he said. His eyes were intense, searching for something.

"I," she stammered and felt the heat rush to her cheeks. She inhaled sharply. "I don't know what to think. One minute you're kissing me; the next minute you're yelling at me. It's a blur." She waved her hands in the air, praying her face wasn't beet red and that the glare from her mask dulled her embarrassment. "It's not important anyway. We've got a job to do here. Let's just forget it ever happened, okay?"

"I'm wounded." He stabbed an invisible knife to his heart. "My ego is forever shattered at being thought forgettable."

Cassidy laughed. "You're a pain in the ass is what you are." Good. If they teased one another, then the kiss didn't mean anything. Glancing down at the linoleum, she bit her lip. It'd take her more than a few hours to forget the flash of desire his lips ignited. With a sigh, she lifted her eyes and smiled brightly.

He tapped the edge of her mask. "Trust me, Sunshine. Next time will be unforgettable."

It saddened her for some inexplicable reason that he'd reverted to calling her Sunshine. It placed them back on familiar ground. She should be happy about that, right?

"Let's get these results over to the CDC."

Jake connected to the Internet and sent the results over a secure line. "What next?"

Cassidy surveyed the mess on the necropsy table. She sighed. "Let's clean this up. Verify all the other wolves are in similar condition, and remove that bullet for Ethan."

"What are you entering as cause of death?"

She chewed her bottom lip. "Dehydration followed by internal bleeding is the official cause of death. We need to understand that virus before we claim that it's the culprit. Regular parvo isn't necessarily a death sentence; besides, the skull anomaly is baffling."

They spent the next several hours mimicking the necropsy from the first wolf. Jake verified that in each blood sample, the odd parvo virus appeared. Cassidy recorded her findings and shot photographs of the damaged internal organs.

Stretching, she put away the last piece of equipment and they exited into a small alcove. She pressed a button, and the area sealed itself and provided a fast decontamination wash for their suits. They stripped off their protective gear and stowed it appropriately.

The relief of being without a mask had Cassidy inhaling and exhaling in joy. "I hate those things. They always make me claustrophobic."

Jake reached over and tugged the end of her ponytail. "Let's get out of here."

They left the vehicle and locked it. Cassidy dug a small key that

Steve had handed her out of her pocket and opened a six-by-six junction box on the exterior of the camper. Flipping a large red switch, she initiated the decontamination of the inner camper.

Turning, she followed Jake as they made their way back to the inn. The sun pierced the mist on the lake, dissipating the vapor into thin fingers of steam. Cassidy paused for a moment to soak in the beauty of her surroundings. Then the chill and exhaustion seeped in, and she shivered and yawned. "This profuse bleeding isn't a normal symptom of parvo."

"I realize that."

"And did you note the thickness of all the blood, even what remained within the bodies? It was clotted enough to appear congealed."

"Realized that, too." Jake yawned. "I think we both need to sleep before we begin spinning hypothetical solutions."

Cassidy couldn't agree more. They entered their suite. All was quiet. Peering into her bedroom, she groaned. Steve and Michelle were sprawled across the top of her covers snoring in remarkable synchrony. "I guess they're as tired as we are."

"Come on, Sunshine." Jake grabbed her hand and tugged her toward his room. "I'll share."

Even through the fog of exhaustion, her hormones attempted to spark. "Are you sure this is a good idea?"

"No. But I'm too damn tired to think clearly."

Cassidy smiled. "Tired is good." She eyed the queen-sized bed, debating whether to climb beneath the covers or simply collapse face first. Her brain froze, obviously as tired as her body. She placed her palms on the end of the bed and crawled onto its surface, sighing in appreciation.

Jake chuckled. He stretched out and turned to face her. "Sleep."

Already burrowing into her pillow, she murmured her response. "Uh-huh."

Jake pulled her close to his chest and she snuggled her back against him, not thinking or caring. Her eyes drifted closed, and she smiled foolishly when he kissed her hair and whispered against her ear. "Good night, Cassidy."

A loud bang snapped Cassidy from her sleep and she bolted upright, smashing her head against Jake's shoulder. "What? Who?"

Steve popped his head around the corner of the bedroom door and smiled at them. "Wake up, sleepyheads. The circus has arrived."

She blinked, trying to clear the sleep from her eyes. "You stole my bed."

"Yeah, sorry 'bout that. I used your shower, too."

Cassidy glared at him, feeling as if he'd stolen her last piece of candy. This was her bathroom he'd admitted to messing up. "You'd better not have left wet towels on the floor." A clean and tidy bathroom meant an invigorating and inviting shower.

"Quit arguing, kids. It's too damn early." Jake grumbled and focused on his watch. "Hey, Sunshine, we managed to sleep for three whole hours."

She sighed. "That's a record." The clamor and banging that had viciously stolen her from paradise continued outside the window. "What's going on?"

"The circus." Steve answered.

"Circus?"

"Of scientists."

"Scientists?"

"Get some coffee, Cass. Maybe you'll lose the echo." Steve shut the door, leaving Cassidy and Jake still sitting on the bed. A sudden rush of shyness washed over her as she realized how close together they'd slept.

He knocked his shoulder against hers, creating that bubbling belly effect again in her stomach. "Morning."

"I noticed you left the good out of that."

"There's only one kind of good morning that follows three hours of sleep. And, Sunshine, we didn't even come close." He gave her the big puppy-dog eyes, making her giggle. Giggle? She hadn't done that since high school.

Sobering, she stared at Jake. He didn't once break eye contact, ratcheting up the emotions that squeezed tighter in her chest. Despite her best efforts at not encouraging his advances, Cassidy knew what she wanted. The intimacy of sleeping within his arms and the overwhelming need to feel alive after witnessing the ugly side of death shattered Cassidy's reserve. "You bother me."

His lips twisted in a wolfish grin. "Is that a bad thing?"

"Yes." Caution flew out the window, and she crawled over to straddle his lap. His eyes widened, and desire flickered within their deep blue depths. She bent her head and rubbed her lips against his then moved closer, pushing herself against his chest and seeking the warmth of his mouth. He responded with a hunger that momentarily stunned her. His fingers ran through her hair and he held her tighter, jacking up the stakes to an almost irreversible level.

Cassidy disengaged, drawing in deep breaths. She traced a finger along the line of his jaw. "I don't want to be forgettable." She gasped when he moved his hips upward rubbing between her legs.

"That'll never happen."

She tugged at the hem of his T-shirt. Glancing at his face, Cassidy hesitated. His breathing stilled, and his face tightened. Insecurity pounded her chest. "Too fast?" Her voice was nothing more than a whisper, but it shot across the room with the power of thunder.

Jake reached over and twisted a strand of her hair around his finger. "You might not like what you find."

Cassidy grinned, relieved, and pulled his shirt up and over his chest. "I doubt . . ." Her voice trailed off as the edge of a tattoo caught her attention. Sunshine glittered against the emblem of an American flag split asunder by a lightning bolt. She knew this tattoo. She'd seen it not long ago, in a dark tent, on a horrible night. Her hand shook uncontrollably when she traced the symbol with the edge of her finger. She heard Jake's sharp intake but ignored him.

Betrayal. Anger. Sadness. Heartache. Too much to absorb.

Cassidy felt Jake move and before she could protest he'd flipped her off his lap and onto her back, her head cradled in his hand and the vivid blue of his eyes piercing her soul.

With a growl, he bent his head and touched his lips gently to hers. "It doesn't matter."

Cassidy sighed, wanting to make all the bad emotions fade beneath the power of her blossoming awareness for him.

But deceit hurt.

Anger burned.

Betrayal destroyed.

And pride wouldn't allow her retreat.

He tilted his head; his fingers slid through her hair, gently picking at the tangled mess of curls. "You started this, Dr. Lowell."

"And I'm ending it." Cassidy pushed against his chest and jumped off the bed, dashing toward the bathroom before she relented to the passion in his eyes.

Her hand slid onto the cool metal of the doorknob. Before she had a chance to escape Jake's presence, the bedroom door crashed open, slamming against the interior wall with a resounding thud.

Beyond the quiet reserve of their suite, she heard the bellow of deep male voices and her name being shouted as if it were a curse. "What's going on?" She hated the way her voice squeaked, resonating with the sudden sense of dangerous foreboding that tightened her chest.

Ethan Connor darkened the open doorway, a gun pointed directly at her heart.

CHAPTER 23

CASSIDY STARED DOWN THE BARREL OF THE PISTOL, TRYING TO make sense of the bizarre situation. "Ethan, put that gun down."

He shook his head and narrowed eyes, which burned with anger. "How could you, Cass? How could you destroy something you worked so hard to create?"

She avoided glancing at the movement beyond Ethan's shoulder. A finger signal from Jake silenced her, as he silently slid off the bed. "Why you holding a gun on her, Connor?"

"She's under arrest."

Jake approached Ethan, but he swung the pistol and pointed it at Jake's chest. "Back off, Anderson. I'm taking Dr. Lowell into custody. She's charged with treason and first-degree murder."

Cassidy shook her head. "Treason? Murder?"

Ethan approached Cassidy, handcuffs in one hand, gun in the other. The room dimmed slightly as her mind processed his words. A hand reached from behind Ethan's back, jabbing into the arc of his neck and sending the park ranger sliding to the floor. Steve grinned at Cassidy and shrugged his shoulder. "Always wanted to be a bad guy."

He tossed a weapon in Jake's direction and a bundle of clothes at her chest. "Time to move out, Captain."

Cassidy couldn't comprehend the significance of his words, but her survival instinct kicked into place. She quickly donned the shirt, sweater, socks, and shoes Steve provided and was on Jake's heels and out the window in sixty seconds flat.

She didn't resist when Jake reached back and grabbed her hand, keeping her close as they ran along the edge of the inn. Panic and confusion threatened to overwhelm, but Cassidy concentrated on her surroundings. The laughter of innocent youth drifted from a window above their heads, blending with the cacophony of wildlife that trickled beyond the edge of the woods. Steve pressed a warm hand against her back and urged her forward.

The rising call of the righteous thundered behind them and demanded they surrender. Cassidy tugged on Jake's hand. "We should stop. Explain ourselves. This is all a mistake, Jake."

"Don't kid yourself, Sunshine. There's no mistake here." Jake pushed her down and shielded her from a sudden onslaught of gunfire. Bullets pinged off the brick building and tore into the soft ground at their feet. "How far, Steve?"

"Beyond that tree line. I'll go fire it up." Steve dashed forward, staying low to the ground and zig-zagging against a shower of bullets.

"This is insane." Cassidy raised her voice to be heard above the gunfire and commands being shouted behind them. "We need to call Sharpe."

Jake turned and stared at her, a cool reserve only half masking the surprise and anger that flared within the depths of his baby-blues. "Don't fight me on this. There's a chopper beyond that tree line." He bent his head and swore when she frowned and glanced over her shoulder. "Cassidy, something's gone terribly wrong. Turning yourself over to Dudley Do-Right will be the end of your career and perhaps life."

"I don't understand."

"Neither do I, Sunshine. But our best bet at finding answers is about five hundred feet that away." He pointed toward the pine trees that edged a gravel road to their left.

Hesitation rarely encroached upon Cassidy's life, and this moment wasn't a time to allow it in. She nodded, placed her hand in his, and prepared to run. "Let's do it then."

Jake tilted his head, closed his eyes, and listened. Cassidy mimicked his actions and heard a faint thump of rotor blades. Before she opened her eyes, Jake yanked on her arm and they raced across the gravel road. Bullets whizzed by, striking stone and grass. Her heart pounded in her chest as she ran as fast as her legs would carry her. Sliding around the edge of a tree, she braced herself with her hand but Jake pulled her onward; the rough bark snagged at her tender skin and scraped the length of her wrist. Swearing, she stumbled forward attempting to match his pace.

They ran.

She heard Ethan's voice behind her, and fear snatched her breath away. Jake pulled harder on her arm, and she forced her legs to move faster. They broke through a clearing, and the helicopter hovered above ground less than fifty feet away. Jake pushed her toward the chopper and dropped to one knee, firing his gun at the woods. Cassidy tripped, her legs weak and rubbery; she winced as dirt and rocks bit into the bleeding flesh of her palms. She righted herself and raced for safe haven.

Her legs and arms burned from exhaustion, but she used her last burst of energy and threw her body into the interior of the helicopter, curling into a ball as she rolled and slammed against the back wall. She felt the chopper rise and panicked when she realized Jake wasn't aboard.

Cassidy scrambled to the edge of the chopper, the scene and circumstances all too familiar. This time she'd make a difference. Jake hung suspended from the rung, his legs kicking in the air as Steve lifted them higher above the ground. Bullets flew, striking metal but not penetrating. She reached over the edge and grabbed Jake's arm.

He glanced up in surprise, then narrowed his eyes in anger. "Let go of me. Get back where it's safe."

Cassidy glared right back and pulled with all her strength. She felt his weight shift slightly. His hand gripped her shoulder as he propelled his body through the opening and into the helicopter. Without thinking, she launched herself at him and slammed her fist into his chest. "Don't do that again. You almost fell."

He pulled her into a hard embrace, and she smiled as the deep rumble of his laughter warmed her ear. "You're a piece of work, Goldilocks."

Two cups of coffee later, Cassidy felt more in control. Steve had flown the chopper straight out of Yellowstone and into a safe house provided by the Black Stripe unit of ZEBRA. She'd changed into a pair of faded, well-worn jeans and a standard ZEBRA polo shirt, not bothering to ask how her belongings had managed to appear within a short time after their arrival.

It'd taken her longer to brush the knots from her hair and braid it securely down her back than it had to put on clean clothes.

Jake stepped out of the small bedroom. The scent of his spicy cologne mixed with baby shampoo drifted toward Cassidy. An intoxicating combination. He walked up to her and accepted the mug she held out to him. He tossed her a wicked grin and winked as he brought the mug to his lips. She felt herself blush and turned away.

He moved closer. Her back brushed against his chest. She glared at him, fighting the unwanted attraction. He'd lied to her.

"Space?" Cassidy asked.

Jake's lips curved upward. "No thanks. I'm fine."

Cassidy's eyes widened at his glib comment and she attempted another glare, making Jake tilt his head back and laugh at the expression on her face. She felt ridiculous and silly. It grated against her skin.

"How you holding up?" he asked.

"Confused."

Jake walked into the center of the small lodge house they'd confiscated. "My Black Stripe unit is assigned to monitor your actions and determine any connection you might have with New World Petroleum."

"Unit? As in Steve?" Disbelief filled her voice, and it raised an octave higher than normal.

"Yes. ZEBRA has been laundering money for NWP. We want to know why."

Anger quickly replaced disbelief. "And you think I can tell you?"

"Two of your team members from Africa are dead, and you're being framed for the supposed release of a biological weapon. Yeah, I think you can tell us."

Cassidy sat, finding it difficult to process everything. She bent her head and rubbed at the sudden throbbing in her temple. Her voice was low, barely audible. "Who?"

Jake frowned and tilted his head. "Excuse me?"

Staring into his face, she spoke louder. "Who is dead?"

"The bodies of your two geologists were found in Port Harcourt a few days ago."

Cassidy closed her eyes, her body tingling as if she'd run into a wall of needles. Charles and David. Gone. She stood, rubbing her arms up and down in an attempt to recirculate blood, which felt thick and coagulated within her veins.

The fax machine beeped, and she wandered over to review the sheet it spit out, her mind trying to wrap around the information from Jake. Sitting on the edge of a floral wing chair, Cassidy read the fax for a second time. "I know where we're going next," she said to no one in particular.

"Where's that?" Jake stepped up beside her, too close again.

"Montana. Apparently a subsidiary of NWP owns a piece of property there."

Steve entered the room and handed Cassidy another stack of papers. She shuffled through them quickly. They were press cuttings of the charges filed against her. Rage built quickly and almost exploded in a scream as she flipped to the last page. Instead, Cassidy inhaled several deep breaths and handed the sheet to Jake. "This is bogus. A total setup. This has NWP's handiwork written all over it."

Jake nodded. "I agree."

She needed to focus on the virus and ignore what the false charges meant to her career. Cassidy lifted her head and signaled to Steve with her hand. "Where do we stand with the CDC?"

"Their team isn't fully together yet. They've set up camp just beyond the RV and are attempting to isolate and diagnose the genetic composition of the parvo virus you extracted from the wolves. They've received notice of additional human contamination."

Cassidy's eyes widened as her mind digested the ramifications of Steve's words. The CDC and ZEBRA often worked assignments simultaneously. Their relationship was one of trust and respect, facilitating the ease of transferring responsibilities. "How will we be kept apprised as the situation escalates?"

"Colonel Price has a pipeline direct to the CDC. As far as they're concerned, you're the only suspect and the balance of our pod are still good guys."

Cassidy smirked, digging out the emotional shield of sarcasm. "Great. I've always wanted to be a wanted woman."

Jake snorted and whispered beneath his breath. "All you had to do was ask me."

The fax beeped again and another sheet spit out. Jake picked this one up and read its contents before passing it to her. "This isn't good."

Their fingers touched briefly. She swallowed, ignoring the tingle. "What?" Cassidy read the document. "That's impossible." She raised her head and gazed at him. His eyes clouded with concern.

He shrugged. "I know, but they've run the test three times."

"What's going on?" Steve asked.

She turned toward him and handed over the document. "Apparently the dead woman was also infected with the same mutated parvo virus as our wolves." Cassidy's mind began to tick off solutions as to how this could possibly happen. "I thought that media stuff linking the death of that woman to the wolves was nothing more than a fabricated tie-in to trump up more charges against me."

Steve paced in a tight circle. "Parvo isn't transferable to humans, is it?"

Cassidy shook her head. "No. Fifth Disease is the human version of parvo, and it's relatively harmless." Standing, she followed him and paced in her own tight circle.

Jake furrowed his brow. "That woman had a rash on her upper chest. Isn't that indicative of Fifth Disease?"

Cassidy stopped mid-stride. She felt nauseated. "We're not talking parvo or Fifth Disease. This virus is a blend of the two of them with an added ability to mutate the thickness of blood." Glancing at Jake, she noted her own fear mirrored in his face. "This is more than a wolf version of the bird flu and definitely supports a bioterrorism theory."

"Explain," he said.

She walked over to the coffee table and pulled over a pad of paper. Drawing a stick figure of a man and a dog she penciled in a vertical line beneath the human body. "Although both versions of parvo require dividing cells to reproduce, when Fifth Disease attacks a human body it latches onto cells found in your skin or bone marrow. There are specific proteins on the surface of the virus that determine what it can attack."

Cassidy flipped the sheet of paper around so that everyone had a clear vision of the diagram. "Now, parvo attacks here." She drew a circle around the intestinal tract zone of the stick dog. "As well as the animal's immune system." Sitting back and thinking, Cassidy chewed on her lower lip. "In other words, parvo goes after immune and intestinal systems and Fifth Disease targets areas making red blood cells."

"This ability of the virus to attack both human and canine cells couldn't have happened naturally?" Jake asked, staring at her sheet of paper.

Cassidy shook her head. "No way. This is laboratory-induced mutation. These two viruses are as different as night and day. They couldn't mutate into one without help."

"Dehydration, intestinal damage, and rashes can be explained as symptoms of either parvo or Fifth Disease, but what about the blood?"

Fear of the unknown knotted Cassidy's stomach. "I don't know, Jake. I honestly don't know."

CHAPTER 24

Balancing a bag of groceries on his knee, Edward unlocked his hotel room door. He shuffled inside, ready to settle on the
bed and catch up on world news. His shoes discarded and clothes loosened, he scooted onto the mattress and aimed the remote at the TV.

It felt like weeks rather than a day since his altercation with Jason.
He reached onto the table beside the bed and pulled his laptop close,
flipping the lid open. Edward verified the phone line hadn't loosened
then clicked onto the Internet. With a few keystrokes he reassured
himself that his flight to Richmond was still on schedule for first thing
in the morning.

Glancing at the television set, he felt his stomach flip over at the
familiar scene. A young newscaster with slicked-back hair and high-
heeled shoes stood in front of Old Faithful, a gathering of people behind
her waving at the camera. The geyser erupted and she smiled into the
lens, beginning her report.

Edward stared at the screen, ignoring the pain that squeezed his
chest. His ears buzzed, the noise blocking the sound of the television
set. All his carefully laid plans disintegrated into a pile of worthless

schedules and intent. Smashing his fist into the bag of chips, he fought against the urge to weep.

He glanced at the television set and turned the volume up a notch. They were giving a brief bio on the zoologist they insisted released a biological weapon into Yellowstone. Edward reached for a notepad and jotted down her name. There must be a damn good reason Dr. Cassidy Lowell suddenly became the perpetrator of CPV-19, and he was going to figure it out.

"Cassidy Lowell," he said, tapping the computer screen, "you will be my bargaining chip."

Nick Fowler approached the cottage, glancing around for any signs of life. He snatched a crumpled piece of note paper from his back pocket and verified he had the right address. It didn't make sense.

He'd imagined Edward Fiske's laboratory would be housed in a large facility. But what stood before him was nothing more than a disheveled cottage surrounded by small, decaying buildings. The grass surrounding the exterior of the house was overgrown and tangled with weeds, sprouting a foot high against the edge of the front porch. He slowly turned in a circle and examined the layout of the land. A wide stretch of rough cut lawn, brown and crisp from lack of rain, spread to the left of the house and slanted downward disappearing behind a small slope.

The only thing that sparkled and shined was the lazy bend of the Yellowstone River. It glittered against the back of the house like a twinkling jewel. The air smelled fresh and clean except for the faint tinge of smoke from the mountains, an unfamiliar scent to a man who'd spent the better part of his younger years neck high in 'Nam marshes that seethed with rats, snakes, and the devil-only-knew what else beneath its bloody water.

Bodies, swollen and mangled, were the fragrance Nick preferred. To hell with nature and cleanliness.

Where the fuck was Jason?

Nick impatiently stomped around the cottage, peering in windows and banging on doors.

He stepped onto the rickety front porch and called Jason's name. No answer. He turned the knob on the door and entered the small house. He didn't bother absorbing his surroundings; he didn't care. A few paces later, he was in the center of a tiny kitchen with blue and gold wallpaper and yellowed linoleum.

He swore, did an about face, and strode back to the front porch. Squinting against the sun, Nick noted a small brick building and log cabin off to the left. He crossed the grass and made his way through a patch of trees until he stood before the brick structure. It was about five feet in height and had a two-foot metal door.

Opening the door, Nick peered inside. There was nothing but a large pile of ashes. Must be some sort of incinerator. He slammed the door shut and leaned against the structure. Where the hell was the lab tech?

Nick bent down to pluck a blade of sweet grass from the ground. Focusing his eyes on an irregular pattern on the lawn, he crouched and ruffled the spiky leaves. There were patches and large blotches of crusted brown material splattered in a haphazard fashion.

Blood from the good doctor.

Here was the proof the tech at least completed his assignment before performing his vanishing act. Standing, he sighed and scanned his surroundings. Heading toward the dilapidated log cabin, Nick cursed in annoyance.

Fucking amateurs.

He pushed open the door and entered the log cabin. A light shone brightly from an opening in the floor. Nick pulled his gun from its halter and approached the hole cautiously, calling Jason's name. All he heard in return was the echo of his own voice.

The dank smell of the upper room tickled his nose, and he muffled a sneeze. He tested the metal stairs for soundness, then climbed down into the lighted room below.

"Well, I'll be damned." Nick spun in a circle, absorbing the laboratory. He moved along the counters, opening and shutting drawers and cabinets. The place was spotless. He couldn't find any evidence of the CPV-19 production. Nothing.

Climbing back up the stairs, Nick made his way outside and down the path to the incinerator. He glanced toward the river, noting a trail of broken grass. Something metal flickered in the sunlight. Walking over, he bent and picked up a cell phone. With a flip of his wrist it opened and displayed a number.

"Fuck."

It was the same number he'd been calling all morning. Jason's number.

He opened his own phone and dialed. Shaking his head, he flung Jason's phone into the air. This assignment couldn't get any more screwed.

"Yes?" Cole answered.

Nick took a quick breath. "There's been a complication."

"Like what?"

"There's no one here at the lab. I found dried blood and signs of a body being dragged to the river. The lab assistant's cell phone has been discarded on that same path. The lab is spotless. Shit. There's no sign of life whatsoever or of CPV-19." He waited and prayed none of this would be blamed on him.

"That is a bit of a complication. Do you think Fiske is still alive?"

"His car isn't here, and Jason's is. So, yeah, I think Fiske is among the walking."

There was silence. "The lab assistant isn't smart enough to double cross us. Let's assume that the good doctor turned the tables on his demise and is on the run. I'll track him from here. I want you to destroy everything there."

Nick frowned. "Why? No one knows this place exists."

"And I want to keep it that way. Make sure there's absolutely no evidence of that underground laboratory left behind."

Nick blew out a mouthful of air. "That's no easy feat."

"That's why we pay you the big bucks."

Fucking jerk. He flipped the phone shut and went to scrutinize the laboratory. How the hell was he going to destroy it? He sniffed and smelled the smoke from forest fires too far away to do any damage. A thought crossed his mind and his lips curled upward. He'd been trained to use his surroundings as a weapon, and that's exactly what he intended on doing now.

Beauty.

It abounded in the endless flowing waters of Yellowstone River. Sun glittered in fairy wings of diamonds upon its surface, causing an unexpected pang of longing within Cassidy. She craved a lazy day by the river and the security of her mother's voice.

Jake stepped into her line of vision, another beautiful sight. He spoke rapidly into his cell phone. His eyes roamed everywhere, searching for danger. They rested a beat too long on her, and her pulse did an invisible Irish jig.

Cassidy wanted to snap her blinders back in place. She desired to return to a life that revolved solely around work and held her heart and emotions at arm's length.

But that choice was no longer hers. Instead, a kaleidoscope of longing for a life she'd never attain threatened her normal stoic resolve.

Jake approached, studying his compass and consulting the sunlight and lay of the land. "We have about a one-mile hike to reach the edge of NWP's holdings."

"I think I can handle that."

"We'll be there before the sun sets."

Cassidy picked up a canvas backpack that rested at her feet. "What's Steve doing?" Disappointment and an edge of uncertainty still rankled her after watching Steve fly off into the distance. His affiliation with Black Stripe grated and irritated what she'd considered the most solid relationship she'd ever been a part of.

"I've sent him to confiscate the transport plane and brief the rest of the pod."

She studied his face. Her trust still less than comfortable. "You're pretty confident he won't be arrested."

"Sunshine, he'll never be seen." Jake headed toward the riverbank. "Time to find a piece of the puzzle."

Cassidy followed his path. She had to admit she liked him, definitely too much for her own comfort. Somewhere in the past two days he'd found a way past her carefully placed emotional barriers and snuck in, rooting himself firmly beneath her skin. Beneath his brash and cocky persona, Jake was smart, funny, and intuitive . . . a dangerous composition of qualities that enticed Cassidy.

But he'd deceived her. "Thank God I didn't sleep with him."

Jake turned around, slowing his pace and walking backwards. "Excuse me?"

Cassidy blushed and shook her head. "Talking to myself again, Captain."

He narrowed his eyes at her use of his military rank title, then spun on his heels and resumed their previous pace. Cassidy grinned. She'd irritate him. Good. They moved quietly, settling into a comfortable silence. The sun filtered through the trees on their right, burning the top of her head.

Jake paused, checked the compass, and dropped his backpack on the ground. He sighed and ran his fingers through his hair. His T-shirt was soaked in sweat, the heat of the afternoon making conditions uncomfortable. Cassidy averted her eyes and attempted to ignore how his muscles rippled beneath the clinging cotton. "We're almost there. Just around that bend is the edge of the homestead."

"This could be a wild goose chase." She sighed and tried to balance her emotions. "I mean, what do we honestly expect to find?" Cassidy wanted answers, but it felt as if they were simply chasing a whisper of hope.

Jake squeezed her shoulder and offered her a lopsided grin. "A miracle?"

She rolled her eyes, stretched, and inhaled. The scent of cool water drifted off the river. "Let's make our way around that bend, then." Ahead of them was a small bank of thick grass that swept around a cut in the river.

They moved forward and rounded the bend; before them lay a large clearing with an old farmhouse to the left and a number of dilapidated outbuildings toward the edge of the woods. Cassidy squinted and touched Jake's shoulder. She pointed toward the side of one of the outbuildings. A shadow moved.

Nick Fowler crouched behind the cabin and watched Jake Anderson jog around the bend. A thin line of sweat dripped down his cheek, and he wiped it on the edge of his shirt. The afternoon had been long and arduous, and the appearance of Anderson and Blondie complicated an already unbalanced agenda. First Fiske's vanishing act and now this surprise visit. The day continued to spiral down into another level of hell.

He flipped open his phone and called Cole. "They're here."

"Who?"

"Anderson and that girl."

Silence. Nick tapped his foot and twisted a small wire between his forefinger and thumb. He could hear a scratching noise through the line and figured Cole was scribbling as he threaded this recent intrusion through his mind. "They can be eliminated."

He lifted his hands toward the sky, then clasped them together. "You sure?"

"Yes. The media's been alerted and her reputation sullied. At this stage of the game, anything she might submit to OPEC would be disregarded as petty."

Nick cursed himself for possibly ruining his chances at playing but decided he'd rather be upfront than face the repercussions later. "I haven't found that geological survey you wanted."

"Don't snuff before you have it; is that clear?" A deep rumble of laughter filtered through Nick's phone. "Once that's done, shut the bitch up and get back here."

Nick's lip curled up. "Thank you." He raised his fist holding the phone to the sky, punching the air in excitement. Placing the phone back to his ear, he verified the facts. "I'll have this area cleared within the next fifteen minutes, including Anderson and the doctor."

"The geological takes precedence. Don't focus on the kill. We haven't been able to pinpoint the whereabouts of Fiske. When we do, you'll need to be dispatched to whatever location he's at. If Anderson and the girl don't give up the survey, leave them. They'll be taken care of later."

"Roger that." *My ass.* He hummed to himself, excited about the prospect of dirtying his hands.

He jogged around the outside of the log cabin, verifying all his charges were in place. The ground had been soaked with gasoline, so when the lab imploded the entire estate would quickly be consumed in flames. With it being dry, the fire would spread in rapid waves beyond this area and consume the woods. By the time the firefighters made their way to this quadrant, the laboratory would be completely demolished and hidden beneath the burnt remnants of its surroundings.

Nick peered around the bend in the river. Anderson and the woman were in a heated discussion. He smiled, his heartbeat increasing at the thought of pulling on her hair and staring into her eyes. He'd waste only a bullet on the man. But Blondie . . . she was special.

The ground vibrated.

A muffled explosion echoed from the section of the property they'd been monitoring. Jake grabbed her hand and raced across the field. An old log cabin shook on its foundations then collapsed, bursting into a huge ball of fire.

"What the hell?" Jake and Cassidy ran toward the house in the distance, the fire blazing a fast wave across the dried grass. He stopped as a figure stepped from the tree line, pointing a gun in their direction. The gunshot was swallowed by the sound of the raging fire, but there was no mistaking the thud in the ground next to their feet.

Cassidy tugged on Jake's arm and pointed toward the river. He shook his head. The water was running much too quickly for them to cross. She continued to tug on his arm. He ducked beneath the gunfire and followed her down the embankment.

"Help with this kayak!" Her voice was thin against the raging fire, and he had to strain to hear her. Flames burned across the yard, consuming the house with another explosion. "That fire is moving too fast for us to outrun. It'll burn straight across that road. We'll be trapped unless we make our way downriver."

Another bullet whizzed past their heads. "This guy is relentless." Jake helped Cassidy drag the kayak to the river edge.

"I'm jinxed. The world is out to get me." Cassidy huffed and pushed against the back of the small boat. "What have I ever done to deserve being shot at? This is becoming a daily habit of mine."

He grinned. "Call me an optimist, but I'm thinking we stumbled on something pretty damn important. This is no natural fire." Jake tossed her a paddle and pushed them off the shore. The man behind them pursued, grabbing another one of the kayaks. "And I'm also thinking this guy is more than just an angry homeowner. Looks an awful lot like Cole's right-hand man to me." He dipped his paddle in the water.

Cassidy held herself low over the bow, paddling on the opposite side of Jake. "Yep. It's Nick Fowler."

Jake remembered the hired killer from the night of the attack on Cassidy's campsite. The expression of pure hatred mixed with lust as Nick had stared at Cassidy sent a cold chill down Jake's back.

He noted she matched her rhythm to his, skillfully guiding them down the river. Bullets skimmed the water to their left. "Ugly son of a bitch."

They navigated the river like pros. Although the frigid water splashed against his skin, Jake felt the sweat bead on his forehead. If he was already tiring, Cassidy must be exhausted. She never broke stride.

Bullets continued to rain around them. This was more than a trespassing problem. This guy wanted them dead.

"Hold on!" Cassidy yelled.

Jake snapped his head up and gasped. The kayak skimmed across the top of the water and plummeted down what felt like miles of icy waves. Cassidy steered the front. Jake balanced the back and helped her maintain position. The rapids tossed them around, soaking into their clothing.

The raging river shot them out at the end of a turn and the bottom of the boat slammed into something solid, flipping them beneath the churning water.

CHAPTER 25

THE CURRENT DRAGGED CASSIDY BENEATH FRIGID WATER, chilly liquid flooding her mouth. She tumbled over and over, unable to fight the turmoil, choking and gasping for air. Her forehead smacked into something hard. She cried out and swallowed another mouthful of water.

Reaching up, her arm connected with an object and she grabbed on, pulling herself to the surface. Her lungs burned. Holding onto the log, Cassidy hauled herself above the water heaving in great gulps of oxygen and hacking a mouthful of foul river out. The current spun her in circles, giving an entirely new meaning to a mad teacup ride. She twisted her head, searching for Jake.

Her eyes rested on the odd-shaped log she clung too. It wasn't wood. Cassidy wiped back the mass of hair that hung across her eyes in thick strands. Her fingers clutched the edge of a frayed shirt. An eye-watering stench of decay assaulted her nose, and she screamed.

Shock vibrated from the tip of her toes. She released the dead body, backpedaling and pushing it as far away from her as she could. Another rapid tugged at her legs; she inhaled deeply and felt the draw of the current as it hauled her down beneath its watery blanket.

Tired and numb, she couldn't battle against the pull of the river.

Blackness closed around her eyes and she relaxed, following the current like a rag doll. She blinked when a hand reached down and yanked her out of the water. Struggling and fighting to breathe, she clawed at the arm. She didn't want to die. And in a split second, Cassidy realized she was no longer being swallowed by water and it was sweet air that burned her lungs. Her savior threw her onto hard ground, pressing rough hands against her chest.

Coughing and gasping, Cassidy opened her eyes and gazed into a fierce set of baby blues.

"Cassidy," Jake gasped her name then brought her roughly to his chest, smoothing her hair back. "Don't ever do that again." He rested his forehead against hers and swore softly.

They were both shaking uncontrollably.

"What did I do?"

He stared at her and grinned. "Scared me." Jake shook his head and shivered. "Don't do it again."

She grimaced and pushed herself to a sitting position. "I feel like I've been beaten by a meat tenderizer." Cassidy reached for Jake's hand and entwined her fingers with his, passing in silence the words of her heart.

He shivered and kissed her temple. "I hear ya."

"We need to get out of these clothes or else we'll be the only people known to die of hypothermia in the middle of July."

"This isn't a good place." Jake turned and glanced upriver. "I don't know where Fowler went, but I can't trust that he'd be so lucky as to drown."

"Let's get away from the river." Fighting back the hysteria of kissing death smack on the lips, she rubbed her arms. "There's a dead body floating out there."

Jake's eyes focused and sharpened on the river. "You sure?"

Cassidy nodded. "Uh-huh. Positive."

"I'm not diving in and following it downstream. We'll call it in."

She smacked his arm. "With what? Smoke signals? I doubt our phones will work after that water ride."

He tilted his head and opened his mouth to speak, then closed it again. "What?"

"I have a better phone than you. One of the Black Stripe perks. Let's find somewhere to dry off; then we'll figure out where we are, okay?"

They struggled to their feet, sodden and freezing. As they made their way up a rocky incline, Cassidy pointed toward a small, sunny clearing. "There's a cabin."

"Out here?"

"Sure. It's probably owned by one of the outfitters that bring tourists out to hunt and fish and have exciting river adventures just like ours." She pushed him forward.

"Funny."

Jake knocked on the door and when there was no answer, he picked the lock with his pocketknife and opened it. "After you, madam."

Cassidy entered the small one-room cabin. There were bunks against one wall, a kitchenette on the other, and a huge fireplace in the center of the two. "We can't have a fire. It would give away our location." She turned and faced Jake; the heat in his eyes tingled along every inch of her skin. She swallowed.

"Want help getting out of those clothes?"

Cassidy choked on the lump in her throat. "How can you even think about something like that when we're stranded in the wilderness being hunted by a madman?"

He lifted a shoulder, the side of his lip curving upward. "Men think about it all the time. Didn't you read the survey?"

Suppressing a giggle, Cassidy pointed behind her at a small door. "I'm going in there."

Jake chuckled, the warmth of his laughter filling the tiny room.

"You do that, Sunshine."

Cassidy turned on her heels and headed into what she assumed was a bathroom. Pushing on the door with the palm of her hand it slowly creaked inward. The room was dark. She reached above the toilet and twisted the blinds, allowing natural light through the window. Surveying her surroundings, Cassidy sighed. It was simple but clean; they couldn't be too far off the beaten path.

Cassidy jiggled the handle on the toilet and was surprised when it flushed. She opened a small closet door and almost screamed in delight. Towels and blankets were stacked neatly, each covered in clear plastic. Whoever owned this place maintained a classy operation. Ripping open one of the bags, her fingers dug into the warmth of the wool blanket.

Cassidy stripped out of her clothes. She ran clean water from the tap and splashed it on her face. Shivers and shakes caused her hands to tremble and teeth to chatter, but she withstood the cold for a few moments, verifying she'd survived relatively unscathed. Wrapping the blanket around her, she sat on the edge of the toilet and gathered her strength.

The warmth generated by body heat and wool seeped into her skin, calming the violent shakes. She inhaled and exhaled, trying to ease all the unanswered questions that rattled her brain.

Cassidy stood and opened the medicine cabinet. There wasn't much, but she did find a small toiletry package that contained a comb, toothbrush, and toothpaste. She yanked the comb through her matted curls. After several minutes of torture and ten broken plastic teeth, she hurled the stupid thing into the garbage can.

She left the bathroom, feeling that a small modicum of sanity had returned. "There's running water. It's not hot though. We can't be too far from a road if they've dug in a septic and well system." Cassidy glanced at his sodden T-shirt. "Why don't you get out of those wet clothes and grab yourself a blanket. I'll fix the bandage on your leg."

Jake raised his brows. "I think it's best if I do that myself." He picked up the first-aid kit from the table and headed into the bathroom.

Cassidy sighed and walked around the cabin. She stared at the wet bundle in her hands and headed outside, leaving the confining walls of the small room behind. The afternoon sun beat down and caressed her shoulders. She adjusted the blanket wrapped around her chest and bent to lay her clothes upon the ground.

A limb snapped beyond the edge of the forest. She spun around, certain that Fowler had found them. The woods were silent. Cassidy backed toward the cabin, her eyes scanning the clearing for any sign of danger. A high-pitched cackle echoed from the trees, and she sighed in relief when a crow flew off a low-lying branch and rose into the air.

"It must be close to two o'clock," Jake said, stepping outside the cabin. "I'll haul over some branches to hide our clothes."

Cassidy turned and inhaled sharply, her pulse suddenly performing a wild Mexican hat dance. "Is that all you could find to put on?"

Jake glanced down at the towel wrapped around his waist and shrugged. "Don't worry, Sunshine. I won't take advantage of you."

Cassidy lifted her hand and pressed it against her heart. It hurt. She realized in a flash of insight that she wanted to be taken advantage of. The need to feel his warmth and heat and be reminded that life was more than the troubled moments of the past few hours struck at her core. Something must have crossed her face because Jake's steps faltered. "Don't look at me like that, Cassidy."

She bit the bottom of her lip. "I can't help it." Her voice trembled, making her curse silently. "I'm scared."

He lifted one brow. "Of me?"

The woods dropped into silence, their breathing the only sound she heard. "Of the way you make me feel."

Jake turned and placed his clothes on the ground beside hers. He held his hand out toward her, and she reached back. Their fingers entwined, flashes of electricity raced from his touch and spread a wave of heat that rivaled the burning land they'd left behind. He pulled her toward the cabin. "It's not safe out here."

She glanced around and decided against admitting to her recent fright. "He'd have to be psychic to figure out the exact point we left the river."

"He wasn't far behind us." Jake opened the cabin door. "I'll feel better when our clothes are dry and we're back on the move."

Cassidy followed him inside and clasped her hands together when he released his hold. She needed control. This certainly wasn't the time or place to act on the instincts that were raging through her body.

Jake moved through the cabin, securing the lock on the front door and placing his gun within easy reach. "Your gun still work?" she asked, wondering where the heck hers went to.

"Yeah. Yours?"

She shrugged. "I guess it's at the bottom of the river." Cassidy sat down at the small wooden table, resting her elbows on its surface.

Jake moved to the window beside the front door, dragging a chair across the floor and sitting on it. He scanned the perimeter. Cassidy watched his muscles bunch and tighten as his head moved back and forth for a full view of their surroundings.

"What are we going to do?"

Jake glanced at her and offered her a half smile. "Nothing until our clothes and my phone dry."

She stood and paced. "We need to hike back upriver and check out that fire. What the hell was that place?"

Jake nodded. "I wish I understood the motivation behind the charges against you."

Cassidy moved off her chair and went to stand next to Jake. "I know why they're doing this."

"Nigeria?"

She nodded. "They want to discredit me. Ruin my reputation.

That way all my accusations regarding the Niger Delta will be reduced to nothing but the ramblings of an insane mind. And, more importantly, NWP wants me eliminated. Make my findings in the Niger Delta null and void by dishonoring me and permanently shutting me up."

Jake's eyes narrowed and he focused on her, his body taut with tension. "Why do you say that?"

"Nick Fowler." Cassidy sighed, running a shaking hand through her hair. "Cole's shadow and hired killer."

"You truly believe that NWP would go this far?"

Cassidy nodded. "Absolutely."

Jake snaked an arm out, wrapping it around her waist. He pulled her close so that she stood between his legs. Cassidy reached out and allowed her fingers to trace the same path she'd watched him do, running them through his damp hair. He closed his eyes and inhaled her scent. "Do you think they planned this all from the beginning?"

Cassidy bit her lip, fighting the sensation of his skin against her palm. "No. I think they saw an opportunity and acted. Ruining my reputation is easier than killing me." Jake twirled the ends of her hair around his forefinger, tugging her closer.

"Jake?"

"You are beautiful," he whispered, his attention suddenly snapping from her face to the window. "And a damn distraction." He shoved her to the ground. "Something's on the edge of the tree line."

CHAPTER 26

JAKE SWORE TO HIMSELF. HE'D SLIPPED. PRESSING HIS SHOULDER against the corner of the window, he peered outside. A shadow wove between the trees. It paused and then moved forward, casting a large black silhouette upon the grass. Jake exhaled. He hadn't even realized he'd been holding his breath.

"A bear."

Cassidy smiled. "Really?" She moved to stand beside him. "Wow. Take a look at that."

Jake leaned against the window and watched as a huge brown bear ambled into the sun. Less than two paces behind, a small cub followed. He glanced at Cassidy; her face sparkled with a wide smile. "You like bears?"

She winked. "I don't normally have the opportunity to study a grizzly."

Alarm snaked across his shoulder blades. "That's a grizzly?"

Cassidy grinned. "Uh-huh. Isn't she beautiful?" She pointed out the window. "See the heavy mane of hair framing her face and the light color of her hide? If you weren't certain about the size, that alone would mark her as a grizzly. The black bear is smaller in stature, more prominent in these parts and slightly less aggressive. She'd tear your head off in a second if she thought you threatened her or her cub."

"Okay, then. We'll just stay right here."

Cassidy laughed, causing a sudden blast of desire to strike his gut. What the hell was the matter with him? "As soon as the bears leave, I think we should dress and head out of here." Jake walked over to the refrigerator and retrieved his cell phone from the top, where he'd stashed it next to the medical kit.

"But to where?" She turned and stared at him. "Did you see the heavy line of smoke coming from the north? I don't think there's any way we'll be able to make it back to that house and cabin. And we certainly won't be able to pick around the ashes without proper equipment and gear." She frowned at him. "Is it working?"

He flipped the phone open and verified he now had signal. "Are the bears still out there?"

Cassidy moved to the window and shook her head. "All clear."

Jake smiled. "Call Steve while I go check my bandage. I think it needs changing." He headed into the bathroom praying that by giving her some of her authority back she'd begin to trust him once more. Attraction wasn't an issue. The sadness tainting her eyes killed him. After a few moments of self-condemnation, he headed back to Cassidy.

"Steve answered," she said, cocking her head and gazing at him thoughtfully. "After locking on the signal, he thermal imaged the area. There's no sign of that guy chasing us. But he clearly saw a whole horde of firefighters battling the flames beyond that small ridge to our north. Luckily, the fire is being blown away from our location. He thinks the roads will be passable in about five hours. At least, that's what the fire department indicated."

"What about the chopper?"

Cassidy shook her head. "Too risky. Water planes are working the air."

"So we wait?"

"Yes, I suppose we wait."

His insides burned, and Jake kicked himself for the path his hormones insisted on pursuing. "No bad guy?"

She swallowed and shook her head. "Nope."

"We're all alone? No way out of here?"

Cassidy shrugged. "We could hike south for thirty miles. There's a road that intersects with Route 89."

"That would take us roughly six hours, right?"

She nodded. "Seems silly to do that when Steve will be here within five."

"Yes, it does."

The heat in Jake's eyes tingled along every inch of her skin. Cassidy's pulse raced. He raised one brow and approached her. Jake growled something she couldn't make out, but with a flip of his wrist her blanket was off her body and on the closest bunk. All thought was obliterated when he pulled her hard against his chest.

She needed this. For once, Cassidy decided to relent to her emotions, seek what she desired. To hell with sanity. Her hands splayed against his chest, and she gazed into his eyes. The power that lay within their blue depths didn't frighten; it invigorated and caused heat to flare in places she'd forgotten ever existed.

"Cassidy," he whispered into her ear and nibbled her lobe. "You're killing me."

Oh, boy. She chuckled and rubbed her cheek against his skin. "Likewise."

Her senses spread, the scent of stacked firewood by the hearth and

Jake mingled into one. She'd never be able to make a fire without remembering this one . . . this human pyre his kisses ignited. Cassidy tugged at the edge of his towel, and it disappeared. Her hands explored, touching what she'd forbidden herself to consider possible.

Jake ran his hand through her hair, pausing her finger walk across his skin. She gazed into his face; desire and need mirrored the sparks and electricity coursing through her veins. Cassidy bit her bottom lip, running her tongue along the edge of her teeth.

His head dropped down, and his lips touched hers. Nipping and sucking in tiny pieces, his mouth commanded and directed. Jake's hands moved across her skin, caressing and exciting. He trailed tender kisses down her neck; then everything exploded. They were no longer two separate entities.

They twirled through the room, their shadows casting a sensual dance of entwined limbs. Cassidy inhaled, her breath catching as every touch of his hand seared and branded. Jake lifted her against his chest. He bent and swiped the towel off the floor, moving them toward the narrow bunk. His whispered words were lost against her skin.

Cassidy sank into the mattress, surrendering to the demands of her body. No more thoughts; only action. She gazed into Jake's eyes, reached for him, and for the first time in forever submitted to a power greater than her mind. Jake moved slowly; her eyes fluttered closed as she soaked in the pleasure of their unity.

"Cassidy." He nuzzled her neck.

"Don't talk," she murmured.

His chest rumbled with laughter, sweat glistening and mixing with hers. She moved her hips and lost herself in the essence of Jake. Her mind and body blasted beyond the border of reality, careening her through wave after wave of pleasure.

Jake collapsed beside her, pulling her into his embrace. Cassidy fought for air, the emotion that ricocheted inside her chest difficult to absorb. Jake kissed her temple. He placed a knuckle beneath her chin, forcing her to gaze into his eyes. "That was more than physical." His eyes darkened, and the ramifications of their actions and his response alarmed and warmed her heart.

Cassidy tilted her head and stared at anything but his face. "I don't know how we fit."

Jake laughed; it filled the cabin and made her smile. "I thought we fit just fine."

She shoved his shoulder and risked a glance at his face, the sparkle of humor that glittered in his eyes a more familiar sight than the expression before. "You know what I mean."

"I do?"

"Well, what I meant to say is in my head. I just haven't let it out yet." More laughter and this time she joined him. Cassidy couldn't believe what a moron she was being. "It's complicated."

"Only as complicated as you want it to be, Cassidy." He bent down and rubbed his lips against hers. "We have some minor details to work out, but I bet there'll be a day when you turn to me and fall into my arms. No second guessing. No troubled eyes."

Cassidy pushed a lock of hair off his face. "I doubt it." She grinned when he growled his outrage.

Jake nipped at her earlobe, sending shivers racing up and down her spine. "Face it. I've gotten to you."

She sighed and snuggled closer for warmth. "I can't argue with that, Jake Anderson." Her heart skipped a beat, and she bit her bottom lip. This couldn't be happening. She needed to rein in her emotions. "We're moving too fast."

Jake rolled his eyes. "Lord have mercy, woman, is it going to kill you to let loose a bit?"

Cassidy offered him a small smile and ran her finger along the edge of his jaw. The scratchy prick of his afternoon shadow felt sexy and dangerous and way too intimate. "Yes."

He touched his lips to hers and breathed her name against her mouth, sending a rush of emotion through her system. She suddenly felt heated and flushed and entirely uncomfortable. This wasn't desire or lust he aroused; it was more. And alien. And scary.

"Rest, Sunshine." He pulled the blanket around her shoulders and draped his leg over hers. The comfort and heat coupled with her emotional and physical exhaustion did her in. Cassidy surrendered to oblivion, frowning as she held tightly to the only solid thing in her life. Jake.

She resisted the final pull of sleep, reminding herself this didn't mean she needed to be in love. The feel of Jake's skin beneath her hand was simply a comfort, something physical and nothing more than that. A thought rolled to the forefront of her mind, insisting she was incapable of simply having sex. Cassidy yawned, pushed it away, and finally relented to weariness.

Robert leaned past Nick and grabbed the bottle of fifty-year-old scotch. Nick watched as he poured himself two fingers and cradled the thick, crystal glass in his hand. The door of the limousine opened, allowing a thin streak of light into the dim interior. Drew Sharpe climbed in, eyed Robert's glass, and seated himself beside Nick.

"I have the environmental report. I forged Dr. Lowell's signature."

Nick hid a smirk as Robert ignored Drew's envious stare at his scotch. "Not important now. What about the survey? Do you have that?"

Drew pursed his lips and shook his head. "Not yet. I'm still looking. I've widened the search, as you suggested earlier, to include her computer and its components." He cast a quick glance at Nick and frowned. "The media's done well. She'll not be able to make a move without us knowing."

Nick growled, finding it hard to sustain his distance. "Let me eliminate her."

Robert swore beneath his breath and glared at Nick. "No. I've altered the plan. I need her back in the delta."

Drew scooted forward and adjusted his tie. "Nigeria? I thought you wanted her arrested and disqualified as a reliable scientist. Haven't we accomplished that?"

A wide smile curved Robert's lips. "I think pretty Miss Lowell deserves to witness the future of the Niger Delta up close and personal."

Shaking his head, Drew sat back, his body smacking into the leather of the seat. "You can't do that. She'll die for sure."

Robert pointed a finger at Drew and clucked. "Exactly. And infect others before she dies initiating my plan. That land belongs to me."

Drew inhaled sharply. "I never agreed to this level of danger."

Robert glanced quickly at Nick and nodded once. Nick grinned, excitement bubbled in his chest, then he stilled and inhaled. With an indiscernible move of his arm to the left, he reached over and snapped Drew's neck with a quick jab of his elbow. The heat of the kill flooded his system, sending him into a state he considered better than sex. He laughed and shoved Drew's body away from him.

"Now you do." Robert sighed, then tilted his head back and joined Nick's laughter.

CHAPTER 27

Jake splashed cold water on his face. It ran in thin streams across his cheekbones and onto his bare chest, causing him to shiver.

He wasn't proud of the reflection in the mirror. He'd broken his own code of ethics and become emotionally involved with a suspect. With a flick of his wrist, he traced a large bull's-eye on the surface of the mirror. "Way to go, Anderson." Black Stripe came first, and there'd be no disclosing unnecessary details of this mission or baring his soul for her forgiveness. If she knew he still considered Black Stripe top priority, she'd consider the act of wrapping her fingers around his neck and squeezing until he stopped breathing rather lenient.

Jake exited the small bathroom. Cassidy lay sprawled on the bunk, her hair fanned across her face and hiding the curve of lips he'd become very familiar with. The gentle rise and fall of her chest indicated she slept. Padding quietly, he was careful not to disturb her. With a towel wrapped back around his waist, Jake left the cabin to check on their clothes.

It was late afternoon and the sun had dropped behind the tree line, no longer shining its warmth on their garments. The burning forest fire perfumed the air with a pleasant smoky pine scent, and if you forgot the damage and danger it represented it was almost soothing.

Their clothes were dry. Boots, however, still squished with retained water. Nothing could be done about that. Gathering their things up and turning toward the cabin, the door creaked open and Cassidy walked toward him wrapped in her blanket. She smiled, a light blush touching her face. Her curls cascaded down her back, a breathtaking tangle of gold.

"Hey there, beautiful." Jake's gut twisted painfully. His instincts told him she held back vital information. Cassidy's predicament shot a new angle on his investigation. There was more here at stake than her reputation. Jake's lips curled up in a half smile. Somewhere buried beneath all the trivial facts in her brain was the answer. He was confident she knew more than she realized. Uncovering the nature of the relationship between New World Petroleum and ZEBRA relied on determining what those facts were. "Your clothes are dry," he said and tossed her stuff over.

She dropped her blanket and dressed, giving him a cheeky grin as he whistled between his teeth. Jake paused a moment and watched her graceful moves; the way she flipped her hair back and knotted it without the aid of a hair clip amazed him. It was a messy mane, but the soft curls that escaped framed her face like an angel's halo.

She snapped her fingers and broke the spell. "That look in your eyes, Romeo, isn't going to help us move forward."

Chuckling, he followed her example and tugged on his jeans and shirt, immediately feeling more in control.

"What's so funny?"

He winked. "Nothing. Just thinking to myself that it's much better to be wearing jeans when in dangerous situations."

She smiled and walked over, entwining her fingers with his. His heart stopped and then started with a rapid beat that had him swearing silently. He reached up and twirled a stray strand of her hair around his finger. "Cassidy, we need to talk." Jake inhaled and felt sick to his stomach. He sat down and pulled her onto his lap.

"I know. I thought of something." She nestled between his legs and he wrapped his arms around her, holding her tight.

"What?"

"We need to determine the connection between Sharpe and Cole."

Jake nodded. "We've been working that angle for quite some time without any success." He gazed at her with steady eyes.

"You think I know?"

"What were the geologists doing for you?" Jake didn't like the sudden evasive expression that crossed her face. He felt a spark of anger.

"Trying to prove that Port Harcourt was sinking."

Jake pushed her off his lap and stood up. "And that was worth killing for?"

Cassidy stared at him as if he'd grown an additional head. "Why are you so angry?"

"Because you're not telling the truth." He inhaled a sharp breath as she gasped at his accusation, and tried to rein in his temper. "What are you hiding?"

She leapt to her feet and pointed a finger at his chest. "Don't think that because of our little romp in the cabin, you know me or can judge whether I'm telling the truth or not. Because you don't know me. And you can't judge what you don't know."

His cell phone rang, and he answered it with a curt hello. Listening to Steve on the other end gave him a momentary reprieve to calm his anger and think clearly. He flipped the phone shut and turned to face Cassidy.

"That was Steve. He's downloading coordinates for our rendezvous point. We need to get a move on; the hike will take us about an hour, and daylight is fading." Cassidy worried her bottom lip. He bent over and kissed her tenderly, easing the frown that wrinkled her brow.

"Sorry, Sunshine. You're right." He'd readjust his approach next time.

"Are you positive Charlie and David were not simply victims of the raid on the ZEBRA camp?"

He wrapped his arm around her shoulder and pulled her close. "I don't want to talk about this anymore." Jake flipped open his phone and read the coordinates. Following the built-in compass, he led them into the woods and away from a topic he no longer felt like tackling. If Cassidy still held this much resentment against him because of his deceit, he needed more time to gain her trust.

Cassidy understood Jake's anger. But, right now, it made absolute sense to her to remain quiet regarding her concerns about Charlie and David. The geological survey was the only trump card she held. Running her fingers across the smooth bark of a quaking aspen, she traipsed after him. She grinned as he stepped over a fallen log, his jeans tightening perfectly across his butt.

He glanced back at her and winked. That prompted her stomach to tense and an uneasy tap dance of attraction to lodge in her gut. She bit her lower lip. "I'm starving."

"For?" he asked.

"Food." She laughed when his shoulders dropped.

"Damn. I thought we'd have a little quickie right here in the middle of nowhere."

"That sounds appealing. Just think, chiggers and ticks and all sorts of funky earth creatures can join us. I think we'd better refocus our minds on the nightmare that has become my life. I know you think I'm holding back, but I'm not. We have to consider what our options are."

Jake shrugged and held a branch back for her. "Okay. How about the level of involvement of our fearless leader, Drew Sharpe? Why would he aid in the warrant issue?"

"I have no clue." Cassidy accepted his hand as he guided them through a narrow pass. "He's always supported everything I do. And he, for one, should know I couldn't have brought a virus back. For crying out loud, I didn't even receive my bag until I'd been home for a week."

Her boots were still wet, and her socks rubbed a raw spot on the side of her foot. Night hadn't fully settled. She breathed deeply in an attempt to smooth out her emotions. The woods held that odd glow that she always associated with the gloaming. It was her favorite time of day. She could feel the earth sigh in relief as the heat of the sun diminished and the cool embrace of the evening beckoned those afraid of the light.

They made their way up a steep incline, and the trees began to thin. Cassidy glanced over her shoulder and paused, soaking in the view. Yellowstone River flowed in the distance. It wound its way through thick groves of lodgepole pines, then spread in a wide path of blue ice before twisting around a bend and disappearing from view.

Jake was directly behind her and turned to follow her line of vision.

"This land takes my breath away. You can almost step back in time to the era of the fur trappers like Jim Bridger and Osborne Russell. The thousands of trails that wind themselves through this region allow us an unusual perspective into the past, don't you think?"

He tilted his head. "You mean a time before terror filled the world in the form of toxins and bullets? Yes, I can certainly appreciate the appeal of that."

"Did you know we were the first to use biological warfare? We handed the Indians blankets contaminated with small pox and wiped out entire tribes. I guess man has always tiptoed along the edge of the evil canyon."

Jake sighed as if caught in the clutches of indecision. With a quick swipe of his arm, he pulled her roughly against his chest, kissing her mouth. His lips seared and burned a wide path of desire that sparked every nerve ending in her body. She clung to his shoulders, unsure of how to respond. His kisses were angry; then they faded into a tender caress, singing to her heart. Jake pulled away slowly, inhaled a deep breath, and walked past her.

The thump of rotor blades intruded upon the wilderness and snapped her out of the stupor he'd left her in. She followed Jake through the last line of trees and into the clearing, where the chopper lights flashed in the distance.

She pressed her hand against her chest. Pain curled within, making it difficult to breathe. And she didn't know why. She didn't understand the tears that burned her eyes or the despair that suddenly tied her guts in knots. But she'd be a fool not to recognize the emotional wall that existed between her and the only man to ever push beyond her defenses and open a door into a realm of existence Cassidy thought only belonged in fairy tales and romance novels.

Jake knew it was over. If not this second, then it would be within the hour. He needed to use all measures at his disposal to determine the knowledge she withheld.

Striding toward the helicopter, he nodded at Steve. Jake signaled for him to move to the passenger seat with a point of his finger, and climbed behind the controls. "She's holding back" is all he said. They waited for Cassidy to catch up. She walked slowly across the clearing, her hips swaying in unison with the gentle breeze that moved the trees.

He allowed her the time to collect herself. She wasn't ignorant, and he was certain she'd understood the meaning of his kiss. He frowned. At least he thought she did. Did he properly convey *"I am who I am. Sorry."*

"Where have you set up base camp?" Jake focused his attention on work and not his heart.

Steve cleared his throat and handed him a sheath of papers. "I've successfully commandeered the plane. Valerie has left Yellowstone and returned to headquarters. They've been instructed to search the building and network for whoever the mole is."

Jake glanced up sharply from reading the press releases Steve had provided. "Mole?"

"Sure. This is an inside job. You'd have to have pretty high clearance within ZEBRA to know the details that were leaked to the press, right?"

"Sharpe did it, right?"

"Colonel Price believes he's not acting alone."

"Is that how this was done? By the press?" Jake sighed. "It just keeps getting better. Did you bring the gear I asked you to?"

"Yeah."

Cassidy climbed into the back of the helicopter. "Where to now?" she asked, crossing her legs and sinking against the wall.

Jake glanced over his shoulder. He cursed silently at the dull glaze to her eyes and sudden demeanor of defeat. Frowning, he guessed he'd conveyed a different message with his kiss than the one he'd meant to. "We're going north. If you have the energy, I'd like to snoop around that property that exploded on us."

"I have the energy."

Steve twisted in his seat and whispered something to Cassidy. Her light laughter sparked a wave of jealousy. He flipped the ignition switch and lifted them into the air.

He felt Cassidy grip the back of his seat, but she didn't say a word. Another bad omen.

Steve spouted directions, and within fifteen minutes they crested a rise and faced a blackened and scarred corner of Earth. No one spoke. They exited the helicopter and moved to retrieve the axes and other paraphernalia Jake requested. Each person grabbed a small green duffel bag containing flashlights, evidence containers, and an instant camera.

The fire had moved past this zone hours previously. A soft rain began to fall, hitting the ground with a sizzle and kicking up a fine mist. "I think the cabin was in that direction," Cassidy said. She led the way past the charred remains of the main house.

"Steve, take watch. I don't want to be in anyone's crosshairs."

"Ten-four, Captain." Steve jogged to the left, his gun stretched out at arm's length. He scoped the tree line and then moved toward the shore.

Cassidy glanced over her shoulder. "Captain? I can't get used to that."

Jake didn't need this now. "Just think of Kangaroo. Come on, Sunshine, let's see what was so damn important it needed blowing up." The silence irritated Jake. It was a testament to all that the evil hand of man ruined. After days of having his senses awakened to the power of the wild by Cassidy, he became acutely aware of the lack of its existence in the wake of the fire.

They made their way to the pile of ashes that sat in what Jake considered the general vicinity of the cabin. He walked around its perimeter and stepped back toward the angle of the river. "I think this is definitely it."

"Okay." Cassidy kicked a pile of charred debris and moved in a slow circle. She paused and glanced up at Jake. "Forensics 101?"

He scanned their surroundings and nodded. "It shouldn't be much different than how we approach unusual kill sites." Shutting down all personal involvement, Jake stepped into his professional skin. "How do you want to proceed—spiral, grid, or zone?"

"I think we should begin in the center, then expand our spiral outward."

Jake nodded. "Go for it, kiddo." He followed her into the heart of the debris, scanning the ground for anything unusual.

Cassidy dropped to one knee and examined a small circular object. "I think I've found something." She stood, turned toward him, and disappeared in a cloud of ashes.

———

Cassidy felt the earth give way and reached her arms out to find something to stop her fall. They gripped nothing but air. She fell downward, landing with a jaw-jarring thud. Her heart beat hard against her chest, and she fought back a tide of panic.

"Cassidy?" Jake's voice rang loud and clear, but she couldn't see a damn thing.

She patted the ground around her, searching for the bag she'd been carrying. Nothing. But her fingers latched onto the object she'd retrieved from above. "Down here." A thin beam of light flickered from above, and she glanced up.

"Are you okay?"

Cassidy did a mental check and figured that besides the shock of performing an Alice-down-the-rabbit-hole stunt, she was fine. Her back and butt would be a canvas splashed with black and blue, but vanity wasn't one of her stronger characteristics. "I'll live. I've lost my bag. Can you toss down a flashlight?"

"Hold on; let me get Steve." She heard Jake's voice echo above. Cassidy decided against any form of movement until she had a visual of her surroundings. "Okay, I'm lowering Steve's entire bag."

Cassidy felt rather than saw the bag float down from above. When her hands touched the canvas, she dragged it to her. Searching within, her fingers felt the cool metal of the flashlight. She flicked the light on and spun it around the interior of her cave. "Wow."

Twisted metal bent dramatically at uneven angles, glittering in the narrow beam of light. She smelled damp earth and flipped her flashlight to the left. Silt trickled from the walls in slow streams of grain and rock, pooling on the ground in bumpy mounds.

"What?"

"This appears to be some kind of lab, which goes right along with the lid of a petri dish I found topside." She flipped the light up toward the area where she'd fallen and smiled when it lit Jake's face. "You look like you've lost your favorite toy."

He grinned and cocked his head. "I have."

"Go grab a rope from the Jeep, Chuckie. I'm going to investigate this place."

He winked. "Be careful. This entire area is unstable."

She nodded and turned her attention to her surroundings. It was obvious that whatever had been used to destroy the cabin had originated from this area. She kicked aside fallen wood and skimmed the light across the cracked surface of granite. The counters and cabinets were twisted and mangled, and there was glass everywhere. Careful of her steps, she ran a finger across the edge of what appeared to be a cryogenic storage container.

A soft thud startled her, and she spun around. Jake stood in the beam of her flashlight. "Didn't want you to get lonely," he said.

"This is a state-of-the-art laboratory."

"Fifteen feet below the surface and nicely hidden." Jake clipped a small halogen lamp to a piece of suspended metal. It lit the entire interior. "Very suspicious."

She nodded to her left. "Take a look at that. The way the wall divides these two areas and the amount of glass on the floor, it'd be my guess that we're facing a negative airflow chamber."

Jake scooped something from the rubble. "Mechanical arm?"

"That confirms that supposition."

"Hey, you two, I think you need to get out of there." Steve's head popped through the opening. Cassidy's eyes widened as she felt the earth move and heard a loud wail emanate from the cracks in the foundation.

Jake grabbed her hand and shoved her at the rope. "Go!"

She scrambled upward, moving hand over hand as the walls of the laboratory cracked and gave way. Her heart beat fast. "Hurry up, Jake!" she called, praying he was right behind her. Steve's hand reached down and he pulled her through the hole, pushing her off the blackened mound.

"Run!" Jake's voice reached her from the edge of the hole, and she spun on her heels racing away from the decimated cabin. The ground rumbled and shook, knocking her off balance. Falling to her knees, she twisted around and watched in horror as dust and ash rose behind the running figures of Jake and Steve. The earth shrieked one last time and then collapsed upon itself, leaving nothing behind but a crater full of soil and cinders.

"I guess that's that," Steve panted and dropped to the ground next to her.

Jake kicked the ground and swore violently. "That was probably our only lead to whatever is happening in Yellowstone."

"We'll have to excavate," Steve said.

Cassidy turned toward him. "And how are we going to get approval for that without alerting NWP that we know about this lab?" She didn't like the look that crossed between Jake and Steve. "What do you two know that I don't?"

Jake reached down and helped her to her feet. "Nothing, Sunshine. Let's get out of here."

"Where to?"

Steve laughed. "I've confiscated the plane."

Cassidy raised a brow. "You have? I'm impressed."

They headed back toward the helicopter. She needed a shower. Glancing at the two men next to her, she sniffed the air. They all needed a shower. Cassidy figured among the three of them, they carried about five buckets' worth of black residue.

Jake leaned back from the pilot's seat. "You okay, Sunshine?" His eyes softened and for a brief instant she thought he was going to reach over and wash her troubles away with one of his mind-blowing kisses, but he moved back.

Cassidy glanced down, hiding her disappointment. "I'm fine." She didn't touch him even though every fiber in her being wanted to reach out and hold on.

CHAPTER 28

EDWARD STRETCHED. HIS BACK CRACKED, AND HE TWISTED his neck to ease the strain of the past hours spent on the computer. He peered into a small portable microscope and studied the sample of blood he'd extracted from the dead wolf on the banks of the river.

His eyes skimmed toward the suitcase containing the vials of CPV-19, and a deep biting pain of regret bunched in his chest. So close to success but still a league away. The consistency and level of coagulation puzzled him. Not to mention the physical mutation of that last wolf. He needed to isolate the result to the mutation of Fifth Disease and parvo, making certain that his modification technique didn't trigger any of the symptoms. Damn the board for rushing!

The hard drive on his computer hummed, but nothing transferred from the scope to the monitor. Edward disengaged the cable connecting the microscope to the computer and reattached it. He turned his computer off and rebooted. When his screen finally loaded, he kicked off the program that analyzed the genetic composition of the blood.

The results were then sent to another program created by Jason. It synthesized the progress of CPV-19 within both human and canine.

Edward waited. His computer screen flickered, dimmed, and then displayed the results in glaring red letters.

He leaned forward and rested his elbows on the table. Edward rubbed his face and pursed his lips, focusing on the ideas in his head. He picked up a pen and began jotting down notes.

Virus failed to act as desired.

Why?

Side effect of erythropoietin production.

Why?

DON'T KNOW.

Physical mutation evident.

Why?

"Because I'm a damn idiot," Edward yelled to his empty room.

He swore and kicked the leg of the table, causing his microscope to wobble. *Think, Edward, think.* His process of modifying the genetic composition succeeded, but the end result failed. Understood. He sighed and rubbed the back of his neck. This meant it hadn't failed 100 percent. *Right.* "Too damn bad you're dead, Jason. I sure could use your help right now."

Keep going.

These were side effects that inhibited his claim of successfully controlling genetic modification of a virus and accurate calculation of its interaction with cells.

Edward pulled up a new window on the computer and retrieved another file. He ran his finger down a mathematical diagram. "There you are." He tapped the screen. The numbers he studied disclosed the cell division rate of CPV-19-infected red blood cells. The virus spread at an expected rate for a period of time, then escalated to five times the norm.

This is what had bothered him when Jason had rudely interrupted yesterday. He glanced at the case containing vials of CPV-19.

It was deadlier than he'd originally anticipated.

Flipping back to the other window, he noted the human figure infected with CPV-19 showed an increased production of erythropoietin from the kidneys. The mutation of CPV-2/B-19 triggered this.

Why?

Edward moved the mouse to the right and watched the virtual progression of the disease. The heart ceased its ability to pump the thickened blood, its arteries collapsing beneath the pressure. Veins containing the coagulated cells forced the gelatinous substance out of every orifice in the body much the same as the geysers releasing their heated water.

Success was still years away.

Yes, he'd managed to alter the genetic composition of a virus and accomplish the impossible. He'd forced the virus to recognize specific cells and attach itself victoriously; however, he hadn't eliminated the appearance of side effects.

He hadn't discovered a miracle. He'd created a monster.

Hitting a series of key commands, Edward tilted his head and studied the virus as it spread through the canine system. Same as the virtual display on the human diagram. Thickened blood, arteries collapsing, artery overload. Frowning, he leaned forward and studied his monitor.

He pushed back from the table and stood up, exhausted and frustrated. Edward walked to the front door and opened it, inhaling the crisp air of early evening. The sun had long since disappeared, but the busy street remained bathed in the glow of twilight. Darkness remained an hour or so away.

Disappointment rattled his nerves. Edward verified the access card to his room was in his pocket and stepped onto the concrete walkway. The lure of fast food drew him down the stairs. He turned and glanced back at his room, pondering what lay within.

He'd created a damn good biological weapon but hadn't managed to achieve his goal of scientific brilliance. Edward cracked his knuckles. After dinner, he'd attach his findings to an e-mail and send it to Dr. Lowell.

He had no patent, at least not yet. What he needed to do was save his own life. There was no doubt in Edward's mind that when the board discovered his location, they'd be here to collect the virus and eliminate his existence.

He prayed Cassidy Lowell had connections in high places and would be able to prevent his murder. An idea niggled at Edward's brain. Something about Fifth Disease. The answer to deactivating the virulence of CPV-19 lay there. He just needed time to figure it out. And that was one thing he didn't have.

Edward glanced at his watch and then back at the room where a metal briefcase of death lay waiting. He swallowed against the bile that rose in his throat.

What if his future patent was contained within those glass tubes? Edward turned and headed toward the golden arches. If he were a stronger man, he'd ignore that temptation and destroy CPV-19.

Cassidy shuffled in the tiny confines of the shower. Hot water pounded from the shower head, pelting her body with stinging drops. It soothed. A new confliction regarding the geological survey began to plague her mind.

Black Stripe. Was it really all that it appeared to be? It seemed so; however, the anguish in Anna's dying face never ceased to haunt her nights. If Black Stripe were all good and patriotic, wouldn't they have rescued everyone that night? Cassidy turned the nozzle, determined to save a small amount of hot water for the men as self-defense against their stinkiness.

She slipped out of the shower and quickly donned clean jeans and a shirt. How her things continued to show up at every location amazed and astonished. Cassidy dug into the interior of her makeup bag and found the flashcard containing the geological survey. Not wanting it on her, she hid it once more. Tonight, when everyone slept, she'd slip this into the computer and study its contents.

Her eye caught a pink cylindrical container. Smiling, Cassidy once more retrieved the flashcard from her makeup bag and slipped it into her tampon case, a safe male deterrent.

A flash of Jake's tenderness invaded her troubled mind. *Don't go there.*

Cassidy inhaled and exhaled several times. "Not going there."

Wrapping her fingers around the small latch on the bathroom door, she pushed it open and stepped into the alcove that surrounded the back of the plane.

She moved forward, convincing herself she could play this game of charades. Cassidy glanced at Steve and refused to dwell on the fact that he was also Black Stripe. It was too complicated and horrifying to consider. Sitting down at one of the computers, she tapped the keys and logged in. "I'm checking my e-mail."

Steve walked over and sat next to her. "Good idea. Also pull up the news articles regarding your arrest warrant."

She frowned. "News articles?"

Jake joined them, handing her a bottle of water. "Apparently the media received the information before the law enforcement officers." He sat across from her, stretching his legs out and crossing them at the ankles.

Jake didn't fool her. His fingers were in constant motion, and the corner of his right eye twitched. It made her feel a bit more in control that his deception caused him stress.

Cassidy wrapped her professionalism around her emotions and decided to move past the brief moment of physical weakness. Sex didn't constitute a relationship; therefore, the time in the cabin need not be a complication or distraction.

Focused on the computer and the tangle of lies that threatened her career, she glanced at Steve and he nodded toward the laptop. "Okay." Cassidy searched for her name, and a string of Web sites lit up the screen. Clicking on the first one, she scanned the article. "Not a lot of meat here; just accusations." She pushed a stray lock of hair off her forehead. "It says I brought this unknown virus back from Africa and infected the wolves at Yellowstone. No info on how, what, or when."

Steve peered over her shoulder. "Not surprising."

Cassidy read several more articles without gaining enlightenment, then clicked on her e-mail icon. The frustration of being out of the loop, not in charge, alienated from everything familiar, sent a sudden flood of alarm through her body. She broke into a cold sweat and pushed back from the computer, shaking out her arms to relieve the sudden numb tingling of a black reality.

Jake placed his hand on her knee, kicking off an entirely opposite reaction from the icy grip of panic. "You okay?"

Cassidy swallowed, closed her eyes, and counted to ten. "Fine." She stretched her fingers out and opened and closed them a few times, pretending to be working out stiff joints. "Just tired." She leaned forward, concentrated on her screen, and willed his presence beside her into nothing more than a shadow. Cassidy clicked on her e-mail icon; an unfamiliar name glared on the screen. "This is odd." Her heart raced as she skimmed through the e-mail, and a sudden rush of excitement blanketed all other emotion.

Jake moved closer. "What?"

She hit the print button and glanced up from her screen. "Some guy called Edward Fiske has sent me an e-mail claiming responsibility for this virus." Jake reached behind his chair and snagged the pages of the printer. "And his claims sound rather legitimate."

Jake studied the printout and glanced at her. His forehead was creased in a deep frown, and he shook his head slowly. "He says that he developed it during his research for mutating a virus capable of attaching to red blood cells. Why would he do that?"

Cassidy sighed, disappointed by Jake's words. But he was right: the solution couldn't possibly be this simple. "It's probably just some lunatic trying to earn his ten seconds of fame but . . ." She picked up the e-mail and read it once more, then began a quick search on the net. "If he were capable of attaching specific genetic qualities to our red blood cells, he could work miracles within the immune deficiency field of science. The scientific approach is valid. I'm not willing to dismiss this yet."

She flipped through the search engine results, scanning information and trying to connect the dots. "Makes perfect sense to me," Cassidy stated. "I'm searching for him now. But if you think about it, he's isolated essentially one disease. They operate differently from human to canine." She glanced up at Jake, her eyes widening in understanding. "He made them act as one. If he's for real, this guy discovered a way to force the virus to recognize specific cells. That's amazing."

"What would be more amazing is if we could find him. Anything?"

Cassidy glanced back at her computer screen. "He's definitely a biologist. Scientific America has a brief bio on him."

"Any idea where he is now?"

Cassidy tried not to snort. "Why not just ask me for a cure to this virus? I haven't a clue as to his location." She paused, then held up her hand. "Let me see that e-mail again." Scanning the last page, Cassidy handed it back to Jake. "The e-mail states he'll contact me tomorrow."

Jake picked up his phone and dialed a number. He glanced at Cassidy, who raised her eyebrows, questioning his call. "I'll trace the origins of the e-mail."

She nodded and returned to her internet files. "It looks like for the past several years he was funded by a board of corporate investors." Digging deeper into the net and Edward Fiske's background, Cassidy discovered a link to a Web site. It was from a scientific conference dating back a few years with pictures of the attendees and their groups. Her eyes rested on one particular face.

Their first piece of the puzzle. "Bingo."

CHAPTER 29

CASSIDY HIT THE PRINT BUTTON. RUNNING HER HANDS through her hair and shaking her shoulders to loosen tight neck muscles, she stood up and walked around the chairs to the printer. "Boys, I'd like to introduce you to Robert Cole." She picked up the printed pages and handed them off to Jake, an excited giggle escaping her lips.

Jake accepted the sheet displaying the picture she'd discovered. "New World Petroleum's president?"

She grinned and nodded, suddenly feeling validated. It wasn't imagination or supposition. The facts were in Jake's hand; this entire nightmare centered around NWP and Robert Cole. "I see you've done your homework, Dr. Anderson." She grabbed the black marker Jake had used earlier and drew a line beneath where he had written New World Petroleum on the whiteboard and scribbled the words *Robert Cole* in large letters. "It says here that NWP's board of directors is insistent on maintaining a strong presence in the world's scientific development." She paused and glanced up at Jake. "This would explain their involvement at Yellowstone. They'd use that as a cover for Fiske's lab, right?"

Jake nodded, a thoughtful expression wrinkling his forehead. "Perhaps."

"We have NWP's connection with the virus, but we don't have ZEBRA's connection anywhere." She chewed on her bottom lip, tapping the marker against the metal arm of a chair. Excitement incited by finally uncovering at least one mystery made her fidget.

"Are we confident that ZEBRA has crossed to the dark side?" Steve asked.

Jake shrugged and rose to his feet. His calmness and matter-of-fact approach at the information irritated her.

She spoke up. "The answer is close. I can feel it." But uncertainty had her biting her bottom lip.

Jake glanced at her briefly, then turned to study the whiteboard. He moved nearer to her; the electricity of his presence escalated her restlessness. "Colonel Price is convinced there's a link. He didn't elaborate any further."

"Well then . . . " Cassidy tossed the marker at Jake. "I think you need to confer with your colonel because we're at a dead end." The focus on work helped her immensely. Emotions and hurt feelings had no place within an investigation, and she relished the fact that unraveling the puzzle allowed her a few moments of escape from the uncomfortable memories of the cabin that kept parading around her head.

"Not so dead, Sunshine. We have a lead on the virus."

"There were two attachments to the e-mail from Fiske. I'll pull them up and see if they have anything to do with a cure. Although based on their file names, I think they contain more mysteries."

Steve waved her back into her seat, and she clicked on the first file, titled "Anomaly." Cassidy read the diagram several times, processing the details and analyzing the facts. "I think from these numbers and notes in the addendum that our infamous Dr. Fiske didn't succeed with his experiment." She double clicked on the next file, titled "Failed Results."

Cassidy motioned for Jake and Steve to close in around the computer. She ignored the jump in her pulse when Jake rested his hand on her shoulder but she didn't shrug off his touch, instead allowing the warmth from his fingers to ease the tension in her shoulders. *Stupid me.* It wasn't as if he personally was the one who had yanked her from the Niger Delta and left Anna behind. What if he was the good guy he seemed to believe himself to be? Frowning, Cassidy moved her shoulder away from his touch. Her line of thinking straying down a path she didn't want to take. He'd used her. Lied to her. Manipulated her.

This was not the beginning of a healthy relationship. But what about the chemistry? And his intelligence? And irritating humor? "Shut up," she said and then cringed when she realized she'd spoken out loud.

Steve bent his head to hide a grin, and she glared at him. "I didn't say a word," he said, raising his hands in protest.

Jake tapped her shoulder. "I can hear your brain revving into overtime. Care to fill us in?"

Cassidy gaped at him. He was reading her thoughts? "I'm not listening to myself right now, thank you very much."

A glint of amusement sparked in Jake's eyes, and she blinked back the traitorous response in her own. He leaned over her shoulder and tapped the computer screen. "Fill us in on what these diagrams mean."

"Yes, of course. That's exactly what I was thinking about." She dipped her head down, praying neither man could see the brilliant red that burned her cheeks. "This first diagram indicates a severe jump in the speed and voracity of the dividing blood cells." She flipped to the second screen. "And this baby shows us exactly what the outcome is of the rapidly dividing cells."

"Coagulation and bleeding out," Jake said.

"Right. My guess is that this wasn't intentional. It's a side effect."

Steve whistled through his teeth. "Curable?"

Cassidy shrugged. "I don't know. He didn't send enough data for me to analyze." She spun around and faced Jake. "He doesn't have any hypothesis regarding the physical traits of the wolves."

Jake touched the tip of his finger to her nose. "I do."

Her eyes widened in shock. "You do?"

Jake nodded and paced in a small circle. "The virus seems to have developed its own personality. Not only has it thickened the blood but it's triggered"—he paused to lay emphasis on his last word— "a mutation within the wolves."

Cassidy frowned. "Triggered?"

Grinning, Jake sat down beside her and whispered. "Recessive genes."

She smiled and wagged a finger at him. Smart man. "Like the werewolf?"

"Such silliness from a well renowned zoologist like yourself? Sunshine, I'm shocked."

Cassidy tilted her head and considered the avenue Jake's statement opened. It should have concerned her how easily she folded away her normal argumentative trait and adapted to his line of thinking, but it didn't. "Not silliness. Some believe that the birth of the werewolf legend is founded in a group of wolves born with a recessive gene." She waved her hands in the air to emphasize her next statement. "Not man to wolf and vice versa. But one that creates a bigger, more dangerous breed."

Steve leaned forward and studied the computer screen over Cassidy's shoulder. "But these wolves weren't born this way. They mutated."

Jake sighed. "It's possible."

Steve pushed back and walked to the other end of the seating area. "It'll take months to determine what gene has triggered these mutations."

Twisting in his seat, Jake faced Steve. "We don't have months."

Cassidy crossed her arms and wiggled her fingers, trying to tap out a rhythm of sense. "You're right. We've got to find Edward Fiske and discover a way to stop this thing from spreading. My take is that the gene research can be done later. It's not going to provide a key to anything right now. But the virus . . ." She sighed and stretched her arms to the ceiling. "That's got to be stopped." Cassidy glanced at Jake, ignoring the comfort and security his presence created. "Can you somehow get this to the CDC without ZEBRA or anyone searching for me finding out?"

Jake nodded. "I don't work for ZEBRA, Cassidy."

Her eyes widened. "You don't?" Another brick in the wall; one more reminder that he wasn't who she'd thought.

He tilted his head and smiled. "Well, in a roundabout way I do. But they don't sign my paychecks."

"Who does then?"

"Now if I tell you that, I'd have to kill you."

Cassidy glared at him, fighting a flash of loneliness. "Very funny. I suggest you keep your snide comments to yourself in the future, Dr. Anderson. You're already headlining my most-irritating-person-in-the-world list."

"I can't do anything about that, can I?"

She stretched her arms again battling back exhaustion and waggled the tips of her fingers, pulling and tugging on the kinks in her back to loosen her shoulders. "No. Don't even bother to try."

"Get some rest, Sunshine. It'll be a few hours before I can pull my team together."

"Where are we going?" If she rested, her mind and tug-of-war feelings might right themselves.

"To find ourselves a geneticist."

She yawned. "Good plan." Cassidy flipped the computer switch off and headed toward a more comfortable seat. A few hours of sleep would help to banish the emotional cobwebs clouding her head.

Cassidy twisted her neck to the left, trying to break free from the chains of her nightmare. Scared. A buzzing noise tickled her ears, and she whimpered. Fear flashed, and the pressure of being held stole her breath. "No. No." Blue eyes pierced her heart with a vicious jab, and she bolted upright, wide awake and sobbing. Her forehead connected with a hard object, prompting a masculine grunt to emanate from above. Pain slashed through her temple and blurred her vision.

"Cassidy, be quiet."

She heard Jake's words, and it was a few seconds before she realized he held her pinned to the chair, his hand gently covering her mouth. Cassidy blinked twice and focused on a pair of vibrant blue eyes. The curve of his cheekbone and set of his chin familiar and frightening.

"It was you," she said when he released the light pressure on her mouth.

"Be quiet. There's someone outside the plane."

The meaning behind his words didn't penetrate. "You killed Anna." More shock. More disillusionment.

His eyes hardened, and an angry fire burned within their depths. "So you've said."

"No," she argued. "I never thought it was you." A tear slipped from the corner of her eye. She didn't think there was anything left in her heart to break.

She was wrong.

Cassidy gazed into his face, unable to break eye contact. The emotion that flickered within the depths of his eyes triggered a traitorous response from deep within her soul, but she refused to acknowledge it. Didn't want to consider what it meant. Who was he?

"I thought you'd already guessed it was me." He held his fingers to her lips. "Please be quiet. I've sent Steve to search the perimeter."

She turned her head to the side and dropped into silence. The only light in the plane emanated from tiny amber globes that lit either side of the center aisle. She needed to distance herself from Jake. He gripped her arm when she attempted to slide from beneath him.

"Don't move."

Gazing into his eyes, everything about him finally made sense. Her awareness of him went beyond the normal déjà vu experience. The feel of his hands upon her skin and rough edge of his cheek, his stance and arrogance all wrapped into the package of someone she'd targeted to despise.

Another tear followed the salty trail down the side of her face. "I believe my humiliation is complete."

"Cassidy, you don't know everything." His voice was low and hushed within the confines of the plane. He touched her chin with his thumb and dropped a tender kiss upon her lips. She fought the need to take more, taste more. "For whatever it's worth, that is real." Jake pulled her hand between them and placed her palm upon his chest. She felt the beat of his heart beneath her fingers. "And so is this."

"Captain?" Steve popped his head around the corner of the door and wagged his brows. "We're not alone."

Jake frowned and nodded. "Duh." He slid his body off Cassidy and reached down to pull her to her feet. "How many?"

"Only shadows, but it appears to be about a half dozen."

She followed him down the aisle, ducking to peer out one of the windows. "I don't see anybody."

Jake's shoulders were tight and his body bent forward in preparation for attack at a moment's notice. He was tense and on high alert, which scared Cassidy. "I don't think they'd be parading around in plain sight." Jake frowned and held her hand. "Stay close."

Cassidy glanced down at the vice grip he had on her and rolled her eyes. "Like I have a choice?"

He tossed her one of his snarky grins and winked. "Not if I have anything to say about it."

They reached the top of the stairs, and Jake peered out. He surveyed the area then slipped away from the opening, pointing at Steve and signaling where he wanted them positioned. Jake turned in her direction and pointed to the hatch that led into the compartment below the plane. "Go!"

Before Cassidy could react, a blinding light shot through the door. Jake pushed her to the ground, rolling them both back toward the other side of the cabin. Men charged through the door. Cassidy heard a familiar voice, and fear stole her breath.

"You make my job incredibly easy." An ominous ripple of masculine laughter filtered within the confines of the plane.

Cassidy turned to say something to Steve. His face was emotionless, anger twisting the warm brown of his eyes into hard wood. Nick Fowler slammed the butt of a machine gun into his temple, and Steve fell to the ground.

The brutality of the scene stunned her, and she struggled to calm her breathing before she hyperventilated. "Steve!" Cassidy reached for Jake but was yanked to her feet and blocked by a man who appeared from behind the plane door. His breath stank of stale beer and cigarettes. He leered at her, then spun her around and secured her hands behind her back with rough-edged rope.

Terror at being bound and incapacitated had her pulling against the cuffs. Her heart felt as if it were about to break out of her chest. She gasped and was slammed against the wall as Jake rushed Fowler. Her forehead snapped against a hard edge, bringing forth a flash of dark then thousands of shooting stars beneath her eyelids. Cassidy shook her head and blinked away the pain. The NWP lackey pointed a gun and fired.

Cassidy screamed. "Let go of me." A surge of emotion slammed against her chest, and she struggled against her restraints to reach Jake.

Foul breath hit her face-on. "Quit yer whining, bitch. He's not dead." Fowler gripped her arm painfully.

Shivers of relief cascaded down her back as she focused on the slumped body of Jake. There was a dart jutting out of his shoulder. A tranquilizer. Cassidy felt her knees buckle and leaned against the wall of the plane for support.

"We have time for a little fun?" The disgusting brute who'd secured her hands ground himself against her backside. She twisted around and planted a solid foot smack into his family jewels.

"Get off me." She spun on her heel and began another drop-kick, but Fowler intercepted her. He gripped the edge of her foot, twisted, and threw her flat on her back before she could retaliate. The restraints on her arms made an even battle ground difficult. "What," she gasped, "is going on?"

Fowler knelt and pushed her hair from her face. "Sorry, bitch. You should of just done as you were told in Africa."

Cassidy tamped down the burning terror that had her senses whirling and shook her head. Her heart pounded and adrenaline coursed through her veins, making clear thinking difficult. "You're behind the release of this virus into Yellowstone?"

"Stop whining." He bent forward and whispered against her cheek. Her stomach clenched, and she gagged. "You need to provide us with a bit of information, and when you do maybe you'll get to live."

"What information?"

He yanked her roughly to her feet and pushed her down the plane's exterior stairs. She stumbled against the railing, the cool metal biting into her arm. With a resolve that was entirely concocted, Cassidy moved confidently down the remainder of the metal steps. When she reached the bottom, he dragged her to the left. Her eyes widened at the sight of a military-looking helicopter.

She glanced around, searching for hope but found only deserted hangars. Her stomach heaved again as the dire situation ballooned into a full-fledged nightmare. No way out. Fowler picked her up and tossed her roughly onboard. She struggled to her feet and landed heavily on a wire mesh bench. Cassidy watched, stiff with terror, as Nick signaled to the men dragging Jake and Steve across the tarmac. She ran a million and one escape plans through her mind and discarded every single thought. *Don't panic.* But the wild beating of her heart and short breaths contradicted that statement.

Fowler reached down and pulled Jake onto a bench opposite her. She glanced at the line of blood dripping across his forehead, her fingers itching to feel his pulse. His vulnerability undid her. She stared at him and willed him awake, wanting nothing more than to see that snarky grin light his face. But he didn't move, and she bit her bottom lip in despair.

"You see," Nick spoke in a matter-of-fact tone, interrupting her thoughts. She detected the hard anger that lay behind his words, and it chilled her. "There are things happening within the Niger Delta. No more will our country be dependent upon others. But you "—he shoved his rifle into her gut—"wouldn't write the fucking report the government wanted. Instead," he sighed, "you screeched about the dangers of oil production."

Cassidy began to fit the pieces of the puzzle together. "How much?"

"Money?" A man spoke from behind her, and Cassidy twisted in her seat to face him.

She tried not to gape, but the sudden appearance of New World's president scattered what little sense she'd been making of this situation. With a will she didn't know existed, Cassidy shut down her fear. The exposure of Cole's identity didn't bode well for her predicament. "Cole."

He laughed, and the rest of his men joined in. "It's not about the money, Dr. Lowell. It's about freedom from OPEC and the ever-rising fuel costs. It's about being in the forefront of the twenty-first century gold rush."

She closed her eyes and tamped down on a fresh bubble of terror. "So you're going to shoot me because I wouldn't write a damn report? Don't you think that's a bit extreme?"

He bent over and dropped a wet kiss on her cheek. She moved her head away, swallowing against the nausea his damp lips provoked. "I'm not going to kill you, sweetheart. I'll just offer you a helping hand out of the chopper."

"And them?" Cassidy nodded toward Jake.

"Them, too. After all, I'm not a monster. You should have some company during your slow death in the wilderness."

Cassidy furrowed her brow. What the hell did he mean? She was afraid to ask.

The silence of predawn was shattered by the rhythmic whirring of helicopter blades. Cassidy bent her head and whispered a soft prayer, calling on the soothing memories of her mother. The machine vibrated, and she dug her fingernails into her palm as it rose from the tarmac and swept into the sky. A blast of cold air snatched the ends of her sleep-tossed hair, whipping it around her head in Medusa-like tendrils.

She swore against the idiocy of not having refastened her hair the instant she'd awakened. Small details gained advantages. With her hands tied, there was nothing she could do about the thin strands of hair striking her face and blinding her.

Cassidy blinked and twisted her neck, clearing a mass of tangles from her eyes. She scanned the interior of the chopper, ignoring the lewd gestures and words being spouted by the occupants. *Think. Think. Think.* Four men dressed in black camouflage outfits sat on the narrow metal benches that flanked the interior of the helicopter. The largest and most threatening man was positioned directly to her left. Nick Fowler.

His eyes roamed across her body, stopping often at the curve of her neck. The fire within their bleak depths spoke of a lunacy Cassidy could only guess at. Death wasn't indifferent to him. It was a neighbor, a trusted friend.

Steve and Jake were directly in front of her across a narrow stretch of riveted metal. Jake's head lay slumped to the side, his hair hanging in matted clumps across his face. Cassidy worried her bottom lip. She ignored the fear that raked her heart at the thought of his death and convinced herself her concern lay solely in their combined safety.

Her stomach flipped as the chopper flew through the turbulent wind current of the Tetons. Cassidy swallowed and fought against the bile that rose in her throat. She glanced across the aisle. Steve sat next to Jake staring out the open door, his face hard and unreadable. She didn't recognize him. He held himself straight and still, no foot tapping or fidgeting. His quick smile and easy laugh were gone, replaced with anger and hatred. He glanced in her direction and shook his head, indicating she needed to remain quiet.

Cassidy's mind churned over the past few years. Glimpses and pockets of their numerous late-night chat fests whirled in her mind. She concentrated but found no trace or link to this side of him. This soldier.

Robert Cole sat on Steve's other side. He held a gun loosely upon his lap, pointing it directly at Jake's heart. Cole turned his head and stared at her. Cassidy didn't flinch, didn't offer a silent plea. She'd be damned before she laid her fear at his feet. His eyes were cold and flat. Another blast of air whisked through the doors and forced her to bend her head and block the stinging lashes of her hair.

She felt rather than heard Cole approach her. His black scuffed boots were less than six inches from her bench. He grabbed a fistful of hair and yanked her head back. Her eyes watered, and she glared defiantly into his face. "What?"

He didn't answer but gathered her hair, pulling and yanking on the wild locks. Robert stripped a bandana off his neck and secured the mess of golden curls on top of her head.

"I suppose I should say thanks, but somehow I don't think that was an act of kindness."

He grunted and motioned with a lift of his chin to the brute seated next to her. "Better, Nick?"

The strange man laughed bitterly, sending a sliver of fear down her spine. "If it hit my face one more time I was gonna shove her out that door ... now."

Cole shrugged. "Those aren't my orders."

"Fuck the orders."

"Fuck you." Cole turned and grabbed his gun from one of the other men's laps. He seated himself back in place, prodding the tip of the cold metal into Jake's stomach. The biologist didn't move.

Cole and Fowler debated softly, their attention temporarily averted from Cassidy. She swept her eyes across the interior of the helicopter, noting a cluster of bags at her feet. By their size and shape, she figured they were basic gear bags that contained flashlights and other miscellaneous small items. The why and what questions as to the necessity of these bags tickled her mind, but she shoved them away.

She moved her foot until it rested on top of the nearest bag. With slow purposeful twists of her ankle, the lumps beneath her boot moved around. They appeared long and rectangular, confirming her theory of flashlights and such.

Either that or it was a bagful of dynamite. Cassidy decided to take her chances that the bags were exactly what they appeared to be. Military gear backpacks.

Something told her the exit from the helicopter wasn't going to be an easy one. She inched toward the door and snuck her foot into the shoulder loop of the top backpack and then repeated her action on the one below. She tugged the bags closer; a small flame of hope sprung from this action and stopped her from completely falling to pieces.

Moving her leg back, she repeated the steps, making sure that she'd snagged both bags. No one paid attention; they were deep into a discussion about their search for Edward Fiske.

Nick's voice carried across the compartment. "They traced the Internet connection to a hotel in Salt Lake City. We'll dump these two and head over there." The man smiled, flashing nicotine-stained teeth. Cassidy's skin crawled.

The meaning of his words penetrated her mind. How did they have knowledge of Fiske's whereabouts? She tugged the bags closer. If they were going overboard, so was this gear. Cassidy twisted her back to the foul creature beside her and focused her attention on Jake. They'd tied his hands but not his feet. She worried if the gash on his head was deep enough to cause concussive results. He still hadn't opened his eyes. Cassidy stared at him, once more attempting to will him awake. His finger moved.

Her heart nearly burst out of her chest. The chopper tilted to the left and she braced her feet, preventing herself from sliding into stink-bag Nick. Her eyes never left Jake's lap. His thumb curved upward. Cassidy concentrated on not showing the relief that flooded her system. Jake was fine, simply playing unconscious. She swept her gaze to his face and noticed his lashes flutter beneath the thick mane of hair that dropped across his cheekbone. Jake pointed at the bags and she allowed herself a smug grin at having figured that one out on her own.

The helicopter dove toward the right. Beneath the full moon, tree-tops glistened on the ground. She leaned closer to the door, attempting to determine their location. A meaty paw grabbed her shoulder and shoved her hard against the back of the helicopter. She growled her frustration and turned toward Cole.

He approached her and clung to the arm loop above her head. Sweat bled from his armpits, staining an oblong patch on the black shirt he wore. Cole's hair was slicked back except for one thin strand that split his forehead with needle-like precision. Cassidy glared into his face.

"Don't look at me like that, Dr. Lowell. You did this to yourself. You have something I want." He ran his thumb over her lips, and she bared her teeth to bite him. "That's not very nice. Where's the report?"

"What report?"

"The printout of the geological survey your worthless assistant gave you."

Cassidy attempted to cover her surprise. Her mouth went dry as her mind tumbled through the ramifications of what he wanted. "I don't have it."

"I'm not a patient man, Dr. Lowell. Where is it?"

She glared at him, her brain whirring in a thousand different directions. The damn geo-survey. That's what this was all about? "I don't have it."

Robert's eyes never left her face. Her heart skipped at his icy stare, then stopped completely as she watched his arm raise and discharge the gun. Steve's head snapped back and blood splattered everywhere, coating Jake's shocked face.

Cassidy sat stunned, staring at the red pattern seeping down the metal wall of the helicopter. Her nose burned, and her voice disappeared. She screamed Steve's name, but nothing came out. She watched, frozen, as his body slumped forward and fell to the ground, motionless. Lifeless.

Pain engulfed her heart, and it threatened to send her spiraling into oblivion. She shifted her gaze away from Steve's body and glared at Robert Cole. Hate and anger replaced her grief. Kill him. Kill the bastard. Her mind raged and screamed, but her voice wasn't responding.

Cassidy's eyes blurred with tears, and she collapsed forward keening softly. Rocking back and forth, she attempted to gather her shattered emotions together. *Don't let them see you like this. If they see, they hold power.* Sitting back, she averted her eyes and turned so that Steve's body didn't cause her conviction to waver. "You bastard."

She pushed forward, fighting against her restraints. *Kill him. Kill the bastard.* The helicopter dipped toward a jagged outcrop. Cassidy shoved back the ball of grief that lodged itself in her stomach as they crested Upper Falls and moved east. She felt her body begin to shake and a deep chill spread across her nerves. She inhaled several times, her nostrils flaring as she attempted to draw in the oxygen that would save her from succumbing to shock.

She glanced up, and Jake stared at her. Sadness softened his eyes, and she held onto the sight of him as if he were a life raft. His eyes glistened with moisture, and Cassidy swallowed hard. She stared and pulled strength from his presence. He moved his head, and she followed his gaze outside the chopper. Her brain kicked into gear, and survival became top priority. If she wanted to dump someone in the middle of nowhere, Mirror Plateau wasn't a bad choice. It was outside the main caldera and remote. The chopper dropped lower, and even under these circumstances the beauty of Yellowstone stole her breath. A waterfall fell in cascading curtains of white ribbons, crashing against the rocky riverbed below.

Steve was there now, within the twinkling stars that hovered above the jagged peaks. She needed to believe that, to hold onto her faith, or else they'd never survive.

Cole shouted. "Now where's my damn report?"

The chopper dipped toward the falls, floating about ten feet above a narrow ridge to its left.

Cassidy inhaled and screamed as loud as she could. "I don't have it, you son of a bitch." Her throat was raw, and she bit her lips to stop them from trembling. "Damn you, I don't have it!"

Nick grabbed Jake, dragged him to his feet, and hustled him toward the door. Jake head-butted him, breaking loose. Twisting to find Cassidy, he locked eyes with hers. He nodded, and she offered him a tight smile. She knew exactly what he wanted. They were going to jump under their own power. Ignoring the tug on her heart and warmth that spread from her toes to the top of her head at the trust that crossed his face, she stood up.

Cole swore loudly and Nick reached for her, but Jake charged straight ahead, slamming into her chest and pushing them both out and over the rim of the helicopter. Frigid air and fear snatched at her throat and Cassidy gasped, fighting to control her panic. Arms flailing, she felt the bags smacking against her legs. On reflex, she twisted and tucked and struck the ground with head-splitting force. Opening one eye, she bit back the pain that filtered from every inch of her body.

"Jake?" Her voice came out as nothing more than a meek whimper. "Jake!"

Nothing.

She flopped on her back and gazed at the helicopter. The turbulence from its rotors kicked up dirt and debris across the ground, causing her to cough and choke. Her eyes widened, and fear froze her in place. Nick aimed a rifle at the center of her chest. Cassidy glanced down, following the movement of the small infrared dot until it rested on her heart. She inhaled deeply, anger melting away the fear. She stared up at him, her eyes daring him to pull the trigger.

CHAPTER 30

THE THOUGHT OF STEVE'S ASHEN FACE FLOODED CASSIDY'S mind, igniting a tornado of hatred that raged through her system. "Kill me, you chicken-shit asshole!" she screeched at the helicopter, not caring that she sounded more like a wounded hawk than a fierce lion. Chaotic wind, whipped into a frenzy by the helicopter rotors, yanked her hair from the bandana and slashed it against her face in painful lashes. She didn't avert her eyes from the figure of Nick Fowler.

He shifted the angle of his shoulder and aimed at her head. "You bitch."

Staring into the eye of the machine gun didn't scare her anywhere near as much as dealing with the loss of her best friend. She gasped at the anger that twisted his face into a gruesome mask and saw the flick of his finger that ignited a bright line of firepower.

Cassidy twisted to the left. The bullets struck the vicinity of her feet, pummeling the gear bags. She swore and rolled into a tight ball, glancing over her shoulder and watching in amazement as the helicopter banked away from her position. It was leaving.

Jake.

She struggled to her feet and hobbled on sore legs in the direction of the chopper, her gaze flickering over the bullet-ridden bags. Black nylon with wide gashes spewed leaky bottles of water and an assorted cluster of items not clearly visible in the darkness onto the hard-packed earth. Ducking her head, she pushed her cheek against her shoulder attempting to free the hair that clung to her face.

Cassidy glanced up at the helicopter and felt an instant kick of relief when Nick was yanked away from the door by one of the other men. She opened her mouth and screamed as loudly as she could, releasing her fear, hatred, and grief in a call of the wild and dispossessed. It burned her throat but lightened the crush of despair.

The helicopter rose into the night and drifted away.

Cassidy collapsed to her knees, her roar of hopelessness softened to a low-pitched keening. Rocks jabbed into knees and roots bit into soft flesh, but she barely felt the pain. Fire burned beneath her skin from bumps and bruises that made her eyes water; she inhaled, allowing numbness and a sense of detachment to act as a Band-Aid. Leaning forward, she touched her forehead to the ground and clenched her hands into tight fists as if the action would block Steve's death from immobilizing her.

Chill mountain air curled around her shaking body, triggering uncontrollable shivers. Cassidy closed her eyes and concentrated. She searched for her center, that core of existence she needed to find in order to cross the bridge from insanity to survival. Blue eyes flashed, and her mind lunged for the oasis they offered in her swirling chaos of emotions.

Jake.

Cassidy struggled to her feet and called his name.

Beyond the noise of the pounding waterfall a faint timber filtered across the distance. "Here," he answered from an area outside her line of vision.

His voice filled a void, becoming an orchestra to her shocked mind.

She swallowed, tipped back on her heels, and stood. Her legs wavered, weak and physically jarred by the fall. She bit her bottom lip, breathed deeply several times, and listened carefully to her surroundings.

Survive.

Blood and death knocked and demanded entrance, but she refused. Sorrow and tears insisted on release, but she denied. Hate and revenge filled her soul, and she smiled.

Survive.

Cassidy glanced around. Moonlight cast a soft glow, allowing her eyes to see beyond darkness and shadow. An arc of thickly forested hills rose to her right and banked into the distance. She tilted her head and listened. The roar of the waterfall lay to her left, cascading down a ravine she couldn't see. She marked everything in her mind, then crouched down and twisted at an awkward angle. Her fingers brushed against the cuff of her jeans and she wiggled, forcing them farther down until they felt the hard edge of plastic. Her knife. She bent at an uncomfortable slant and whispered her thanks for years of hard workouts that helped block the pain of her contortions.

Jake's voice drifted across the distance, distorted by the strain of her actions. "Cassidy, don't panic. Take a few deep breaths to gain control and then scrutinize our surroundings."

She swore and puffed out a breath of air in exasperation, every bruise screaming its location as she reached toward her feet and edged the knife from its holster.

"I know how frightened you must be, Sunshine. But you can do it."

She glanced in the direction of his voice and rolled her eyes, beads of sweat burning her eyes. "Are you hurt?" Her words came out strangled because of the current circus act taking place. Cassidy's fingers touched the sharp edge of metal that signified she'd worked past the handle and reached the blade. "Thank God." She inched the knife the rest of the way out, grabbing it quickly before it fell to the ground, and went to work on the ropes securing her wrists.

The strain in Jake's voice was evident. She could hear a tinge of breathlessness and edge of gritted teeth. "I'm not hurt; just kind of hanging on."

Cassidy frowned, sawing back and forth on the ropes. Too bad she didn't have her BFK, otherwise known as *big friggin' knife*. These ropes would be history in two seconds with that blade. "What does that mean?" She tried to raise her voice, but she was working hard at the bindings. It came out more like an exhausted gasp.

"Cassidy, Sunshine — please take those deep breaths. Don't be afraid. I've been in worse situations. Once you realize that you're all right and that we're here together, things won't seem so bad. I need you to think clearly."

Her wrists broke free and she rose slowly to her feet, dusting herself off. Steve's death didn't linger far from her mind but for now grief became imprisoned by anger, which suited Cassidy. She gazed at the sky and reached her fingers toward the stars, stretching her muscles and issuing a silent prayer. A flash of sadness tightened her throat, but she inhaled sharply rejecting the tears.

"Cassidy, don't despair. Pull yourself together."

Pull myself together? "Shut up, Anderson." She glanced down at the shredded ropes pooled around her feet. Irritation flashed, and she grinned at the familiar sentiment Jake's arrogance triggered. "Pull myself together?" Her voice was soft and didn't carry across the distance separating her from the current object of her aggravation. "I'm about as pulled together as Miss Piggy."

She walked to the left and picked up the shredded gear bags, shoving in the items that had spilled across the ground. "Where are you?" She heard several rocks skitter down the stony outcrop. She jogged in the direction of his voice, keeping the echo of the waterfall to her left.

"Over the edge. But don't be scared. It'll be okay. I just need a little help."

Cassidy peered over the cliff. The moon held his face in shadow, making it difficult to discern his eyes. "Shut up, Anderson." His arms were trapped by a scraggly bush, which definitely saved his life, but made it impossible for him to move. "Hang on." It was good to be near him again, but she ignored the warmth that heated her heart from isolation. She maneuvered herself over the edge, her fingers digging into the side of the cliff. Cassidy carefully tested each handhold before shifting her weight to the next position.

It didn't take her long to find a foothold next to Jake. The tree branches trapping him were small but solid with ragged bark that chafed against the palm of her hand. Jake moved his body, securing her between his chest and the chill rock. She nodded her appreciation and relaxed her hold on the mountainside, adding more power to the knife.

He anticipated every action she took as if his body were an extension of her own. His scent wrapped around her, and Cassidy drew comfort from his presence. Her knife sawed through the rope, one twine at a time.

She wrapped her fingers around his wrist and guided his hand to a sturdy branch. "Hold on. I'm cutting the last rope." As his right arm swung free, Jake moved to the side and gripped the ridge of rock beside her arm. He pulled her tight against his chest until her hold was once more secure.

They stayed there for a moment, catching their breath. "Ready?" Jake asked.

Cassidy ignored the urge to not move, to remain close to him. "Yeah. I'll go first."

They climbed up the edge of the embankment. Cassidy scooted over the ridge and rolled onto her back, catching her breath. She glanced up into Jake's grinning face, ignoring the spark of energy he caused.

"How'd you cut yourself loose?"

"Contrary to popular opinion, I'm not a scared, quivering female." *At least, I'm trying not to be.*

Jake had the decency to look contrite. "Sorry 'bout that." He held his hand out and helped her to her feet. "Damn, woman, you're going to steal my heart with all these hidden talents."

Cassidy turned and offered him a cheeky grin. "I thought I already had." Focusing on anything but the loss of her friend helped to build a wall against the grief. She realized that her internal struggle against Jake acted like a bandage against the sorrow that bled her heart. For once, she welcomed the confusing elements he sparked.

His expression sobered and she bit her bottom lip, suddenly feeling entirely too vulnerable. Jake reached out and caressed her cheek. "Without a doubt."

She fought the flush of pleasure spreading from the tip of her toes all the way to the roots of her hair. Cassidy averted her eyes and stepped back, not wanting him to see how he affected her. Jake's shoulders dropped and he rubbed a hand across his face, swearing softly. Exhaustion and sadness painted a side of him she'd never seen before. Cassidy hesitated then succumbed to need and reached for him, wrapping her arms around his neck and pulling herself tightly against his chest. His arms enclosed her, creating a cocoon of safety.

"I . . ." Her voice hitched, and she swallowed. "I was afraid for you."

Jake brushed her hair from her face and tipped her chin upward. "I'll never leave you."

His lips touched hers and she melted against the warmth, stealing a moment of pleasure. When they separated, a sad smile curved her lips. "But I'll leave you."

He shook his head slowly and bent to whisper in her ear. "I dare you."

Cassidy allowed a soft laugh to escape and reluctantly pushed away from Jake. He didn't believe her, but it was the truth. Their lives were too different, the water under the bridge too deep. If she didn't leave, his world would swallow everything she'd fought for and achieved in life. Self-preservation would win out in the end. Of this, Cassidy was certain.

"Where are we?" Jake asked, breaking the silence.

Cassidy allowed a flash of pride to dominate the I-refuse-to-be-in-love thoughts. "Actually, we're in a damn good position. Cole's arrogance and haste prevented a solid background check of this area. We're on Mirror Plateau. There's a ranger outpost not far from these falls." Cassidy shivered, the sudden memory of Steve slamming into her mind and rendering her immobile. "I can't believe he's gone."

Jake pulled her close once more. He held her against his chest, rocking back and forth. "I promise there'll be time to mourn." He released his hold and tipped her chin up with his forefinger, offering his own courage from the depths of his eyes. "Now, it's time for revenge."

Cassidy laughed, a bitter edge turning it sour. She pushed away and spun in a circle. "What is it with you and guns and danger? Oh, right, this is your life." Her words caught, and she stared at him. He stood still, not apologizing, not making excuses. Jake danced with the devil, welcoming danger and challenging death. No matter what she felt for him, it wouldn't work. He scared her. A fresh batch of tears welled and Cassidy swallowed, willing them away. Yes. She'd leave.

Opening her arms wide and spinning in a circle, she yelled to the stars. "I'm so freakin' pissed off it's not funny."

Jake kicked the ground by her side and ran his fingers through his hair. "Pissed is good. Of all the places in Yellowstone, don't you think it's odd that he plops us down next to a ranger station?"

This she could answer. "I'm certain not on purpose. The wolves follow the migrating elk here around this time of year. It was one of my favorite observation posts. I know this country like the back of my hand."

Jake frowned. "Ranger post. Wolves. Ethan Connor?"

Cassidy tossed a backpack at him. "Jealous?" He scowled, making her laugh. The amusement released some of the emotion that had a vice grip on her chest. "Let's get going. We're southwest of Specimen Ridge. That tributary over there that's creating the waterfall forks off the Yellowstone River. Once we cross the river, we have about an eight mile hike to the main road and from there we can head north for about another five miles to the ranger station —" she paused and inhaled. "There'll be a phone." She held up her smashed cell phone. "Hopefully, one in better condition." She watched Jake feel around for his own cell phone, but he came up empty handed. He did, however, reach down and unbuckle his belt.

"I have a better idea."

Cassidy's eyes widened, and her breath caught. "This isn't the time or place."

Jake's eyes snapped up and pinned her in place; then a slow, sexy grin spread across his face. "Not what you think. Homing device. I'm too tired to hike." He flipped open the cover of his belt button, fiddled with some unseen buttons, and snapped it together. A soft red light pulsed from the edge of the metal clasp. "Someone will be here soon."

Cassidy nodded, relieved. She sat down, crossed her legs, and stared at the brilliant stars that winked above their heads.

Jake settled himself beside her. "Tell me about the report Cole was asking you for."

Cassidy hesitated, her heart skipped a beat, and she swallowed as a horrifying thought crossed her mind. Grasping at anything to bide her a few moments to think, she held her hand up for him to wait and bent to tie her bootlaces. Her motions were exaggerated as she untied the laces and pulled at each hole to stretch the worn leather.

Her mind twisted around this latest troublesome thought. Was it possible Jake was in cahoots with Cole? How had the bastard known her whereabouts, the location of Fiske, and her friendship with Steve? Standing, Cassidy took another second to secure her hair with the bandana given by Cole. Jake waited patiently, glancing around and studying their surroundings. She should trust him.

Cassidy worried her bottom lip, recognizing that under the current situation all of her senses and instincts were warped and discombobulated. A soft breeze rustled the leaves of a quaking aspen, filling the night with the sound of sandpaper. This mission had cost Anna her life, flushed Cassidy's career down the toilet, and torn her best friend from the land of the living. What had Jake sacrificed?

Nothing.

She smiled when Jake turned toward her and raised an eyebrow for her to answer his question. "Cole wanted a geological survey."

"Why?"

A branch cracked and echoed loudly through the canyon, answered only by the muted calls of nature. Cassidy and Jake froze and turned toward the edge of the tree line. A wolf padded into the clearing in a blazing glory of enraged yellow eyes and windswept fur.

Cassidy felt the power; the fury floated across the small distance. It mesmerized her. She hunched over and reached for her knife, gripping it in her palm—poised for an attack. Jake glanced down at the tiny silver blade and back up at her. "What're you gonna do? Clean its teeth?"

She suppressed a grin and grabbed his arm, slowly rising to her feet "It's not infected anyway."

They watched in silence as the wolf sniffed the air, growled, and spun on its haunches, racing back into the forest.

Jake exhaled loudly. "That was a heart-stopper."

Cassidy laughed and released her own shaky breath. "Too bad we can't live off adrenaline."

"How'd you know that wolf wasn't infected?"

"Well, it definitely wasn't one of those mutated wolves. That was obvious. I figure that the healthy sheen of its fur and bright, inquisitive eyes pretty much screamed safe. I could be wrong, but I don't think so. It didn't smell sick." Work-related conversation helped ease the tightness in her chest, and she felt a semblance of normalcy return. She needed to tell Jake about the survey.

Jake shook his head. "Smell sick? Sunshine, they tossed out the plans when you were born. You are one hell of an original."

The night was filled with cries of wild animals. Owls screeched, and the underbrush rustled with activity. Cassidy concentrated on deciphering each individual sound, refusing to allow her mind a moment of rest. Coyotes sang to the moon in the distance, and the familiar sound wrapped a blanket around her heart. "My father and I used to play a game." Her voice sounded loud compared to the music of Mother Nature.

"What was that?"

Cassidy stifled a laugh as Jake's words were even louder than hers. "We'd sit on our roof and listen to the coyote. Then we'd take turns creating an imaginary adventure. Were they hunting or simply celebrating a coyote holiday?"

Jake's voice dropped to a whisper. "Were you close with your parents?"

An unbidden smile curved her lips upward. She placed a hand out to push a branch aside and waited until Jake reached the same area, then released control of the tree to him. "Yes."

He grinned at her. "I have a big family. Our get-togethers often sound very much like those coyotes."

Cassidy laughed, imagining a group of Jake-like personalities bossing one another around. "I bet you do."

Minutes passed, and the moon grew brighter. After a while the nocturnal animals began to shift their activity into a slower, more sedate speed that dropped the noise level to a minimum. Cassidy gazed beyond the edge of the pine trees and noted the shifting of the light. Morning wasn't too far away.

Jake's voice made her jump. "Cassidy?"

"Hm?"

"You never answered my question about the survey."

Cassidy paused and turned to face him. She gazed into his eyes and felt the pull of attraction and something else, something that felt oddly like a desire to bond. It unnerved her. She squared her shoulders and decided brutal honesty was the right path.

CHAPTER 31

CASSIDY SEPARATED HERSELF FROM THE INTIMACY OF THEIR surroundings. A distant hum signaled the approach of their rescue unit.

"Well?" Jake insisted.

"I have the survey."

Jake's eyes darkened, and he ceased moving. "Go on."

Cassidy rushed her words together, hoping to mask her insecurity and misgivings. "I've had the survey all along. But I honestly didn't realize that this entire fiasco revolved around its existence."

"Cassidy . . ."

She held up her hand, realizing how tangled their lives had become. "I'm sorry I didn't tell you." Pointing toward the distance and refusing to glance at Jake's face, she positioned herself ten feet away. "The chopper's here."

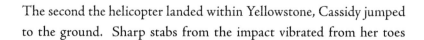

The second the helicopter landed within Yellowstone, Cassidy jumped to the ground. Sharp stabs from the impact vibrated from her toes up through her spine, resonating off every bump and bruise. It'd only taken them fifteen minutes to reach their destination, but her muscles tightened and contracted painfully, forcing her to exhale several deep breaths. She waved a thank you to the park ranger flying the helicopter and shaded her face from the dirt being kicked up by the rotors.

Yellowstone National Park headquarters.

The oblong, wood-sided building with its green metal roof was an oasis that appeared as luxurious to Cassidy as the Ritz. She followed Jake toward the park offices and stared in surprise as they passed a collection of military vehicles surrounding the place. Jeeps, Hummers, and trucks were parked in haphazard fashion all displaying the insignia of the United States Army.

"What's this?"

He shrugged and pushed the door open, holding it for her as they entered the building. "My guys."

It took a moment for her eyes to adjust from bright daylight and her ears to absorb the number of voices and clicking of computers. When they did, her throat caught. Ethan's territory had been invaded by soldiers. They were everywhere.

Lining the wall with makeshift computer stations.

Grouped around a bulletin board splattered with maps and tactical instructions.

Huddled over a large silver coffee dispenser.

The quiet offices of Yellowstone's park rangers resembled a scene she'd only ever witnessed in movies. Jake's presence was acknowledged with respectful salutes and a group of men in military dress waved him toward Ethan's office. "I have to be debriefed."

Debriefed.

It sounded ominous to Cassidy. Another strange aspect of a world she'd never been privy to. "Yes, of course. Go."

He nodded stiffly and turned toward the other end of the room.

293

Jake hadn't spoken a word to her since the confession of the geological survey. She watched him enter the door to Ethan's office. A woman in a black tank top and military camouflage pants patted his back, displaying a mirror image of Jake's tattoo on her upper shoulder.

Black Stripe.

A shudder ran through Cassidy as she studied the muscular curve and athletic build of the female soldier. Her eyes widened as Jake returned a salute. He'd discarded the last thread of his biologist disguise and slipped into full soldier mode, barking orders and demanding answers. It disconcerted her.

The woman turned, her profile familiar. She lifted a hand in Cassidy's direction and smiled. Cassidy tensed in shock. Cold shivers suffused her and her world tilted to the left, causing her to place a hand on the corner of a nearby desk to steady herself.

Michelle.

Reality finally hit her head-on. Her ecologist was Black Stripe. Steve had been Black Stripe. The entire mission in Yellowstone was being driven by Jake's team. Cassidy suddenly felt out of place; the Army personnel that moved past her intent on their responsibilities were alien and invasive.

Michelle approached her and offered a sympathetic smile. "You okay?"

Cassidy nodded. *Be a scientist. That's who you are.* "Fill me in on the status of the wolves, the progress of the disease, and the circumstances of my arrest warrant."

Michelle sat on the edge of the desk and crossed her arms. "We've quarantined the entire northern quadrant of the park, including the area around the ranch where the CDC reported a possible outbreak. Since yesterday, there's been no more progress on the wolves as you were the one handling that element." She uncrossed her arms and pointed a finger at Cassidy. "As for you, you have been remanded into the custody of Captain Jacob T. Anderson of the United States Army." She grinned. "He's a good man, boss."

Cassidy absorbed everything Michelle said, ignoring the jump in her stomach at her validation of Jake. "Remanded into custody? What exactly does that mean?"

"Where he goes, you go. You're his responsibility."

She frowned and chewed on her lower lip. "Don't know that I like that."

Cassidy glanced around, surveying the men and women in the room. Coffee percolated on a stand beside the window, and her mouth watered at the scent of a fresh pot.

"No choice there," Michelle answered lightly.

"Where's Fiske? I assume you've been apprised of that aspect of the investigation."

"Yes, ma'am. I've followed that link. He's in Salt Lake City. They've repaired the transport carrier, and it's being fueled and prepped as we speak."

"Where we going?"

"After Salt Lake City, we'll be departing for West Africa."

Her heart skipped a beat at returning to the Niger Delta. A mixture of excitement and despair blended together, creating an unsettled feeling within the pit of her stomach. "Good." Cassidy twisted her hands together and scrutinized the walls. They were paneled in dark, worn wood that sported large maps of Yellowstone National Park. One of the maps contained thick red marks over the northern quadrant. She rose and walked over to the map, studying the quarantined area. "We can't leave without another ZEBRA pod replacing us. The wolves are still at risk, and so are all the inhabitants of this region."

"Liv Somers is already on her way. The moment you were compromised, corporate triggered the backup group. Black Stripe is also sending replacements for myself, Jake, Steve and Valerie."

"Wow," Cassidy said and sat down in a desk chair, her emotions even more tangled than her hair. "All of you are Black Stripe?" This late in the game, a sense of betrayal shouldn't be an issue. But there it was, curling its evil tentacles around her heart and squeezing. She caressed the worn leather of the chair arms, feeling the soft hide slide beneath her fingers.

Jake strode across the floor waving a hand at Michelle, dismissing her. "Where's the survey?"

Cassidy swallowed and nervously tugged on her ponytail. Her voice caught and she cleared it, knowing she'd created an irrevocable shift in their relationship. "With my things on the transport plane."

He narrowed his eyes and studied her face. Anger and disappointment highlighted his expression, causing her breath to hitch. She blinked and squared her shoulders. Jake shook his head once, turned, and strode out of the office. She heard him bark several commands and followed him out the door. He glanced over his shoulder, pointed at her, and then snapped at one of the soldiers. "Get her to the transport plane."

Cassidy inhaled sharply at his dismissal. She empathized with his emotions, remembering all too well the betrayal and disbelief he'd caused when she discovered his allegiance with Black Strike. "No. I'm going with you."

"Like hell you are."

The cold disdain that laced his words felt like nails in her coffin. "I've been remanded into your custody, Captain Anderson. Where you go, I go."

He ran his hand through his hair and swore softly. "Get to the Jeep parked out front. I'll be there in a second."

Cassidy nodded and dashed for the door before he changed his mind. Exiting the building, she inhaled several deep breaths and combed the parking lot for a ZEBRA Jeep.

The sun sat high in the sky and rather than climbing into the Jeep,

Cassidy sat on the hood and allowed the heat to bake her shirt. She chewed on her bottom lip, scene after bloody scene playing through her mind. Anna and Steve. Steve and Anna. What had she done?

Jake ran out of the building, the door slamming behind him. She glanced up and watched him stalk toward her. His chin was set firmly and the easy, relaxed grin she'd become familiar with existed only in her memory. A soft breeze kicked up from the ground and ruffled his mop of hair. He pushed it back and motioned with one hand for her to climb into the vehicle.

Cassidy should welcome the cold distant soldier persona, but it hurt. Hurt her heart and her soul. He jumped behind the wheel of the Jeep, cranked the engine, and sped out of the parking lot.

She glanced at him, nervous and insecure. "I'm sorry I didn't . . ."

Jake held his hand up. "Don't go there. I can't begin to process all the trouble your inability to confide in me has caused." He turned to her for a second, and the anger on his face stole her breath. "If I'd known about this, maybe Steve wouldn't be dead."

Cassidy inhaled sharply at his accusation. "Don't you think I blame myself enough for that? I don't need your holier than thou attitude. For crying out loud, the image of his body haunts every second of my day."

"What I want to know is . . . were you distrustful of me because I'm Black Stripe or because I've gotten to a part of you no man ever has?"

Cassidy couldn't speak; her temper raged from a simmering storm into a full-fledged category five hurricane. "You son of a bitch."

Jake glared at her. "Name calling doesn't suit you, Dr. Lowell."

She gripped the edge of the vinyl seat and turned to gaze out the window. The Jeep headed south toward Yellowstone Lake and the inn, passing a portion of the caldera where buffalo grazed on sweet grass.

Cassidy clamped down on the angry words she wanted to spit at Jake, choosing the path of silence instead. Jake's accusation that Steve's death was her fault kicked her stomach into rolling waves of nausea. A cell phone rang, which startled her out of her moment of woe and self-pity. Jake must've been provided an extra cellular.

She missed her phone.

She dropped her head down, and a lone tear escaped and splashed on the edge of her arm. She missed the sound of Steve laughing at whatever idiotic thing she said, and his voice crackling across a static connection from Atlanta to Africa or wherever the hell she'd been stationed.

Jake snapped the phone off his waistband and answered. He listened to the voice on the other end, nodding and mumbling back. Lines creased his face, and weariness stole his tan and replaced it with pale fatigue. He hung up and slowed the Jeep, pulling off to the side of the road. When he switched the ignition off, Cassidy closed her eyes and turned away from him. No good would come of this discussion. She felt the warmth of his hand on her neck and tensed her shoulders. "What now?"

"Ethan Connor's in critical care at the hospital. Apparently, he was one of the rangers called to the scene of attack last night and Fowler's men intercepted him."

She swallowed and drew several deep breaths into her lungs. Emotional overload shut down her heart. She'd long since forgiven Ethan for attempting to arrest her. Jake didn't know how close his label of Dudley Do-Right matched Chief Ranger Connor. "We need to get to that survey. What if Cole went back to the plane and searched for it?"

"Cassidy . . ."

With a shake of her head, she pointed to the keys. "Start this damn thing. Without that survey, we're screwed."

Jake stared at her for a moment then removed his hand, leaving behind an intense chill. With a flip of his wrist, he fired up the Jeep and pulled back onto the road. The hum of the engine and movement of the vehicle soothed more than she'd anticipated. No more hiding things. No more mistruths. It was time to lay it all on the line and fight. Not for herself, but for the Niger Delta and all the innocent lives lost because of Robert Cole's devious activities.

"Tell me, Jake. What exactly do you think is going on?" Cassidy turned and faced him, pushing back on anything that remotely resembled an emotion.

"Be more specific."

She ignored his military, clipped manner and pushed beyond the pain caused from his lack of warmth. "Why was Cole in Wyoming, and what the hell does he have to do with this virus?"

Jake tapped his fingers against the steering wheel and cast her one quick glance. "I believe that New World Petroleum is using you as a scapegoat for this virus. I also believe that they are planning on releasing CPV-19 into the Niger Delta, killing millions." Jake bent his head to the side and raked his fingers through his hair. "It's obvious that they have an inside contact within ZEBRA. Who that is, I don't know. The information and rapid arrest warrant regarding your involvement with NWP and Yellowstone contains data that only a ZEBRA executive would know."

He shrugged and drummed a soft beat against the plastic of the dashboard, frowning at whatever crossed his mind. Cassidy followed the motion with her eyes, assimilating the information he'd divulged.

Jake glanced at her, a troubled expression deepening the furrow between his eyes. "Drew Sharpe has disappeared."

Her heart skipped, and she felt another wave of nausea attack her insides. "I don't want to believe he's involved."

"That last statement was a fact, not a theory." He didn't back down —just pinned her in place with conviction written on his face.

"Why? Why would New World Petroleum, one of the largest oil producers in the world, risk their reputation and entire business by releasing a deadly virus? And why would Drew Sharpe toss away his career to help them?"

"That," Jake said, "is the million dollar question."

"And the answer is in that survey." Cassidy twisted her hands together, picking at pieces of dirt lodged beneath her nails. "New World Petroleum already rules the local government; they have no need to kill millions of Nigerians."

Jake shrugged. "I don't know their motivation, but this is where the facts of my investigation lead. NWP is planning on destroying the people within that region."

"I don't believe that. The Niger Delta is already theirs."

"How so?"

Cassidy sighed. "You were there. Didn't you see that the living conditions are deplorable? Oil production has already killed that place."

"Maybe so. But it hasn't killed the will of the people."

Cassidy's mind immediately turned to Anna. Her conviction and dedication to saving the home of her ancestors were sentiments shared by many within the Niger Delta. She needed to think. She stifled a yawn. She needed sleep.

Jake didn't remember the last time he felt this void of all emotion. He wrapped the feeling tight around his heart and decided it was for the best. The mission remained his top priority. When, exactly, had his heart become involved?

He snapped his soldier armor in place and pushed personal feelings aside. "Where's the survey?"

"In my saddle bag."

Jake glanced at her, remaining distant and professional. "Where exactly?"

"My tampon case."

Choked laughter escaped Jake's mouth, and he shook his head at her. "Your what?"

Cassidy frowned. "It's a small pink cylinder. You'll see it."

"Er, sure." Jake decided to allow her to retrieve it. Searching a woman's personal hygiene objects left him uncomfortable and slightly embarrassed. He closed his eyes and realized the brilliance of her hiding place. "Smart girl."

She glanced across the Jeep and smiled shyly. "Thanks."

Jake watched the road ahead. "What's on the survey, Cassidy?"

She shook her head. "I don't know. I remember studying it that night you pulled me from camp but, for the life of me, can't pinpoint whatever it was that bothered me. I'm certain the trauma of the evacuation has hindered my brain."

Jake ignored her small jab. He'd like to believe she knew him well enough to know he hadn't left those people to die. "If you didn't realize it was important, why'd you hide it?"

Cassidy shrugged and shook her head. "Gut feeling, really. Charles had sent David upriver to research some sort of anomaly, and then Sharpe questioned me about the existence of a geological survey right before my briefing on the wolves, and it struck me as odd. So I hid it, kind of like squirreling away something sweet for after dinner."

Cassidy sat in silence, listening to the melancholy music on the country western station. Jake drove the Jeep at top speed toward Jackson Hole airport. A small bubble of excitement mixed with curiosity made her fidget in her seat, and she struggled against displaying these emotions.

He'd been distant and uber-professional, but Cassidy saw the undercurrent of his emotions spring forth in his restrained movements and short, emotionless answers. Jake struggled with his feelings, and it warmed her heart.

She sighed and turned toward him. "Any news on the identification of the first CPV-19 victim?"

Jake nodded. "Yes. Apparently, she was on sabbatical from the zoology department at the University of Florida. She'd been spending the past six weeks tracking and observing the Net Pierce pack."

Cassidy smothered a laugh. "Nez Perce?"

He shrugged. "Whatever. The CDC discovered a jagged scrape wound on the palm of her hand. There were traces of rock and debris inside the cut, along with wolf feces."

Of course. "Part of tracking is determining the source of fecal matter. She must have picked some up in order to classify how long it'd been there."

"You zoologists are gross."

Cassidy ignored him. "Parvo is absorbed through fecal matter. Normally, it's ingested by other animals and contracted that way. However, the strain of this virus is extraordinarily virulent and must have transferred immediately into her bloodstream." She glanced up at Jake. "Just like Fifth Disease."

"Scary."

"I couldn't agree more." Cassidy gazed out the window of the small helicopter. A disease as deadly as CPV-19 being released within the jungles of the Niger Delta frightened her beyond belief. Infection of both animal and human meant absolute genocide.

Seated within the comfort of the ZEBRA plane, Cassidy rested her head against the edge of the chair. She couldn't remember the last time she'd felt this worn out. Her body ached from the numerous bumps and bruises collected from her fall into the lab and her impromptu flight out of the helicopter. Her mind was taxed beyond belief by the fear of the virus and concern for the inhabitants of Yellowstone. Unanswered questions and solutions to the open ends of the investigation plagued her constantly.

The moment they entered the plane, Cassidy sat down at a computer and wrote everything down. Theories. Facts. Questions. Everything. She bent her head in frustration as the system responded in slow motion to each entry she typed. Cole's men had irrevocably damaged their equipment during the abduction, leaving behind only one working computer. And it was a dinosaur. The system didn't even have a USB port for the flash drive. She'd been reassured laptops would be delivered the moment they arrived at Salt Lake City.

Jake walked over and slipped into the seat next to her. She twisted her neck and stared at him. He'd been deep in discussion with the pilot when they'd returned and then spent an additional hour on the phone with his superior officer. His presence filled the plane, and she tried to block out the effect it had on her emotions.

Cassidy turned her concentration back to other matters. She remembered one of her notations. "Have you sent people to excavate the lab?"

"Yes." Jake answered. "And headquarters called to inform us that your arrest warrant has been revoked."

She frowned and sucked her bottom lip between her teeth. "That was fast. You must be able to pull some pretty powerful strings."

Jake shrugged. "I'd love to take responsibility, but the petri dish lid you found at the lab site contained traces of parvo."

"Plain parvo?"

"Yes. And combined with everything else we've put together, it was enough to smash through the erroneous claims of your involvement with CPV-19."

Cassidy bent her head from one side to the other, snapping the kinks in her neck. "Good." She should feel more relieved, but her mind was numb.

"We're ready for takeoff. You okay flying out of here?"

She grinned, relishing the brief drop from his military bearing. "Hell, yeah. This is a walk in the park compared to everything that's transpired the last couple of days." And it was the truth.

The engine hummed and vibrated through the body of the plane as it taxied toward the runway. Cassidy buckled her belt. Jake remained seated beside her, and she swiveled to face him. "Don't you have somewhere else to be?"

He stared at her, tilting his head. "Like where?"

Cassidy pointed to Michelle, who was seated toward the front of the plane. "There."

"But I like you more."

He stated his words in a serious manner but there was a glimpse of something familiar in the depths of his eyes, and it eased the pain and regret that refused to allow her stomach to settle. "I meant shouldn't you be coordinating our plans or whatever it is you Black Stripes do before embarking on a dangerous mission?"

"Don't worry. It's in the works."

The plane raced down the runway and rose into the sky, banking its wings and gracefully turning toward the mountains. Cassidy gasped and inhaled sharply as the turbulent currents dropped their elevation slightly.

"It's fine," Jake whispered.

"I know." She offered him a half smile. "Some habits die hard."

Her fear subsided, and she gazed out the window as the plane flew through the Tetons. Dark shadows glittering with snow winked at her from beyond the barrier of her window. They rose above the peaks and Cassidy smiled, placing her face as close to the small opening as possible. The mountains were breathtaking. Exhilarating. Their wild beauty unchanged for centuries.

This bird's eye view is what her parents saw.

She'd be back. When her responsibilities were complete, she'd return home and put to bed the rest of her demons. Cassidy's eyes watered. Pressing her fingertips to the glass, she whispered a soft prayer. "Bye, Mom. I love you." Her father, too, but it was her mother's wisdom she missed the most and the comfort of her forever-forgiving heart.

Cassidy felt Jake rise and leave her in peace. The confliction of her feelings toward the exasperating man too complicated to untangle, she closed her eyes and slipped beneath a blanket of exhaustion. Safe for the moment, her mind rested and her body reached for the regenerative powers of sleep.

CHAPTER 32

THE RUMBLE OF LANDING GEAR AGAINST TARMAC JOLTED JAKE from his half sleep. He stretched, slipped his hand down, and flipped open the metal clasp of his seat belt. Standing slowly and working the kinks from cramped muscles, he glanced around the interior of the transport plane.

Michelle was already on the phone, moving alternately from her seat to the fax machine. She held a stack of papers in her hand, waving them at Jake. He nodded and moved down the aisle, gracefully absorbing the motion of the plane with his legs. The engine slowed and stopped and dropped the interior into a hushed silence. "Michelle, go down and coordinate our transportation with the local PD. They should be waiting for us."

"Yes, sir." She turned, resting her hand against the wall of the plane, and waited while the ground crew connected a set of rollaway stairs to the exterior of the door. When everything was in place, Michelle pushed a series of numbers into a keypad and twisted the metal latch. With a loud hiss the plane's door swung open, swamping the interior with sunshine.

Jake trailed his fingers along the top of the headrest of Cassidy's seat. He bent over and studied her face. Her head rested against the window, a curtain of golden curls trailing along her cheekbone and across her shoulder. Ignoring the sudden tightening of his chest, he moved his hand down and pushed her hair back. She stirred, and he frowned at the rim of bruises against her neck. Jake closed his eyes and smoothed away the sudden desire to kill Robert Cole. His personal feelings must remain separate from the mission.

Jake slid into the seat next to her and gently shook her shoulder. "Cassidy, we're here."

"Hmmm?" She inhaled and stretched her arms to the ceiling. "Already?"

A light scent of lavender crossed the distance between them, reminding Jake they'd only had a brief moment to change clothes and hand wash the dirt and grime away from their fall out of the helicopter. "Sorry, Sunshine. It's a short flight from Jackson to Salt Lake City." He stifled a laugh at the childish pout which crossed her face. "You can stay here, if you like." That snapped her awake.

"No way." Cassidy straightened in her seat and reached down to tug her boots on. Jake glanced at the ceiling, not wanting to feast on the curve of her breast or the patch of bare skin exposed beyond the edge of her T-shirt. "Do you know where we're going?"

He couldn't have her any more than he could lay claim to the sky above his land. The sting of her distrust faded as they approached the next leg of their investigation. He needed her cooperation and her brain. Jake decided allowing a small amount of his true feelings out would work miracles in gaining her full trust and solidifying their teamwork. "Yes. I established the results of the traced Internet connection, but unfortunately the local PD already received a call of suspicious behavior at that address. They investigated and found nothing."

Cassidy ran a brush through her hair, turned, and stared at him.

"Nothing?" She scooted forward, searching the seat for something. Her hand dug into the back of the chair, and with a triumphant smile she yanked out a ponytail holder. "Knew it was here somewhere." With a flip of her wrist, she twisted her hair through the black band and refocused on Jake. "You're sure? They didn't find a thing?"

He rose and stepped into the aisle, allowing her to proceed in front of him. "Nothing."

"No dead body?"

"Nada." Jake followed her. "But don't get your hopes up. There's no telling what they've done with him."

"I know. But still"—she smiled at him over her shoulder—"it's a positive thing. No body."

They stepped onto the top of the stairway, and Jake smiled as Cassidy inhaled deeply and spread her arms wide. He admitted the blue sky and fuel-tainted air were a welcome contrast to the climate-controlled interior of the plane. Jake placed his hand against her back and gently pushed her forward until she moved under her own power and jogged down the metal stairs of the transport jet.

The noontime sun beat a steady heat onto the tarmac, creating a hazy wave of jet fuel along the horizon. But it didn't block the view of the distant mountains that cradled Salt Lake City. He turned his attention to their welcoming committee. A large, beefy man in a rumpled suit moved from the small crowd and met them at the base of the stairs. "Captain Anderson? I'm Lieutenant Dulaney."

Jake absorbed the arrogant twist of the man's lips and immediately pegged him as a man of great self-importance. He didn't mind playing to the Lieutenant's ego to speed along the investigation. "Pleased to meet you, Dulaney. This is my associate, Dr. Lowell."

Cassidy reached in front of Jake and shook the man's hand. "Thank you, Lieutenant, for your time and cooperation. We appreciate your assistance in this matter."

Jake smothered a smile of pride at her intuitiveness. The man shrugged and pointed at a dark blue Crown Vic. "Let's get this over with."

Jake followed Dulaney across the tarmac and slid into the front passenger seat. Cassidy's hand brushed his shoulder as she climbed in the back and a shiver of awareness snaked from the base of his neck and tingled across his scalp. The lieutenant pulled onto the main road, following another unmarked vehicle containing his deputies and Michelle. "I understand you located an abandoned helicopter. Have you processed it yet?"

Dulaney snorted, rolled down his window, and spit a wad of mucus onto the road. "Started. But the feds arrived about an hour after it was reported."

Not wanting to find himself in the middle of a territorial pissing contest, Jake nodded and dropped the subject. He'd contact Colonel Price and make sure all evidence was piped into his computer. "We're heading to the Holiday Inn on North Temple, right?"

"Yes, sir." Lieutenant Dulaney picked up his radio and confirmed his coordinates with central dispatch.

Jake glanced over his shoulder at Cassidy. She stared out the window, her shoulders slumped and an odd air of detachment written across her face. "You okay, Cass?"

She turned and faced him. "Oh, sure." But her quick smile didn't cover the grief or fear that clouded her emerald eyes. "Just pondering my future employment opportunities . . ." *And the loss of my best friend, you jerk.* It didn't take a rocket scientist to finish her sentence.

Jake decided to ignore what he couldn't fix and instead flashed a cheeky grin. Her face blushed, which made his grin spread into a full-fledged smile. Dammit if he didn't affect her. That made things slightly better. "Don't worry. ZEBRA's not going anywhere."

"Even without Sharpe?"

Jake frowned. "I'm sure of it. It's a worldwide organization."

She raised her brows. "And a cover for an elite military group?"

He glanced sharply at Lieutenant Dulaney. The man seemed oblivious to their conversation, humming along to his radio. "This isn't the time or place to discuss these things."

Cassidy's face reddened, and she bowed her head. "I'm sorry."

Jake swore. He hadn't meant to embarrass or chastise her. "Don't be, Sunshine." Before he made matters worse, he twisted around and faced the front. The highway was flat and straight shooting past the city's skyline. Salt Lake was nestled between two mountain ranges, one to the east and another to the west. Billboards for the tabernacle and a multitude of recreational resorts displaying sparkling white snow and golf courses scattered the edge of the interstate.

"What you guys hoping to find at the hotel anyway?" Dulaney spit another gob of mucus out the window and tossed Jake a questioning glance.

Jake hid his disgust at the man's obsessive need to hawk and spit. "I don't know," he answered honestly.

"Well the feds are there now."

Jake nodded and dropped into silence. He pretended to study the passing surroundings, but his mind kept returning to the woman in the backseat. Damn. Cold air blasted from the car's vents. He frowned and wondered if there'd be a chance of getting Dulaney to turn it down a notch. Glancing at the man's paunch and meaty fingers, he decided the evidence of too many donuts would negate his request. If he'd quit lowering the window and spitting, the car could maintain an equitable temperature instead of blasting frigid air into Jake's face.

It didn't take more than ten minutes to reach the hotel. They turned off the interstate and drove along a road lined with strip malls, motels, and fast-food joints. Dulaney pulled his Crown Vic up to the curb in front of a two-story Holiday Inn and shut it off. They exited the vehicle, the heat and bright sun of early afternoon ricocheting off the black tarmac and ratcheting the temperature up an uncomfortable notch. Jake reached for Cassidy's door, but she was already out and heading up the stairs.

He jogged after her. They flipped their IDs to the two federal agents that blocked the front door and were waved into the interior.

"The place hasn't been ransacked," Cassidy said.

Jake scanned the corners, confirming her first impression. Two chairs cushioned with a burlap fabric remained upright and in position around a small pedestal table. The dresser and Edward Fiske's suitcase appeared untouched. "Sheet looks stained."

"Urine," a lab tech said, exiting the bathroom. "Who are you guys?" He was a slip of a man, with curly black hair cropped short. Small eyes were expanded by the wire-rimmed glasses perched on his nose.

"ZEBRA."

"Right. The chief told me to expect some zoo animals."

Cassidy glared at the skinny man, approached him, and planted her feet, blocking his path. "Considering our clearance is about fifty grades higher than yours, I suggest you cooperate and explain what's been found here." She tapped her finger against his identification tag. "Or is that too difficult for your pea-brain to absorb?"

Jake turned his head and tried to muffle his laughter. The lab technician backed off, holding his hands up in front. "No insult meant, ma'am."

"Doctor," Cassidy said.

"Doctor, ma'am. You might want to take a look in there." He pointed to the bathroom and Cassidy pushed past him.

Jake shook his head and sighed. "You picked the wrong person to call a zoo animal."

The lab tech bent and gathered his tools together. "She sure is testy. It's prolly that . . ."

Jake gripped the man's shoulder, digging his fingers into nothing but skin and bones. "I wouldn't go there if I were you."

"Yes, sir. We discovered a power cord that appears to belong to a laptop, and at first glance there doesn't seem to be anything unusual within his suitcase." The tech pulled a clipboard over from the bed and read from the top sheet. "Pants. Shirts. Socks. Underwear. That's it. I'm running tox screens on the urine."

"Good. Any other trace found?"

"Hair and prints. This is a busy hotel, which will make isolation difficult. Oh yeah, and I gathered everything in there as well." He signaled over his shoulder with his thumb. "Where do you want the lab results sent to?"

Jake nodded toward the door. Michelle remained outside, chatting amicably with the federal officers. "She'll tell you."

The technician stared at Michelle, his eyes resting on her gun. "Jesus," he whispered.

Jake chuckled. "You'll be fine. But I'd suggest you refrain from any animal remarks."

"Yes, sir." The tech gathered up his clipboard and collection kit, heading toward the door with tentative steps.

"You need to see this." Cassidy called from the bathroom.

Jake turned and walked through the narrow door. The small room heightened his awareness of Cassidy and he purposely flipped the all-business switch on in his head, refusing to acknowledge the light lavender scent that wafted upon the air.

She bent over the sink and stared at some odd markings on the mirror, the edge of the counter biting into her waist. Her jeans stretched across her rear, and Jake averted his eyes to focus on the glass in front of her. He moved closer for a better view of the scratches on the mirror but remained at a safe enough distance. "What's that?"

"A message written in soap."

"Clues to where he's being taken?"

Cassidy shook her head. "Clues to the composition and possible antidote for CPV-19." She pulled a pad out of her back pocket and copied down the white lettering. "I don't think Edward Fiske was an evil doctor. Everything he's done to date points to the fact that he honestly felt he was performing a task that would benefit humanity."

Jake shrugged. "He did, right?"

She glanced at him and frowned. "Well, technically yes. But what was created from his experimentations is atrocious. He definitely walked a fine line between genius and monster." Cassidy snapped her notebook closed and shoved it back where it belonged. "However, it appears that he had every intention of developing a cure or prevention of the virus."

"How do you know that?"

"Because"—she pointed to the mirror—"this formula neutralizes the Fifth Disease factor of CPV-19."

Jake's brain kicked in, and he studied what Edward Fiske scribbled on the mirror. "But we don't know if it'll prevent the coagulation or intestinal failure prompted by the parvo."

Cassidy shrugged. "In theory, it should. Parvo is attacking the intestinal cells because they divide at a rapid rate. Fifth attacks red blood cells because they also divide at a rapid rate, conveniently breathing life into the virus. Something within the genetic makeup of Fifth Disease has thrown the dividing cells into overdrive. If we shut down that aspect, we can concentrate on battling the parvo strain through correcting the dehydration and electrolyte imbalances." She sighed and leaned against the wall. "In theory, that should work."

Jake hated to burst her bubble. "Cassidy, parvo attacks the bacteria in the intestinal tract, and unless we catch it early enough before it moves into the bloodstream we won't be able to save the infected. Not to mention, the survival rate of the young, the old, and the weak will be zero."

"I know, Jake. I'm not underestimating the danger of being infected with parvo. But the young, old, and weak are a small percentage."

He stared at her, knowing his next words weren't going to be received well. "Not in the Niger Delta." The pain that crossed her face was exactly what he expected, and he softened his voice. "This is a start, though. It's a great start." Jake crossed his arms and stared at her.

"What?"

"Why wouldn't Fiske send this with the e-mails? If he's truly attempting to help us, he'd have given us all his information on CPV-19."

Cassidy worried her bottom lip and nodded in agreement with him. "I thought that too. But if he'd sent us this stuff"—she pointed to the mirror—"would we be here now?"

Jake narrowed his eyes, thinking about her statement. "Probably not. We'd have gone straight after Cole."

"Right." Cassidy exited the bathroom. "And his chance of rescue eliminated." Her excitement faded and was replaced with a shoulder-drooping defeat. "Whichever way we turn, we're screwed. They have the virus and the man who can provide an antidote. What do we have? Nothing."

Jake chuckled. "We're close. They have a plan, and I'm afraid it includes us." Cassidy's eyes widened, but she didn't voice any argument. He guided her out the door, reaching for his sunglasses. "I doubt very much they'll be releasing the virus the second they step foot within the Niger Delta."

"God, I hope you're right."

"I know I am," but the twist in his gut spoke his doubts. New World Petroleum's motivation regarding CPV-19 remained an anomaly, and until that mystery was solved there'd be no guessing at a timeline for their agenda.

CHAPTER 33

CASSIDY EXITED THE POLICE CAR, GLAD TO BE REMOVING HER-
self from the lieutenant's presence. His affinity for spitting out windows
reduced the grumbling in her stomach to nothing. Dark green delivery
trucks marked with the insignia of the United States Army sat beneath the black-and-white-striped transport jet. Boxes stamped with
an assortment of lettering that made no sense to Cassidy were being
unloaded and carried up the ramp and into the belly of the plane by a
group of uniformed men.

"What's going on?" she asked Jake.

He tilted his head and gazed at her as if she were out of her mind.
"Loading up for our assignment?" Jake smiled and winked at her, creating an irritating flutter in her belly. "I doubt we'll be able to purchase
this stuff in the local villages over there."

Cassidy rolled her eyes at her stupidity. "Right. Of course."

"You ready?"

"This is my life. Planes, choppers, and automobiles. I suppose I
should be thankful that this mode of transportation has all the com-
forts of home." She followed Michelle up the metal stairs and into

the plane. She paused for a moment, barely recognizing the interior. Valerie bustled down the aisle, converting the comfortable seating sections into sleeping quarters. She lifted her head and smiled at Cassidy. "Good afternoon, Cassidy."

"Hi, Valerie. Did you arrive with the supply committee?"

Chuckling, Valerie continued to pull levers and snap dividers into place. "Something like that."

Cassidy watched the quick efficient movements of her administrator. This woman was in her early fifties and Black Stripe? If someone asked her to place a bet on that question, she'd certainly lose. Valerie's khaki slacks were neatly pressed, and the white collared shirt with a small zebra embroidered on the left breast pocket screamed corporate America, not international espionage.

"Where's your tattoo?" The words blurted from Cassidy's mouth, and she felt a wave of embarrassment color her face.

Valerie paused and laughed. "Honey, if I so much as walked into one of those places I'd faint from fear."

"But everyone else has tattoos."

Valerie put her hands on her hips and studied Cassidy. "Only the field ops. I'm administrative."

Cassidy worried her bottom lip. "You perform the same duties for Black Stripe as you do for me?"

She shrugged. "Similar. I just have a higher security clearance. It's my job to coordinate tactical and make sure my boys"—she smiled at Michelle, who was busy arranging her bags in the compartment she'd chosen—"and girls come home safely." Valerie patted Cassidy on the arm. "Between you and me, I much prefer the White Stripe assignments."

"White Stripe? I'm classified as White Stripe?" This was news to her. She covered her mouth, hiding a yawn. Her temple pounded and heralded the arrival of what she knew to be an intense headache. She rubbed the corner of her forehead and gazed longingly at the sleeping quarters Valerie finished arranging.

"Here you go, honey." Valerie slid the curtain she'd hung to the side. "Why don't you rest while I make sure dinner preparations are underway."

Cassidy felt Jake's presence the moment his shadow blocked the daylight from the open door. He moved up behind her and scrutinized the interior of the plane. "Nice job, Valerie."

She sighed and followed his line of vision. "I do enjoy the innovative ideas ZEBRA incorporates. I've rearranged the back end to service your working needs."

Jake nodded and placed his hand on the back of Cassidy's neck. She resisted tilting her head toward his touch and luxuriating in the light pressure of his thumb to the base of her hairline.

"I think you need to take Valerie's advice and rest."

Cassidy shook her head. "If I fall asleep now, there's no waking me. I think I'll grab something to drink and get cracking on the geological survey. Did you get me a laptop?"

"Yes, ma'am. It's with your stuff in the back." Jake stepped aside and allowed her to pass into the back compartment, which had been organized to seat everyone conference-style. She found her bags and laptop secured in one of the storage compartments that flanked the rear wall. The scent of fresh brewed coffee had her mouth watering. "Valerie," she called over her shoulder. "You're a saint."

Cassidy poured herself a steaming mug of energy and settled into one of the chairs. Flipping the laptop open, she plugged it into one of the jacks that allowed her access to the Internet via an onboard satellite system. The machine whirred to life. She accessed her personal directory through the Internet and scanned the list of files that contained all the data on the Niger Delta.

Her eyes skimmed downward, and she narrowed her gaze on the messenger bag. No. The geological survey needed to wait. Without reacquainting herself with all her mission details, she might miss whatever it was on that survey that turned Robert Cole into a killer. Warm honey eyes swamped her memory. "I'll make him pay, Steve. I promise."

She began rereading everything compiled over her six-month tenure in Africa. It didn't take long before the words on the screen pulled her in and blocked out all activity within the jet. Cassidy clicked from one window to another, typing in notes and observations that might be useful. Beyond her bubble of concentration, she absently acknowledged the plane's soaring into the sky with a frustrated sigh at having to hold her laptop steady.

Stretching her arms to the ceiling and bending forward to shimmy her shoulders and work circulation into the frozen muscles on her back, Cassidy stared at the screen before her. She rubbed her temple, refusing to relent to the stabbing pain of her head. With a quick glance out the small window, she noted the darkness. How long had she been at this?

The geological survey was next, and then she'd quit. Tired brain resulted in less than acceptable work.

Moving her hand down, she slipped it beneath the leather folds of her messenger bag. She glanced around to verify no one watched. Other than Jake, Cassidy didn't know whom to trust. Her fingers dug for the tampon container. She felt the plastic surface on the cylinder and slipped the top off, her eyes never leaving the interior of the plane. A thin metal card touched her fingers and Cassidy quickly retrieved it, popping it into her USB port on the laptop before anyone noticed.

Cassidy clicked on the icon to open the file and a geological study of the southern region surrounding Port Harcourt popped up. This was the report from Charlie that Anna left her the day before she died. Cassidy recalled pulling the statistics up regarding the erosion of the section of coastline along Port Harcourt, but beyond that she'd been too tired to finish reading and decided to leave it for later. "I guess now is later." That blank brain cell scratched at her mind, but she couldn't isolate it beyond a foggy idea that she should be remembering something else.

"What was that, Sunshine?"

She glanced up, and her eyes widened as Jake placed a steaming bowl of soup in front of her. "My hero." Until that moment, she hadn't realized how starved she was.

"Wait, you'll love me more in a second."

Spooning the tomato-based vegetable and pasta stock into her mouth, she closed her eyes and savored the subtle taste of oregano and red pepper. She didn't know where Valerie unearthed it, but she was in heaven. "Not possible," she said between mouthfuls.

Jake grinned and handed her a bowl of warm rolls salted with garlic and onion. "Oh heavens"—Cassidy swallowed—"you're right." She snatched a roll and inhaled the yeasty aroma. "I am so hungry."

"Gee," Jake said. "I don't know why. Could it be you haven't eaten anything other than protein bars in close to eighteen hours?"

Cassidy chewed and nodded. "That could be it."

Jake sat down across the table from her and dug into his own bowl of soup. "So what've you found?"

Cassidy dropped her voice to a whisper. "Nothing yet. I'm about to start on the geological report. Anna"—Cassidy swallowed back the sadness—"handed it to me the night before . . ." She glanced anywhere but at Jake's face. Exhaustion was getting the better of her emotions. She didn't want to see his blue eyes or believe that the coldness of the soldier she'd met that night and experienced again today was him.

"The night before?"

Cassidy felt her anger peak. "The night before she died." She pushed her soup away and turned back to study the report. *This will never work. I want him. I hate him. I want him. I hate him.* "Oh for crying out loud, would you please leave me alone?"

Jake's face registered shock, and then his easy grin and relaxed nature slipped away. "Of course, Dr. Lowell. I'll be happy to. However, the moment you have an understanding as to Robert Cole's agenda, I expect to be informed."

His face held distrust, and Cassidy sighed. "I won't hold anything else back from you, Jake, if that's what you're insinuating."

"Not suggesting a thing, Dr. Lowell. Just want to make certain you're clear on the chain of command."

Cassidy bent her head and swore repeatedly until her temper and frustration calmed to a dull roar. Her computer indicated it was almost nine o'clock. Where had the time gone? The remnants of her soup were no longer appetizing. How could a man make her feel complete and whole one moment, then lost and angry the next? "Damn him."

Valerie stepped out of the small kitchenette behind Cassidy. "Are you still hungry, honey?"

"No, Valerie. Thanks. It was delicious."

"How about some cookies?"

Cassidy grinned at the other woman's motherly demeanor. She stood and stretched. "I'm fine. Actually, I think I'll just take this to bed with me."

"Honey, if I had a man looking at me like Captain Anderson looks at you, the last thing I'd be taking to bed is a laptop. That hard drive compared to that hard drive . . ." Valerie pointed in the direction of Jake. "No comparison."

Cassidy gasped. "Valerie, I can't believe you just said that."

"It's the truth."

Cassidy shook her head, smothering her smile. "Have I no respect anymore?"

"Just telling it like it is. And that man *is*."

Cassidy gathered up her laptop and stepped around Valerie. "He's not for me is what he is." She ignored the sadness that crept onto the older woman's face. "And that's a fact." She left the conference area and headed toward the small compartment containing her bed.

Jake blocked her path. "Turning in?"

His face was unreadable, but as Cassidy stared into his eyes she saw a whirlpool of emotion. It mirrored all the silent conflicts between her heart and her brain. "Yes. I'll think clearer after a few hours of rest, but first I'm going to review the survey. I'll let you know the second I have something."

"You have a solid twelve hours before we even approach the coast of Africa."

Cassidy smiled. "Thanks. I'll set my phone alarm."

Jake grinned. "Do you know how to do that?"

Smartass. She'd been given a new phone, one that resembled the model Jake carried. Her suspicion regarding its origin was confirmed. *I have no clue how to set my alarm.* Cassidy squared her shoulders and answered him. "Yes, of course I do. I'll see you in the morning or afternoon or whatever time of day it'll be when we hit the African continent."

He stepped aside, and she skirted past him. Jake placed a hand on her arm, sending waves of fire up her nervous system. She swallowed and slowly raised her eyes to meet his.

"Cassidy, I . . ." His voice was low and hoarse, and he coughed to clear whatever prevented him from speaking.

She shook her head. "Don't go there, Jake." Cassidy freed herself from his burning touch and dove into her compartment. Her hands trembled, and she inhaled several times to calm the conflicting sensations running through her system.

With a flip of her wrist, Cassidy tossed the portable computer onto the edge of her bed. She made sure her curtain was closed as tight as possible and then slipped out of her jeans. The makeshift bed felt wonderful to her tired and aching muscles. She flipped on the overhead light and pulled up the report. Resting her head against the pillow, Cassidy battled against the fatigue that insisted she sleep.

She scanned the first page, which basically detailed the area around Port Harcourt that contained shale, as well as the prolific oil centers. Tracing her finger along the section designated as the oil-rich belt within the Gulf of Guinea, she followed it from the northwest offshore region through the southeast offshore and then inland and past Port Harcourt.

Cassidy clicked to the next page and frowned at the diagram. It contained a dark red shade, setting it apart from the brown of shale and green of oil. Red spread in large ovals above the oil fields of Port Harcourt and west into the heart of the Niger Delta. She studied the fine print, squinting at the tiny letters. The terminology was difficult, spouting geological eras and the development of the delta proper. She only had a cursory understanding of geology and would require additional documentation to explain specifically what the text meant.

The pages blurred, and a frustrated sigh escaped. Sleep was imminent. Moving the computer onto the floor beside her head, Cassidy reached up to flip her light off. If she rested for an hour, maybe she'd be able to see what it was her brain insisted was in the report. Before her fingers caught the switch, her eyes focused on the data lighting the monitor. She twisted to close the lid and paused. The beginning paragraph was titled *Hydrocarbon Trap/Jurassic—Paleocene*.

Cassidy reached over and snagged the laptop off the floor, reading the details. Her eyes widened at the ramifications of the text, and her heart raced.

This was it. Her brain kicked into gear as she realized she'd been reading this prior to going to bed that last night in camp. What highlighted her monitor was the information she'd been trying to remember and the anomaly Charlie had alluded to. The puzzle became clear. She stood and pulled her jeans back on, her body humming with excitement and a disconcerting sense of doom.

New World Petroleum didn't want to control the Niger Delta; they wanted to own it.

CHAPTER 34

JAKE ENTERED THE CONFERENCE AREA INTENT ON DISCOVER-
ing the source of the rich coffee scent that woke him an hour before
his alarm was scheduled to go off. He moved around the chairs and
reached for the pot of brew on the sideboard. A flash of gold caught his
attention. Glancing to his left, he swore a string of curses the colonel
would be proud of.

Cassidy was sound asleep, her head resting on a pile of papers and
arms sprawled across the table. He walked over and gently shook her
shoulder. "Sunshine, wake up."

She stretched and yawned, her hair falling across her face in a tangle of golden curls. "Morning."

He pointed over his shoulder. "Something wrong with your bed?"

Cassidy twisted her shoulders and ran a tongue across her teeth,
smacking her lips together. "I need a shower." She rose, pulled a flash
card from her computer, shuffled the papers together, and offered him
a cheeky grin. The snap of humor that touched her eyes made him
very uneasy.

"What gives?"

"I have a theory of what New World Petroleum's up to."

Jake's attention immediately sharpened. "And that would be?"

She yawned again and shook her head. "I think they've found a new source of oil, but I can't confirm it." She pushed past Jake and headed in the direction of her compartment. "I'm taking a shower. But you need to make some arrangements."

"Such as?"

Cassidy turned and stared him straight in the eye. "We have to go upriver. To the last point David was known to be. My gut says Charles followed him, which is why he wasn't in camp the night of the attack. There's something there, Jake. It's our something worth killing for."

Cassidy felt almost brand new. A few more hours of sleep would probably aid in returning a bit of color to her face, but there wasn't time for luxuries.

Jake drilled his fingers against the tabletop then stood up, running a frustrated hand through his hair. "Why wouldn't NWP proceed with staking a claim at this site the normal way instead of all these backhanded, dark-allied maneuvers?"

Valerie dropped a large basket of muffins in the center of the conference table. "I can answer that."

Cassidy and Jake responded at the same time. "You can?"

Her mouth curved up in a secretive smile. "You didn't think I just pushed papers, did you?" Valerie slid into the chair next to Michelle and picked up a blueberry muffin. Peeling the wrapping off its bottom, she glanced at Jake. "I've received Cassidy's security clearance."

Cassidy frowned. "Why do I need security clearance?" Michelle inched the basket of muffins in her direction.

"That way we won't have to whisper behind your back," Jake said, reaching behind her and palming the same type of muffin. He held a chair out for her, and she sat down.

"I appreciate that," she said, not quite certain she was comfortable with the classification that allowed her into the inner sanctum of Black Stripe. "Tell us what you know, Valerie."

"Right. One of my assignments was to filter all information regarding your mission in Africa. The official statement of purpose was for you to research and generate a positive report regarding the effects of oil production within the Niger Delta."

Cassidy rolled her eyes. "Mission impossible."

"What you didn't know was the reason for that report."

"I know that OPEC requested it. I assumed it was a ploy for more payoff money."

Valerie shook her head. "Not quite. New World Petroleum requested rights for the area you designated up there." She pointed to the whiteboard. "The officials in Port Harcourt refused unless NWP provided a positive report and steps for improving the livelihoods of those within the Niger Delta."

Cassidy frowned. "That doesn't sound right. Why would they do that? It's in their best interest to turn the other cheek and accept blood money."

Valerie popped the last piece of muffin in her mouth and chewed thoughtfully. "From what I could unearth, the pressure from OPEC, stemming from the unrest sparked by the rebels, prompted the local government to take affirmative action. That way it would appear they were protective of this region and fighting for its people's right. If they refused to take affirmative action, OPEC could step in and take a stronger hand in governing this zone."

Jake sighed and nodded. "Makes perfect sense."

"But I didn't write the report," Cassidy added. "Why didn't they hire someone else?"

"Because ZEBRA is the who's who of environmental studies," Michelle mumbled, chewing on her muffin.

Cassidy glanced at Jake, and he offered her a half shrug. "Possible," she said and pushed back from the table. Collecting her discarded muffin wrapper, she tossed it in the garbage can. "We believe we know what they want but how are they going to achieve control?"

Jake leaned back in his chair and uttered one word. "Genocide."

Cassidy gaped at him. It had been a theory, but facing the realism was an entirely different matter. "How could they possibly accomplish that without creating a worldwide upheaval?"

He left his chair and stood in front of the whiteboard. Picking up the black pen, he made an X to the north of Port Harcourt, another X above the red square Cassidy had drawn, and a final X to the left of the Warri dot. "This is where they've purchased land."

"How does that point to genocide?"

Jake drew a line and connected the marks he'd made. "You build a wall."

Michelle snorted, then coughed when she inhaled muffin crumbs. "That's a bit far out, don't you think?"

"Yes," Jake agreed. "But it's why they pay us the big bucks. Thinking outside the box is our expertise."

Cassidy stood and stretched. "It's still a theory. Once we reach the coordinates pinged on the geological survey, we'll know more. If what Jake believes is true, there'll be evidence."

"Speaking of the Niger Delta, we'll be landing in Principe in approximately two hours. I suggest we change into our tactical gear and prepare ourselves."

"Tactical gear?" Cassidy didn't have any such thing. She glanced down at her jeans and shirt and wondered what else she was supposed to wear.

Valerie waved at her. "I took the liberty of ordering you a kit. I'll dig it out from the supplies and bring it to your compartment."

"If you say so," Cassidy replied, still confused as to what tactical gear encompassed. "I'm going to organize all this paperwork and make a few calls. I'd like an update from the CDC as to the status of CPV-19." She began shuffling loose papers together and stacking them in neat piles. Reaching her laptop, she shut the lid and unplugged it.

"Did you get any sleep last night?"

She turned her head and grinned at Jake. "Sure. I'm used to snoozing on conference tables; it's one of my favorite pastimes."

"I'm not joking."

Cassidy bent down and picked up her canvas bag. "Neither am I." She shoved the laptop into its compartment and then filed the papers into another sleeve.

"We have two hours. You can nap."

"Stop it. You sound like Valerie." She gathered up the power cord from her computer and placed it into a side pocket. "One mother aboard is enough."

Jake sighed and mumbled something derogatory under his breath.

It made Cassidy feel all warm and fuzzy that he cared, which irritated her.

Valerie popped out from behind a door Cassidy never knew existed. She handed Cassidy a small black duffel bag. "There ya go."

"This is my tactical gear?"

"Yes, ma'am. Everything you need will be in there." She disappeared back through the door, humming a Garth Brooks tune.

Cassidy scrutinized the bag, holding it at different angles. "What's in here?"

Jake grinned. "Clothes and other stuff." He whistled the same tune Valerie hummed and left her alone.

"It's the other stuff that concerns me." Cassidy picked up her canvas bag and hefted the tactical gear on her shoulder. She headed into her compartment mentally cursing Valerie for sticking a tune in her head. Singing softly, she smiled. "Love this song."

She dropped the bags on her bed. Cassidy tugged the gear bag closer and yanked on the zipper. Within the interior she discovered camouflage military clothes. She grinned when she pulled out the pants and tank top. Never in her life did she think she'd be sporting the muted splotches of a soldier.

Cassidy dug deeper and unearthed a large knife with an ankle band attached to its canvas case. "I like this." She slipped the blade from its cover and twisted it in the light, admiring the sharp jagged edges. "Very pretty." She tipped the gear bag upside down, and all sorts of goodies spilled onto the bed. Canteen. Glock. Holster. Bandana.

Cassidy stripped out of her jeans and polo shirt and pulled on the pants, tank top, and over jacket. There were pockets galore. She strapped the knife to her ankle, gun to her waist, and shoved the other paraphernalia into accommodating folds in her clothes. The socks made her hum in delight. They were made of a blend of cotton and lycra, making them lightweight and breathable. A definite advantage over the thick wool socks she normally used.

She bent and pulled her boots on and laced them up. "Thank you for not replacing these." Cassidy couldn't imagine breaking in new shoes over the next few days. Her shoulders shook in revulsion at the mere thought. "Can we say bloody blisters?" A watch with a large face and built-in compass was next, and she secured that around her wrist.

Cassidy gathered her hair in her fingers and quickly French braided the curly mess, pulling it tight and neat against her head. She snapped a hair band in place at the end, then wound the bandana around the braid and secured it at the bottom. "Wish I had a mirror." G.I. Jane reporting for action. Smothering a giggle, Cassidy stepped out of her compartment.

"I like you in my colors," Jake said from the conference room.

Cassidy glanced down at her outfit. "I think the green is a bit over the top."

Michelle chuckled and moved past Cassidy to sit at the table. They were dressed identically except for the bandana. The ecologist wore it on her head, cap style. "Valerie says there's a call from the CDC with an update on the virus you requested."

"Okay." Cassidy nodded. "Let's get them on video conferencing."

Michelle pushed buttons, and it was only a few seconds before an image flickered on the screen. A group of people in heated discussion gathered around an oval table. Cassidy leaned forward and moved the mike closer. "Liv, is that you?"

Liv Somers, ZEBRA biologist, glanced up and beamed a large smile in Cassidy's direction. "When the chips are down, you call in the best. How the hell are you, Cass?"

Cassidy bent her head and smothered a smile. Jake rolled his eyes at the woman who was originally assigned to Pod Gray Wolf before Black Stripe became involved. "Tell me where you're at?"

"Let's see . . . the first thing on my list is a note from the park rangers. The body you discovered on Yellowstone River is one Jason Gold. Heard of him?"

Cassidy shook her head. "No. What did his background check unearth?"

"Not much if you discard the fact that he's a brilliant scientist specializing in DNA replication." Liz smiled.

Cassidy nodded. "Any connection with Edward Fiske?"

"According to one of the scientific Web sites, he's his lab assistant. They've been working on a methodology to successfully introduce new DNA to red bloods cells."

"That follows in line with everything we know to date. Speaking of which, what's the news on the virus?" Cassidy pulled out her notepad and scribbled Jason's name on it.

"This is one nasty son of a bitch. The formula you discovered written on the bathroom mirror in Salt Lake City has been helpful. Dissecting the genetic composition, we've been able to isolate several areas where a possible vaccine will work. However, you do know that there's no known cure for parvo, right?"

Cassidy and Jake both nodded. "Of course, only reactive treatment for the symptoms," she said.

Liv flipped a document onto the top of an overhead projector, and two images of the virus were displayed on the screen. Red and green were predominant colors within the body of the upper virus, whereas the lower sample appeared to contain less of the red strain. "We've isolated Fifth Disease and injected the non-mutated version of the virus into an infected wolf." The biologist paused and took a small breath. "The cell on top is prior to the injection, and the cell on bottom is after."

"The prognosis?"

"We've been able to cut back on the blood thinners. Heart rate is still elevated but not in the danger zone. It appears that the clean strain of Fifth Disease attacks and neutralizes the viral component of its counterpart in CPV-19." Liv flipped off the overhead projector and stared at Cassidy. "They have a fifty-fifty chance."

"It's better than nothing." Cassidy pulled out her notepad that she'd shoved in one of the leg pockets of her pants. She flipped it open and scanned her writing. "Any more infected humans or canines?"

Liv shook her head and grinned. "I think your immediate response to the situation has prevented farther migration of the virus."

"How about the wolves?"

Liv glanced down at a piece of paper that was handed to her. "It appears that the numbers we received regarding the diminishing packs of wolves were erroneous. A technical guru from the FBI fiddled with the park's GPS tracking system and, *voilà*, instant wolves."

Cassidy frowned. "I don't get it."

"Don't misunderstand me. There's definitely depletion in the northern packs surrounding Gardiner. We haven't determined that the virus has spread beyond that quadrant as of this date. I can reassure you, though, that the numbers to the east and south of Gardiner remain unchanged."

Cassidy jotted some notes down in her pad and then focused back on Liv. "Have you isolated the transference aspects of CPV-19?"

"Yes." Liv paused and conferred with the person beside her. "This is Doctor Michael Rothwell from the CDC. I'll let him finish."

Cassidy smiled at the young man. His close-cropped curls and large eyes provided an almost angelic feature to his face, but the moment he began to speak the seriousness of the situation was loud and clear in his voice. "Beyond the normal parvo transfer, i.e. digested feces, we discovered spores within the wolves' nostrils."

Jake and Cassidy sat forward and glanced at one another with panic in their eyes. "Are you saying this thing is airborne?"

Dr. Rothwell folded his hands and nodded. "That's exactly what I'm saying."

CHAPTER 35

EDWARD HEARD MUFFLED VOICES, THE FOG OF A DRUG-INDUCED sleep shadowing his mind. He struggled upward through the thick blankets of confusion and disorientation. His thoughts slurred, and he battled against the urge to release himself to the comfort of sleep. A deep metallic hum vibrated against his ear. Edward concentrated on the noise and broke through the last barrier created by the narcotic injected into his veins.

His eyes fluttered open and he blinked in rapid succession, attempting to clear his vision. It was dark. A thin line of natural light flickered along the edge of one wall. Edward craned his neck and followed it to the source. He squinted, making out the rounded edges of what appeared to be a small porthole.

With a quick scan of everything that ached, Edward realized his hands were no longer tied. They'd obviously dumped him in here and cut the ropes before leaving. He moved to a sitting position, rubbing first one wrist and then the other. Circulation returned, and his fingers no longer held that tingly numb sensation from when they'd first been bound behind his back.

Edward felt the wall his back rested against. It was cool and smooth. As he tapped his nail against the surface, a high-pitched echo resounded. Metal. Another sound merged with the constant hum. It reminded Edward of the time he'd spent exploring an old naval ship-yard with his father. That day had been cold and damp, making a young Edward crave the sunshine along the beach. He'd fantasized that the waves lapping against the hull of the dead ship carried mer-maids on their watery carpet. Edward felt a brief surge of affection for a man he normally harbored hatred for. Because of his father, he knew his location.

He was on a ship, and the sound that mixed with the hum of what must be an engine was that of water.

Standing up and walking with small, hesitant steps, he ran his hand along the wall. When his fingers brushed against a vertical crack, Edward followed the line down to the floor and back up. A door. He spread both hands wide and searched for the knob.

He found it and twisted. To his surprise, it wasn't locked. Edward opened the door, allowing a small amount of light into his cell. His eyes adjusted, and he opened it more. Inch by inch, beautiful light filled the room. When he felt confident enough, Edward stepped beyond the door and into a brightly lit room.

The first thing he noticed was a thick glass panel separating him from the men in an adjoining room. Edward gazed at his surroundings, absorbing the laboratory atmosphere that was remarkably similar to the one in Gardiner. This one, however, appeared to place him on the other side of the negative airflow chamber.

He recognized the figure of Robert Cole and the thug who'd dragged him from the motel in Utah. They were hunched over a com-puter terminal in a heated discussion with a young man in jeans and a baseball cap. Edward rapped his knuckles against the glass divider.

The three men turned around, studying him.

"Dr. Fiske, how nice of you to join us. Please"—Cole waved a hand in the direction of a lone chair in the center of his side of the room—"have a seat."

Edward's knees wobbled, and he considered sitting with these people a better alternative than fainting. He stumbled toward the chair and sat down. "What am I doing here?"

"Research," Cole said and turned toward the young man typing rapidly on a keyboard. "What's the matter?"

"It looks like they've broken the code I created with Jason that interrupted the signal feed from the tracking devices on the wolves."

Robert moved closer and peered over the technician's shoulder. "It was a matter of time." He patted the young man's shoulder and once more faced Edward. "How do you feel?"

He was thirsty. But instead of answering, Edward glared at him. "I'm not answering another question until you tell me why I'm here, behind this glass partition."

The man raised one brow and beamed a gracious smile at him. "I felt you were of value, of course. One of my associates indicated that you e-mailed Dr. Lowell with some concerns regarding CPV-19."

"My concerns have nothing to do with the virus. I simply need to complete more testing to verify the validity of the modification technique."

Cole tilted his head back and laughed. "Of course you do. And I have to say I appreciate an honest man. My onboard geneticist confirmed that very fact."

Edward glanced left, then right. Why was he separated? If they understood his data that was sent to Dr. Lowell, why keep him alive? "Why am I in this negative airflow chamber?" Edward responded, wondering what game these people played.

"Dr. Fiske, how else am I to test the antidote?"

Edward bent his head, suddenly feeling woozy and sick to his stomach. "I found a way to help millions of people. You're a monster. You've twisted my research into something evil."

Cole sat down and poured himself a glass of water from the pitcher on the table. Edward's mouth felt like sandpaper, but he wouldn't show these people his thirst. No weakness.

"I'm not a terrorist. I'd never approve biological warfare on my own soil. The ability to gauge the virulence in real-world situations created by your laboratory assistant was priceless. Yellowstone is an isolated area. I have every faith that between the CDC and remaining ZEBRA scientists, the disease will be quarantined and eliminated."

Edward bent forward. "And what of the lives lost before that happens?"

"Collateral damage."

The man focused his attention away from Edward toward a man sitting in front of a computer screen. "Have you tracked Lowell and Anderson?"

"They reached Yellowstone at approximately 0900 hours yesterday. My ability to track beyond their flight plan has been compromised." The technician twisted in his chair. "They know Sharpe is missing. Our contact is on high alert, unable to feed anymore information."

"Hold on one fucking minute." The brute who sat on the other side of the computer operator pounded his fist on the table. "Anderson and Blondie are still alive?"

"Of course, Nick," Cole answered. "I told you we needed them." Edward cringed inwardly as Cole bent his head and laughed in a deep wicked tone, then glanced at the man who'd been ready to put a bullet in Edward's brain. "I've already explained to you, they were meant to survive that fall. I only wanted to buy time."

The big man mumbled something unintelligible, then dropped back into silence. His presence at the table made Edward uneasy. There was nothing pleasant about him. If Death were human, he'd be his twin.

Cole leaned forward and addressed the man at the computer.

"When do you think they'll arrive?"

The tech answered. "They're about a day and a half behind us."

"Which," Cole interrupted, "is exactly what we planned."

"Are you certain this is smart? Leading them back here?" Fowler questioned, flexing his fingers.

The NWP president glared at the man. Edward felt blessed not to be on the receiving end of that man's wrath. "If you had managed to intercept that geological report before Anna Kuffae wrapped her meddling paws around it, we wouldn't be in this position now would we, Nick?"

"I didn't receive no fuckin' notification about the geologist until it was too late," the man defended himself. Edward mentally locked away the tidbits of the conversation. He'd ponder them later.

"Nevertheless, if that report had been buried, then you wouldn't have been required to release the Kill-and-Go squads, which in turn would've prevented the involvement of Black Stripe."

Nick rose from the table and crossed his arms. "Maybe you should have been more in tune with ZEBRA and its secret society."

Cole pointed a finger at Nick. Edward remained silent, watching in astonishment. "Don't push me, Fowler." He sighed and seemed to be silently counting to ten. "We're both tired, and a lot's at stake. I'll forget this attitude indiscretion." He turned to face the computer tech. "Have you heard anything on the status of the survey?"

"No, sir. Like I said, communication has been sketchy."

Cole tapped his finger against the top of the metal table and turned toward the other man. "Is the doctor ready?"

Fowler nodded and glanced in Edward's direction, making him feel suddenly like a lab rat.

"Good," Cole responded. "And the amount of CPV-19 is adequate for our needs?"

Nick rose and tapped the computer tech on the shoulder. "Run the figures for the Delta, would ya?"

The tech's monitor sprung to life with a map and then a soft red glow over the portion of what appeared to be . . .. Edward rose and strode toward the glass. He squinted and focused on the outline of West Africa.

Edward froze. They were releasing the virus in the Niger Delta? He frowned.

Robert clapped his hands and nodded. "Fantastic. Anderson and Lowell will land in Principe and then make their way towards us. With a twist of fate forced by my hand, Cassidy Lowell will weave through the villages to the west of Port Harcourt leaving death within her wake. Poor pretty bird, she doesn't seem to know when the cards are stacked against her."

Edward sat back down with a heavy sigh. They spoke as if that's where they were: in Africa. His heart stuttered when full realization hit. He wasn't going home . . . ever.

Everyone in the room laughed.

The door to his left hissed, and Edward spun in its direction. A man in full protective gear entered the room, carrying a syringe in a plastic case. He approached Edward. Robert Cole's voice boomed through the intercom, sounding tinny and distant beneath the shock permeating Edward's mind.

"Edward, be a nice man and roll up your shirt sleeve for the good doctor."

He turned and stared at the smiling face of Robert Cole. "What are you doing?"

Cole lifted a shoulder. "Why, infecting you, of course." He turned and spoke to Nick Fowler. "How else are we supposed to verify the accuracy of the antidote?"

Edward's stomach seized and he gagged, pushing down his nausea. "And if it doesn't work?"

Robert tilted his head to the left and shook it sadly. "Now, Edward,

337

I have every faith in you. Of course it'll work."

Edward felt lightheaded. *They must be pumping some type of nitrous oxide through the vents.* The howl of amusement echoing into his chamber faded as a black tunnel of oblivion closed in and ended his session with consciousness.

Cassidy glanced down at her pad of paper, the hastily scratched notes from the previous teleconference blurring into an unreadable scrawl. She squeezed her eyes shut and rubbed the dull ache that attacked her temple. She was tired. The few hours of sleep she'd succumbed to the night before hadn't been enough.

Jake sat across the table, barking orders into his cell phone. Tangled emotions continued to invade her soul, but she did her best to hide them. In the end, they would part and return to their respective lives. Within the harsh light of reality, betrayal, distrust, and lack of comprehension regarding one another's actions didn't even place a ripple in the pond of incompatibility. They existed in separate worlds. He twisted in his chair and gazed at her, tilting his head and raising his brows in a silent question.

She shook her head, wishing fervently for that sliver of light that would break away the chains on her heart. Cassidy didn't like admitting the possibility she'd fallen in love or that suddenly it didn't matter what he'd done or who he was. She didn't know how to close the wound he'd opened or move beyond the thought of living without him by her side.

Peering out the small window, Cassidy saw a tiny cluster of islands dot the surface of the Gulf of Guinea. Sao Tome and Principe, a group of volcanic islands that comprised a portion of the Cameroon line. They sat off the shores of Gabon and were a mystery to Cassidy beyond what the textbooks described. She frowned, wondering where they'd hidden an airport. "Are you sure there's a place to land down there?"

"Yes," Jake said and laughed softly. "I've been here before." He leaned forward and motioned to her seat belt.

Cassidy grabbed the ends and buckled them around her waist. "You have?"

"The island is on the brink of economic disaster and has leased several acres to the Army. We use it as a jump-off point within this region. It's small but effective."

"I see."

"Do you know anything about the island?"

Cassidy grinned. "From what my one last brain cell remembers, it's about 386 square miles, relies on cocoa exportation, and has over 700 breeds of orchids. Also there are numerous birds that are endemic to its locale."

Jake smiled and shook his head. "You never cease to amaze me. To be exact, that would be 727 orchids as of last week."

Cassidy grinned, deciding not to query him further as to how he knew exactly how many orchids were on the island. "I'll fess up. I'm no wonder child. But in doing research for my assignment here, I ran across an interesting article. These islands were never a part of the African continent, which makes their flora and fauna entirely different than any other region around here. I found that fascinating." Cassidy shrugged. "Just little details that stick in my brain. I'd love to try and grab a few photographs. How long do we have before taking off to the Niger Delta?"

Jake shook his head. "Not long. I have a crew assembling our equipment. I'll have to review whatever intel they've managed to unearth."

"I understand." At least I think I do. Cassidy frowned and focused on the descent. Lush tropical undergrowth met the plane at an uncomfortable rate of speed. Tires collided with the runway and Cassidy held her breath as palm trees and an assortment of other plants rushed past her window, their wide leafy stems swaying and bending beneath the power of the jet engines.

They slowed, and the plane turned off the primary runway and coasted toward a small grouping of metal buildings. The engines stopped and Cassidy went to unbuckle her belt, offering Jake an apologetic smile. "Sorry about the nail marks on your hand." When had he reached over and entwined his fingers with hers?

He grinned. "No worries, Sunshine." Jake turned toward Valerie and Michelle. "It's time to rock and roll. Valerie, you're welcome to join us at base camp or you can stay here. Whatever you choose. Make sure the communications equipment is up and running and give us an hourly update on the status of the wolves and virus."

"Aye-aye, Capiton." She chuckled when Jake frowned at her. "Take care of your girl. She's not one of us."

Cassidy rolled her eyes. "I can take care of myself."

"Michelle," Jake called as the ecologist headed out the door. "I want up-to-date information on the movements of the squads. Also, coordinate tactical information with the Black Stripe squad assembled. Let them fill you in on our last mission."

"Yes, sir." She turned and jogged out of sight.

"And me?" Cassidy asked.

"You're going to the shooting range."

Of all the things she'd expected to hear, that wasn't even close to being on her list. "I'm hopeless."

Jake shook his head. "Get your gear. I've seen you throw a knife and understand your comfort level with that weapon. However, it's not functional for where we're going. If you don't learn to shoot straight, you're not coming along."

Cassidy stepped into her compartment and grabbed her gear bag. "Honest, I'm fine with the knife."

She turned to leave the small cubicle, but Jake blocked the doorway. "Trust me, you won't have time to chase your knife down after every throw." He grinned when she frowned.

"You've got a point there."

"Let's go, Sunshine. We have two hours before Colonel Price arrives."

Cassidy followed Jake out of the plane and paused, the humid atmosphere strangling her after the controlled temperatures of the plane. Stripping off her lightweight jacket, she understood the selection of a tank versus tee. "Hot," she exhaled.

"Yes, ma'am."

She scanned her surroundings. The runway was at the top of a high peak. In the distance, she could see bright orange and green tiles dotting the landscape. There didn't appear to be an abundance of roads, and the noise from the surrounding tropics was a symphony of bird songs. The fumes of oil and gas were all that permeated the air around the small landing strip, but Cassidy imagined the perfume of the myriad of flowers and tropical plants would be sweet nectar.

"Santo Antonio," Jake said, following her line of vision.

"I don't suppose we're going there."

He winked. "No, we're not."

"How about the beach? I hear it's lovely this time of year."

"Sorry, Sunshine. No bird watching. No beach. And no shopping."

She narrowed her eyes and sashayed past him. "You're *no* fun."

Cassidy spotted a military truck parked close to the first metal building. "Is that ours?"

"I believe it is."

They approached it and tossed their bags in the back. "Michelle's already gone?"

Jake paused before revving the engine. "Cassidy, this is a covert mission. If I didn't think you were necessary for its success, you wouldn't be here."

"I figured that," she responded, her voice taking on the icy undertone of her aggravation. She wasn't a child. "I've been in dangerous situations before."

"No," Jake said, shaking his head. "You haven't. Not like this."

"I'll do what I'm told."

"I don't doubt that. But I want you to remember we're going to war. Are you prepared?"

She stared at him, unable to voice the words lodged in her throat. Was he asking her if she was prepared to die? "No."

"Good. That's exactly how it should be. Don't get cocky, and don't get bossy." He started the ignition, backed the truck up, and sped across the tarmac.

"I suggest you take your own advice."

"No need, Sunshine." He grinned at her. "I'm the man in charge, which makes me automatically bossy and most certainly cocky." His eyes glinted in amusement, and she stuck her tongue out at him.

Cassidy sobered, her mind turning to the events about to unfold. "How many men will you have?"

"Only a handful. This is extreme covert ops. The United States imports 33 percent of their oil from Nigeria. If the Nigerian government were to catch wind of this infiltration into their land, they'd stop exportation."

"I see."

"Our rescue mission of your crew a few weeks ago was sanctioned by OPEC because you were there on their behalf. Otherwise, we would have had to leave the choppers behind and come in by foot."

Cassidy chewed over this information. "But we're no longer sanctioned?"

Jake shook his head. "Nope. You never know which way the wind blows when it comes to third world governments. This will appear as just another attack by rebel forces."

"And if we fail?"

"We won't."

Cassidy sighed and gazed out the window. His confidence didn't appease her uncertainty. If anything, it accentuated exactly how unprepared she was for this mission. He pulled off the road onto a winding dirt path. Through the wide branches of the palm trees, Cassidy spied several military tents interspersed with metal modular buildings. She immediately recognized the ZEBRA logo that was painted on the buildings. "Is this base camp?"

"Yes. But we're going to the range first. It's only a few clicks more."

"Okay." Cassidy closed her eyes, allowing the warm breeze to caress her face. They were far beyond the hot tarmac of the tiny airstrip, and sweet fragrances from a plethora of orchids and lilies tickled her nose. "They speak Portuguese here, right?"

"In the late fifteenth century, the Portuguese explorers Pedro Escobar and JoAo Gomes discovered these islands." He knocked his shoulder against hers. "I know a few things, too."

She offered him a cheeky smile. "Yeah? Did you know that these volcanic islands are one of Africa's smallest countries?"

"Yes," Jake laughed. "I did know that. Over the past six months, I've spent quite a bit of time here."

Six months? Cassidy frowned. "I don't suppose that time span has anything to do with my assignment in the Niger Delta."

Jake frowned. "Now you know if I tell you that, I'd have to kill you."

"I have security clearance. Valerie said so."

"Only for this mission."

She hated being in the dark. What the hell had he been doing in the Niger Delta? If he'd been there that whole time, then he certainly would've been prepared enough to save Anna and Georgie.

"Cassidy, stop that thinking."

Shocked at his intuitiveness, Cassidy frowned at him. "I'm not thinking."

Jake didn't bother to hide his grin, and it irritated her. "Yes, you are. You're trying to figure out exactly how long I've been here and whether or not I was spying on you. And if I was monitoring your actions, then why the hell didn't I prevent the invasion of your camp?"

Her mouth dropped open, and a soft hum reverberated through her body. There was a certain comfort level in having somebody know you so well he could read your mind. "I can't help it."

He parked the truck at the edge of a short grassy plain. Turning toward her, he stared into her eyes. "The Niger Delta is a military hot spot. The United States is very concerned with rebel forces and the depth of corruption within the government. Your assignment allowed our people to move freely within the area. Many of the employees on staff belonged to this unit." He reached over and rubbed a thumb against her cheek. "You weren't alone in your fear for the safety of that region."

Cassidy didn't know how to respond.

"That's how we operate, Sunshine. We weren't there to watch you. You were our cover. An important aspect of our mission. And whatever you were working on, our actions in no way infringed upon your assignment."

"How did you know about the strike?"

Jake offered her a half smile. "We have our informants."

"And Anna? Why couldn't you save Anna?"

"Who says I didn't?"

Cassidy frowned and worried her bottom lip. "I wish you'd be straightforward instead of giving me all these half-truths." She didn't understand the scope of his work, and it was apparent from his description of ZEBRA's presence on this island that she wouldn't be privy to any details.

Jake sighed. "Can we just go shoot and quit arguing?"

"I guess so." Cassidy followed Jake and stopped when he turned around and stared at her. "Are you forgetting something?"

344

"No. But you are."

She tilted her head and put her hands on her hips. "I am?"

He tipped his head back and raised his arms to the heavens. "Please help me." Fixing his sight on her, he pointed back to the truck. "Your gun."

"Oh, right." A soft giggle escaped her mouth, followed by the flush of embarrassment on her cheeks. "Sorry. You can take the girl away from zoology, but you can't take the zoologist out of the girl—or something like that. I'll be right back." Spinning on her heels, Cassidy raced back to the truck and retrieved her gun from the gear bag. She'd stored it there before landing, uncomfortable with its weight around her waist.

She secured the Glock in its holster and went to turn around, but a flash of color distracted her. Twisting her head, she stared at the dusty path they'd driven down. Beyond the canopy of trees, a few buildings from the ZEBRA camp could still be discerned. With only a small portion of the island at their disposal, it appeared to Cassidy that ZEBRA crammed everything around the hub of the encampment. The gun range was less than half a mile from the cluster of buildings.

The figure of a woman dressed in jeans and a bright red tank top walked in her direction. A large white bandage bound across her upper left chest stood out against the cocoa complexion of her skin. Cassidy's heart stopped. She recognized the woman, but it was the young boy tugging and straining against her grip that sprung tears to her eyes. "Cassidy!" the boy cried. "Doctor Cassidy!"

"Georgie," she whispered and ran to meet him halfway. He flew into her embrace, wrapping his bone-thin arms around her neck and squeezing with all his might. Tears poured down her face as she rocked him back and forth, thanking the Lord for the sweet scent of bubble gum.

CHAPTER 36

CASSIDY REACHED OUT HER ARM AND ANNA DROPPED TO HER knees, wrapping both Cassidy and Georgie in her embrace. Tears ran in rivers down Cassidy's face, but she didn't care. She squeezed Anna's good shoulder and kissed Georgie's forehead. Such sweetness. "Damn, I thought you were a goner." For this one second in time, the world brightened.

"It'll take more than a bullet to the shoulder to bring me down." Anna reached over and pried Georgie from Cassidy's arms. "I've been worried sick over you. I saw your vehicle pass the outskirts of the camp and decided to take a chance that you were heading out here. I knew you couldn't be far. The road dead ends around that bend."

Cassidy stood up and brushed the dirt from her knees. "I'm thrilled you found me because that's nothing compared to what I've been feeling." Cassidy hugged her friend, then turned to Georgie. "And how did you get here, young man?"

Georgie pointed over her shoulder. "Him."

Cassidy spun around and faced Jake. He stood beside the truck, his hands shoved into his pockets. His shoulders were relaxed, but Cassidy felt the tension cross the distance faster than an arrow. The joy

346

at finding Anna and Georgie alive wiped out her immediate reaction to throttle the lying son of a bitch. Why hadn't he told her?

"Cassidy, get a move on. We're running out of time."

She glanced at Anna, then back at Jake, and shrugged. "Can't it wait?"

The steel expression that slammed down over his face caught her by surprise. What was his problem? She'd been the one running around the past three weeks with a mountain-sized gorilla of grief hanging on her back.

"War waits for no one." He turned and motioned for her to follow.

War. Cassidy rolled her eyes at his dramatics and offered Anna a slight smile. "We'll catch up later."

Anna nodded. "I'll be back at camp when you're ready."

Jake called her name and even though the tropical foliage softened his voice, she heard his anger loud and clear. "Gotta run." Jogging in his direction, she thought of a few choice words to stick up his tight military butt.

Jake reined in his temper and counted to five. The expression on Cassidy's face burned into his mind. Her happiness and relief at finding her friend alive softened her features and smoothed the worry lines he'd spent the past week memorizing.

Until that very moment, he hadn't believed she honestly thought he'd allowed Anna Kuffae and her son to die. His stomach twisted, and for some insane reason he felt betrayed. This strong reaction to the realization she didn't trust him shocked and scared him.

Swearing and kicking the dirt, he yelled for her again.

"I'm here," she called and broke through the hedge line into the clearing. "Quit your caterwauling."

He glared at her. "I don't caterwaul."

"No. You bellow like a wounded rhinoceros." She tilted her head and offered an expression that begged for his rebuttal.

He wasn't about to enter into an insult contest. Jake drew her attention to the targets lined up on the other end of the shooting range. "Shoot."

"Just like that?"

Jake nodded. "Yeah, just like that. I want to see your style."

"Okay. But you'd better duck."

He bent his head and smothered a grin. Even with all the bullshit going on, she still got to him. "I think I'll be fine. I'm right next to you."

She shrugged. "Don't say I didn't warn you." Cassidy jammed a clip into her gun, flipped the safety off, aimed, and fired.

Jake watched in amazement.

"I'm glad I've stunned you into silence. What shall I do next to entertain?"

He stared at her and grinned. "Open your eyes."

"What?"

"Open your eyes." Jake stepped behind her, guiding her arm and the gun in the direction of the target. He ignored the sensation and immediate heat of her body. "When you pull the trigger, don't close your eyes."

She spun in his arms and flashed him an annoyed frown. "I don't close my eyes."

"Yes, Sunshine. You do."

Sudden realization dawned on her face. "That's because I was taught to throw a knife that way."

Jake shook his head. "I don't think I want to understand that comment. You can throw a knife; now let's see if you can shoot a damn target from forty feet."

She nodded and shoved her elbow into his gut. "Stand back." Cassidy moved her shoulders back and forth. "You have real personal space issues."

He crossed his arms and lifted his chin in the direction of the targets. "Shoot."

Cassidy fidgeted for awhile, raising her gun then shaking her head and pointing it back at the ground. With a deep breath, she aimed and fired. When the bullets hit their target, she whooped with delight. "I did it! I did it!" Turning, she jumped into Jake's arms and hugged him.

He stepped out of her embrace. "Now do it again."

She tossed him a cocky smile and spun to face the target. He stepped farther away and settled against the base of a palm tree. Jake watched her aim, fire, reload. Aim, fire, reload. After a while, her shots became consistent and he smiled at the confidence of her stance.

The alarm on his watch chimed, and he glanced at its face. "Time to go. The big man is here."

She peered over her shoulder and nodded. "Okay." Walking toward him, Cassidy opened her mouth to speak but Jake turned and headed back to the truck. He didn't want to hear her accusations or apologies or whichever current emotion topped her list regarding transgressions-by-Jake. Right now, he was making a list of his own.

Cassidy, her face troubled, slipped into the seat beside Jake. He wanted to ignore the feeling in the pit of his stomach and concentrate on only his mission, but it wasn't possible. He flipped the ignition and pulled slowly onto the dirt road. "I never really thought you believed I'd left Anna and her son behind."

Cassidy stared out the window, her back toward him. "No. You probably didn't. And I never believed you capable of blaming me for Steve's death. But I've healed that wound and moved forward, so I suggest you do the same."

Jake's heart stopped. What the hell was she talking about? "I don't blame you for Steve's death." He jammed his foot against the brake, and they lurched to a stop. "Explain yourself."

She twisted around and faced him, her face flushed with anger. "You accused me right after I told you about the geological. You said if you'd known I had this, Steve might not have had to die."

Jake closed his eyes and rubbed a hand across his forehead. "Those words were said in anger, Cassidy." He swore when her eyes welled with tears.

"I didn't even know that's what Cole was after, so how could I have told you about the survey?"

He rubbed a thumb across her cheek. "I'm sorry."

She sighed and shifted away from his touch. "Too late. Let's just move forward and complete our mission."

Jake didn't like her response but agreed on the last bit. They had a job to finish, and he prayed doing so would leave her heart open to his affection. They drove the rest of the way in silence. Jake pulled the truck between two large canvas tents. The tall figure of Colonel Price dominated the space to the left. He signaled for Cassidy to follow him and entered the command tent.

"Colonel Price." Jake saluted.

"Anderson, damn good to see you, boy!" He reached forward and squeezed his shoulder. "And I presume this pretty little lady is Dr. Lowell?"

Jake turned his head to hide the grin at Colonel Price's description. If he concentrated, he bet he could hear the prickling of her skin.

"Yes, sir. That would be me, the pretty little lady."

Swallowing his laughter, Jake moved toward the center table that housed a mock-up of the Niger Delta. "Have you reviewed my plan of attack?"

"Just about to. Why don't you explain?" Colonel Price said. He walked toward Jake and signaled for Cassidy to move ahead of him.

"This region is where they will expect us to infiltrate." He glanced up at Cassidy and winked. "Standard operating procedure is to find the

350

quickest route to our target while remaining one with the environment. Under normal circumstances, I would direct my men to be dressed as locals, blend in with the Port Harcourt crowd, and move toward the coast. I'm figuring that Cole will be informed of this due to their inside connections." Jake walked around the other edge of the table and pointed to an area above the space Cassidy thought held the new vein. "We're going here." He paused and pointed at Cassidy. "Just you, me, and Anna."

"Run that one by me again?" she asked.

"Because of the suspected mole, my squad will be heading out an hour after us following the original game plan. We're going in alone."

Cassidy frowned, her suspicions regarding the Black Stripe team validated by his concern. "I figured something was up. Glad you're not the turncoat Anderson."

Jake glanced up in surprise, then shook his head and ran his hand through his hair. The colonel crossed his arms over his chest waiting to hear Jake's response. "You could've just asked."

She shrugged. "We don't always tell one another the truth, so what good would that have done?"

Jake rolled his eyes. "Here's my take. No one but Black Stripe knew we were on the transport plane. So how did Cole find us?"

"And how did they know about the location of Fiske?"

He nodded. "Exactly."

Cassidy paced in a tight circle, muttering to herself. "And you don't know who the traitor is, so you're sending us in alone?" She worried her bottom lip. "The squads will be on high alert. They've flanked the entire coastline and roam in packs through every region of the Niger Delta. How will we avoid them?"

Colonel Price stepped forward. "I have to brief the president. I'll leave you two to hammer out the final details."

Jake saluted and Colonel Price grinned, causing an intense wave of irritation to flood Cassidy's body. The second the colonel left the tent, she pointed an accusatory finger at Jake. "Explain what you're doing about the Kill-and-Go."

"Anna's been in touch with an Ijwo militant group. They say they'll help."

Cassidy frowned. "The rebels are young, inexperienced kids with big guns. You can't expect them to become fierce warriors overnight. And they're not known for being the most cooperative bunch."

"It'll work." Jake answered. "They'll cover our investigation."

"How?"

Jake shrugged. "By doing what they do best."

"Which is?"

"Killing."

CHAPTER 37

EDWARD RAN HIS NEXT STAGE OF TESTS. HE DIDN'T KNOW HOW long he'd been locked in the laboratory, but his adrenaline held him together and pushed his brain into overdrive. Once he removed the aspect of his ego, he found an interesting level of detachment. The antidote had worked. His blood was clean of CPV-19. Cole had demanded he produce another hundred vials, and he'd agreed as long as he was allowed to continue testing the DNA modification and inconsistencies.

The pounding in his head caused by his bullet-wounded ear became a dull background noise.

Stretching his arms wide, Edward tipped his head back and yawned. He moved his shoulders and decided to stretch his legs. His butt was numb from spending hours on the round cushion of the lab chair, and there were still resounding effects of CPV-19 running through his bloodstream. A drop of blood trickled from his nose, and he picked up a tissue to wipe it away.

The door opened, and a man he remembered as the computer technician entered. "Doc, I need you to fill these vials with your magic potion." He dumped a bag of glass tubes screwed into small spray bottles.

The rotor blades of the chopper spun dirt into small funnel clouds, kicking pebbles and grime at Cassidy's legs. "Let them go first."

"What are they doing?"

He motioned for her silence.

The men finished hauling the last item onboard and Jake followed it, jumping into the interior of the helicopter. He reached down and held his hand out for her. She hesitated for a moment, glanced up at his face, and inhaled in surprise at the sudden panic within his eyes. Cassidy stepped forward and grabbed his hand. He pulled her up and into the helicopter, their gaze never wavering. "You have to trust me," he said, his voice harsh within the metal interior of the helicopter.

Cassidy blinked and bent her head. "I trust you with reservation. We don't exactly have the best track record with one another."

She turned away at the flicker of hurt in his eyes and sat down, buckling her belt and frowning when Jake settled next to her. He circled his hand above his head, and the pilot nodded. The chopper lifted off the ground, churning up deeper layers of dust and ruffling the edges of the camp tents.

Georgie waved madly from the ground below. Cassidy smiled and waved back, then stole a glance at Anna. Tears glistened in Anna's eyes, and Cassidy's heart went out to her.

Cassidy turned her attention to Jake. "So why the public exit on a Red Cross transport?"

"If we're tagged by the Nigerian government, we'll be under the disguise of an emergency medical supply drop."

"That the reason you're basically advertising our departure?"

Jake grinned. "Just treating it as a normal run." He handed her a small box.

"What's this?"

"Something a bit more substantial than that granola bar you just wolfed down."

She shook her head. "I'm not hungry."

"You need energy."

"Trust me," she said. "You don't want me to eat."

Jake frowned at her. "Cassidy, we need to put our personal feelings aside and concentrate on this mission."

He stared at her, and she kept her face as unemotional as possible. "I am concentrating on this mission." The flips and dips her stomach was doing had absolutely nothing to do with him. Nothing at all.

The helicopter flew low, beneath radar level. It hummed across the Gulf of Guinea. Cassidy could see the glow of the gas flares far below dotting the dark water like fireflies. The chopper banked north and sped past the shoreline in the direction of the heart of the jungle. Cassidy rested her eyes, concentrating on not throwing up. Anna chatted with the soldiers on either side of her, as calm as a cool summer evening.

I will not hurl.

She checked her watch. They'd been airborne for close to two hours. "Do you have any idea what these rebels are capable of?" she asked Jake.

"Do you believe they'd do anything to jeopardize their own people?"

"Hell, yes." She slapped her palm against her forehead. "But you don't, do you? You're thinking that the drums and rituals will be what pulls everyone together and focuses them on the Kill-and-Go only." How could she have been so foolish? "This is all so . . ." Cassidy waved her hand in the air. "Half-assed."

"Fear is crippling," he answered.

She wrapped her fingers around his forearm. "Jake, listen to me. This is nothing to sneer at."

"I would never consider belittling someone's beliefs or goals for freedom."

She tugged on his arm. "You're not listening to me."

He patted her hand. "Yes, I am. You don't believe the Ijwo will follow through on their promise."

Cassidy nodded. "If they don't, your ass is dead. Do you get that?"

"Stop." His face flushed a deep red, and the edge of his eye twitched. "Who's being condescending now? This is what I do, Cassidy. I'm a trained soldier, not some snot-faced biologist. With or without the Ijwo, this mission will be completed."

Her breath caught, but she couldn't argue. He was right. This was his world, and if he chose to party with the devil then there was nothing she could do to stop him. She turned and listened to Anna's idle chatter. The rhythmic thumping of rotor blades drowned most of the conversation taking place across the aisle, but the drone of their voices lulled Cassidy.

Remaining in that plateau where reality touched only the surface of the mind, the minutes passed quickly. With a jolt, Cassidy realized they'd dropped lower and the jungle lay directly beneath. Anna stood and held onto a strap to keep herself steady. Cassidy staggered to her feet, allowing Jake to guide her into position. He rested his hand on her shoulder and gently pushed her forward.

The helicopter hovered over a small clearing, never fully touching the ground. Cassidy jumped, her duffel bag gripped securely against her chest. A quick whiff of humid air and then her feet crashed into the ground. She bent her knees to absorb the impact and rolled to the side, making room for Anna and then Jake. Her fingers dug into cool earth and damp leaves as she pushed off to stand.

The chopper drifted away, and the jungle settled into its normal nighttime activity. Isolation and a feeling of disembodiment descended upon Cassidy. A pounding rhythm filtered in their direction; the pulsing of ceremonial drums. Cassidy shivered, dread washing across her skin.

"Come on, Sunshine. We have no time to waste."

Cassidy focused on him as he turned and ran into the woods. She jogged after Jake, followed by Anna. Their footsteps were lost beneath the beat of drums, but Cassidy heard her own ragged breath and that of Anna's as they struggled to maintain Jake's pace. There was a narrow dirt path before them that cut through the jungle, used by the villagers to reach either the river or the road. As Jake approached the fork, he paused.

Cassidy moved beside him, holding her side and pinching at the stitch that burned. "What?" Cassidy kept her voice low, but it sounded loud and harsh against the natural music of the jungle. Jake tugged on her arm, pointing to a small area beyond a cluster of trees, indicating that she and Anna take cover.

She grabbed Anna's hand, and they moved where he pointed. Cassidy kneeled, adjusting her weight to avoid sharp rocks. The spidery fingers of the mangrove root gave her a handhold. A bead of sweat trickled down the corner of her cheek, and she rubbed her chin on the edge of her shoulder wiping away the moisture.

Her heart pounded furiously. Fear. Cassidy inhaled deeply and calmed her breathing. She wasn't cut out for this line of work. The enormous cavern that separated the two worlds she and Jake occupied loomed before her eyes. His calm detachment anchored his familiarity and ease in covert and dangerous missions. Cassidy suddenly felt like a scared rabbit. Something brushed against her shoulder, and her heart almost burst from her chest when Jake's whisper followed the touch of his hand. "It's all clear," he said.

"Jesus, Mary, and Joseph," Cassidy exhaled, her hands shaking from the adrenaline surge. Jake led them in the direction of the pounding drums.

A small village appeared before them. There were rows of crude concrete buildings, their doorways containing nothing more than a blanket to prevent the invasion of mosquitoes. Life here wasn't easy.

357

Darkness of night glowed with fires. In this remote corner of the delta proper there were no oil wells, which meant no gas flares. They felt the pollution in the form of acid rain and diminished river life. If Cassidy remembered correctly, there were a few pipelines that cut to the east. But there hadn't been a spill in this region for twenty years.

If what she feared lay upriver, it would all change. New World Petroleum would rip through this jungle devouring everything in its path. Within the center of a clearing, a mass of bodies swayed to the power of the drums. They chanted and banged their feet in rhythmic steps upon the hardened earth. The women wore strands of beads braided within their hair. The multicolored decorations knocked against each other, creating a beat within a beat.

The men sported colors and tattoos in varying pictures. Each tribe held its rituals sacred. Some had piercings that must be unbelievably painful; others wore a simpler display of their culture—with only one line of paint highlighted by a few white dots.

Amazing. Cassidy stared in astonishment at the blend of tribes.

The one thing that remained common among these people was their conviction and fervor to banish the evil that controlled their soil. The band of rebels, guns slung carelessly over their arms, circled the edge of the worshippers, moving and singing along with their people.

A group of men surrounding the dancers noticed Jake and signaled across the fire. With a single cry, a large drum pounded twice and the dancing stopped. Bodies swayed and the circle opened; seven men approached them. Their hair appeared wild and gray, interwoven with feathers. Fangs and claws of the jungle were strung like beads around their necks, heads, and waists. All held staffs and their eyes burned with fire, red replacing the whites around their pupils.

Cassidy swallowed, not wanting to show fear.

They circled the Black Stripe squad, and Anna stepped forward speaking to the assembly in their native tongue. After several moments of what appeared to be intense negotiations, Anna nodded and returned to Jake and Cassidy. "They say that evil flows from the north and they won't go upriver."

Cassidy frowned. "Evil? As in NWP?"

Anna tightened her lips and moved her eyes to caution Cassidy against speaking too loudly. "I don't know. But they're spooked. The Ijwo will head downriver and spread across either side of the banks. They'll hold the Kill-and-Go to this location."

Jake gripped Cassidy's shoulder. "This isn't what I'd bargained for. I wanted them to cover our backs upriver. It's too dangerous. We need to call in backup."

She stared at Jake and shook her head. "We don't know who the mole is. We're better off going it alone." Cassidy placed her hand on Anna's arm. "Stay here and keep us apprised of any threat that breaks through the Ijwo defense."

Anna exhaled and pursed her lips. "This is too dangerous, Cass. David and Charles . . ."

Cassidy didn't let her finish her sentence. "We have to be sure of what NWP's doing, Anna. I can't show up to OPEC and throw out unfounded accusations. If we're shutting this operation down, I need facts. Hard facts. Or else every life . . ." She choked, Steve's smile flashing through her mind. "Every life lost because of NWP will be in vain. No . . ." Cassidy straightened her shoulders and turned on her heel. "We're going upriver. Without backup and without the Ijwo." She shifted the weight of her pack from one shoulder to the other and moved back toward the jungle. The flow of trepidation coursing through her veins belied the brave front she'd shown Anna. Cassidy was beyond her comfort zone and completely terrified.

CHAPTER 38

THEY APPROACHED THE RIVER. JAKE MOTIONED DOWNWARD with the palm of his hand, and Cassidy slipped to the edge of the path, pressing herself against the base of a mangrove. She watched Jake scout the area until his body blended with night and he disappeared against the shadow of the river. A light breeze kicked off the water and fanned across her face, bringing with it the acidic tingle of oil she associated with the Niger Delta.

Jake appeared before her and held his hand out. He spoke with a half whisper. "The boat's ready."

Cassidy nodded and followed him to the edge of the embankment. She waded into the water, inhaling sharply at the chill bite of the river. As gracefully as possible, she lifted her leg and slid over the top of the thick rubber boat, tumbling inside and quickly righting herself. Jake pushed them off from shore and jumped aboard. He ignited the small outboard motor, and they began their journey upriver.

Fog thickened as Jake maneuvered them into the center of the river. It cloaked their presence but hindered their vision. Cassidy unzipped her pack and retrieved a small flashlight, map, and compass. Spreading the map on the base of the boat, she hunkered down and flipped the switch of the light. Shielding the light with her body, Cassidy placed the compass upon the map and mentally calculated their position.

"We've about ten miles to go before heading back to the shoreline." She kept her voice soft and quickly shut off the light.

Jake patted the floor of the boat and she nodded, shuffling back to seat herself between the warmth of his legs. She held tight to the compass and map.

He bent forward and spoke into her ear. "You never really explained exactly what it is we're looking for."

"I think a new drill site, but I'm not absolutely certain."

Jake sighed. "Yeah, I understood that part. But something's got your knickers in a twist, Sunshine. Why is this new drill sight so threatening?"

Cassidy nestled back against his chest and lifted her face to stare into his eyes. "Charles' data shows an incredible amount of collected oil, but it doesn't show the source—that's the anomaly."

"I don't get it."

"During the Jurassic period the sea level of the African continent lowered, leaving behind an enormous section of land to the evolutionary process. Until the middle Tertiary the fauna and flora of Africa were distinct from those of Eurasia and the rest of the world, creating this unique pocket of organic material."

Jake nodded. "That's what crude we're extracting now, right?"

"Correct." Cassidy shifted her weight, and rested her elbow against Jake's leg.

Jake leaned forward and she held the compass up for him, flipping on the flashlight for a moment so that he could verify they were on course. "And why would this oil be different than all the other sites that are being drilled?"

"Because the stats Charles recovered display only vacuous space beneath the oil."

"A canyon?"

Cassidy lifted one shoulder and stared into the night. "A very big canyon." Cassidy's nose wrinkled, and she rubbed it against her arm. "What stinks?" She coughed and gagged as the scent became stronger, making breathing difficult.

Jake pulled the bandana off her braid and handed it to her, signaling with his hand that she should tie it around her nose. She nodded and mirrored his actions. He idled the motor and grabbed her flashlight, flipping a beam of brightness across the water. "Would you look at all these fish?"

"Dead fish."

"There must be thousands."

Cassidy reached overboard and plucked one from the water, holding it underneath the flashlight Jake beamed in her direction and performed a cursory check. "Gills are full of silt." She tossed it back and peered through the fog. "How close are we to shore?"

"A couple hundred feet. Want to check it out?"

She retrieved the flashlight from Jake and consulted the map. "We're not far from our coordinates. I think whatever we find here"—she pointed at their destination—"will explain this. It seems counterproductive to investigate when my instinct says it's nothing more than erosion created by excavation of the land."

"You sure?"

Cassidy nodded. "I've seen this before. Not quite so bad, but I've seen it. When you strip the mangroves from the shoreline, the soil erodes contaminating the water and strangling the fish."

"Let's move on then." Jake fired up the engine and continued upriver.

The rubber boat moved through the water, each bump and sway heightening Cassidy's anxiety. They dropped into silence, both caught within their own dark thoughts.

"This could be a suicide mission. No backup. No nothin'. We don't know what the hell's waiting for us."

Cassidy refused to respond, her voice unable to carry any words that would dissipate the sinister edge of Jake's statement. He was right. She glanced up, startled when he flipped the engine off. "What's going on?"

Jake pointed over her shoulder. "We're here."

Cassidy ran her palms along the cool metal that framed the levy. She couldn't see more than a few feet in front, but she felt the power and span of the dam by the sheer vastness of empty space beyond the railing. "This is amazing."

"What's it for?"

Biting her bottom lip, Cassidy smiled when another puzzle piece fell into place. "A portable oil rig."

"This place feels abandoned."

Cassidy nodded in agreement. "NWP would be foolish to maintain a presence in an area they don't own. It would draw too much attention. I think we're safe to explore."

Jake stopped her from moving down the ladder they'd located. He bent close and stared directly into her eyes. "David wasn't safe. Don't get cocky."

She gripped the edge of the crudely built ladder, ignoring the prick of splintered wood. "Don't worry, Captain. I'll be careful."

Jake grunted something unintelligible, pulled a length of rope off his shoulder, and tied it to the edge of the railing. He allowed it to unravel, and Cassidy watched as it fell gracefully downward. "What're you . . ."

Her words trailed off when Jake touched his lips lightly to her cheek and whispered, "Don't take too long, Sunshine."

She bit back an indignant shout as her eyes trailed his graceful leap off the edge and fast rappel into the belly of the levy. "Cheater," she hissed and quickly began climbing down the ladder.

When her toes touched solid ground, Cassidy exhaled a shaky breath. She was grateful for the darkness. If she'd realized exactly how far down the base sat, her descent would've been riddled with panic and hyperventilation. Jake moved close and tapped a finger against her nose. He pointed two fingers at her eyes and then pointed them back at his own eyes. When she opened her mouth to speak, he shook his head with a sharp motion and then did the funny finger signal again. Cassidy frowned and bit her bottom lip. He rolled his eyes and repeated the eye poking maneuver, causing Cassidy to bend over and stifle nervous laughter. She'd watched enough movies to finally figure out this meant keep your eyes on me, but being an actual participant threw her out of reality.

With a few deep breaths she gathered some control and nodded at Jake, mimicking his finger signal and sucking in her lips to prevent another bout of giggles. He shook his head in defeat, then spun on his heels and jogged into the darkness. Cassidy followed, matching his pace. Her normal curiosity was curbed by the blanket of night. Visibility remained limited.

She felt the grade of earth shift as they headed upward, out of the levy. Jake paused at the top and motioned for Cassidy to retrieve the map. She laid it on the ground, and he focused a tiny beam of light on the area where her finger rested. Cassidy attempted to gain a clearer picture of their surroundings, but he flipped off the flashlight.

The moonless night left them victim to protruding roots and uneven ground. Jake kept their pace slow and methodical. Cassidy ignored the caress of foliage as it brushed against her face, not wanting her mind to stray to all that crawled upon its surface. Her line of business alerted her to the full dangers of what lurked within the dense jungle.

Jake paused. Cassidy slammed into his back, distracted by her attempt to listen for snakes and the like. He grunted but remained still. She tilted her head and peered around his shoulder. The jungle opened to a cleared area of land. There were shapes and shadows of things piled on the earth that were indiscernible in the darkness. A soft hum filled the night air.

Jake glanced over his shoulder and held his fingers to his lips. Cassidy remained silent. He dropped to the ground and she followed his actions, belly crawling across the clearing and in the direction of the odd noise. She felt a vibration and paused. Cassidy turned her head and put her ear against the dirt.

The vibration was real. It shook the earth and reminded her of the time as a teenager she'd tested Hollywood and placed her ear to the ground, listening for approaching horses. Her father had laughed but Cassidy sought the truth, intent on proving to the world how smart she was. Sure enough and much to her surprise, the approaching herd of Cutter horses she'd seen in the distance caused the earth to echo the pounding of their hooves.

Lost in the sound that hummed from below, she didn't hear Jake's whistle until a rock hit her forehead. Rubbing the sore skin, she glared into the darkness. His low whistle reached her ears, and she scooted forward.

"Don't do that again." He ground the words out through gritted teeth. "I can't see you in this darkness."

"The earth is vibrating," Cassidy hissed back.

"No kidding. Stay close."

She stuck her tongue out at his back and moved behind him. He stood and reached down to help her to her feet. "There appears to be a cave here."

"No sign of life."

Jake tilted his head and searched their surroundings. "That we can see."

They slipped between two leafy bushes and into the cool entryway of the cave. Cassidy felt the damp stone beneath the palm of her hand as she stepped forward; it soothed for some unknown reason. Her foot caught on a soft mound jutting from the base of the wall and caused her to stumble. Jake flipped on the flashlight and spanned the ground.

"David's backpack." Cassidy dropped to her knees, recognizing the worn green fabric and bright orange initials he'd embroidered into the canvas himself. Her fingers traced the smooth stitching, and she swallowed against the sudden lump that formed in her throat. "I remember when he did this. He hated that Charles kept grabbing his pack by accident so he picked the loudest thread he could find and sewed on his initials." She gasped when Jake's flashlight highlighted what appeared to be a dark patch of blood against the rock wall. Standing, she scrutinized the area. "There's some scalp and hair here." She ignored the sudden dip in her stomach at the site of the matted hair and dried brown substance.

Jake pulled out an envelope and small knife. "I'll collect DNA."

Cassidy nodded and disregarded the trepidation that crawled along her skin. They moved farther into the cave, every step cautious, every breath silent. Her heart pounded in her ears in direct competition with the mechanical humming that drew them deeper and deeper into the cavern.

"Over there," Jake spoke softly into her ear and pointed over her shoulder.

She followed the angle of his arm and nodded when she saw a small red light secured against the cavern wall. "Modernization."

Jake led them across a narrow ledge. The humming notched higher as they passed the red light, rumbling and vibrating through the rock. They rounded a small bend and faced the source.

"It's a generator." Jake approached the large ten-by-ten green box and circled it warily. "There's switches and controls along this back wall."

366

Cassidy flipped her flashlight beyond the shadow of the generator and inhaled a sharp gasp. A lake spread farther than the scope of the beam of her narrow light, its surface rippling in murky waves. She staggered forward, kneeling at the edge of the basin. "Look at this . . ." A loud bang sounded, and Cassidy blinked as the cavern brightened to an uncomfortable level.

"And let there be light." Jake whistled softly, gazing over Cassidy's shoulders.

She followed his line of sight and shook her head slowly from side to side. "This is a lake—no, it's a sea . . ."—her voice dropped to a whisper—"of oil."

"Amazing. No drilling. No methane. Just gallons and gallons of crude ready for shipping."

Cassidy sighed. "But the source?"

Jake signaled for her. "Maybe these maps will help." He pointed toward a wall behind the generator that sported large geological renderings and what appeared to be some type of station schematics.

"You think it's safe to keep these lights on?"

"Probably not." He flipped the switch, and they sank into darkness once more. "Wait for your eyes to adjust before making your way over here."

Cassidy grumbled. "You could've waited until I'd gotten there."

"Sorry, Sunshine. Wasn't thinking."

She moved the beam of her flashlight around the interior and began walking in Jake's direction. Trailing her fingers along the edge of the generator, she guided herself to the back wall. Cassidy began with the geological survey farthest to the left. She studied the drawings, glancing back and forth from the color-coded template in the bottom right hand corner and then tracing her fingers along the survey.

Next, her eyes absorbed the map that displayed a blown-up section of the Niger Delta. "Okay . . ."

Jake inched forward and offered her his full attention. "This is the shoreline of the Niger Delta." She moved her hand toward the bottom of the picture and ran it upward in an arc from the edge of Port Harcourt up and past the area where they stopped at the levy. "Here's Port Harcourt in the south and Warri in the north." Cassidy placed her hand over the center of the line. "This is the middle of the delta proper. This appears to indicate that during the Jurassic period the earth shifted, forcing this section down and into a bowl shape."

"Okay," Jake said, although the tone of his voice indicated he was uncertain of what she implied.

Cassidy twisted around and faced him. "This date here . . ."—she tapped her nail on a crudely scribbled date written in red pen—"shows that this bowl of crude oil reached its full capacity two years ago, shifting the fault planes and leaking into existing veins of oil from the Paleocene era. But the pressure was too powerful and forced another shift in the earth's crust."

"And?"

"That lake, sea, whatever . . ."—she gripped his arm and pointed back over her shoulder—"is all oil. It's endless. Jake, this resource of crude is not only the purest in the world but an amount larger and greater than anything within the Middle East or the rest of our continents."

Jake sighed, shaking his head. "Which means that NWP would control the world's largest source of oil?"

"Worth killing for?"

He shrugged. "If you're into that sort of thing. But yeah, I guess for a guy like Cole it's worth killing for."

"We need to grab a sample, take pictures, and deliver it as proof to President Nuna. If mined properly, this oil could provide Nigeria with steady income for hundreds of years. The potential of bringing West Africa out of its third world status is here."

Jake didn't answer immediately, but when he did, his words froze the blood in Cassidy's veins. "Along with the potential of igniting World War III and bringing more blood and destruction to the Ivory Coast." He sighed and stepped away from her. "It's ironic. A land so rich in resources yet so scarred by death."

His words echoed within the cavern, bouncing back at them until they faded beneath a more ominous sound.

The rapid staccato of an AK-47 machine gun.

CHAPTER 39

JAKE PUSHED HER ROUGHLY AGAINST THE WALL. "STAY HERE."

Cassidy frowned as he made his way toward the entrance of the cavern. "Like hell." He glared over his shoulder but didn't prevent her from following. The gunfire was random, flowing in a wild rhythm, stopping completely, then trickling into a few final bursts.

"I don't think these are NWP men."

Gunfire was gunfire to Cassidy. She didn't care whose finger itched the trigger, the end of the story remained the same. Dead. Deader. Deadest. Not good. "Let's get back to the boat."

"What about your sample?"

Cassidy chewed her bottom lip. "This is too dangerous. Our lives aren't worth it." Frustration and indecision made her voice harsh in the silence of the cave. "We'll come back." Jake stared at her for an excruciating amount of time. She shuffled from one foot to the other and pointed toward the cave entrance. "We'll come back." This time her voice was stronger, more committed.

Jake gave her a sharp nod and proceeded toward the mouth of the cave. Gunfire still wavered on the night air, but now it broke the silence above an area farther north of their location. The grounds clear of in-vaders, Jake signaled her to follow.

Cassidy paused before exiting the cavern. Her fingers gripped the edge of the rock, and sadness welled from the very bottom of her soul, slicing through her chest with the viciousness of a machete. Because of this, she'd lost half her heart, half her world. She'd lost Steve.

A warm hand reached for her, strong fingers intertwining between hers. Cassidy tilted her head up, gazed into Jake's eyes, and saw the other half of her heart.

Jake and Cassidy returned to the rebel camp. Exhausted, but in turn jubilant at their discovery.

"I need to contact Colonel Price and formulate our next course of action." Jake moved to the edge of the woods and signaled for Anna to follow him. "I'd like you to update me on the whereabouts of the Ijwo and their actions tonight."

Cassidy smiled as one of the native women approached her with a crudely carved wooden bowl. "Wine," the woman said and handed it to Cassidy. "Go sit against that rock. It will relax you."

Not wanting to offend the woman, Cassidy accepted the bowl of fermented fruit and headed in the direction she pointed.

She settled against a large rock, content to watch the graceful moves of the women and old men as they leapt in a circle and sang to their gods for deliverance. Cassidy's eyes drifted closed, and she allowed herself a brief moment of respite from the uneasiness that plagued her mind.

A rustle of leaves behind the boulder shot a bolt of fear through her heart. Cassidy sat up, glancing around the rock.

Nothing.

She laughed softly at her nerves and rested back against the hard surface. She thought the hum of native singing and percussion of drums must be echoing through the jungles, creating strange noises.

A twig snapped.

She moved quickly and crouched in a defensive attack position, studying the dark patch behind the rock. This was not her imagination. "Who's there?"

No answer.

Cassidy reached down, feeling along her jeans for her knife. An eerie sound drifted across the night. A soft melody that contrasted with the wild beat of native drums. "Hush, little baby, don't you cry . . ."

Cassidy inhaled sharply as the breath was knocked from her chest. An arrow of pain shot across her breasts, burning and searching for a place to escape her body. She dropped her knife, tilted her head back, and screamed into the night, but her throat was dry and no sound emerged.

Fire. Her veins were on fire. Cassidy dropped to the ground, turning her head and staring into the eyes of Michelle. "What?"

Michelle brandished an empty needle, then tossed it behind her. "Salutations from Robert Cole."

Jake traipsed after Anna, following a group of men into the jungle. The soft ground muffled their steps, and the men before him became ghosts floating silently between the clusters of mangrove forests. They paused at a clearing, and he signaled for the rebel leaders to approach. Anna stood beside him in case she needed to translate. The beating of the drums added an eerie background noise and he swore softly, wishing this feeling of dread and fear would unknot his insides.

Motioning to the men, he crouched and listened to their individual reports. A man lifted his head and spoke above the others. "I am Sunday. I'll be watching you until you leave this area. We found only large gatherings of Kill-and-Go to the south. They didn't head your way, and we didn't cause any bloodshed."

Jake smiled, hiding his concern. "Thank you, Sunday." If Kill-and-Go were congregating in the south, then Robert Cole must be close, which meant the virus had definitely reached the Niger Delta.

"If you need me, you must whistle."

Jake nodded and clapped the man on his shoulder, thanking him. He watched as Sunday broke the men into separate groups and thanked them for their participation. With a quick glance over his shoulder, the man's face split into a wide smile flashing bright white teeth at Jake. He brandished his gun in one hand and lifted a sharp-edged machete in the other. "We go." They melted into the night until only Jake and Anna remained in the clearing.

He frowned and found himself chewing his bottom lip. Rolling his eyes and shaking his head that he'd succumbed to Cassidy's habit, he pointed back toward the direction they'd come from. "Let's go get Cassidy. I want you to remain in the village until morning in case something crops up that I need to be aware of."

Anna nodded and headed past a cluster of mangroves. "That'll be fine."

Michelle withdrew a gun and dug it into Cassidy's temple. The woman's eyes reminded Cassidy of Nick Fowler's. Wild and unrestrained. Evil. "You have more personalities than Cybil." Cassidy spat in her face, attempting to block out the ramifications of what she thought ran through her veins. "I take it this is a little taste of what was cooked up in Yellowstone?"

Michelle hissed and pinched Cassidy's arm where the needle had penetrated. "Oh yeah. But, hey, take heart. You're gonna be famous.

You'll go down in the history books as the mad scientist that killed the Niger Delta." Her gaze narrowed, and Michelle gripped Cassidy's arm. "Now, I've lost patience. Where's the survey?"

A flash of the punching bag entered her mind, and Cassidy remembered her vow. Better, stronger, smarter. Strength in pain. *Oh, no, sister. I'm not going to die alone.* Cassidy twisted toward the woman, her elbow slamming into Michelle's chest and knocking the gun from her hand. She grabbed the ecologist's arm, wrapping her fingers around the woman's wrist with an iron grip and yanking Michelle toward her. Cassidy sank her teeth into flesh. Her jaw locked and she pushed deeper, making certain the skin burst and the salty taste of warm blood flooded her mouth. "Salutations from me, bitch." Cassidy spit blood and torn flesh onto the ground, wiping the back of her hand against her mouth.

Michelle screeched in pain and swore, clipping Cassidy under the jaw with the sharp edge of her knuckles. "You fool. I'll return to headquarters and inject the antidote while you lay here dying, alone and unloved with these disgusting natives you care for so much." She bent forward and lowered her voice. "If you give me the survey, I'll consider sending you back the antidote."

Cassidy was no fool. She concentrated on fighting the automatic urge to check the swatch of packing tape that secured the survey in place. The flash drive she'd taped beneath her breast felt as if it weighed a million pounds and blinked on and off like a neon sign. "I don't have it," she lied.

"Bitch. I know you do. It was on the plane."

Deciding to switch tactics, she softened her voice. "How could you possibly turn your back on ZEBRA after all your years of service?"

Michelle swiped her arm against the sweat forming on her forehead, leaving a red smudge on her cheek from the bite Cassidy had inflicted. "Robert Cole is an incredible man. He's going to make the world sit up and take notice."

Realization dawned, and Cassidy's eyes widened. "You're in love with him?"

"Give me the survey, Cassidy, and I'll come back. I promise."

Shaking her head, she hissed at Michelle. "Never. When Sharpe finds out about your betrayal, you'll be blacklisted and alone. Think of that." Cassidy gazed beyond Michelle's shoulder, noticing that the villagers had ceased dancing and were staring in her direction.

"Drew?" Michelle laughed softly, glancing over her shoulder nervously. "He's dead."

Cassidy lost her breath and struggled to swallow. "What?"

"Such a shame. It appears he couldn't stomach the idea of your part in this little adventure."

"My part?"

Michelle sat back on her haunches and retrieved her gun from the dirt. "Sure. In awhile, you'll be too sick to talk. These people care for you; they'll take whatever measures are necessary to make you better." She bent closer and whispered in Cassidy's ear, her breath hot and feeling as dangerous as a viper's bite. "You're going to spread this disease, Cassidy. It'll be you. You'll kill the Niger Delta." Michelle's patience snapped, and she yelled. "Where's the damn survey?"

The echo of the ecologist's voice drew the attention of the villagers. Several men headed in their direction.

Michelle swore.

"You'll be stuck here with me," Cassidy said. "No chance at that antidote." She gazed beyond the woman at the crude weapons carried by the tribal elders. Michelle's eyes were wide with indecision, but the urge for survival won and the woman backed away, disappearing into the wavering shadows of a mangrove tree.

Cassidy whimpered, a tear slipping down her cheek. Her blood a river of fire as it poured poison into her veins. She needed to stay conscious long enough to warn off the villagers.

Edward rested his head upon the cool surface of the sterile laboratory counters. His body ached from the rough handling of his captivity, and the crude stitches in his ear were not holding up. Blood seeped onto his arm, but he ignored it. Over the past few hours, he'd succumbed to the truth of his future.

There was none.

The laboratory door opened, and a slender woman in her mid-forties entered. She wore all black, which accentuated the curves of her body. He lifted his head and sat up, struggling against the threat of fading into a faint.

"Fiske?" Her voice cut the silence of the lab in two.

"Yes."

"Give me the antidote for CPV-19."

Edward slid off his chair and shuffled toward the silver briefcase. He snapped open the lid and handed the woman a vial.

"Syringe?"

Alarmed, he studied her face. A thin line of blood leaked from the edge of her ear and her breathing appeared labored and thick with mucus. He twisted around and grabbed a sterile syringe from a box on the counter. "Here." Edward pushed it in her direction.

She snatched it up, broke the end open, and plunged it into the vial of antidote. "How much?"

"One cc."

The woman released the plunger, expelling what she didn't need, then jammed the needle into her arm. She moved forward and gripped the edge of the countertop as the antidote flooded her veins. Edward knew from personal experience the burning sensation followed by cold numbness that raged through the woman's body.

After a few moments, she lifted her head and moved into the center of the room. His eyes widened when he recognized the insignia on her shirt. ZEBRA. "Are you here to rescue me?"

She smiled and nodded. "Yes. I'm here to deliver you to your Maker."

Her arm lifted, and he peered down the barrel of a gun. Edward closed his eyes and said a final prayer. He felt a wave of relief at no longer having to carry the burden of the horrible disease his ego created.

Gunfire sounded, and the world went black.

Jake moved through the trees, alerted by the cessation of the ceremonial drums. His pulse beat rapidly, and fear grabbed his gut and twisted painfully. He paused, his hand resting lightly on the slick bark of a mangrove tree. The tempo of the village had changed since his departure. No longer were figures dancing and singing around a center pyre; they were gathered and pacing in worried circles. Jake searched the area for Cassidy.

He swore. Her blond hair should be a lighthouse among the dark-skinned Ijwo. One of the medicine men stepped forward and grabbed Jake by the elbow. "Come here."

Jake glanced back at Anna, who shook her head, as confused and worried as he was. "What's going on?"

"Your woman . . ." The man pointed toward one of the low-rise concrete buildings.

Jake's breath caught, and he shook off the man's hand and ran toward the building. He went to enter, but another man grabbed his shoulders. Jake struggled, shouting Cassidy's name. He broke through the web of hands and crashed into the building, slamming the door open.

"Come no closer," a loud voice commanded from the dark interior.

Jake squinted and recognized the man in the ornate beaded shirt with feathers and bird claws hanging from his dreadlocks as the one who'd approached Cassidy earlier that night and asked her to stay. "What's the meaning of this?" Jake's eyes searched the dim light of the room, and he spied a streak of golden hair in the far corner. Jake moved forward but the black man held his arm, the power of his grip stopping Jake. "Let go."

"No farther."

Jake heard a rustle and squinted through the darkness at Cassidy. She struggled to her elbow, holding her palm out in his direction. "Stop, Jake. Listen." Her breathing was ragged, and he could hear the pain in her voice. "Michelle. She infected me." His heart clenched as her entire body shook with the energy she used to speak. "Antidote at NWP."

He swallowed and inhaled, calming his panic. "Cole has an antidote?"

Cassidy nodded weakly. "Go. Hurry." She collapsed back against the thin mattress.

Jake closed his eyes and reached a hand in her direction, pointing an accusing finger at her. "I told you not to do this anymore."

"Do what?" Her voice drifted into a soft chuckle.

He couldn't stand facing her illness. Jake spun on his heels and headed out of the building, yelling over his shoulder. "You know what." He paused outside the building and pointed a finger at the two witch doctors conversing softly in their singsong version of Pidgin English. "She dies. So do you."

The man who'd prevented him from moving closer to Cassidy gripped his shoulder. "Bad mojo running through her body. She try to keep me away, but I tell her my life for our land is an easy sacrifice. Be swift so that we may fight this black magic."

Jake nodded. "Keep her alive." He ran into the clearing, moving around the bodies of the concerned villagers. Fighting back their questions, Jake fled into the jungle, keeping his pace steady. He whistled through his teeth as he ran. Time. *Damn.* How long did he have? His brain ran through a million scenarios, and not one was satisfactory. He'd never realized he'd been lonely, not until her touch and warm laughter claimed his heart and his world brightened beyond anything he'd dreamed possible. Without Cassidy, the future felt empty.

He paused, bending over and heaving in deep breaths. Glancing around wild-eyed, he swore at himself for running headlong into the jungle without bothering with direction. The rustle of leaves and a cracking twig snapped his attention to his left. Sunday stepped from the shadows of an overgrown fig bush. "You need help?"

Jake laughed bitterly and pushed his hair off his forehead. "Hell, yes. Can you lead me downriver?"

Sunday nodded. "Your woman?"

"Poisoned."

Concern and alarm invaded the man's eyes. "Bad mojo."

Jake snorted, checking his gun and other ammunition strapped to his body. "So I've been told." A sweet scent drifted in their direction; it smelled musky with a tinge of sandalwood.

"The medicine men are calming her spirit. They will burn away what they can. Their powders are potent, pulled from some of the most poisonous frogs in the world. If nothing else, it'll give her the rest her body needs to fight the poison."

Gazing at Sunday, Jake decided not to contradict the man. "Let's go."

Jake and Sunday moved to the banks of the Niger River. Stepping over the claw-like roots of the mangroves, the two men climbed aboard the rubber boat Jake had pulled onshore upon his and Cassidy's return from the cave.

Sunday sat in front navigating as they silently paddled through the murky water. He refused to use the motor. Kill-and-Go swarmed this zone like flies on cow dung. The jungle flanked both sides and vibrated with the power of the drums as they resumed their steady beat.

Thick foliage ruffled in the breeze, bringing with it the mixed scent of burning fires and dank composted earth. Jake said a silent prayer for Cassidy and focused his energy on the task before him.

Now this is worth killing for.

CHAPTER 40

Terrified screams filled the air as Sunday's men spread across the jungle, killing all in their path. Sunday glanced over his shoulder, and Jake nodded in understanding. The Ijwo were performing as promised, eliminating the Kill-and-Go squads and protecting those to the north.

"How much farther?" Jake's voice was barely a whisper on the breeze.

Sunday studied the coastline and responded in the same hushed tone. "We've passed into the western coastal plain. The beach and barrier islands are straight ahead."

They slipped from the relatively calm current of the river into the turbulent surf of the Gulf of Guinea. The skyline flared with the preternatural light of hundreds of gas flares. Jake's vision adjusted to the sudden glare, and he leaned forward tapping Sunday on the shoulder. "That's it. That freighter up ahead. Can you swim back from here?"

Sunday nodded and silently slipped overboard, leaving Jake alone to paddle across the choppy water. Sulfur and methane poisoned the air. He unwrapped a bandana from his arm and tied it across his nose. After several excruciating minutes, the rubber inflatable brushed against the side of the hull of the mammoth ship and Jake moved quietly and efficiently to secure the attachment lines.

Waves smacked the hull with a rhythmic slap that ratcheted up his anxiety. Like the hands of a clock, ticking Cassidy's time away. He grabbed the anchor rope and shimmied up to the first deck.

Jake crept along the bow of the ship, keeping low. He frowned at the ghostly feel of his surroundings. For a freighter this large there should be men everywhere. Heading down a center corridor, he picked up the bitter scent of burning coffee. Fluorescent lights were dark upon the ceiling, leaving only the dull amber glow of generator-operated bulbs.

According to the map Cassidy had prepared for him, the conference room, offices, and sleeping quarters all originated in one sector. He twisted the handle on the door she'd indicated was Robert Cole's office.

Empty, except for an odd shadow cast upon the carpet.

Jake pushed the door open a bit farther, placing his back against the jamb and sliding through the gap gun first. Silence.

He followed the black silhouette back to its source. A body lay sprawled before a mammoth desk, arms splayed to the side. Fluorescent light filtered from outside, flickering against an all too familiar tattoo. Michelle. Dark spots splattered across the rug, and a puddle of blood seeped into the fabric. He cautiously stepped around the wet material. Kneeling down, Jake felt the pulse at Michelle's neck. Remorse didn't register a one on his emotional scale. In fact, if she'd been alive he'd probably have killed her himself for poisoning Cassidy. He patted her down but found no items of worth or clues to the whereabouts of the virus.

Jake stepped back and silently exited the office.

He proceeded forward and checked the conference room and then the small cafeteria.

Empty.

His stomach tightened, and his gut screamed loudly. This wasn't right. He frowned and moved toward a door that filtered a small sliver of light into the corridor.

Jake tested the knob. It was locked. He pulled out his Army knife and picked the lock. Jake opened the door slowly, aiming his gun at the interior of the room.

A man sat in the center slumped over the edge the counter. His hands and feet hung loosely, and his head rested at an odd angle. Jake moved cautiously. He reached forward and checked his pulse. Dead. The head flopped back, and Jake noticed the outline of a bullet hole in the man's temple. Glancing at the rounded figure and manicured hands, Jake guessed he faced Edward Fiske. A quick glance at the laboratory surrounding him and a pad of scribbled notes with the scientist's signature confirmed his supposition.

Stepping back, Jake noticed a metallic briefcase on the counter. He flipped it open and counted a dozen vials marked CPV-19 and a dozen more marked antidote. "Bingo." Jake spun on his heels and exited the small room.

Nick strode through the door of Robert's office with his gun drawn and eyes wary. His boss glanced up and then stared at the drawn gun. "You sure he's onboard?"

Nick nodded his head once. "Cameras caught him."

He couldn't help the smile that tugged at the corner of his mouth. "Set the charges."

"It seems a waste to blow this place up."

Robert stepped around the desk, carrying a suede satchel. "You filmed Michelle shooting Fiske?"

"Fuckin' A. A bit twisted, that one. Shot herself up with the antidote, then put a gun to the doc's head, kissed his mouth, and blew the fucker away." Nick shrugged. "Too bad you offed her."

"I don't need her anymore."

Nick nodded, quietly opposed to the death of Michelle. She'd proven to be a wealth of information, coercing Drew Sharpe to their side and wiping the blood off their money by washing away NWP's connection with the Nigerian government.

Cole sighed. "She failed to find me the geological survey. It was my only course of action. ZEBRA will be blamed. It'll be an international incident that will close their doors for good. The survey will be buried."

Nick tightened his mouth. "I've hooked up the live feed video."

"Excellent. In the lab?"

"Yes."

Robert headed toward the door. "The feed has been programmed to my computer in Port Harcourt. You sure your man can alter the image?"

"To show Anderson setting the charges and placing the virus on-board instead of stealing it?"

"Exactly."

Nick followed Robert out the door. The two men walked down a thin corridor and began climbing steep metal stairs. "Yes. He'll do that."

They reached the top, a blast of ocean air tossing Robert's neatly combed hair into a frenzy. "Superb. That's all the evidence I'll need to incriminate ZEBRA."

Nick paused and surveyed the near empty ship. There were a few workers ambling about, but nothing more than a skeleton crew. Collateral damage.

Robert broke the silence. "What are we waiting for?"

Nick grinned. "I'll start the fireworks."

Jake pressed his back against the wall of the corridor; he could feel the rivets of the soldered metal through his shirt. The cool metal of the briefcase was a comfort in his hand, his fingers gripping it in a solid hold. He placed one foot in front of the other, his ears tuned to any noise that would signal the approach of his enemy. His gun faced forward, ready to slay anyone that attempted stopping his escape.

A muffled boom echoed up one of the stairwells. Jake tensed and cocked his head, listening for the source of the noise. A dark cloud of smoke flooded the stairs ahead, and panicked screams echoed from below. Jake slipped quickly down the corridor, pausing at the stairwell. Another explosion ripped the silence, this time followed by several smaller detonations. *What the hell?* The ship listed, tossing Jake backward and slamming his shoulder against the edge of the wall. A concert of groans and creeks from strained metal filled the corridor.

The barge was breaking apart.

Running as fast as the lurching craft would allow, Jake navigated farther down the hall and toward the exterior deck. More booms interspersed with bright flashes of light cascaded across the ship. The heat of fire reached his face. Skidding on his heels as the ship dipped and dove in the opposite direction, he exited into the night at mid-ship.

Swinging his head from fore to aft, Jake saw nothing but pandemonium. Whatever crew had been hiding when he arrived was now yelling for help and racing for safety. Men streamed from the belly of the metal beast, swarming in panicked circles around lifeboats. Others, dressed in khaki security uniforms, fired their weapons into the air in an effort to gain control. Bursts of orange flame blasted from portholes and stairwells as the lower levels of the barge began to disintegrate and take on water.

Another explosion and the ground dropped from beneath Jake's feet. He hit a lower deck, rolled to his right, and jumped up. Jake clutched the suitcase, ducked his head, and ran toward the railing. He choked and covered his mouth as he passed a fiery hallway. Blinded by the smoke, Jake reached his gun hand forward and searched for the metal railing. His arm connected with something solid and he blinked, momentarily confused by the block in his path.

A fist connected with his jaw and his neck snapped back, sending bright flashes of white before his eyes. He stumbled but kept his hold on the briefcase. Jake dropped beneath the line of smoke and crouched, gazing through the haze at his attacker. The other man coughed and moved forward, his arms out and ready to seize Jake by the throat.

Blinking and shaking his head, Jake angled away and crawled to a non-smoke-infested area. The sound of heavy footsteps and muttered curses alerted Jake to the fact that he was being followed. He turned, his gun held steady and aimed directly at his pursuer.

A heavyset man with a jagged scar across his face broke free from the black smoke. Jake recognized him immediately. He lifted his arm and pointed the muzzle of his Glock at Nick Fowler's face and fired. The ship lurched to the side and cast his bullet astray.

The man sneered at him and lunged.

Jake made a wide arc and circled around the man. Nick shook his head and pointed at Jake, laughing maniacally. "You didn't really think we'd allow you to take those, did you? So long, mother fucker."

A gun discharged and Jake felt his shoulder rip open, numbing everything from his upper arm to his hand. He cursed, releasing the suitcase. Jake spun around in the direction of this new shooter and aimed the Glock, ripping rapid fire and slicing through the man until he collapsed in a heap of blood and shattered bone. Jake flattened himself on the ground, reaching for the metal case containing the CPV-19 and antidote.

Nick kicked it away, walked forward, and ground his foot into the open and bleeding wound on Jake's arm. Howling in pain, Jake snapped his legs in a scissor kick, pushed off the deck using his back and leg muscles, and faced Fowler.

Jake attacked the NWP employee, ignoring the blood that coursed down his arm and the numbing pain that made his movements sluggish and off kilter. Nick Fowler played dirty; he didn't want to encourage a brawl but fed off Jake's weakness. He continued to attack Jake's wounded side, taking advantage of the injury.

Jake fell to his knees, heaving in much-needed air. The throbbing in his shoulder made his head dizzy and stomach nauseated. "Cassidy." His throat burned as he said her name. But it helped, filling him with energy. Jake staggered to his feet. But Fowler was quick and unhindered by a wounded arm. He slammed his fist into Jake's face, then shoved him against the railing. Jake's back bent over the metal pipes; he balanced precariously on the edge of tipping over and dropping to his death.

Another large explosion sent decks tilting and shattered metal flying. Jake steadied himself, gripping the iron railing as his feet slid from under him. Blood poured from his arm, making his hands slick and sticky. He shook his head clear and focused on the NWP man. He'd backed off and was flashing Jake a cocky grin. Waving the briefcase in the air, he turned away, his laughter ringing loud above the chaos of the sinking barge.

Jake tore a strip of cotton from his shirt and wrapped it tightly around his gunshot wound. He gathered his strength and centered his mind. In the distance, Nick ran toward a set of stairs leading up a level. The whirring of helicopter blades drew Jake's attention. A helicopter sat on a helipad several stories up.

He swore and raced after Fowler.

Hot wind blasted his face from fires burning in all directions. Acrid smoke blinded him and made breathing difficult. Jake ignored the biting pain of his bullet wound and stumbled up the stairs after Nick Fowler. He crested the top of the platform and burst toward the helicopter, pumping as much energy into his legs as possible.

The blades of the chopper whipped the salty sea air into a frenzy; it burned and stung like a million bees against Jake's exposed skin. He pushed against the wind, raising his arm and shielding his face from the cutting air.

Nick climbed onboard and took the controls, lifting the craft upward. Jake stared in frustration as Robert Cole leaned over the edge, flipping him the finger. Cassidy's life was flying away, and that wasn't in the deck of cards Jake knew belonged to him. He dashed to the center of the helipad and snagged a length of coiled rope, tying one end into a lasso. Twirling it above his head, he snaked the end over a running board and held tight as the helicopter banked to the left and dragged his body above the burning wreckage of the ship.

His shoulder and entire left arm screamed with pain, but sea-green eyes kept Jake focused. Hand over hand, he battled the swaying rope and ascended toward the running board of the helicopter. Bullets flew past his head as Robert Cole stretched beyond the open door, firing line after line of deadly metal in his direction. The movement of the chopper aided Jake by swinging the rope in a pendulum motion, but it made climbing upward feel impossible.

Beyond the desire to pummel the NWP men into smithereens, the life of his woman spurred Jake to push past his body's limitations. His palms were slick with sweat and blood, and he cursed as his hands slipped and he lost a precious few feet. Wrapping his legs tighter around the rope, Jake once more gripped the bristled, twisted hemp and pulled himself upward.

Hand over hand.

His vision blurred as salty wind whipped against his face. Taking advantage of Nick's attempt to shake him by sending the chopper into zigzagged turns, he forced the rope into a wide arc. Lifting his legs before him, Jake swung onto the foot of the helicopter, temporarily

blocked from Robert's bullets. He shimmied beneath the open doorway, where Nick Fowler sat behind the controls of the helicopter.

Jake inhaled deeply, focused his mind, and rolled himself around,
pulling up and planting his feet firmly on the thin running board. His
stomach was a knot of pain, but he fought past it and concentrated on
the metal case and its contents. He winked when Nick glanced over
at him, shock blanching his enemy's cheeks stark white. Jake didn't
hesitate; he hammered his fist into the asshole's face, sending him into
oblivion. He followed with a swift jab to Fowler's neck to ensure the
man's incapacity and then reached and yanked his seat belt loose.

He bit back the burning pain of his shoulder and used his left arm
to steady himself as the helicopter dove toward the black water. Jake
focused on the controls and tugged on Fowler's arm, dragging him
halfway out of his seat. Swearing beneath his breath, he inhaled and
anchored himself more strongly with his wounded arm.

Jake gripped Fowler's shirt and yanked him fully out of his seat.
The man's unconscious body was deadweight, but Robert's screams and
movement in the back of the chopper sent a rush of adrenaline and Jake
pulled with every ounce of his energy. Nick Fowler sprang from the
cockpit and flew into the air, falling gracefully through the night sky
and landing with a resounding thud on one of the oil barges below. The
reverberation on the metal deck ricocheted upward, and Jake smiled
with satisfaction.

"One down. One to go." Jake's nostrils flared wide as he inhaled
much-needed oxygen. "Hold on, Sunshine, I'm almost there."

Jake dove behind the controls of the helicopter, pulling back on the
stick and bringing them upward. Feeling the weight of Robert's hand
on his neck, he ducked, jabbing his elbow back and connecting with the
man's stomach. Robert struggled forward, but Jake had already had
enough. He lodged his knee to hold the rudder steady and turned to
face his enemy.

"You son of a bitch." Jake lifted his chin and challenged Robert. "Come here." He motioned his enemy forward with his hand. A wide gash split the corner of the man's temple and blood pumped down his face in a swath of red. "Did you hurt yourself, old man?"

"Fuck you." Robert wiped the back of his hand against the crimson river trickling into his eyes. "You'll never win."

Jake narrowed his eyes, centered his line of sight, and smashed his fist into the bridge of Robert's nose, breaking it instantly. The man's head snapped back; then he fell forward against Jake, his hands scrambling to reach the helicopter controls. Jake shoved him back, but the loss of blood to his left arm made it a halfhearted attempt.

He shifted his stance, transferring his weight to the right, and swung his fist upward toward Robert's chin. The man chopped at his wounded shoulder, sending fireworks across Jake's line of vision. The NWP president ducked and smacked his elbow against the rudder. "Son of a bitch," Jake swore, shoving Robert backwards, battling now not only the man but also gravity as the helicopter went into a tailspin.

Out of the corner of his eye, Jake saw the silver briefcase slip toward the door. He lunged over the seat and rolled to his feet, grabbing its handle and bringing it up with a hard left swing, clipping Robert in the side of the head.

"Get . . ." Jake rushed forward. "The fuck . . ." He head butted Robert. "Out of . . ." His fist shot upward and dove into the tender skin beneath the man's chin. "My chopper." Jake charged forward shoulder first, sending the NWP president sailing out of the helicopter, arms flailing and screams dying as he fell.

Without a second to collect his breath, Jake jumped behind the helicopter controls, righting the chopper an instant before it smashed into the watery depths of the gulf. He pulled it back into the air and banked to the left. His entire body shook, and he had to bite his lip to concentrate on holding the rudder steady. Turning the craft toward the jungle, he glanced down.

Robert Cole's landing hadn't been pretty. His body hung suspended over the Gulf of Guinea, impaled by one of his own gas pipes. Jake shook his head as a gas flare shot into the night, incinerating the head of New World Petroleum. "Youch. But I can't say you didn't deserve that."

Navigating over the jungle, Jake said a silent prayer. How much time had he wasted? Would she be okay? How fast did the disease progress? "Shit," he swore again and again, combating the wave of blackness that kept wrenching him toward unconsciousness.

Jake flew low over the treetops, concentrating on the bends of the Niger River. He recognized the fork that was flanked with a steep cliff and glanced beyond it to the lazy half-moon curve. Hovering briefly, Jake absorbed the terrain below. A fire reached its blazing fingers toward the night, and he grinned. "Almost there."

Spinning the helicopter in the pyre's direction, Jake sped forward counting the seconds until he began his descent into the clearing where the night had begun. Turning the ignition off, he waited a beat before falling out of the cockpit. Anna ran forward, kneeling at his side. He shoved the case at her. "Go."

"You're hurt."

Jake glared at her and grabbed her arm with such force she winced. "Go, dammit. I'll be fine." Anna's eyes widened and she nodded, seizing the case and racing like the wind to the building where Cassidy slept.

An Ijwo rebel stepped forward, his face sporting its own bruises and deep gashes. Jake grinned when he recognized Sunday. "You have fun tonight, my friend?" Jake asked, then bent forward choking on a wad of bloody mucus.

"I see not as much as you." The black man knelt beside Jake. "Your wounds are bad."

"I'm fine. My woman?"

Sunday glanced to the ground, then back up toward the stars. "Bad mojo."

Jake's heart clenched, and he struggled to stand. Sunday helped him, and the two limped toward the concrete building. Jake's eyes filled with tears and he shook his head, trying to settle the pain in his chest that had nothing to do with his wounds.

Before he stepped into the building, Sunday stopped him. He reached out and produced a wet cloth from somewhere Jake couldn't see. "You don't want to frighten her into leaving this world."

Jake snorted and choked once more. He wiped his face and allowed Sunday to wrap his shoulder and staunch the flow of blood. Jake smiled and lifted a brow. "Did I break any teeth?"

Sunday laughed out loud, the warmth and camaraderie helping to heal Jake's battered soul. "No, mon, you's still ugly white man."

Jake tipped his head back and laughed, then turned and strode into the building ready to face whatever lay within. Anna sat at the edge of the bed, her head down and hand gently wrapped around Cassidy's. She wouldn't be close if the antidote hadn't begun to work, right?

Approaching softly, Jake's heart twisted at Cassidy's pale and seemingly lifeless face. Blood dripped from the corner of her ear, and another red streak stained the edge of her pillow. He paused and gazed heavenward, adding another prayer to the multitude of ones he'd been chanting all night.

A needle prick burned on his arm and he flinched, turning to fight. The witch doctor who'd been overseeing Cassidy's care held a hand up. "If you're in here, then you need the antidote." The man offered a gap-toothed grin. "Better safe than sorry."

Jake reached a hand out and touched Anna's shoulder. Anna glanced at him and offered a small shrug. "I don't know" is all she said.

But it sounded like heaven to Jake. It wasn't a "she's gone," or "there was nothing we could do."

He dropped to his knees and pulled Cassidy into his arms. She moaned. It was music to his ears. "Come on, Sunshine. No woman of mine quits this easily." Jake felt her hand against his wrist; it burned with fever but caressed him with love.

"Yours?" she whispered, her eyes remained closed.

Jake dropped a line of kisses against her forehead. He ignored the heat that burned his lips and concentrated on the fact that she was alive. "Did you have any doubt, Cassidy?"

Cassidy sighed and tilted her head back to stare at him. He winked and touched his lips gently to hers. "You look like hell." Her voice was soft and hoarse, and he frowned when another thin trickle of blood escaped the corner of her mouth.

He grinned. "Yeah, I know. That's what you get for playing with the devil."

She lifted her hand and gripped his arm. "But this land is the devil's gold no more, right?" Her eyes fluttered and closed, and she collapsed against his chest. Jake glanced at Anna and the medicine man and they both shook their heads, sending a lightning bolt of terror through Jake's heart.

CHAPTER 41

A BEAM OF LIGHT SPLIT THE DARK NIGHT AND GREW BOLDER. She rocked gently back and forth in a hammock. Frowning, Cassidy couldn't remember being anywhere near a hammock. A familiar voice sang softly beside her. The chant grew louder, and she recognized the sweet pitch of Anna's soprano melody. Blinking her eyes again, she tried to focus. Heat and a steady beat thumped against her right ear.

A musky scent familiar and belonging to . . . Cassidy's head hurt. Belonging to . . . whom? She closed her eyes tightly and concentrated.

Jake.

She sighed and rested her head against his chest, no longer fighting or trying to figure out what was going on. In Jake's arms, she was safe.

"Don't pass out on me again, Cass." Jake's chest rumbled as he spoke.

She smiled at him, feeling very woozy and lightheaded. "Okay."

The song grew louder and she fluttered her lashes up, twisting her head toward the sound. Anna walked beside Jake and smiled at her. "Hi, boss. Glad to report you're free and clear of that nasty stuff running through your bloodstream."

"You are a bad girl," Cassidy scolded. "I told you to leave." At least she thought she had. Cassidy remembered Jake's visit when she'd told him about the antidote, but everything after that was a blur of pain and fever.

"Hush. You're going to be fine." Anna prodded at the tender skin around Cassidy's needle mark. "She's lost a lot of blood."

"I have not," Cassidy responded. "It's only a pin prick." The world spun, and suddenly she was floating. Turning her head, she stared into the concerned face of her lover. "Hi there, big guy." Oh, she wasn't floating. He was carrying her. That's right.

Jake frowned. "What's the matter with her?"

"Shock and adrenaline and everything else that comes with narrowly winning the race against the man with the hood and scythe," Anna answered from somewhere over her own shoulder. "We need to get her back to Principe now."

"I think that's a good idea," Cassidy said. "Where's that two-timing bitch, Michelle?"

Jake's chest rumbled, and she rubbed her cheek against the comforting sound. "Dead," he said. "I found her body on Cole's barge." She felt him turn around, her legs swinging from the motion. "Have we called and ordered an extraction?" Jake asked, sighing and moving his arm to shift her weight.

"Give her to someone else," Anna demanded. "Blood is seeping through that bandage."

"No." Jake paused and kissed Cassidy's forehead.

She smiled and inhaled, a wave of warmth and security welling in her chest as she now knew without a doubt that it was Jake she smelled. A stab of worry suddenly burst her comfortable fuzzy buzz. "You hurt?" She narrowed her eyes and glared when he shook his head.

"Just a flesh wound."

Cassidy struggled, but he wouldn't release her. "Relax, Sunshine."

She tried to disobey, fought against the lull of his voice and Anna's

singing. But it didn't work. Closing her eyes, she drifted off to sleep.

Jake sat in a hard-backed chair, resting his feet on the edge of a narrow cot. Cassidy slept. Her face was pale and the IV that pumped healing fluids into her veins made her appear fragile and weak. Damn her.

The doctor indicated that she'd recover in time. His greatest concern was her physical exhaustion. Her body had been pushed to its limits, he'd explained to Jake, leaving her immune system low and system open for infection. The doctor's concern over the needle mark on her arm and possible contamination twisted Jake's forehead into a scowl.

A movement caught his eye, and he leaned forward. Her eyes fluttered open. She turned her head and stared at him, her lips curving in a half smile. "You still look like shit."

He tilted his head to the side, a grin sliding into place, her humor warming his heart and reinforcing what he'd been fighting against the past week. He couldn't live without her. "You don't look so hot yourself, Sleeping Beauty."

Cassidy glanced down and shuddered. "Why do they always make hospital gowns out of ugly prints?"

Jake ignored her complaint. "How do you feel?"

She struggled to sit up, and he helped her by shoving some extra pillows behind her back. "Like I've been drowned, dumped from a helicopter, and had a deadly disease slammed into my blood system."

He nodded. "That's good. I thought for a moment there you were hurt."

Cassidy reached for his hand. "While I've been sleeping like a lazy hound dog, what's been going on? Have you ferreted out Michelle's connection?"

He shook his head. "We're still trying to unravel that, but I have a feeling once we trace the wired funds we'll understand more." Jake entwined his fingers through hers. "The freighter owned by New World Petroleum has been totally destroyed. CDC has flown out, as well as the World Health Organization. They've taken control of CPV-19."

"They didn't get rid of it?" She inhaled and bit her bottom lip. "That's so dangerous."

Jake nodded and shrugged. "I think they believe that whatever Edward Fiske was working towards warrants further experimentation. CPV-19 will be stored safely within the control of the CDC."

Cassidy sighed. At least with the existence of an antidote, it nullifies some of the virus's deadliness. "How about Drew—what were his plans?"

Jake's heart ached at the sadness in her eyes. Was it the betrayal of people she once cared for or the thought of leaving him that made tears well in her eyes? He poured her a glass of water and held a straw to her lips. "I believe he was simply a pawn. Someone Michelle used to reach her goals."

"I didn't infect any of the villagers, did I?"

Jake smiled and shook his head. "That was their objective, though."

Cassidy nodded. "Under the barbaric conditions of those medical centers, the virus would have spread at a violent rate."

"In theory." He ran a thumb along the edge of her cheekbone. "They were going to repeat the same procedure using other innocent people."

"And the cave?"

Jake shrugged. "That's the Nigerian government's problem. We have no authority over that."

Cassidy pursed her lips. "Will they implement my steps toward bettering the environment?"

Pushing away from the bed and standing up, Jake put distance between them. He couldn't stand this idle chatter. The urge to demand she tell him how she felt made his insides all twisted and unsettled.

"I don't know, Sunshine. We can only hope."

Cassidy reached beneath her gown and fumbled with something around her breast. Jake raised a questioning eyebrow and tried not to grin. "Anything I can help you with?"

She glared at him and produced a small flash drive. "The geological survey."

Jake eyed it. "I wondered where you were hiding that little sucker."

Cassidy smiled and winked at him. "Only you would've been able to find it." She paused and sighed, worrying her bottom lip. "I think under the circumstances the Niger Delta is better off without this." Snapping the metal in half, she tossed it at Jake. "Burn that. Maybe we'll buy this place some time to uncorrupt itself before they discover the gold mine resting beneath their shores."

Jake picked up the shattered pieces. "I hope that happens."

Cassidy sank back against the pillows. "And you? Why are you still here? Shouldn't you be out saving the day somewhere?"

He moved toward her bed. "I'm right where I want to be."

Cassidy averted her eyes and stared out the window.

Jake's heart sank. He swore and sat down on the edge of the bed. Tipping her chin towards him, he stared into her eyes. "I can't change who I am."

A lone tear tipped her lash and snaked down the edge of her face. He traced it with his finger. Cassidy reached up and placed her hand upon his. "And I can't change wanting more. I want the whole package or nothing."

He swallowed. "You have me."

"No," she shook her head. "I don't."

Swearing, he rose to his feet and strode to the door. If she couldn't accept who he was, then this was a waste of time. "I guess I'll go find something to save." He turned the knob, battling against the pain in his chest. "See you around, Sunshine."

Cassidy pressed her fist against her heart. Tears streamed down her face and she hiccupped, her breath becoming difficult to catch. Damn him. He was all she wanted but she deserved all of him, didn't she? Cassidy refused to live with him unless she shared his entire life, all of what shaped him into the man she loved. As long as he was Black Stripe, that was impossible.

The door opened, and for a brief moment her world lightened. But when the face of Anna Kuffae came into view, Cassidy slumped back against the pillows.

"Gee, I don't think I've ever gotten that warm a welcome," her friend laughed and came to sit beside the bed.

"I'm sorry," Cassidy sniffled.

Anna reached over and dipped a wash cloth in water, then handed it to Cassidy. "Don't let that man walk away."

"And what do you propose I do?"

Anna grinned. "Love him." She pushed Cassidy's hair away from her face.

Trying to calm her breathing, she stared at Anna. "How did he rescue you from our old camp?"

"I don't honestly know. The Kill-and-Go squad dragged Georgie and me into the center of the village, and then everything went black. I think I passed out. Georgie says that Jake walked through fire and swept us off the ground." Anna laughed. "He thinks Jake moves the earth."

Cassidy swiped at a fresh batch of tears. "He never told me."

Anna patted her hand. "Honey, my understanding of this crew is that everything they do is very hush-hush. And now that their ranks have been breached, things will crack down even more."

"I know. I can't live like that." She hiccupped and reached for her water.

"Like what?"

She stared at Anna, her heart shattering beyond repair. "Never knowing if he's dead or alive."

CHAPTER 42

CASSIDY WALKED ACROSS BASE CAMP. SHE PLACED HER HAND above her eyes, shielding against the sun. A camera hung around her neck and despite the heat of the day, her plan to locate and photograph the giant sunbird panned out. Her mouth still felt constantly dry. But today was the day she received her clean bill of health. And as far as she was concerned, it was ten days too late.

Entering Colonel Price's command tent, she slipped into the first available chair. Her eyes adjusted to the dim interior, and she nodded at several of the Black Stripe members. She knew the second Jake entered. Her heart slammed against her chest, and she turned her head in his direction. Her ability to breathe ceased to exist.

He didn't occupy the empty chair beside her but stood against the far wall, placing the entire width of the room between them. Neither did he return her stare. Cassidy bit the bottom of her lip and bent her head, scrutinizing her nails. The application to Black Stripe she'd submitted to Colonel Price must have been denied. Therefore, self-preservation kicked into place and a return to her safe, work-consumed life lay before her.

"Ladies and gentlemen . . ." Colonel Price entered the room and immediately took command. "I wanted to have a final briefing before we scatter to the four corners of the world."

Cassidy glanced up and thought she caught Jake staring at her. His eyes shifted and focused on Colonel Price.

"As you know, we have begun an investigation into ZEBRA. Valerie Baxter has returned to Atlanta and is in the middle of an ass-deep analysis of the corporation, its structure, and employees." Colonel Price glanced at Cassidy and grinned. "Of course, we have one or two members here that don't require that intense level of study."

Cassidy sighed and offered him a polite smile. Nothing seemed to excite her these days. She'd attempted to invigorate her interest in the fauna of Principe, but even the success of actually witnessing a giant sunbird elicited only a slight rise in her normally exuberant quest for wildlife.

Colonel Price moved to the front of his desk and sat on the corner. "Everything that has transpired over the past three weeks was, in reality, just the beginning of our mission. The only aspect that we've managed to conclude is the gray wolf and Yellowstone. Dr. Lowell, would you care to update the squad on that area?"

Cassidy nodded and rose to her feet. She walked toward Colonel Price and turned to face the remaining members of the Black Stripe squadron, acutely aware that Jake was no more than three feet to her left. "Liv Somers has concluded that the northwest quadrant of Yellowstone did, in fact, suffer a drastic loss of gray wolves. There are eight packs that were infected with CPV-19. Those wolves didn't survive. With the aid of Dr. Fiske's research and the CDC, along with many man hours by the park rangers and a . . ." Cassidy paused, frowning. "White Stripe?" Colonel Price nodded, and she continued. "And a White Stripe pod, they have confirmed that the remaining packs are clean of infection."

Colonel Price bent forward and glanced at her. "Any chance of a reoccurrence?"

Cassidy shrugged. "According to the CDC, the virus has played itself out. If there is a future outbreak, we have the resources to contain and eradicate it."

"Excellent." Colonel Price beamed at her, then nodded his head toward Jake. "Anderson? What's going on in the delta?"

Jake stepped forward and moved past Cassidy to stand at the side of his superior officer. "We've completed negotiations with the Nigerian government. They've agreed to allow us back within the realm of the Niger Delta. Dr. Lowell will be leading the response team. I have assigned most of you to her pod as I'm not fully comfortable that the threat from the Kill-and-Go has been eliminated."

Cassidy nodded and glanced at the men and women who were to be her backup for the implementation of ecological rehabilitation. "This is an eight-week rotation. If there are any that feel the time spent here would be a hardship, please don't hesitate to request reassignment. We have a tremendous amount of work ahead with very little reward."

Colonel Price clapped his hands once. "I think that's it. Dr. Lowell, your ride will be here within the hour. Quit picking at your nails, and get the hell out of here."

Cassidy sighed and felt the instant heat of embarrassment flush her face. She hadn't realized she'd been fidgeting. "Yes, sir." She mock-saluted the colonel and headed out of the tent.

She resisted the urge to glance over her shoulder. Refused to allow herself one last look at her heart.

"You can do this, Lowell. It's the right thing. No attachment. No pain." Cassidy bent her head and swiped in frustration at the tears. "It's the right thing."

"Don't you think you should go after her, Anderson?" The room had emptied and it was only Jake and the Colonel within its shady interior.

"She needs space."

Colonel Price squeezed Jake's shoulder. "Not too much, okay? I'd hate to have to put up with this solemn and grumpy soldier forever."

Jake grinned. "Have no fear, Colonel. When the time is right, she won't be able to resist me." He frowned and hoped this was the truth. Cassidy needed to clear her head and once she did, she'd realize they were meant for one another. He understood her hesitation regarding his line of work and with the aid of Colonel Price was making progress in correcting her concerns. Jake turned toward the Colonel. "I think."

Colonel Price grinned. "Good. Then you won't have a problem working with her again?"

Jake narrowed his eyes. He had started the necessary paperwork to cross over to the civilian side and garner White Stripe status, but he hadn't expected results this quickly. In all honesty, he didn't know if he was ready. "What have you done?"

"Nothing that wasn't asked for." The colonel reached into his pocket and retrieved a small pin. It was an identical match to the tattoo Jake sported.

"What's this?"

"It's for your new partner."

Realization dawned, and the weight gripping his chest disappeared. "Cassidy?"

Colonel Price nodded. "Go get her, son."

———

Cassidy dropped her duffel bag on the dirt outside her tent. She checked her watch, then scouted the airspace above camp for her ride back to the Niger Delta. Nothing.

Glancing across the courtyard, Cassidy recognized Jake's figure. He strode toward her, his shoulder's straight and body prepared to attack. "Hoo boy, what did I do to deserve this?" She muttered beneath her breath.

"Dr. Lowell," he barked at her.

Cassidy swallowed and answered, keeping any inflection of want or need out of her voice. "Captain Anderson."

His snarky grin slid into place, and he held his hand out in her direction. "I believe you forgot something."

She narrowed her eyes, not trusting one iota of his attitude. "And what would that be?" Jake flipped his hand over and opened his palm. Cassidy stepped forward and peered at the pin resting against his skin. She picked it up and scrutinized the Black Stripe emblem, her heart immediately acknowledging everything the tiny metal decoration represented. "I forgot a pin?"

"No, Cassidy." Jake leaned down and tipped her chin up, staring into her eyes, his gaze deadly serious and full of emotion. "You forgot me."

She sighed, her eyes welling with tears. Shaking her head, Cassidy snaked her arms around his neck, pulling him down to steal one of his mind-blowing kisses that would now belong to her forever. "Not possible. You're unforgettable."

His chest rumbled with laughter as he whispered against her lips. "Told you so."

"**Chernobyl Murders** is a page-turner of the highest order: from the compelling characterization to the vividly described landscape of a devastated Ukraine to the stunning cover art, Beres has penned himself a winner."

—**Paul Goat Allen,** *Chicago Tribune* **(September 13, 2008)**

1985, a year before the Chernobyl disaster. Hidden away in a wine cellar in the western Ukraine, Chernobyl engineer Mihaly Horvath, brother of a Kiev Militia detective Lazlo Horvath, reveals details of unnecessary risks being taken at the Chernobyl plant. Concerned for his brother and family, Lazlo investigates—irritating superiors, drawing the attention of a CIA operative, raising the hackles of an old school KGB major, and discovering his brother's secret affair with Juli Popovics, a Chernobyl technician.

When the Chernobyl plant explodes scores of lives are changed forever. As Lazlo questions his brother's death in the blast, Juli arrives in Kiev to tell the detective she carries his brother's child. If their lives aren't complicated enough, KGB major Grigor Komarov enters the fray, reawakening a hard-line past to manipulate deadly resources.

Now the Ukraine is not only blanketed with deadly radiation, but becomes a killing ground involving pre-perestroika factions in disarray, a Soviet government on its last legs, and madmen hungry for power as they eye Gorbachev's changes.

With a poisoned environment at their backs and a killer snapping at their heels, Lazlo and Juli flee for their lives—and their love—toward the Western frontier.

ISBN# 9781933836294
Hardcover / International Thriller
US $25.95 / CDN $28.95
Available Now
www.michaelberes.com

THE
FRONT PORCH
PROPHET

RAYMOND L. ATKINS

What do a trigger-happy bootlegger with pancreatic cancer, an alcoholic helicopter pilot who is afraid to fly, and a dead guy with his feet in a camp stove have in common?

What are the similarities between a fire department that cannot put out fires, a policeman who has a historic cabin fall on him from out of the sky, and an entire family dedicated to a variety of deceased authors?

Where can you find a war hero named Termite with a long knife stuck in his liver, a cook named Hoghead who makes the world's worst coffee, and a supervisor named Pillsbury who nearly gets hung by his employees?

Sequoyah, Georgia is the answer to all three questions. They arise from the relationship between A. J. Longstreet and his best friend since childhood, Eugene Purdue. After a parting of ways due to Eugene's inability to accept the constraints of adulthood, he reenters A.J.'s life with terminal cancer and the dilemma of executing a mercy killing when the time arrives.

Take this gripping journey to Sequoyah, Georgia and witness A.J.'s battle with mortality, euthanasia, and his adventure back to the past and people who made him what he is—and helps him make the decision that will alter his life forever.

ISBN# 9781933836386
Hardcover / Fiction
US $25.95 / CDN $28.95
Available Now
www.raymondlatkins.com

It began with lies.

One-quarter Nez Perce, Cord Sutton attempts to hide his Indian blood by adopting the life of a gentleman. As part of the ruse, he intends to gain respect by buying the Lake Hotel, an island in the Yellowstone wilderness that offers elegant accommodations to travelers on the Northern Pacific Railroad.

When Chicago heiress Laura Fielding is rescued from a stagecoach robbery in Jackson Hole by a rugged looking mountain man in rough clothing, she hides the fact she is wealthy. She does not know the man traveling to the park with her is, in fact, Cord Sutton.

Nonetheless, during a three-day wilderness journey their alliance is sealed. Upon arriving at the Lake Hotel, Cord and Laura learn each other's true identities . . . and the fact Laura's father is backing a rival to purchase the hotel.

On opposite sides, Cord and Laura find bigotry, arson, and the desire for revenge threatens their growing love, and their lives. If they survive, Cord must learn to embrace his heritage and Laura must turn her back on her father's luxurious world . . . IF they survive . . .
The Lake of Fire.

ISBN# 9781933836218
Mass Market Paperback / Fiction
US $6.95 / CDN $8.95
Available Now
www.readlindajacobs.com

For more information
about other great titles from
Medallion Press, visit

medallionpress.com